IRISH
SODA BREAD
MURDER

IRISH SODA BREAD MURDER

Carlene O'Connor
Peggy Ehrhart
Liz Ireland

Kensington Publishing Corp.
kensingtonbooks.com

KENSINGTON BOOKS are published by

Kensington Publishing Corp.
900 Third Avenue
New York, NY 10018

Library of Congress Control Number: 2024943023

ISBN: 978-1-4967-5108-9
First Kensington Hardcover Edition: January 2025

ISBN: 978-1-4967-5110-2 (ebook)

10 9 8 7 6 5 4 3 2 1

Printed in the United States of America

Contents

IRISH SODA BREAD MURDER

Carlene O'Connor

Chapter One

Tara Meehan balanced her plate of Millionaire Short-bread as she descended from her loft down to her Uncle Johnny's salvage mill, Irish Revivals. Today was the annual psychic fair slash bake sale, and she could hear the excited voices of their talent echoing in the massive space below. One voice rose above the others, and she recognized it immediately: Ronan Stone, arguably the most sought-after psychic in Galway City.

"A photo is worth a thousand words, darling," he belted out.

"I think you mean, picture," another man said, topping off the comment with a nervous laugh.

"You'll always know what I mean because I say it," Ronan replied.

As Tara reached the bottom of the stairs, a woman draped in colorful scarves chased another woman clad in a black dress with sequins. "Why aren't you referring clients to me anymore?" she whined.

"I'm doing me best," the woman in black said. "But if you were as skilled as you say, you'd be able to answer that for yourself." With that the woman in black disappeared into the first booth, marked SLOANE STARGAZER. The other woman must be Deirdre Palms, the palm reader, and sure enough she slipped into the second to last booth, the one set aside for Deirdre.

A petite woman standing near the colorful neon auras looked at the clock and gasped. "Less than an hour?" she said, slapping the top of her head with her hands. "Where are my spectacles? I can't see without them!" She threw desperate glances at people around her, but no one stopped to help her look. "This is going to be a dumpster fire!"

"I have an entire box of spectacles you can rummage through," Uncle Johnny said, emerging from the kitchen with a tray of tins. He jerked his full head of black hair toward the back of the mill. "In the storage room," he said. "But be careful. We just had a new shipment, and the boxes are all piled in front of the windows. I wouldn't go near them if I were you; you're liable to get crushed in an avalanche." He grinned. Tall and broad, the only resemblance her maternal uncle bore to Tara was the signature black hair and blue eyes. With him in his late sixties, Tara suspected he'd been secretly coloring his for some years now; it was the shade of shoe polish and often took on a blue tint. Tara was smart enough to keep her gob shut about it.

Ciara Moon squinted in the direction Johnny pointed, and then hurried toward the storage rooms. "Desperate times," she muttered.

A tall and thin bald man holding a top hat adjusted the bow tie on his tuxedo and then hurried toward the bake sale table where Johnny was arranging his tins of Irish soda bread.

"Not so close, Paddy," Johnny said. "You spread your germs, you buy them." *Paddy Pockets*. The occult magician.

Tara finally reached the bottom of the stairs and brushed past a man dressed in a corduroy blazer and denim. "What a space," he said, looking around the mill appreciatively. Tara recognized his voice from his podcast: Dave the Debunker. His podcast, *Psychic Scums and the Skeptic,* was growing in popularity. Ironically, he was married to Ronan Stone; they'd been together a decade now. According to Dave, Ronan was the only true psychic of the lot. That didn't sit well with the rest of the psychics, and Tara knew his presence was going to stir the pot. The psychic fair was all about fun and charity, and Tara prayed he didn't plan on sabotaging it. "It's massive," Dave said, opening his arms to the mill.

"Thank you, darling," Ronan called out from behind his booth.

Dave threw his head back and laughed, then turned to Johnny. "If you ever want to sell—"

"Not on your life," Johnny said.

Dave shrugged. "Just keep it in mind; you never know."

Tara wanted to pipe in that *she* was first in line or second after Johnny's wife, Rose, but wasn't going to be crass. The old stone mill was absolutely a treasure. Johnny sourced architectural salvage items from all over Ireland, and the historic mill was a short walk or drive from Galway City. A small creek with a water wheel outside added to its charm, not to mention a partial view of Galway Bay. Inside, the three-thousand-square-foot shop boasted architectural salvage items, an old commercial kitchen, Johnny's office, storage rooms, a back patio, and an upstairs loft where Tara currently lived.

As a former interior designer in New York City, Tara had always dreamed of owning this type of space. Industrial yet artistic, and filled with history and charm. She'd only met her Uncle Johnny less than five years ago when she'd come to Galway to spread her mother's ashes. And once she fell in love with the bustling city, not to mention her eccentric uncle, she couldn't bring herself to leave. She'd even opened her own shop in the city, Renewals, where she sold some of Johnny's smaller treasures. And now she was engaged to be married to Johnny's employee, Danny O'Donnell. There was no way Tara could ever leave the wondrous life she had fallen into. Who knew a trip inspired by grief could lead to her living her ideal life? Tara was grateful for it every single day. Her life wasn't perfect, but it was imperfectly hers, and it wasn't just the colorful people who fulfilled her. Tara was in love with Ireland itself, and so far, the relationship was rocky—if the rocky cliffs hanging over the Atlantic Ocean counted.

Ronan Stone poked his large head out of his end booth. "Where's Rose?" he asked.

"She's not feeling well," Johnny said. "But don't worry, she'll still make an appearance."

Ronan gasped. "And spread her germs all over us?"

"She's going to make a virtual appearance," Johnny said with a grin.

Ronan frowned. "And what about her infamous soda bread?" He wrinkled his nose, but Ronan wasn't fooling anyone. Despite the rivalry between Ronan and Rose, he was mad for Rose's Irish soda bread, and everyone knew it.

"I made the soda bread this year," Johnny said. "Rose instructed me step-by-step." Ronan groaned. "I swear," Johnny said. "You won't taste the difference."

"We'll see about that," Ronan said before disappearing into his booth. He could still be heard moaning about it behind his blue velvet curtain.

"I'm going to make you try it," Johnny said. "You won't be disappointed!" Tara glanced at his tins of soda bread. Johnny was eyeing them like a proud papa. Everyone else was a tad worried, given that he hadn't allowed anyone to sample the goods. Tara set her tray of shortbread down on the bake sale table and turned to survey her design work. She'd been up all night setting up the space.

"It looks fabulous," she said. "If I do say so myself."

Johnny muttered an agreement, but his focus was still on his soda bread. "Might even be better than Rose's."

"Bragging must be in the Meehan blood," Ronan Stone yelled out from his booth.

Tara laughed. He wasn't wrong. But Johnny was proud of his Irish soda bread, and she was proud of her design for the event. Booths were situated along the large open floor, decorated with symbols and signs, all announcing the psychic and his or her specific area of expertise. DEIRDRE PALMS: PALM READER had the sculpture of a palm above her booth, RONAN STONE: PSYCHIC MEDIUM had a painting of a crystal ball above his, SLOANE STARGAZER: ASTROLOGIST had a stunning photograph of the night sky littered with sparkling stars, PADDY POCKETS: OCCULT MAGICIAN had a painting of a rabbit popping out of a hat, and CIARA MOON: AURA READER had colorful neon bands around her booth, all representing the myriad of auras that could be seen.

Due to the lush blue velvet curtains, each of the five psychics had privacy, with plenty of room for people to line up in front and enough back access to come and go sight unseen. In the center of the space, a variety of pink, purple, and white crystals were piled high, displayed in an old birdbath sourced from an Irish garden.

Tara glanced at an old clock above the massive exterior doors. The gorgeous piece used to hang in a train station.

They would be open to the public in one hour. A large sign was propped on an easel that would be front and center as folks entered:

BAKED BREAD AND BEYOND
PSYCHIC FAIR AND BAKE SALE
(NO NUTS!)
ALL PROCEEDS GO TO LOCAL CHARITIES

Someone came up behind her, and she knew from the smell of his cologne it was Danny. They had been engaged for a few months, and she still felt butterflies whenever he was near. He began to read the sign aloud. "No nuts?" he said. "I think that ship has sailed."

Tara laughed and gave him a playful shove as he tried to snag a piece of shortbread. "Charity," she said. "I have a batch for you upstairs."

He sighed and ran his hands through his sand-colored hair. He was tall and handsome, hazel eyes flecked with green, and Irish charm for days. A self-proclaimed bachelor, he'd shocked a lot of folks when he'd finally popped the question. They were going to get married on Paddy's Day—one little week from now. *Insane.* "Jokes aside, what's with the 'no nuts' comment?"

"Ronan Stone," Tara said. "He's deathly allergic."

Just then, as if he sensed they were talking about him, Ronan Stone emerged from his booth, still holding a crystal ball. "There's trouble ahead," he said. "Does anyone else sense it?"

The side of his crystal ball had brown smudges. Tara wanted to point this out, but Ronan was known for being mercurial. She'd let someone else break the news. But it was disturbing. How could he see the future when he

couldn't even see that his crystal ball needed a good scrub-
bing?

"I've had a horrible feeling all morning meself," Ciara
Moon said, returning from the back room with a pair of
black spectacles taking over her face. "Losing me spectacles was a bad omen."

"Do you think they all know we're getting married?"
Danny whispered in her ear.

"Perhaps," Tara said. "Shall we call the whole thing off?"

"If the crystal ball says we should . . . I say we smash
it." He kissed her neck.

"I'm starving," Ronan said, apparently no longer worried about impending doom. "Is there not breakfast for
the talent?"

"Wheel me to him," a voice from somewhere in the
mill said. It was Rose's voice; there was no doubt about
it. Tara turned to look for her, but instead of spotting her
aunt, she saw Uncle Johnny. He was pulling a dolly that
had an upright broom attached, and secured to the broom
was an iPad. Rose's image filled the screen. "You're making me dizzy," Rose said. "Can you not jerk me all over
the place?"

"What in the actual . . ." Tara placed her finger on
Danny's lips before he could curse.

"I was wondering that myself," she said. "Let's find out
what this is all about." They hurried over to Johnny and
Virtual-Rose. "Hi, Rose," Tara said. "What's the story?"
Rose, a tiny woman with wavy black and gray-streaked
hair down to her hips, looked larger on screen. Although
Rose normally sported a heavily made-up face and a signature bright red rose tucked behind her left ear, today
Tara could see the red around her aunt's eyes and nose, her
hair pulled behind her, and an understated black wrap. "I
heard you weren't feeling well," Tara said.

"And now you can see it," Rose sniffed.

"Can we ever," Ronan Stone said, sneaking up from behind and shoving his large face close to the screen. Rose glared, and Ronan shrank back. "I'm only messing." Ronan held up his hands as if he was being arrested.

"I'm truly sorry," Tara said. Rose had been looking forward to this event all year.

"I'm going to try Johnny's soda bread soon," Ronan said. "I wonder if it's better than yours." He truly enjoyed riling her up.

Rose ignored him and addressed Johnny. "Did you put the crosses on top?" Some Irish used to believe that putting crosses on top of the soda bread helped keep the Devil out while baking, and poking the four corners let the fairies out. "That's the blessing," Rose continued. "Did you remember the blessing?"

"I did, so," Johnny said. He threw a look to the table. Tara had seen his tins, and he had completely forgotten to put the crosses on top. And although it was traditionally a blessing, the crosses also helped the bread bake from the center out.

"Someone is lying," Ronan said in a singsong voice. "But that's okay. Rose, you're already away with the fairies, and I already have a little of the Devil in me so what's a little more?" He roared with laughter.

"Johnny!" Rose said. "You know that Irish soda bread is sacred!" Johnny glanced at Tara, who gave a slight smile. They both knew what was coming: a history lesson. Rose was hard-core about her soda bread, as were many others. There even existed an organization, the Society for the Preservation of Irish Soda Bread, formed by Ed O'Dwyer. The horror of the famine, which took a million Irish lives, gave rise to the popularity of Irish soda bread. It was quick and easy, and the ingredients were simple: flour, salt, bicarbonate of soda, and sour milk. These days the sour milk was replaced by buttermilk, and soda bread had a variety of forms: brown soda bread; griddle bread; golden soda bread; Railway Cake or Spotted Dog, which contained currants; scones—the list went on. But Rose was a stickler for traditional Irish soda bread, which dated back to the 1840s and contained only flour, bicarbonate of soda, salt, and buttermilk.

"I'm sorry, I'm sorry," Johnny said. "I'll put crosses on them now."

"It's too late now!" Rose said. "The cross helps in the baking process, you eejit."

"I'm no good without you," Johnny said, and Rose immediately softened. She gave a smile and a shrug. Johnny threw a look to Danny. "Live and learn."

"This is an interesting arrangement," Tara said, taking in the broom and dolly to which the iPad was attached.

Johnny grinned. "You like? I made me wife into a robot."

"You're pulling your wife on a leash," Danny said. "Classic."

"Have you done your affirmations yet this morning, Johnny?" Rose asked.

Johnny grinned and pumped his fist. "I'm a millionaire!"

"*We,*" Rose stressed.

"We're millionaires!" He grinned yet again, then turned to Tara and Danny and rolled his eyes.

"What in the world?" Tara said.

"We're manifesting," Rose said. "We've been doing it for three months."

"Nothing so far," Johnny said.

"You have to imagine as if it's already happened," Rose said. "How many times do I have to remind you?"

"I'm a millionaire!" Johnny said. Rose fumed. "We! We, we, we! We are millionaires!" he added.

"Rose Meehan is dead, Rose Meehan is dead," Ronan Stone chimed in. They all turned in horror to see Ronan Stone standing there grinning. "I'm manifesting too," he said. He bent down to the iPad until he was eye to eye with Rose. "Still not working."

Chapter Two

"Hilarious," Rose said. "Someone get that horrible man out of me face." Ronan removed himself and trotted away to the bake sale table. "Pivot me," Rose barked. "Pivot me!"

Johnny sighed and turned the contraption so Rose could see the booths with the names of the psychics with his or her specialty listed above them. She took them in with an appreciative nod. "Nice work, Tara."

"Thank you," Tara said. "But Johnny and Danny deserve equal credit."

"Wheel me out of their earshot," Rose said. Johnny obliged, taking his dolly and broomstick closer to the booths. Tara and Danny followed. Rose pointed at the first booth: DEIRDRE PALMS: PALM READER.

"Otherwise known as 'Sweaty Palms,'" Rose said. She jerked her head to the next booth: CIARA MOON: AURA READER.

"The Dark Side," Rose said. "Every time she reads someone, she insists their aura needs to be cleansed. It's her mouth that could use a good soaping."

"Pot, kettle," Danny whispered.

"What did you say?" Rose barked.

"We're thrilled for your insight," Danny replied quickly.

They moved on: PADDY POCKETS: OCCULT MAGICIAN.

"He's here?" Rose shook her head. "Watch him. He calls himself a magician when what he is a masterful pickpocket."

"Next," Tara said, hoping to move this along.

SLOANE STARGAZER: ASTROLOGIST.

"Star Glazer," Rose said. "As in glazed-over. And not just her eyes. Her predictions are so generic. She's sweet on Johnny too."

"I can hear you," Sloane said from behind her curtain.

"I can as well," floated a voice from behind Deirdre's curtain.

"Me too," Ciara said. "My sight may be bad, but there's nothing wrong with me hearing!"

"I take no offense," Paddy Pockets chimed in last. "And she's right. Watch your pockets!" He howled with laughter.

They all glanced at the last booth. RONAN STONE: PSYCHIC MEDIUM.

He needed no introduction, but Rose couldn't help herself. "Bulldozer," Rose said, shaking her head. "He tears people down, then bulldozes right over them with his dire predictions."

Johnny sighed. "Only messing," he shouted. "We love you all."

Rose was not fazed. "Next year I'm getting better talent. We were so desperate this year, we had to scrape the bottom of the whiskey barrel."

"Ungrateful wench," Ronan called out. "Paddy, do you still make voodoo dolls?"

"Absolutely," Paddy said. "But we'll need a lock of her hair."

"I'd happily rip it out meself," Ronan said. "Even if it meant catching all her nasty, nasty germs."

*   *   *

"If it isn't Dave the Debunker," Rose said. As requested, Johnny had propped Virtual-Rose by the entrance, then he'd scurried away, no doubt wanting a break from his demanding wife.

Dave glanced at the iPad. "Rose, darling," he said. "You're looking better than ever."

"What are you doing here?" she demanded.

"What do you think?" he said. "I'm going to hover over the entire event and make sure that the public is not taken for a ride." He glanced toward Ronan's booth. "And support me bigger half, of course." He laughed at his own joke.

"This is a charity event," Rose said. "It's all in good fun."

"Don't you worry, Rose," Dave said. "Maybe I'm only here for *Johnny's* Irish soda bread."

"I hope it's dry, and you choke on it," Rose said. She really wasn't pleasant when she was sick. But Dave didn't seem put off.

"There's that wicked tongue," he said, waggling his finger at her with a grin.

Johnny popped up behind Dave. "You leave me wife's tongue out of your mouth."

Danny erupted in laughter. Tara couldn't help but join him. Johnny stared at them, clueless.

"Tara! Have you tasted Johnny's Irish soda bread?" Danny said, corralling them all over to the bake sale table.

Tara glanced at the neatly arranged tins. "Not yet."

"Get it into you," Rose said. "I need to make sure he's not embarrassing me."

Danny cocked his head. "I'd say it's a bit too late for that."

Tara stared at Uncle Johnny's tin of Irish soda bread. "I'd hate to be the first to cut into it."

"Allow me." The male voice came from behind. Ronan stood holding a large, sharp knife, hovering over the table.

"Don't you dare!" Rose said.

Ronan stabbed the knife into the soda bread, and then deftly cut a small slice. He plucked a napkin from the table, set the slice on top, and handed it to Tara.

"Thank you," she said.

"Do try not to choke on it," Ronan said. "I can see from here it's terribly dry."

Rose glared. As Johnny stared at her expectantly, Tara took a bite of the soda bread. Ronan was correct. It was dry. Irish soda bread was on the drier side compared to other breads, but this was next level. Had Ronan not warned her, she might not have bitten into it so carefully. Even with the small bite, she could feel it constricting her throat a tad.

"Well?" Johnny said.

She couldn't lie. She wanted to spare his feelings, but she couldn't lie. "It's a tad dry," she said.

"That is a grave disappointment," Ronan said. "I suppose I shall be abstaining this year." Even so, he stared at the tins of soda bread longingly. Paddy Pockets joined the group, huddling next to Ronan. The two of them bent heads together, no doubt exchanging wisecracks.

"I gave you clear instructions," Rose said to Johnny. "How could you do this to me?"

"Maybe the other tins are fine," Tara said.

"Maybe I can serve it with a glass of milk," Johnny said.

"Or a gallon," Tara replied.

"I'll tell you what," Ronan said. He clunked the knife down on the table and reached beneath his heavy cloak to pull out a crisp hundred-euro bill. "I'll buy a few tins and use them as a paperweight." He dropped the money into the donation jar, then stood staring at the collection as if trying to make up his mind.

"I see right through you," Rose said. "You're just trying to get a rise out of me."

"If I can't get it from this soda bread, it might as well be you," Ronan said with a wink. "Here we are." He scooped two tins from the table.

"We don't have any change yet, Big Spender," Johnny said.

Ronan waved his hand. "It's for charity," he said. "Keep it."

Rose gasped. "You're so tight you'll probably build your own coffin!"

Ronan threw his head back and roared with laughter. "Rose, Rose, Rose. Not smelling so sweet today, are ya? But you've got enough cheek for a second arse."

"I should kick you out of the psychic fair," Rose said.

Ronan raised an eyebrow. "For being generous?"

"You? Generous?" Rose said. "Not a chance. What's your real motive here?"

"This event would be nothing without me." Ronan leaned in. "And yet it's going to be a raving success without you."

"Ha!" Rose said. "You couldn't predict the rain even if you were drowning in it."

"If that's true, I'll be glad for it," Ronan said. "Because all morning I've seen death riding in on her high horse. Galloping, galloping, galloping." He leaned down until he was eye to eye again with Rose. "Is she coming for you?"

"If anyone deserves death riding to snatch a reluctant rider, it's you!" Rose was shouting now, and several heads turned their way.

Ronan touched Rose's nose on the screen with his finger. "Boop." With that he whirled around and headed for his booth, tins of Irish soda bread aloft.

"This is already a disaster," Rose said. "Dry soda bread, me nemesis warning of death."

"But we made a hundred euro for charity!" Johnny said.

"Now I'm glad you didn't put a cross on it," Rose said. "The Devil has met his match."

It was nearly time to open the doors. "Thirty minutes until showtime," Rose yelled from the screen. "Is everyone ready?" The past twenty minutes had been a whirlwind of activity, with the psychics each visiting each other's booths to compare them to their own and pepper each other with strained compliments. Now they were nearly ready. That's when the fire alarm blared. Tara covered her ears. Sloane Stargazer came running from the storage room.

"Dumpster fire!" she yelled. "Dumpster fire!"

"That's what I said," Ciara Moon pointed out.

"A *real* dumpster fire," Sloane said. "Seriously! The back dumpster is on fire!"

"Everyone out," Tara yelled. "Hurry." Johnny was already on the phone to Emergency Services. Luckily most of the psychics emerged from their booths, and they headed for the exit. They gathered in the parking lot. Everyone was there but Ronan Stone, Danny, and Johnny. Moments later Danny and Johnny ran out, holding fire extinguishers. Johnny was also pulling Virtual-Rose behind them. He left the iPad with Tara and ran around back to the dumpsters.

"Where's Ronan?" Dave the Debunker said, as if just now noticing his husband's absence.

"Maybe he's wearing earphones and didn't hear the commotion," Deirdre said.

Johnny and Danny emerged from behind the building. "The fire is out," Johnny said. "It never reached the in-side—we should be grand."

"If it smells of smoke, we're going to have to cancel," Ciara said. "My sinuses won't be able to handle it."

"Then you can cancel," Deirdre said. "Some of us need this job."

They all stepped inside and inhaled. "I can't smell a thing," Johnny said. He surveyed the crowd. "Can any of ye?"

They shook their heads.

"Disaster averted," Sloane said.

"Thanks to you," Johnny pointed out. "But which one of you threw a lit cigarette into me dumpster?"

"Does anyone smell like smoke?" Dave said. He began sniffing. "Someone is wearing too much perfume!"

He was met with glares. "You have a distinct soapy smell," Sloane said. "Maybe you're the secret smoker."

"I have a soapy smell? Meaning I showered and used soap?" Dave stood up straight. "I happen to shower regu-larly, and I've never smoked a day in me life."

"I predicted this," Ciara said. "Does anyone recall me yelling 'dumpster fire' this morning?"

"Maybe *you* set the fire," Deirdre said. "Just to boost our opinion of your abilities."

"Maybe Ronan started it," Paddy said. "And that's why he didn't come out." They all stopped arguing and stared at Ronan's booth.

Dave headed for it. "Darling," he said. "You missed all the drama."

"There's only five minutes until we open," Rose said.

"To your booths." The remaining psychics hurried in. Just then the sounds of sirens approached.

"I thought you called them off," Rose said.

"I guess they were already on the way," Johnny replied.

"It can't hurt to have it checked out," Danny said.

Johnny shook his fist. "If I get fined for that cigarette, one of you is going to pay!"

One by one the psychics stepped out of their booths, all but Ronan. Rose rolled her eyes. "Diva," she said, pointing to his booth. "Get out here."

Dave, who had just reached Ronan's booth, popped in. Seconds later he unleashed a blood-curdling scream. "Help! Oh no, no, no. Ronan. My poor Ronan. Help!" Everyone hurried over. The inside of Ronan's booth was a disaster. Tarot cards lay scattered on the floor, the DEATH card front and center. Ronan's crystal ball was the only item on his table. A message in bright red had been scrawled across it: *Peanut Butter*. Ronan Stone was lying on his back on the cold, hard floor, mouth open, hands splayed, with the tin of Irish soda bread near his head. It was half-empty. No one needed a palm reading, a dire horoscope, their star chart, or a crystal ball to see that poor Ronan Stone was stone-cold dead.

Chapter Three

"Who wants to tell me what's going on?" Detective Sergeant Hayes peered at the colorful group through thick spectacles that continuously slid down her long nose. Her hair, cut in a bob, bounced as her head swiveled. She pushed her glasses up with a trembling index finger. She looked nervous. Tara suspected this was her first murder probe. Garda O'Leary stood next to her, taking notes. He looked fresh out of garda college, and from the flush up his neck, he wasn't used to being around a gaggle of psychics. Ciara Moon couldn't stop staring at him. Tara wondered if he had a unique aura. She'd been looking forward to having Danny's read. Was he getting cold feet about the wedding? She'd been looking forward to this entire event. But that wasn't important now that a man had lost his life. It just didn't feel real yet, and Tara's mind kept circling over it, thinking someone was playing a horrible joke. Ronan Stone's body was covered, but they couldn't remove him until the state pathologist arrived to declare it a crime scene.

Ronan had been such a dynamic figure, it was hard to imagine him gone. Was his energy still with them? And how was it possible that a killer could be among them? If not for the words *Peanut Butter* scrawled across the crystal ball, everyone might have thought this was a terrible accident, a careless baker who had overlooked the multiple warnings that one of their psychics was allergic to nuts.

"Why didn't he use his EpiPen?" Sloane said. "He always had it with him."

Heads swiveled to Dave, who was sobbing into his hands. He must have felt everyone's gaze, for he dropped his hands and nodded. "EpiPen," he said. "It's always in his breast pocket." He reached into his pocket and held up an EpiPen. "And I always have the other. But someone started a fire in the dumpster, and I wasn't there when he needed me the most." The sobs started again.

"We checked his pockets," Detective Hayes said. "They were empty."

Everyone looked at Paddy Pockets. "Are you accusing me?" he said. "I had nothing to do with this."

"You did agree that you're a masterful pickpocket," Ciara Moon said.

"And you were huddled next to him at the bake sale table," Deirdre Palms added.

"I play *tricks*," Paddy said. "But murder isn't one of them." He held his arms open. "Go ahead, Detective. Frisk me."

"Everyone calm down," Detective Hayes said. But she nodded to Garda O'Leary, who went over and patted down Paddy Pockets. He began taking things out: scarves, a stuffed rabbit, a magic wand . . .

"We'll be here all day," Sloane Stargazer said.

"No EpiPen," O'Leary declared minutes later.

"I await an apology," Paddy said.

"You probably have hidden pockets," Dave insisted.

"You're doing a lot of deflecting," Paddy said. "How do we know you aren't the killer?"

Dave glared. "You're accusing me of murdering me own husband?"

"It's usually the husband," Deirdre said.

Just then, a crowd outside began pounding on the door. Detective Sergeant Hayes turned to Johnny. "You'll have to inform them that the event is canceled," she said. "Garda O'Leary will accompany you. This mill is now a crime scene." She looked around. "We need somewhere to gather."

"My loft is upstairs," Tara said. "We can go there."

"Upstairs," Detective Hayes said. "Everyone upstairs."

Minutes later they were all gathered in Tara's flat. It was a large, open space, allowing all the suspects to spread out. Tara had gone to town decorating it. She loved running Renewals, her little shop in Galway City, but design would always be her first passion. The space was minimal with clean lines and no clutter, but it was livened up by splashes of color, unique art and artifacts. Tara and Danny had talked about getting a place together, but for the immediate future they would both live here. It was a sprawling loft, and given that Danny worked for Uncle Johnny sourcing architectural items, he would have a very short commute downstairs. She glanced at all the people gathered; she'd never had this many take over her space, yet there was still plenty of room. Johnny and Garda O'Leary headed out to try and soothe the disappointed crowd outside.

Paddy Pockets was pacing behind Tara's leather sectional, which was driving Tara mental, but if the guards weren't going to complain, neither would she. Was this a red flag? He certainly seemed on edge. Then again, there was no right way to react to a murder, especially when all of them were suspects. Soon Johnny and Garda O'Leary returned.

"The coroner is downstairs," O'Leary said. "He's acting on behalf of the state pathologist."

At least the body would be on its way to the morgue.

"The coroner thinks peanut butter was slipped into the Irish soda bread," Johnny said, his voice cracking. "Given Ronan's EpiPen is missing, I see no reason to disagree with him."

"Not to mention *Peanut Butter* is literally written across his crystal ball," Ciara Moon pointed out.

"Is that what it said?" Sloane piped in. "Maybe they can get fingerprints."

"Peanut butter fingers," Paddy said, looking at his own fingertips. "Does anyone want to smell mine?"

"Gross," Deirdre said. "Besides, I'm sure the killer wore gloves and washed his or her hands."

"Dave smells like soap," Sloane said.

"That again?" Dave stopped crying and shook his fist. "My husband was just murdered!"

"If you're innocent, I truly apologize," Sloane said.

"I swear to all of ye, right here and right now," Johnny said, "I did *not* put peanut butter in the soda bread."

"He bought two tins, and they had been sitting in his booth," Tara said. "Any one of us could have snuck into his booth."

"I second what me husband Johnny said," Rose piped up from a corner of the room. "He did *not* put peanut butter in the Irish soda bread." All heads swiveled in the direction of the disembodied voice, including the detective, whose spectacles slid all the way to the floor as she whipped her head around. Dave quickly retrieved them and held them out to her, but she didn't make a move to take them. She was still trying to figure out where the voice was coming from. "Over here," Rose said. "On the broom." The detective took the spectacles and slowly walked over to Virtual-Rose, mouth open in disbelief.

"Who the bleep are you?" Detective Sergeant Hayes asked.

Tara had never heard anyone "bleep" themselves. "This is Johnny's wife, Rose," Tara said. "She organized this event but was too ill to attend."

"She was arguing with Ronan this morning," Dave revealed, pointing at the iPad. "We all heard it!"

"If you think I'm capable of poisoning a man from afar, then you'll have to admit that supernatural powers exist," Rose said.

Not the best argument, Tara thought.

"Besides, it was me husband who made the soda bread." An even worse argument.

"We know, Rose," Johnny said. "I've already addressed that, now haven't I?"

"You argued with the victim?" Detective Hayes asked Virtual-Rose.

"They're huge rivals," Paddy said, momentarily stopping his pacing. It was as if they'd all decided to point their fingers at Rose. Ridiculous given the killer was one of them.

"It's a very competitive field," Deirdre Palms said.

"We're all know-it-alls," Ciara said.

"Can we get back to the murder weapon?" Rose said. "Did you hear me? It *wasn't* Johnny's soda bread."

"How on earth would you know that?" Detective Hayes said.

"Tara was the first to taste it," Rose said. "And she's still alive!"

Now all heads turned to Tara. Danny pinched her, and she yelped. "I can confirm," Danny said. "Still alive."

"Pinch me again and I can't promise the same for you," Tara quipped.

"Tara?" Rose continued. "Did you taste even a trace of peanut butter?"

"No," Tara said. "I swear there wasn't a hint of it."

"See?" Rose said. "Johnny is innocent, and Tara can prove it, and I'm innocent because I wasn't even there."

A gasp rose from Sloane Stargazer. "That's the perfect murder!"

"Ronan purchased a different tin than Tara was eating out of," Dave said. "Two tins, to be exact."

"He paid a hundred euro for two tins even though we were only charging ten euro," Rose said.

"He was being generous," Ciara said. "For charity."

"And that's not like him at all," Rose said. "He was never a big spender."

Dave looked at his shoes. "She's right," he said. "Even I was surprised by his kind gesture." He started to cry once more.

"The only person I know who regularly flashes that kind of money is Paddy Pockets," Sloane Stargazer said.

"True!" Deirdre Palms chimed in. Heads swiveled to Paddy. He instantly turned red.

"You *are* known to have crisp hundred-euro bills in your pockets, Paddy," Ciara said.

"I've already been searched," Paddy said. "Did you see any hundred-euro bills in me pockets?" He looked around as if to gather support. "Come on! Tara insists her slice of soda bread, that Ronan himself sliced for her, did not contain peanut butter."

"I swear," Tara said. "It did not."

"And it was Ronan who chose which two tins he wanted to purchase," Paddy said. "Do we all agree?" Heads nodded. "I'm a magician, not a psychic. If only one or more tins contained peanut butter, out of—how many tins?"

"Twelve," Johnny said.

"Setting aside the tin that Tara ate from, out of eleven tins, how did I get him to choose the one with the deadly peanut butter?" Everyone stopped to consider this. "It's obvious," he said. "The peanut butter must have been slathered on after he purchased the tins. He took them straight to his booth. Someone snuck in and poisoned one of them."

"If anyone could pull off a trick like that, it's you," Ciara said softly.

Paddy crossed his arms and sulked. "We don't even know Ronan was the intended target."

"We *do* know he was the target," Dave said. "You just said someone snuck into *his* booth after he bought the tins."

"True," Paddy said. "I did say that, didn't I?" He looked as if he regretted it.

"Besides," Dave continued. "Ronan is the only one allergic to peanut butter."

"He saw it coming," Rose said with a gasp. "He saw death riding on her high horse."

Galloping, galloping, galloping, Tara thought. It was true; she'd heard him say it himself.

"Ciara is the one who predicted a dumpster fire," Paddy said. "And then minutes later there was an actual dumpster fire!"

"Set by someone who was *smoking*," Ciara said. "I have allergies, I wouldn't be caught dead with a cigarette in me mouth."

Everyone started talking at once, pointing fingers and accusing each other.

Detective Hayes put two fingers in her mouth and whistled. The piercing sound did the trick, and the room hushed.

"I know this is all fun and games with this 'I can see the future' gimmick, but you will not—I repeat, you will *not*—try to infuse any of this parapsychology babble into my murder investigation. Are we clear?"

"As clear as a crystal ball," Sloane said.

"I was dying to have a look at your palms, Detective," Deirdre said. "I suppose that's off the table."

Garda O'Leary couldn't help but glance at his palms. Detective Hayes slapped them down. Tara felt bad for the detective; she was going to have her hands full with this group. The only way she was going to get any clarity at all was if she spoke with them one-on-one. But Tara was not about to interject her opinion into the mix.

"Detective," Rose said. "Don't you think you should question the suspects one-on-one?"

Freaky. Rose had read Tara's mind, and then hadn't thought twice about speaking up.

Detective Hayes squinted at the iPad. "I make the decisions around here." Detective Hayes now began to pace the room. Deirdre Palms was edging closer to Garda O'Leary and glancing repeatedly at his hands as if trying to read his palms from a distance. "Enough of the group chat. I think it's best if we question you one-on-one," Detective Hayes announced as she stopped pacing. She pointed at Johnny. "Your office," she said. "Is there any reason it would be part of the crime scene?"

Johnny shook his head. "I'm the only one who's been in it this morning. However—"

The detective held up her hand. "I don't want to hear it. I intend on using your office as the interview room."

"Are you sure? Because I think you should—"

"I'm sure." She silenced him with a look. "Now then. Who wants to be first in the hot seat?"

Chapter Four

Detective Hayes exited the loft, followed by Dave, who had volunteered to be questioned first. Tara turned to Uncle Johnny. "What were you trying to tell the detective about your office?"

"I think I know," Danny said. "You should have insisted she listen."

"Let's go somewhere private," Johnny replied with a nod. He picked up Virtual-Rose's leash and gestured toward Tara's room. They headed for it. Tara's room had once been part of the open loft, but she'd hired a contractor to add walls and a proper door. Once they were safely inside, Johnny turned to the iPad. "Sorry, Rose, I need the screen. I'm going to have to call you back."

Just as her mouth opened in protest, Johnny severed the call. And as soon as her image disappeared, Johnny poked at the screen and then stepped back. A black and white image of his office appeared. Seconds later the door opened, and Detective Hayes walked in, followed by Dave. She gestured for him to take the seat across from Johnny's extremely messy desk, then she took the seat behind the desk. From her expression she was appalled by the mounds of books and papers littering the surface. She sighed. "Give me a minute," she said as she began rearranging things to make space.

"I installed a camera in my office," Johnny said.

"You don't say," Tara quipped. "Turn it off."

Instead, Johnny turned up the volume. "I need you two to set me straight," he said, "Tell me we should *not* listen in on the interviews."

"We should not listen in on the interviews," Tara said.

Johnny nodded. "However . . ."

"Someone is trying to frame Johnny for the murder," Danny said.

"How do you figure that?" Tara asked.

"They poisoned the Irish soda bread," Danny said. "The bread made by Johnny. And then they set his dumpster on fire."

"You're right," Uncle Johnny said. "That fire was set to draw everyone out of the building."

"Which means shortly before it was set, Ronan must have already taken a bite of the soda bread," Danny said. "Otherwise he would have joined us outside."

"None of that gives us a right to eavesdrop on a police investigation," Tara said. She was dying to listen too, but one of them had to be the voice of reason.

Johnny gave Tara a beseeching look. "This detective looks so nervous a slight breeze could blow her away. But *you've* solved a few murder probes, haven't you?"

"A few," Tara admitted. She'd found herself at the center of a few murder probes in the years since she'd arrived in Ireland, and she'd discovered that just like interior design, cases often were solved by looking at patterns or taking patterns apart and seeing them in a new light. Her expertise as an interior designer had wired her brain to be able to imagine a myriad of combinations. And much like combinations to a safe, sometimes the right one clicked and the case sprang wide open.

"I don't think I can say the same for our detective," Johnny said, gesturing to the screen. Detective Hayes was still tidying up the desk, pushing up her spectacles every few seconds.

"And we both know that Uncle Johnny is innocent," Danny said to Tara.

"And I know ye are innocent," Johnny said. "That makes the three of us the perfect team."

"I take your points," Tara said. "But what do you think would happen if they found out we were playing Nancy Drew and the Hardy Boys? It's going to make us look guilty for sure."

"How would anyone find out when only the three of us know?" Johnny asked.

"There's a killer among us and he, she, or they need to be caught," Danny said. "Whoever it was, this person was bold enough to pull off a murder in plain sight. Even if the detective was experienced"—he glanced at the screen again. Detective Hayes was now scratching her nose with the end of a stapler—"I think we can all agree we are not dealing with your average killer."

Tara bit her lip. She was more of a rule follower than these two renegades. But they were making excellent points.

"If you don't want to participate, I understand," Johnny said. "But I'm listening in."

"Me too," Danny said.

"I want it on the record that I don't think this is a good idea," Tara said. But Danny was right. The killer was way too clever. And the three of them were innocent. Detective Hayes was now touching Biros to the tip of her tongue and testing them on a notepad in front of them, presumably to find one that worked.

"She didn't even bring her own Biro!" Johnny exclaimed.

"Let's just listen to a smidge," Danny said. He went to the door, which was already shut, and locked it. "Lower the volume." Danny returned as Johnny adjusted the volume until it was just loud enough for the three of them to hear.

"—and may I say something about one of our suspects before we begin?" Dave was saying.

"Just a minute. I'm trying to get me recorder set up," the detective said as she fumbled with the device.

"It's about the American woman. Johnny Meehan's niece, Tara."

Johnny and Danny looked at Tara. "Should we stop listening?" Danny said with a grin.

"What could he possibly have to say about me?" Tara swatted Danny's hand away as he reached as if to turn off the iPad.

"Dead bodies follow her wherever she goes. I find that improbable. In fact, she might be a serial killer."

Tara's jaw dropped open. Danny started to laugh. He rubbed his hands together. "I'll be famous," he said. "I can be on that reality show, *I Married a Serial Killer*—"

"Don't give me any ideas," Tara said. Johnny shushed them.

"My recorder is finally working," Detective Hayes was saying. "Let's begin." She spun around for a minute in Johnny's chair before coming to a stop and pushing RECORD on the device in front of her. "Ready when you are."

Dave's knee bounced up and down as his eyes took in Johnny's office. "Would you like me to talk about Tara Meehan?"

"Please state your name for the recording," Detective Hayes said. She didn't seem to be taking the bait about Tara being a serial killer. But Johnny was right. They had to listen in. Whether Detective Hayes knew it or not, she needed all the help she could get. "Your name," Detective Hayes repeated.

"My name is Dave White," he said. "But most people call me Dave the Debunker." He laughed. Detective Hayes did not. "It was Ronan who gave me the moniker." He pulled a handkerchief out of his suit pocket and dabbed his eyes.

"He's still *crying?*" Johnny said.

"His husband was murdered," Tara said. "Be kind."

"How do we know he isn't the killer?" Danny asked.

Johnny put one finger on his nose and pointed the other at Danny. Tara sighed. Maybe this wasn't the A-team after all.

"And what was your relationship to the victim?" Detective Hayes said.

"I already told you that." Dave's voice wobbled. "Ronan Stone was my husband. And business partner." He removed something from his pocket and slid it across the table. They all leaned in.

"It's his calling card," Danny said.

"Unbelievable," Johnny said. "He's using a police interview to promote his podcast."

"You don't know that for sure," Tara said.

"I have a podcast," Dave said. "*Psychic Scums and the Skeptic.* It's very popular. I was here to do a segment on this event."

Johnny gave Tara look. "Mea culpa," she said.

Detective Hayes stopped writing and looked at Dave. "Do you make money on this podcast?" she asked.

"Astute," Tara said. "I think she's on the ball." Danny and Johnny frowned. "If he's losing sponsors, maybe he staged this to create drama," Tara continued. "Drama gets listeners and listeners get—"

"Sponsors," Johnny and Danny said in unison. The three turned eagerly back to the screen.

Dave shrugged. "I'm saving humanity from falling for so-called predictions by unscrupulous folks preying on those who are gullible. Psychic scum! But I don't make a living off it by any means."

"It sounds as if you have some real anger toward the psychic community," the detective said.

"They're monstrous people! Scavengers! Ripping off elderly and . . ." He suddenly stopped, his face red, his breath labored. He held up an index finger. "I'm a passionate man. An advocate for the vulnerable. But my husband wasn't one of *them*. And I wasn't angry enough to kill, if that's what you're implying."

"That's exactly what she's implying," Tara said. "Look how quickly he became enraged."

"He could be the killer," Johnny agreed.

"Take me through your morning," Detective Hayes said.

Dave squirmed in his chair. "What would you like to know?"

"Deflecting!" Danny said.

"Tell me everything that happened from the moment you woke up this morning until the murder," Detective Hayes instructed.

"May I consult my notes?" Dave asked. "And my recordings?"

Detective Hayes snapped to attention. "Notes? Recordings?"

Dave nodded. "I'm a meticulous note taker and planner. Also, I conducted a few mini-interviews this morning as the psychics were setting up." He stared at his phone, lost in thought, then his head pivoted to the detective. "For the podcast," he said. "Strictly professional." He dabbed his eyes with a handkerchief from his blazer.

"I'm going to need you to turn those recordings over to me," the detective said.

Dave clutched his mobile phone to his chest, his mouth open as he shook his head. "It's me livelihood."

"I thought you didn't make your living off your podcasts," Tara and Detective Hayes said at the same time. Danny and Johnny looked at Tara.

"Maybe you should be in with the psychics," Danny said. "You're reading her mind."

"She caught him in a lie," Tara said. "I'm starting to think we're in good hands with her at the helm."

Dave was still clutching his phone. "You will get them returned to you as soon as we've processed the evidence," Detective Hayes said gently, holding her hand out for the phone.

He chewed on his lip. "Whatever you do . . . you cannot erase my recordings. Do I have your word?"

The detective crossed her arms. "Why do I get the feeling there's something you're not telling me?"

Tara was wondering the same thing. Dave blinked at her with the expression of a burglar who had just been caught shimmying up to a bedroom window. "May I take you through the events first? And then me phone is all yours." He stared at her. "If you *promise* not to erase a single thing."

"Because it's your *livelihood*," she said.

"Exactly."

"On the table," she said. "Where I can see it."

Dave set the phone down and held up his hands. "You're a skeptic," he said. "Just like me."

If he was trying to butter her up, it wasn't working.

Now that she had caught her stride, she was all business. "Take me through the events of your morning."

Dave squirmed again. "You don't have a cigarette, do you?"

"A cigarette!" Johnny said, pointing at the screen.

"Maybe he started the fire," Danny said.

"And Sloane Stargazer said he smelled like soap," Johnny said.

"I do not smoke," Detective Hayes said.

Dave nodded, looking defeated. "I quit months ago, but it's not every day your partner is murdered in cold blood."

"Take your time," Detective Hayes said. She glanced at the clock. "But also, hurry it up."

"Every other psychic here was jealous of my husband," Dave said. "I may be a skeptic, but I also fall on my sword when I have to. Ronan was not a fake. He demonstrated a power even I could not explain." He leaned in. "The rest of that lot? Pure scam artists."

Johnny shivered. "Thank heavens Rose didn't hear that."

"Speaking of Rose," Danny said. "Aren't you a little worried she's going to be browned-off that you cut her feed?"

"Not at all," Johnny said. "I'm petrified."

Danny chuckled. "Happy wife, happy life." He gave Tara a pinch.

"I could present evidence of his greatness, if you'd like?" Dave was saying.

"I'm not interested in Mr. Stone's psychic abilities, Mr. White. I would like you to take me through your morning."

He swallowed hard. "Ronan and I arrived early, before there were any other vehicles in the car park. We sat there for a moment watching the building."

Odd, Tara thought.

Detective Hayes raised an eyebrow. "And why is that?"

"Because cheaters often arrive early to eavesdrop on the public—they try and source information from strangers so when they lure them into their booths for a reading they can spring this information on them to impress them. That's called the *hook*." He turned and stared directly at the spot where the camera was hidden, causing the three eavesdroppers to pull back, as if he had just sussed them out.

"In this scenario, isn't Mr. Ronan Stone the psychic who technically arrived first?" Detective Hayes asked.

"He was only there early because of me," Dave said.

"Who arrived next?"

"The Dark Side," Dave said.

The detective stopped writing. "Excuse me?"

"I'm sorry. That's what we called her. Ciara Moon arrived first." He leaned in. "She claims to see auras. Even has a camera that supposedly takes pictures of them."

Detective Hayes stared at Dave, looking over his head and then around his body as if trying to see his aura. "Why is it you call her 'The Dark Side'?"

Dave held up a finger. "That, Detective, is an excellent question. We call her 'The Dark Side' because she drops diabolical predictions on people—calls their aura 'clouded' and 'rage-filled' or 'jealousy-filled,' 'dirty,' anything vile—and then she offers to cleanse them. For a very hefty price." He shook his head. "Despicable people like her and Deirdre Palms are the reason I went into this field to begin with." He blew his nose. "Not wonderful, truly talented souls like Ronan Stone."

"He's laying it on a little thick, don't you think?" Danny said.

"Yes," Tara and Uncle Johnny said in stereo.

"Jinx, you owe me a Guinness," Johnny said.

"I'd like a clearer narrative of your entire morning," the detective said. "I'll only interrupt if I feel it's absolutely necessary."

Dave nodded. "Very well," he said. "Let me start again."

Chapter Five

"As I said," Dave began, "Ronan and I were the first to arrive in the car park. We even beat the sun. There's only one dim light in the car park, but even so we didn't want to be seen, so Ronan parked in the farthest corner near the back of the building. I knew we would have to kill time, which was why I brought a large mug of tea and a lemon bar. I know that might sound ridiculous given I was going to a bake sale, but you see I had no intention of buying baked goods at the sale. When one is a professional like me, and a skeptic to boot, everyone is watching every move, and I feared if I favored one person's baked good over the other, that I would be accused of being 'on the take'—"

" 'On the take' over a lemon bar?" The detective could not hide her incredulity.

"Yes," Dave said, blinking rapidly. "You have no idea how competitive these psychic bakers can be. Downright vicious."

"Go on, so."

"I was sitting in me car, drinking me tea, eating me lemon bar, and listening to me podcast, if you must know—it really helps to listen to your own shows as if you're an audience member—it's the best way to gain insight—have you ever listened to me podcast, Detective? *Psychic Scums and the Skeptic?*"

"No," Detective Hayes said.

"You should have a listen. And if you don't mind, give me a like and a follow."

"The only thing I want to follow is the events of your morning, so I am going to remind you to stick to the facts and only the facts."

Dave looked hurt, but then nodded. "Ciara Moon was the first to pull into the car park. She drives a Saturn." He stopped talking and waited.

Detective Hayes frowned. "And?"

Dave leaned in. "Don't you want to know the first thing she did after she pulled in?"

"Go on, so."

"She headed to the dumpster around the back of the building."

Detective Hayes crossed her arms. "How do you know this?"

"Pardon?" His confidence faltered.

"If you were parked in front of the building—"

"I see what you're doing."

"What am I doing?"

"You're trying to catch me in a lie." He shook his head. "Excellent technique. I wasn't parked in front of the building. I was parked in the car park. It's to the *side* of the building."

"I see." She shrugged. "We pulled up front."

"That's because you're the guards. You can park anywhere you like, I presume. That doesn't make it an official car park."

"Watch your tone with me, Mr. White."

"Apologies, Detective, but why are we quibbling about a car park when I just told you about a very suspicious activity from one of our suspects?"

"I'm trying to establish whether you could actually see the rubbish bin from the car park if the rubbish bin—"

"Dumpster."

She glared. "Are you trying to rile me up, Mr. White? Distract me with nonsense?"

"No, ma'am. *Detective Sergeant.* I am not. But you see, the Devil is in the details, and I am nothing if not precise. If she had simply wanted to throw something into a rubbish bin, why didn't she bring it into the mill and throw it in one of the many rubbish bins located near the baking table or the kitchen?"

"Maybe she did not want to bring garbage into the mill," the detective suggested.

"Good on her," Uncle Johnny said.

"You're missing the point." Dave leaned in. "I'm trying to tell you *what* she threw into the dumpster."

"Are you saying, parked in the farthest, darkest corner of the car park, that you could see *what* she was throwing in the dumpster?"

"She's good," Tara said. "I think we're in good hands."

"We're still going to listen," Johnny said.

"Shhh." Danny leaned in.

Dave was shaking his head. "*While* she was throwing it away? No, I could not see what it was *while she was throwing it away.*"

Detective Hayes crossed her arms. "Don't tell me that Ronan Stone knew what it was through his crystal ball?"

"Of course not. But in order to explain what I did next, I need to tell you what Ciara Moon did after pulling into the car park and hurrying to the back dumpster."

"Go on, then."

"She *left*. She scurried back to her Saturn, and she rocketed off."

"Interesting," Tara said.

"Maybe she forgot something at home," Detective Hayes said. "I do that all the time."

"Did I mention," Dave continued, "she was wearing *gloves*?"

"It's cool in the mornings."

"Or . . . she didn't want her fingerprints on the murder weapon."

Detective Hayes's eyebrow shot up. "Murder weapon?"

"I'm sure you'll understand why I did what I did next. I mean after all that suspicious behavior I just had to see what she was throwing out."

"Let me guess," Detective Hayes said.

"I went to the dumpster."

"I was going to guess that," Detective Hayes said. "And?"

"A jar of peanut butter," Dave said. "Ciara Moon threw out a jar of peanut butter."

Chapter Six

Detective Hayes tapped her Biro on the table as she mulled over Dave's confession. "Let me get this straight. Ciara Moon pulled into the car park. She parked. She got out of her car—wearing gloves—and headed to the dumpster. And then she returned to her vehicle and left."

"She *peeled* out. Like she'd just robbed a bank."

"And then you went dumpster diving?"

"I'd hardly call it 'dumpster diving.' The jar of peanut butter was right on top."

"But you cannot prove she is the one who threw away the peanut butter?"

"With all due respect, Detective. *Quack, quack, quack.*"

"Excuse me?"

"If it walks like a duck and talks like a duck," Dave said, leaving the rest hanging.

"I don't care if it's a duck or a goose," Detective Hayes declared. "In my profession, we stick to the facts."

"I don't think it's much of a leap, Detective. I know she threw away a jar of peanut butter."

"No. You *assume* she threw away a jar of peanut butter."

He pursed his lips. "I hope you'll take this seriously."

"What is your theory?"

"Given she only needed a little peanut butter to do the trick—and she could have tossed it anywhere—my guess is she was hoping to frame someone."

"And what someone would that be?"

"Rose Meehan," Dave said. "If I had to guess."

Tara, Danny, and Johnny looked at each other in shock.

"Say more about that," Detective Hayes said.

"Ciara Moon didn't need an entire jar of peanut butter to kill Ronan. She could have already scooped out a tiny portion. The smallest amount, coupled with the lack of an EpiPen, would have done the trick." He tapped the desk with his index finger. "And who was the one who said something about a 'dumpster fire' nearly an hour before there was a dumpster fire?"

"You tell me."

"Ciara Moon."

"I knew you were going to say that. Does that make me psychic?"

Dave ignored the sarcasm. "And Ciara is the one who supposedly lost her spectacles, which was the purported reason she suddenly needed to rummage through the back storage room—and the back storage room is the very wall that houses the dumpsters on the outside. I think what Ciara was really doing was checking on the fire—seeing if her lit cigarette had done the trick yet."

"You think she threw the jar of peanut butter in to the dumpster just so she could set it on fire?"

"Two birds, Detective. One stone."

"I thought your theory was that she was framing someone?"

Dave squirmed in his chair. "Yes."

"If she was framing someone, then why set the dumpster on fire and destroy the evidence?"

"To make it look as if she *wasn't* framing someone!" Dave was getting worked up. He whipped out a handkerchief and patted his face.

"How did she know Ronan was going to purchase Irish soda bread?" Detective Hayes had softened her tone.

"Because he's addicted to it. He buys heaps of it every year!"

"That's true," Johnny said.

"Continue," Detective Hayes said.

"There was plenty of space behind the booths for the psychics to come and go unseen. Ciara Moon could have snuck into Ronan's booth, poisoned his soda bread, and stolen his EpiPen. Now all she needed to do was wait for Ronan to take a bite. And then she needed time for the poison to take hold, and she needed the rest of us nowhere in sight so we couldn't save him." The tears started again, and Tara couldn't blame him. Even if his theory was correct, the scenario was horrific.

"I understand Ronan was the only one who ignored the fire alarm," Detective Hayes said.

Dave nodded. "I was coming out of the little boy's room when the fire alarm went off. I hurried out, assuming my better half was already there, and of course, it was pandemonium. I didn't realize Ronan wasn't amongst the group until it was too late. By then Johnny Meehan had put out the fire, and soon we were all going back into the building anyway."

"How did the killer make sure that Ronan wouldn't join the others outside?"

Dave shook his head. "I don't know." Dave lowered his head. "Maybe the poison had taken effect, and he was already in distress."

"Let's say that your theory is correct," Detective Hayes

said. "What motive does Ciara Moon have for killing Mr. Stone?"

Dave took a deep breath. "Her nickname. *The Dark Side*. She's not happy with it. In fact, she said it's been costing her business."

"And?"

Dave sighed. "It was Ronan who gave her the nickname. I've already told you this, Detective."

"Tell me again."

"She's trying to catch him in a lie," Tara said. "It's a good tactic."

Uncle Johnny shushed her.

"He's finally opened his eyes to the deceit going on in the psychic community," Dave said. "The scams. The lies. How they prey on vulnerable, grieving people. Ciara Moon was no exception. Her business was failing, so she resorted to the nastiest trick in the psychic playbook."

"And what is that, Mr. White?"

"I told you! Fear tactics! Telling gullible folks that their aura is cloudy. Dirty. Rage-filled. Cancerous! And then offering to clean it up. For a hefty price, of course. That's when Ronan started calling her 'The Dark Side.'"

"And you think she killed him over a nickname?"

Dave gulped. "No," he said. "I think she must have learned that he was going to be the next guest on my podcast."

Detective Hayes shook her head. "And why would that alarm her?"

"Because the podcast was going to expose frauds. Starting with Ciara Moon. He was going to expose her for being the deceitful, evil she-devil she is."

"Do you have proof she found out?"

"Proof? I know she threw away a jar of peanut butter. I know she wore gloves. I know she immediately took off and returned later—as if she didn't want anyone to know she was the one who threw away the peanut butter. I know she yelled 'dumpster fire.' I know she went to the storage room—maybe checking to see what the chances are that the fire could spread inside . . . and I know that she read Ronan's aura recently . . ." He gulped. "And she told him that death was following him—and *kindly* offered to shoo the Grim Reaper away—but said, and I quote, it 'would cost him.'"

Chapter Seven

Tara, Johnny, and Danny pulled away from the screen, mulling over everything they'd just heard.

"He's wrong about one thing," Johnny said. "I'll have to bring it up to the detective when it's my turn."

"Spill," Danny said.

"We all saw her squinting when she lost her spectacles, and when she returned from the storage room, we saw her wearing spectacles she fetched from the box, so I do not think it was a ruse. And more to the point—*I'm* the one who told her to look for them back there."

"All of that could be true, and she could still be the killer," Tara said. "But you're right; you'll have to tell the detective everything."

"It's too bad you don't have cameras near the dumpster," Danny said. Detective Hayes had ended the interview with Dave, donned a protective suit and gloves, and was presumably headed out to the dumpster.

"Little do you know," Johnny said. He clicked around on the security app on his iPhone, and suddenly they were looking at the back dumpster.

"Why?" Tara said. "Just . . . why?"

"Because I'm a salvage mill," Johnny said. "I can't have

dumpster divers! And she isn't supposed to throw peanut butter into me dumpster. I'll have rodents."

"Tell me you don't sit around in your office all day watching your dumpsters," Tara said.

"As a shop owner, you should be doing the same thing," Johnny said. "My rubbish is no one else's business!"

"Can you see who set the dumpster on fire?" Tara asked.

"No," Johnny said. "It's a live feed, but I don't have it set to record."

"Because that would be weird," Tara said.

"Exactly," Johnny said, missing her sarcasm entirely.

"If Ciara Moon did plant the peanut butter," Danny said, "maybe it wasn't Rose she was trying to frame. Maybe it was you."

Tara turned to Johnny. "Does Ciara Moon have a reason to set you up?"

"Not me," Johnny said. "But I agree with Dave. She might have wanted to frame Rose."

"Why would she frame Rose?" Tara asked.

Johnny stood up. "Rose didn't even want Ciara at this psychic fair. They had a terrible row over it. Rose finally relented. But she made Ciara swear that she would not terrify anyone, and under no circumstances was she to employ fear tactics or 'cleansing' offers."

"That means Dave was telling the truth," Tara said. "At least about that."

Johnny nodded. "Ciara finally agreed, but Rose had her doubts she was going to stick to it. She fully intended on tossing her out if she broke any of the rules."

"And if Dave is to be believed, when Ciara first arrived she threw out the peanut butter *before* discovering Rose was out sick," Danny said. "So, she could have been trying to set up Rose."

"She sounds like a piece of work," Tara said. "But she could equally have just been disposing of litter." Tara began pacing her bedroom. "If only I had the time to do a mood board." Mood boards were very helpful in design, and she'd learned equally helpful in solving crimes.

Danny gave her a look. "You're very sexy when you're doing the Sherlock thing. Is there any chance I can get you to do that on our wedding night?"

"Stop that! Don't say anything like that ever again," Uncle Johnny said as he slapped his hands over his ears. Tara and Danny laughed. "Peanut butter," Johnny grumbled. "We didn't have peanut butter in Ireland until you Americans wouldn't stop going on and on about it. Peanut butter this and peanut butter that. Disgusting. Second only to *root beer.*" He dropped his hands and pointed at the screen. "There she is."

They looked at the video feed. Detective Hayes was leaning a stepladder against the dumpster. She climbed it, opened the lid, and shone a torch inside. They were all eagerly awaiting to see what she would find when static filled the screen, and the next thing they knew, the feed cut off and there was Rose again, staring at them, blocking their view. She did not look pleased.

"Darling," Uncle Johnny said. "There you are. We've been calling and calling you." He slid a look to Danny and Tara.

"We sure have," Danny said. "Something must be wrong with the connection."

Rose's face was scrunched, and her mouth was moving up and down, but no sound came out. "I muted her," Johnny said, covering his mouth as he mumbled it. "What's that, Rose? I can't hear you—what is *wrong* with this connection? Maybe I've got the setting for the volume wrong . . ."

He pretended to scroll around the screen, then cut the call and brought camera feed of the dumpster back on the screen.

"She's going to kill you," Danny said.

"Take it from me," Johnny said. "Once you're in the doghouse, you might as well act like a dog."

"Do not take it from him," Tara said.

Danny chuckled.

"We missed it," Johnny said, slapping his hands on his thighs. The ladder was still there, but the detective was gone. "I'd better call Rose back before she decides to come in person and spew her germs on every last one of us just to punish me." He began calling Rose.

"Don't worry," Tara said. "If she had found anything, she'd be setting up crime scene tape around the area."

Just then suited-up guards came into view and began marking off the perimeter around the dumpster with crime scene tape. Seconds later, the image was gone and replaced with a steaming-mad Rose.

"The plot thickens," Danny said. "Much like peanut butter."

Detective Hayes returned to the office, and Ciara Moon was next in the hot seat. Johnny had finally confessed their secret eavesdropping to Rose, and she allowed him to switch her to an iPhone. Now all four of them were guilty of earwigging. Tara still had her reservations, but it was too late to turn back now.

"Please state your name for the recording," Detective Hayes began.

"Ciara Moon."

"Is that your *legal* name?"

Ciara nodded. "I had it legally changed."

"What was your previous surname?"

Ciara frowned. "Is that relevant?"

Detective Hayes shrugged. "I'm the curious sort."

"Oh, I know," Ciara said. "It's written all over your aura."

Detective Hayes glared. "I'm letting all of you so-called psychics know that—"

"—you are not interested in our psychic abilities," Ciara finished.

"She's definitely not trying to make friends," Rose piped up. "Do you see the look on that detective's face?"

They all did. "I'm sorry," Ciara continued. "I won't mention your aura, or anything too 'woo-woo.' Even if it is a fascinating one."

Detective Hayes glanced upward as if trying to see her own aura, then shook it off. "Take me through your morning, starting with what time you arrived at the mill."

Ciara Moon glanced at the door. "I suppose Dave the Debunker already told you."

"I'm not sharing what anyone else told me, Ms. Moon. I am asking *you* to tell me your movements."

Ciara nodded and pursed her lips.

"She's trying to figure out what the detective knows," Danny said.

"Look who's psychic now," Tara quipped.

"I did arrive early," Ciara said. "I was going to park and then walk to the bay. I love seeing the sun rise over Galway Bay."

"What time did you arrive?"

"It was around half-seven. But before I pulled into the car park, I noticed something in the road right in front of me."

"Go on, so," the detective said.

"I had to stop the car to see what it was. It was a jar of peanut butter."

"You stopped to pick up a jar of peanut butter?"

Ciara nodded. "I certainly did. When you litter, or ignore litter, it leaves a smudge on your aura." Ciara stared directly above Detective Hayes's head. "*Everything* we do affects our aura. Good and bad."

"Did you pick up the jar of peanut butter with your bare hands?"

"No. I was wearing me driving gloves."

"You wear driving gloves?"

"Always." Ciara opened her handbag and pulled out a pair of gloves.

Detective Hayes sighed. "Please continue."

"I parked near the dumpster so I could throw out the jar of peanut butter." She shook her head. "I bet the snakes went rooting through the dumpster after I left."

"And the snakes are?"

"Why Dave and Ronan, of course." She stopped, gasped, and crossed herself. "Scratch that. I won't speak ill of the dead."

"After throwing away this jar of peanut butter, why did you leave, Ms. Moon?"

"Because when I saw Dave and Ronan, it made me think of Ronan's crystal ball, and Ronan's crystal ball made me think of my booth, and I realized I'd forgotten my quartz crystal. I need it to cleanse me own aura after reading others." She reached into her pocket and held up a quartz crystal. "I could cleanse this office if you'd like? Especially after Dave's been in here."

"I've already warned you, Ms. Moon."

"Apologies, your honor."

Detective Hayes sighed. "I'm a detective sergeant, not a judge."

"Right." Ciara shrugged. "Although I do feel a little bit judged."

"Let's continue with your morning," the detective said. "After you left the car park, I presume you went home and retrieved your crystal."

"I did indeed."

"What time did you return?"

"I'm only fifteen minutes away. I returned at half-eight."

"That leaves around forty-five minutes. Why didn't you return straight away?"

"I'd missed the sunrise by that time so there was no need to be there so early."

"You are aware that Ronan Stone had a nut allergy?"

"Of course. That's why I threw away the peanut butter."

"I thought you threw it away because you don't like litter."

Ciara squirmed and then gave a shrug with a smile. "That's true as well."

"What then?"

"I came in, I placed two apple pies on the baked goods table, then immediately began cleansing my booth before setting up shop."

"Did you see or speak with Ronan Stone?"

"I could hear him bragging about his crystal ball, we made eye contact and nodded, but that's the extent of it."

"Where was your booth in relation to his?"

"I was second from the entrance," Ciara said. "Ronan was last."

"If you were so far away, I suppose you did not see anyone enter his booth? Catch any conversation?"

"All of the booths are close together. And I did see something. Before Ronan and Paddy were whispering by the bake sale table, I heard them speaking in Ronan's booth.

Paddy was trying to get Ronan to do something, offering him money. I couldn't hear every single word, but now I think Paddy was trying to pressure Ronan into buying Rose's Irish soda bread for a hundred euro."

"Do you have any idea why he would do that?"

"Have you seen the volunteer sign-up list posted by the kitchen?" Ciara asked casually.

Detective Hayes frowned. "I have not."

"I didn't think so. That's why I took the liberty." Ciara reached into her handbag and produced a wrinkled sheet of paper. She smoothed it out on the desk.

"Hey!" Johnny said. "She can't go ripping things off me walls."

"I don't think that matters right now," Tara said.

"It matters," Johnny grumbled.

Detective Hayes was examining the sign-up sheet. "Paddy Pockets, kitchen duty," she read.

Ciara nodded approvingly. "Paddy Pockets *never* volunteers for kitchen duty. I wonder why he did this time?"

"She's right," Johnny said, pointing to the screen. "He did volunteer. And it is the first time. He usually signs up to greet people at the door. Last year it was a fiasco. I told him, 'Nobody wants a dove in their face first thing in the morning.' "

"Words of wisdom, old man," Danny said, clapping him on the back. "Words of wisdom."

Ciara crossed her arms. "And guess who was in the kitchen making Irish soda bread at the same time Paddy was volunteering?"

"Paddy Pockets!" Johnny yelled.

"Shhh," Danny said. "Someone is going to hear us."

"What if it was Paddy Pockets who threw away the jar of peanut butter?" Ciara continued. "Maybe he'd already scooped out what he needed. The jar had definitely been used, Detective. I assume you have it by now."

"If I did, it would be mostly charred," Detective Hayes said. "But continue."

Ciara nodded. "Maybe Paddy volunteered for kitchen duty so he could slip the peanut butter into one of the tins of Irish soda bread, and when that was done, he made some kind of wager with Ronan to persuade him to buy one. Maybe our occult magician intended on making a man disappear. *Permanently.*"

Chapter Eight

"That's absurd!" Paddy Pockets said. "Why on earth would I have paid Ronan a hundred euro for a tin of Irish soda bread that would be selling for ten? And if it was all about the charity, I would have taken the credit myself." He was sitting in the hot seat and looking none too happy about it.

"Now that I believe," Rose said.

"Then how do you explain *this*?" The detective placed a pile of colorful silk on the desk with gloved hands. It still had crumbs on it. She picked up one end and began to pull the pile up, revealing an endless scarf.

"A magician's never-ending silk scarf," Rose said. "I bet at some point he planned on wowing everyone by pulling it out of the bread!"

"His first point still stands," Johnny said. "Why didn't he buy the tin himself?"

"Because then it wouldn't look like magic, you eejit," Rose said. "Someone would have accused him of planting the scarf."

Paddy Pockets was staring at the scarf like it was capable of biting. "Where did you get that?" he said. He patted his own pockets. "It's gone. That's me scarf! Where did you get it?"

"Don't play dumb with me, Mr. Pockets. It was in one of the tins of Irish Soda bread that we found in Ronan's booth."

"But it wasn't the one he ate out of," Paddy said. "Correct?"

"What does that matter, Mr. Pockets?"

"Because I didn't put peanut butter in the tin, only the scarf."

The detective nodded. "And then you convinced Ronan to buy the tin so you could wow everyone by pulling it out at some opportune moment."

Paddy swallowed hard. "Busted," he said. "It would have been a great trick."

"This is a murder probe," Detective Hayes said. "Why didn't you confess this from the beginning?"

"Because a magician never gives away his tricks," Paddy said. "It's a very strict code. And please can we keep this to ourselves? My reputation would be ruined!"

"Did that scarf come into contact with peanut butter?"

"What? No! Of course not." He shuddered. "I loathe peanut butter."

"There were twelve tins of Irish soda bread on the bake sale table. How did you know which one held your scarf?"

"Johnny forgot to put a cross on top while baking," Paddy said. "To keep the Devil out."

"I told him!" Rose said. "I told him!"

Johnny sighed.

"Your point?" Detective Hayes asked Paddy Pockets.

"I marked the tin that held the scarf with a tiny cross. I certainly wasn't going to let anyone else buy it and choke on it! That's why I offered Ronan a hundred euro to buy it for me. If the bread isn't totally destroyed, you'll find a tiny cross in the right-hand corner of the loaf."

Detective Hayes nodded. "And the second tin?"

"I believe Ronan was offered that for free—by Johnny Meehan." Paddy leaned forward. "Maybe *he's* the killer."

"I didn't mind him taking two tins because he was spending a hundred euro!" Johnny said. "Besides, I didn't offer, he simply took."

"And when Ronan was found murdered," Detective Hayes continued, "by the very type of soda bread you admit to tampering with—why did you not come forward?"

"Because I didn't kill him!" Paddy crossed his arms. "If you want answers, you need to speak with Deirdre Palms and Sloane Stargazer."

"I intend on speaking with everyone, Mr. Pockets. But why is that?"

"They came to my house last evening, the pair of them. Saying they were both having visions of a tragedy. Wondering if we should cancel the event!"

This caught Detective Hayes's attention. "Last night, you say?"

Paddy nodded. "They'd learned that Rose was ill and took it as a bad omen."

"Maybe everyone should have listened," Detective Hayes said. "Or maybe ye don't have any more powers to predict the future than the rest of us lowly humans."

"I think the two of them knew something," Paddy said. "I could tell there was more to the story, but I couldn't get it out of them."

"Did you talk them into keeping the event afloat?" Detective Hayes asked.

"I wouldn't ever tell those two what to do. They'd have taken me head clean off. I simply told them that they could stay home if they wanted, but I for one wasn't going to listen to their doom and gloom story."

Detective Hayes sighed. "Is there anything else you'd like to add to your testimony? Now's your chance."

"Just this. Why was Ronan eating the soda bread in the first place? I paid a hundred euro for it. He was supposed to give the tins back to me. I should have known he would betray me. Ronan Stone never could resist a scone."

Detective Hayes called a lunch break. Tara, Johnny, and Danny soon joined the others in the loft. Johnny announced that he was having lunch catered given they were all stuck here. The last thing they needed was a bunch of hangry psychics.

Deirdre Palms and Sloane Stargazer were sitting close together apart from the others. Their heads were bent, and they were whispering. Tara had set up a station on her kitchen island next to the electric kettle, and people were helping themselves to tea and coffee. She wanted to put pastries out, but given what had happened, everyone agreed they would wait until lunch was delivered.

Paddy Pockets, Ciara Moon, and Dave the Debunker were also huddled together. Were they discussing their police interviews? Tara wanted to tell them that wasn't a great idea, but the hypocrisy would have been too much. The next thing she knew, Ciara Moon was marching over to Deirdre and Sloane. Moments later the women joined the three on the other side. "What's the story?" Danny wondered out loud.

"May we have everyone's attention?" Ciara announced. Given the only people not already in the group were Tara, Danny, and Uncle Johnny, it didn't take long to quiet the room. Virtual-Rose had fallen asleep, and although Johnny had not disconnected her, he had muted and minimized the screen. Once everyone was looking at Ciara, she took a moment to scan the room as if looking at each one of their auras. Tara had to admit she'd love to know what hers, and especially Danny's, could reveal. "We've decided that once the guards have completed their interviews, we'd like to hold a séance to connect with dearly departed Ronan."

Tara couldn't help but feel a tingle of excitement. It wasn't every day that one could experience their local psychics having a séance. "If the guards are finished processing the crime scene, we'd love to use the main floor of the mill," Deirdre said. "But given we don't think that's going to happen, we were wondering if we could use this loft?" They all looked to Tara.

"Absolutely," Tara said, hoping she didn't sound too eager.

"The stars will be aligned just right this evening," Sloane said. "It should help facilitate communication."

"A séance," Dave said. "Now this I have to see."

"You're not invited," Deirdre said. "We will allow no doubters into the trusted circle."

"He was *my* husband," Dave said. "And I never doubted him. Not for one minute." He sniffed. "He was the most generous man!"

"Are we talking about the same Ronan Stone?" Deirdre asked.

Dave glared. "If you must know, he was planning on building me a new studio for my podcast." He sniffed. "A lavish one."

"That sounds expensive," Sloane said.

"You can't put a price on love," Dave replied. "But yes. He said he was going to spare no expense."

"Ronan would want everyone involved," Paddy said. "With all our energies combining, Dave's negativity won't disrupt anything."

"We'll need candles for this evening as well," Ciara said.

"Done," Danny replied. "We have loads downstairs."

"And pillows," Deirdre chimed in.

"Pillows?" Johnny said.

"I'm old," Deirdre said. "I can't sit me bony arse on a hard floor for long."

"I have plenty," Tara said. "Everyone is welcome to a pillow."

"Does anyone have any objects that belong to Ronan?" Sloane asked. "We need something infused with his energy."

"I do," Johnny said. "He returned a crystal ball to me this morning. I let him do trade-ins when he gets bored of them."

"How long did he have it?" Sloane asked.

"A year," Johnny replied.

"Wonderful," Deirdre said. "Please fetch it for this evening."

"And wear gloves," Ciara said.

"And don't touch the glass," Sloane added.

Uncle Johnny sighed. "It's like Rose is here after all."

"It's settled then," Sloane said. "We'll commence the séance at dark."

"A sleepover?" Danny said. "Of psychics?"

"Be a good sport," Tara said. "Think of all the stories we can tell our grandchildren."

Uncle Johnny let out a laugh and then clomped his hand down on Danny's shoulder. "Not even married and suddenly you're a grandpa," he said. "How are those feet feeling? A bit nippy?"

"A bit?" Danny shook his head. "I think you might need to amputate me toes."

Chapter Nine

"I do not want to sit for this interview," Sloane Stargazer said. Lunch was over, and the interrogations had resumed. Sloane was standing behind the chair, her jaw working a piece of gum.

"You do not have a choice," Detective Hayes replied.

Sloane removed a folded sheet of paper from her handbag, spit her gum into it, smashed it into a ball, and aimed for the rubbish bin. When it made it in, she pumped her fist in victory. "I mean to answer your questions," Sloane said. "But I would prefer to stand."

"No," Detective Hayes said, pointing to the chair. "Sit."

Sloane sighed, eyed the chair as if it were her mortal enemy, then perched on it. "Sitting is the new smoking."

"I hear you're the one who alerted folks that the dumpster was on fire," Detective Hayes said.

"I wouldn't call me a hero," Sloane said. "But you can."

"State your name for the recorder," Detective Hayes grumbled. Her lunch break had done nothing for her mood.

"Sloane Stargazer."

Detective Hayes sighed. "And that's your legal name too, is it?"

"What is your star sign, Detective? I'm guessing Cancer."

Detective Hayes looked startled, then she narrowed her eyes. "I'm not here for all that psychic stuff." She frowned. "But how did you know?"

"Your symbol is the crab, and your ruling planet is the Moon. That's why you're so moody."

"I'm moody because I'm investigating a murder, Ms. Stargazer."

"I'm very pleased you're on the case. Cancers are very security-minded, and here you are a Guardian of the Peace!" She tilted her head. "Although you do tend to make decisions based on your *feelings*. One needs to be careful of that in an investigation."

"Did you or did you not pay a visit to Paddy Pockets the other day?"

"I did," Sloane said. "Deirdre Palms and I stopped by."

"And what was the reason for this impromptu visit?"

Sloane steepled her hands, clicked her red fingernails, and tilted her head. "It wasn't impromptu at all. Paddy wanted to discuss the psychic fair."

"Go on." Detective Hayes kept a poker face.

"Paddy said *they* came to warn *him* about their premonitions," Danny said. He and Tara were back in her room watching. Uncle Johnny was busy gathering supplies for the séance.

"One of them is lying," Tara agreed.

"Did Paddy reveal the reason for the invite?" Detective Hayes continued.

"Paddy has anxiety," Sloane said. "He said he'd been having feelings of dread as this event approached and he wanted our insights."

"Similar story—maybe Paddy was too embarrassed to admit he was seeking their wisdom," Tara mulled.

Danny nodded. "I suppose if Deirdre Palms backs up

Sloane's interpretation, then it's Paddy who altered the truth."

"Were you surprised at the invitation?" Detective Hayes asked.

"Heavens, no." Sloane shook her head. "We wouldn't be professionals if we didn't give each other feedback. And in retrospect I wish we had paid more attention to Paddy's fears. Instead, we tried to calm him. I must admit there is a bit of bias toward him because he claims he is mostly a magician. Magicians rely on trickery. But Paddy is also highly tuned to the other side. And maybe we should have warned Ronan. Maybe he'd still be alive if we had." She crossed her legs. "And before you ask—no."

Detective Hayes cocked her head. "No?"

"I did not see or smell any peanut butter at Paddy's house. Then again we certainly didn't rummage through his cupboards."

"Did you bring any baked goods to the mill?" Detective Hayes asked.

"I don't bake," Sloane said. "But I do love eating them." Her smile soon faded. "Poor Ronan. Have you found an EpiPen anywhere in the mill?"

"I'm here to ask questions, not answer them."

"I understand. But it's important for you to know that Ronan always had an EpiPen on him. Sometimes he even had a spare. Whoever killed him must have taken it."

The detective nodded. "Do you know anyone who would want Ronan Stone dead?"

"I've been asking meself the same question over and over. He was a big personality. He definitely could stir the pot. But not to the extent where anyone would want him dead."

"Take me through the events of your morning."

"I arrived at eight, just as they were opening the doors for the talent. The public was to be let in at half-nine so that gave me ample time to set up me booth."

"Whom did you speak with this morning?"

"Everyone," Sloane said. "I make it a point to say good morning to everyone. The more positive energy you give out, the more you get back." She smiled brightly. Detective Hayes stared her down until the smile faded. "It's not fool-proof," Sloane muttered.

"And was there anything unusual about your interaction with Ronan?"

Sloane concentrated on the question. "I had tried saying good morning to him but when I approached his booth, the curtains were closed, and I could hear he was having an argument with someone."

"Someone in the booth or on the phone?"

"I only heard his voice," Sloane said. "But it could have been either. Our curtains went all the way to the floor, and they were made of thick blue velvet. I couldn't see Ronan, let alone anyone else."

"What did you hear him say?"

Sloane bit her lip. "He said . . . 'I don't care what it costs. This is war.' *War*," she repeated. "I find that to be a very threatening word. Don't you?"

Detective Hayes straightened her spine. "Are you saying he was threatening someone?"

Sloane considered the question. "Ronan was nothing if not dramatic. However . . . I wouldn't use that word lightly. Not even in jest."

"Did you let him know what you'd overheard?"

"Not directly. When he came into my booth later, I did ask if he was all right. He then grew paranoid that I was commenting on his looks—that he must look *tired*. I debated admitting I'd heard him arguing with someone, but first I had to convince him he looked wide awake—and I eventually just said that his planets were strongly aligned this morning and I was hoping it hadn't given him *too much* energy."

"In other words, you lied."

"Not at all. That was all true. It wasn't the *reason* I asked if he was all right, but the rest was true."

"And if you had to guess what he was talking about—whom he might be warring with—what would you guess?"

"I'm not one to tell you how to do your job—especially when people in my profession are accused of guessing all the time—but don't you think you should simply stick to the facts?"

"Humor me."

"Are you asking me to choose which one of us I think might have killed him?"

"You're welcome to frame the question however you'd like."

"I don't want to talk out of school." She chewed her lips.

"But?"

"There is something up with Deirdre Palms. She's been acting funny all morning."

"Funny how?"

"Jumpy. Shortly after I heard Ronan in an argument, I popped over to Deirdre's booth. Her curtain was open, as if she'd just returned and hadn't had time to shut it. She was ending a phone call. I don't know who it was with, but her face drained of all color. I asked her if she was all right, and she said she needed fresh air. She pushed past me and went outside."

"Was this before the dumpster was set on fire?"

"Definitely." Sloane gasped. "Do you think she went out for a *smoke*?"

"Does Deirdre Palms smoke?"

"I thought she quit a few years ago. But like I said, she wasn't herself at all today. Maybe she's gone back to her old ways."

"What ways are those?"

"Smoking. Drinking. Gambling. You name it. She went into spiritual work after a stint in rehab years ago. From what I hear, she was on the road to ruin."

"Are you saying she started smoking again?"

"I'm not saying it. But after the fiasco this morning, I do wonder."

"What brand did she smoke?"

"I don't have a clue," Sloane said. "Would you like me to do some digging?"

"No," Detective Hayes said. "Do not say a word."

Sloane mimed locking her lips and throwing away the key. "Am I done?" Sloane sprang from her chair.

"Please ask Deirdre Palms to come in."

"Poor Deirdre," Sloane said. "I can only imagine how much she's regretting threatening Ronan Stone with that lawsuit."

Chapter Ten

Deirdre Palms confirmed Sloane's account of their visit to Paddy Pockets, but then she claimed she had no quarrels with Ronan Stone.

"I hear he was cracking down on the psychic community," Detective Hayes said. "Making sure no one took advantage of clients." Deirdre's face showed no expression. "Not to mention his partner is a skeptic. That has to be somewhat awkward."

"Dave the Debunker!" Deirdre said. "He's a nuisance all right. But the only one who took his little podcast seriously was himself. And I fear he was only with Ronan for his money."

"Ronan had money?"

"I'll be honest. I didn't know he had money until I heard Dave say that Ronan planned on building him a fancy new recording studio."

"If you and Ronan Stone had no quarrels—"

"None. Absolutely none. Zero. Nada."

"Then why is it you threatened to sue Dave White last year for . . ." Detective Hayes rifled through some papers. "Slander?"

"Who told you?" Deirdre said. "Sloane was just in here. Was it her?"

"She's stalling," Danny said.

"I can't believe she didn't see this coming," Tara replied. Danny gave her a look. "No pun intended."

"Answer the question, Ms. Palms."

"It was a little misunderstanding," Deirdre said, waving her hand as if trying to swat away the question. "We kissed and made up."

"I find it hard to believe that you had no ill will toward Ronan Stone, given how much you and Dave White are still at odds."

Deirdre uncrossed her legs and recrossed them, switching from right to left. "I wouldn't say we're at odds."

Detective Hayes pushed a button on another recording device, and soon Dave White's voice filled the air.

"The very reason I started this podcast was to expose these leeches preying on the vulnerabilities and grief of the public. Take Deirdre Palms, for instance. She's a scam artist."

Deirdre glared at the recorder. "I am not!"

"I sent the very same man to visit her," Dave's voice continued, "two weeks in a row. But he appeared to be two separate men. In the first visit, he played the part of a wealthy businessman. He was shaved, in a designer suit, briefcase, glasses—he pretended to be a financial advisor."

"I saw right through it," Deirdre said.

"His reading was all about money. How he was good at making it, how he needed to watch his 'riskier' investments, how he needed to rely on spiritual guidance— namely hers. She saw him as a piggy bank."

"I did not!"

"Enough," Detective Hayes said. "Listen."

Deirdre crossed her arms tightly and glared at the recorder.

"But when we sent him in the following week, he presented very differently. His clothing was threadbare, we gave him a beard and a hat, removed the glasses—made him a clerk at a bookstore. He had the exact same palms, mind you, but his reading was all about how down in the dumps he was, how he needed to sort himself out, how he was in danger of all kinds of *bankruptcy*. Imagine! The very man she called adept at earning last week was now a bum without money. If this doesn't show you that Deirdre Palms is a fraud, frankly I don't know what will."

Detective Hayes clicked off the recording. Deirdre's face flashed bright red. "You can see that's clearly slander," Deirdre said. "And furthermore, when the man came in the second time, he *smelled*. In fact, I had an instant headache. I gave him a brief reading because I could not focus with him sitting across from me. They set me up. And I don't even know if I believe it was the same man. We only have Dave's word for it, and I take it with a grain of salt."

"You threatened to sue him."

"Exactly. I threatened to sue Dave the Debunker, *not* Ronan Stone. And if Dave was the one who had been murdered this morning, then perhaps I would have understood this grilling."

Detective Hayes leaned back in the office chair. "They're married; their finances are intertwined. Some might say you sue one, you sue both."

"We settled out of court."

Detective Hayes nodded. "What was the nature of the settlement?"

Deirdre Hayes huffed. "I honestly don't think that's anyone's business, and I am not going to answer it without a solicitor."

"You seem very angry."

"Anger is a common human emotion, Detective. But that doesn't make me a killer."

Danny grimaced. "It doesn't *not* make her a killer," he whispered.

"Before you brought this lawsuit, did you ask Ronan Stone to intervene in your quarrels with Dave?" Detective Hayes continued.

"Did someone say I did?" Deirdre suddenly looked nervous. "I did not specifically ask him to intervene—I may have said a few harsh things—it's very upsetting when some know-it-all slanders you on his podcast."

"What was Ronan's reaction to the feud between yourself and his partner?" Deirdre Palms went mute. Then shrugged. Detective Hayes leaned in. "Did the two of you argue?"

"Everyone remembers that argument. It was epic." The voice belonged to Rose. Tara and Danny turned to see the broom and smart phone positioned directly behind them. This time she was attached to a robot vacuum. "I can control it from here!" Rose said. "Now I can go anywhere I like."

Danny yelped. "You put the heart in me crossways," he said.

"How long have you been there?" Tara said.

"Never mind me," Rose barked. "Have you been watching *all* the interviews?"

"Most of them," Tara admitted.

"Who told Detective Hayes about that argument?" Rose said, zooming a little bit closer.

"I don't know," Tara said. "We didn't hear anyone tell her. Maybe she did some research on her lunch break."

"The podcast was public knowledge," Rose said. "But not the argument."

"Give us the story," Danny said.

"Epic!" Rose said, using jazz hands.

"Come on, then," Tara said. "Tell us."

"I'll need your full attention."

Danny sighed and turned off the interview. "We're all yours."

"Psychics normally stick to a code of silence," Rose said. "But I suppose this is an exception."

"I should say so," Tara said. "A man has been murdered."

Rose nodded and crossed herself. "May he rest in peace."

"Please," Danny said. "Give us the story."

"Well then." Rose grinned. "I thought you'd never ask."

The occasion was Sloane Stargazer's fiftieth birthday party. "I suppose Sloane should have consulted the stars that day because arguments were definitely in the air. I must admit the first argument of the evening happened between Johnny and myself."

What Rose could not see was that Johnny had just entered the room and was standing directly behind Virtual-Rose. He placed his index finger on his lips. Rose touched the top of her head. "Are you staring at me hair? I've been napping, I'm afraid it's defying gravity at the moment."

"You're grand," Tara said. "We're looking at Uncle Johnny."

"Tara!" Johnny said. "You've no loyalty to family."

"Rose is family now too," Tara said.

"Trying to catch me out, is he?" Rose said. "You needn't have bothered. I planned on owning up to me part in the argument."

"Your part?" Johnny said, walking into her view. "The entire argument was you, Rose. Only you."

Rose crossed her arms and glared at him. "If you're going to listen to me story, you're going to have to do it with your mouth shut."

"Fair enough." He sat on the edge of Tara's bed. "Go on, so."

"I'm telling them about the night Deirdre and Ronan had that argument."

"Epic!" Johnny said.

"If you don't start telling the actual story, me hair is going to turn gray right in front of ye," Danny said.

"Johnny and I were getting ready for evening, and I was dragging me feet," Rose said. "You see, Sloane Stargazer is a single woman. And Johnny here is a very handsome man." Johnny looked at them and grinned. "I've told him over and over again—that woman has her sights locked on him. In fact, if I ever turn up dead, I'm telling ye right now, it's Sloane who's done it. And it won't be long before she'll be casting some kind of love spell on me poor widowed husband."

Tara tried not to laugh. It was possible Sloane had a crush on Johnny, but she doubted it. Sloane was a good decade younger than her uncle and a very attractive woman. She could tell by Johnny's lack of denial that he thought so too. "I'm a loyal man," Johnny said. "That's what I told Rose."

"Exactly," Rose said. "You didn't tell me that I'm wrong—'Oh no, darling, she has no interest in me.' "

"Rose."

"And you didn't tell me that you weren't attracted to *her*."

"I'm married to you, aren't I? Shouldn't that be confirmation enough?"

Tara had a feeling they were watching the exact same argument play out.

"I didn't know why you were so insistent on attending the birthday. You'd never wanted to join in on any of our other events."

"Your other events didn't include alcohol," Johnny said. "This one did." He looked at Danny. "Open bar."

"Case closed," Danny said with a grin.

"That was another thing," Rose said. "The only reason I can think of that Sloane Stargazer would have an open bar is to lure you in!" Now she looked at Tara. "It worked."

"I can't help it if I'm a Silver Fox," Johnny said.

"Can we move on from how good looking and 'rich' you are—the pair of ye—and get the story?" Danny asked.

"Millionaires," Johnny said. "We're millionaires."

Sloane's Fiftieth Birthday Bash—One month prior

"A toast," Ronan said. "To Sloane!"

"To Sloane!" the crowd repeated.

Sloane Stargazer wore her signature black sequined dress that sparkled as if it were the universe itself. She took a bow and raised her glass. "Here's to me!"

Deirdre Palms, already several martinis in, stumbled past her, sloshing drink all over Sloane's dress.

"Watch it," Sloane said.

"You're getting grouchy in your old age," Deirdre replied, wagging her finger at Sloane.

"Ladies, ladies, no fighting." Ronan stepped up behind them and looped his arm around the pair. "It doesn't *suit* you."

Deirdre wiggled out of his grasp and stumbled away. "She's a nightmare lately," Ronan said as he watched her go. "I wonder if something is going on."

"Ronan," Sloane said. "I'm so glad you could make it."

"Sorry I'm late. Happy birthday, darling." They air-kissed on both cheeks. Just as they stepped apart, Ciara Moon seemed to appear out of nowhere. "I think someone is suing Deirdre," she said casually before continuing to the bar. "She's been unraveling ever since."

"Suing her?" Paddy Pockets piped up from a nearby table. "Who, what, where, and especially *why*?" He patted the empty stool next to him.

Ciara tilted her head and addressed Paddy. "Are you going to buy me a whiskey?"

"I am if you're spilling the tea," Paddy said.

"We'll buy you as many whiskeys as you'd like, darling," Ronan said.

"It's *my* birthday," Sloane muttered. "But if it means getting the scoop, have at it."

Ronan, Sloane, and Paddy bought Ciara Moon a whiskey and dragged her to the table. Johnny and Rose were sitting directly behind them, and they immediately stopped their own conversation to listen in. If a psychic was getting sued, it was of interest to everyone in the community. What had Deirdre done, and who was taking her to court? None of them were rich. A lawsuit could destroy a career lickety-split. Deirdre ruined the moment by crashing it. She stumbled up to the table, grabbed Ciara Moon's whiskey, and poured it down her own throat. "You're like vultures," she said as she slammed the empty glass on the table.

"That was mine," Ciara said, pouting over the empty glass. "You ruin everything."

Deirdre huffed. "*Someone* thinks that I acted in bad faith when I told a client that she should make sure she went to her doctor for a checkup. I didn't mean to be the bearer of bad news, but I sensed something was very wrong with her midsection."

"Doesn't that apply to all ladies of a certain age?" Ronan said.

"That's rich coming from you," Sloane said, gesturing to Ronan's big belly.

He shrugged. "I'm at peace with it," he said. "That's the difference."

"This wasn't a weight issue," Deirdre said. "I truly thought she had a serious medical issue that needed emergency attention."

"Don't tell me you charged her more to take a deeper dive into the issue," Ciara said.

"She wouldn't!" Paddy replied. They all looked to Deirdre.

"I need another whiskey," Deirdre said as her left eye began to twitch.

Rose had anticipated this; she joined the table and plunked another whiskey down in front of Deirdre. Johnny lurked in the background—he wasn't officially one of them, and he wanted to at least offer them the illusion of privacy. Deirdre downed the whiskey. "The thing is," she said. "I think someone set me up." Her gaze fell on Ronan.

"Set you up?" Paddy said. "Did this person also force you to use fear tactics on a client?"

"They weren't fear *tactics*. I believed the woman had a reason to fear, and I needed to do a deeper dive. Why shouldn't I charge for extra work? I had to go into a deep meditation, and I even borrowed Ronan's crystal ball for our second session."

"She was on the ball," Ronan joked.

"Did this client come back for her second session?" Ciara asked.

Deirdre slid a look to Dave. He stared back. "She came back all right. She asked me to repeat my assessment from our first visit—which I did—that I feared she had an undiagnosed medical issue but that I wasn't able to pinpoint exactly what. And yes, I told her it would be better to see her doctor. That's the *first* thing I said."

"What was her response?" Sloane asked. "And what sign was she?"

"I have no idea what sign she was," Deirdre said.

"I wonder if her aura reflected her illness," Ciara said.

"I would have done a health spread with me tarot cards," Rose chimed in.

"I bet she was a Taurus," Sloane said. "Bullheaded." She slid a look to Ronan.

"Guilty," he said with a grin. "I love being a bull." His gaze went to Dave, whose face turned red.

"Her sign should have been a snake," Deirdre said. "It turned out she was a reporter. Sent to me by one of you! One of you set me up. Now she's threatening to sue *me*!" Deirdre stared at all her fellow psychics. "And I want to know which one of you betrayed me." She looked at Dave. "What about you?"

Dave pointed at himself. "Me?"

"You've done it before," Deirdre said. "You sent that horrible man to me *twice*. First posing as a businessman and then as some kind of vagrant."

"I certainly did," Dave said. "And you gave him two distinctly different readings."

"That was a nasty trick."

"Be that as it may . . . we settled that matter, so why would I do it again?"

Deirdre jabbed her finger at Dane. "We only settled the matter because I threatened to sue you. Maybe now you're getting your revenge."

"It's not me," Dave said, taking her finger and moving it down. "I'm many things, but a liar isn't one of them."

"On what grounds is this reporter threatening to sue you?" Ciara asked.

Deirdre's face was a portrait of guilt. "I didn't find out she was a reporter until after the second reading, after the second payment. By then I had already told her that there was something wrong with her stomach lining." Deirdre sighed. "She should have been thrilled! It wasn't cancer. And the remedies are simple. Anti-inflammatory diet, drink green tea, try a probiotic and essential oils—quit smoking." Deirdre stopped. "I think that's the cannon that sank the ship. Her clothing reeked of smoke."

"I take it she felt the reading was too generic," Ciara said. "I wish I could have seen her aura."

"She called me a scam artist," Deirdre said. "I couldn't help it. I saw red."

Paddy's mouth had already dropped open. "Deirdre," he said. "What did you do?"

Deirdre sighed. "I slapped her." Everyone at the table gasped. "I couldn't help it," she continued. "And I would do it again. It felt bloody great." Deirdre's shoulders slumped. "But now she's threatening to sue me for assault. This is going to ruin me." She gazed at the other psychics through blurred vision. "And one of you did this to me."

"Why hasn't she sued you already?" Dave asked.

Deirdre scoffed. "Get this. She's asking for a ton of money to settle out of court. That's why I smell a con."

"How much?" Sloane asked.

"Fifty thousand euro," Deirdre said. "If I want to save my own arse, she wants fifty thousand euro."

"Whoa," Tara said. Johnny had just finished telling the story, and everyone sat in silence for a moment. It was more explosive than Tara had been expecting. The shock was evident on Danny's face as well. "That's wild," Tara said. "Did Deirdre end up paying the reporter?"

"Did she ever find out who set her up?" Danny added. "He isn't finished," Rose piped up. "Tell them." Johnny sighed. "That night, Sloane Stargazer came up to me. She asked if I would be willing to help out Deirdre."

"Help out how?" Danny said.

Johnny threw his arms up. "I was practicing me manifestation that night. Sloane overheard me saying I was a millionaire."

Danny laughed. Johnny and Rose glared at him. "Sorry, sorry," he said, still laughing. "You have to admit it's quite funny."

"I take it you told Sloane the truth," Tara said.

"How could I?" Johnny said. "You can only manifest something if you act like you *have it already*. If I told her I *didn't* have a million dollars, I'd have to start me manifesting all over again!"

"That's right," Rose said. "We're millionaires, and that's that."

"But now you're millionaires who won't help out a friend in need," Tara said.

"Exactly," Rose said.

"Does this have anything to do with Ronan's murder?" Danny piped up. "I mean it's a good story and all, but aren't we getting a little off track?"

"No," Rose said. "Because the story isn't finished. After Deirdre's revelation, Paddy went on to another pub, Deirdre and Ciara went home, and Ronan and Dave stayed at the bar."

"We had decided to leave as well," Johnny said.

"But I left me mobile phone at the table," Rose said. "When I went back for it, I could hear Ronan and Dave having a very interesting chat."

"They *did* set her up," Johnny said. "It was just as Deirdre said. They were trying to extort her for fifty thousand euro. Ronan was going to pour it all into Dave's new recording studio."

"Fifty thousand euro," Rose said. "For a podcast!"

"He said he needed fancy equipment, a bigger office, and advertising. Any guess who his first guest was going to be?"

"The reporter who is suing Deirdre," Tara said.

"Right," Johnny said, looking disappointed. "You guessed it."

They all sat in silence for a moment. "Are you going to tell the detective all this?" Tara asked.

Johnny nodded. "I'm just waiting for me interview."

"Are you saying you think Deirdre found out it was them, and she decided to poison Ronan?" Tara asked the group.

"Or did Ronan want to come clean, and maybe Dave killed Ronan?" Danny posed.

"They were in a very heated argument this morning," Rose said.

All heads snapped to her. "What do you mean?" Johnny asked.

"Remember when you abandoned me in the middle of the floor?" Rose said. "When everyone had arrived and were just setting up their booths?"

"I didn't abandon you," Johnny said. "I was juggling a million things for you."

"Of course, you were," Danny cracked. "Because you're millionaires." He threw his head back and laughed.

"What did you hear?" Tara asked.

"Dave and Ronan arguing about one of the other psy-

chics. I don't know which one. But I caught the last part—
Ronan said—'This is war. What a disaster! How could
you let this happen?' " Rose looked terrified, even on the
screen. Dark circles under her eyes gave her statements
gravity. "And then Dave said . . ." Rose gulped. " 'Don't
worry. This ends today. One way or another.' "

Chapter Eleven

Tara sat in front of Detective Hayes wondering how much she should share of everything she learned. Some of it the detective knew already, although Tara wasn't supposed to have that information. She knew that Dave and Ronan had set Deirdre up with the phony male client, then Deirdre threatened to sue Dave, then Dave and Ronan settled with her. Tara now assumed that "settling with her" meant they had paid her. And obviously regretted it, wanted their money back, so they sent a second "plant," the reporter whom Deirdre slapped. And bringing them back full circle—the reporter was extorting her for fifty thousand euro.

The only confirmation that Ronan and Dave were behind it all was the argument Rose overheard when everyone else left the pub. Would it be enough proof? Had Rose misunderstood their conversation? But if it wasn't Ronan and Dave, who set up Deirdre Palms? And as far as the murder was concerned, did it matter whether or not Ronan had been in cahoots with the reporter as long as that's what Deirdre Palms believed? Tara would tell the detective everything, let her sort it out. Everything apart from the fact that they'd been eavesdropping on all the interviews, something she was feeling terribly guilty about. But they were not the murderers, and their intent on listening in was to help solve the murder—that gave her a bit of comfort.

But the detective was distracted. She was on the phone, cradling it between her ear and her shoulder, leaving her poor neck taking the burden while she used her hands to rifle through a folder. "Got it!" she said so loud that Tara jumped. "Sorry, luv." The detective then gripped the phone with her hand and swiveled so that she wasn't facing Tara as she murmured into the phone. But it was a small office, and Tara could still hear her. "Are the prints clear?" the detective said. "We'll need to fingerprint all of our suspects. See which one of them had his or her grubby hands on it. What in the world was this person thinking? No, Garda, it was a rhetorical question. I *don't* expect you to be a mind reader. What? Very funny. Call me if you get something useful." She clicked off and swung back around. "Heard that, did ya?"

Tara was taken aback. "It's hard not to."

The detective leaned in. "A set of fingerprints were found on the jar of peanut butter. Now what do you make of that?"

"Me?" Tara could not believe the detective was divulging this information.

"Aren't you some secret Sherlocka Holmes?"

"Sherlocka?"

Detective Hayes waved her hand like it didn't matter. "The female version," she said. "I just made that up."

"You don't say," Tara said. Detective Hayes's smile betrayed her high opinion of her newfound lexicon. "I'm no Sherlock," Tara continued, "but murder probes do interest me. They're like puzzles. It helps if you can see a pattern."

"Pattern," Detective Hayes mumbled. "I'm surrounded by a bunch of psychics, and I still don't know a thing!"

Tara nodded sympathetically. She was still fixated on learning they found fingerprints on the peanut butter jar. Then she snapped her fingers. "Dave said he went to the dumpster after Ciara peeled away. Maybe they're his prints." She chewed on this. "Then again he explicitly said he did *not* take the peanut butter out of the dumpster." But someone had. The killer. Could it be the husband? Wasn't it always?

Detective Hayes leaned forward, her eyes like slits. "And how on earth would you know what Dave White said in his interview?" Detective Hayes pushed herself up, slammed her hands on the desk, and hovered over Tara.

It took all of Tara's willpower not to glance at the camera, but she could already imagine Danny, Rose, and Johnny watching, mouths open in horror. Tara was a total eejit. She steadied her breath. The detective couldn't possibly know they'd been watching the interviews. She could still recover from this. "I'm afraid people like to talk out of school," Tara said. "Compare notes."

Detective Hayes lowered herself into the chair, swiveled for a moment, and then looked defeated. "I should have kept everyone separated," she said. "Then again if they can all read each other's minds, I guess it's hopeless."

"Sometimes it's good to let them talk amongst themselves," Tara said.

The detective stilled. "Say more."

"You never know when someone will say something that could crack the case wide open." Tara leaned in. "Especially if they think they're alone."

Detective Hayes cocked her head and pointed at Tara. "You're getting at something. What is it?"

"When you've finished your interviews and have gone home for the day, the psychics want to hold a séance. To see if they can 'connect' with Ronan's spirit."

"Now I've heard everything," Detective Hayes said.

"We've heard nothing yet," Tara said. "But if they hold that séance, we just might."

"Or it will just be a chaotic zoo."

"I don't think so," Tara said. "I feel we're getting close. There are just a few pieces missing."

Detective Hayes raised an eyebrow. "You think you know who did it?"

"I've heard a few tales that you haven't heard yet," Tara said. "I'm going to fill you in. But I don't want to overstep—"

"Trample away," Detective Hayes said. "I've spoken to another detective sergeant about you. He said you're quite useful. And of everyone you have little connection to Ronan Stone, so I'm going to trust you for now."

"Good," Tara said. "There are a few bits of evidence I would like to look at. I'd like to go over some of the interviews once more—and then hopefully at the séance tonight, instead of the dead we'll contact someone who's very much alive. A stone-cold killer."

"Stone," Detective Hayes said. "I see what you did there."

"I'm also going to ask if we can use some of the recordings from your interviews during the séance." Tara was taking a gamble with this request.

"Why is that?"

"Because some of them may try to lie, and the only way this works is if I can get everyone but the killer to tell the truth."

Detective Hayes nodded. "I think that can be arranged. Now, where would you like to start?"

Tara didn't hesitate. "Rubbish," Tara said. "I'd like to start with the rubbish."

"Me?" Rose said. "You want me to virtually lead a fake séance?" Johnny, Danny, Tara, and Virtual-Rose were all crammed in Johnny's office with Detective Hayes.

"If I announce I'm going to lead a séance, they'll automatically be suspicious," Tara said. "I'm not a psychic."

"Fine," Rose said. "But for the record I would prefer if I *was* leading a séance. I'm sure Ronan has a lot to say to this group." Rose crossed her arms and sighed. "If only Johnny had put the cross in while baking." Danny muted Rose's feed before Johnny could open his big gob and respond.

Tara nodded sympathetically, then turned to Johnny and Danny. "We'll need chairs from the storage room," Tara said. "And I'll show you why it's the perfect place to start."

The psychics were seated in a circular arrangement in Tara's living room. Among them sat a killer. The chairs had been fetched from the storage room, the furniture was pushed back, and Ronan's former crystal ball was set up on a table in the middle of the room. Flickering candles added to the ambience. Tara stood in front of the group, surprised at how on edge she felt. She was about to out a murderer. And even though Detective Hayes and Garda O'Leary were watching from the recesses, she still worried what would happen if something went wrong. Would she be next in a killer's crosshairs?

As if the Irish skies knew what was happening and had decided to join in, a thunderstorm had rolled in. Rain pounded the roof, and every now and again a flash of lightning would illuminate the suspects.

Tara adjusted her red cape. Rose had insisted she wear it, and Tara felt absolutely ridiculous, but compromises had to be made.

"Rose Meehan is going to conduct this séance," Tara began. "Through me."

"You?" Ciara Moon said.

"You mean someone who isn't here is going to try and contact someone *else* who isn't here?" Deirdre asked.

Tara lifted her hair to show her earbuds but then realized the dim lights made it difficult to see. Unfortunately, it also made it difficult to monitor the expressions on their faces, especially the killer's. Tara was going to have to amp up the emotions to get an outburst from the guilty party. "Rose will be speaking to me through my earbuds," Tara said.

"I don't know if Ronan will come to you," Sloane said. "No offense."

"If you would indulge me anyway, we shall see if he reveals his killer." She made sure not to look in Danny's direction; she had a feeling he was never going to let her live this down.

"Reveal his killer?" Dave said. "I want to believe that's possible. I truly do." He looked around. "But we all know that's hogwash."

"One of us needs to lead this," Ciara Moon chimed in. She pointed at Tara. "You are neither a psychic nor a detective." Several in the group stood as if they wished to make a quick exit.

"Spirit knows, and spirit will guide," Rose said into Tara's ear. Tara repeated the statement. Thunder rumbled. The group began looking at each other as if trying to decide whether to stay or go.

"You're free to leave," Tara said. "But the guards *are*

watching. I worry you'll only look guilty if you decide not to stay."

"I say let's do it," Dave said. "If you're all such believers, you'll do it for Ronan."

One by one those standing sat back down. "Let's just see how it goes," Sloane said. "I trust you, Rose."

"Since when?" Rose said in Tara's ear.

Tara chose not to repeat that. "In order for this to work, everyone will have to tell the truth," Tara said. "I will expect that from everyone but the killer."

"You mean the killer will be the liar amongst us?" Sloane asked. Once again heads swiveled as they regarded each other with suspicion.

"Exactly," Tara said. "If everyone *else* tells the truth, no matter how difficult, I believe we will unmask a killer." She already suspected who the killer was, and she was hoping she could set a trap.

"Do we agree?" Johnny said. "Those of you who are innocent owe it to Ronan and myself."

"You?" Deirdre said. "No offense, but why do we owe you anything?"

Johnny was prepared for this question. "Because I graciously hosted you in my salvage mill. And now one of you has most likely tried to frame me for murder, not to mention turned my place of business into a crime scene. Is that enough reason for you, Ms. Palms?"

"I say you made your case," Deirdre said. "I for one shall tell the truth."

"For one or for *once*?" Sloane said.

Ciara Moon raised her hand. "You can just speak," Tara said.

Ciara cleared her throat. "I'd like to suggest that in the spirit of catching the killer we stop sniping at each other."

For a moment, Sloane pouted, but soon all heads nodded in agreement.

"The first person I need to address is Paddy Pockets," Tara said.

Paddy gulped. "Would you like to see a magic trick?" He began patting himself down, pulling a card, then a coin from his pockets.

"No," Tara said. Paddy returned the items to his pockets with a sigh and waited. "I'd like you to tell everyone about the scarf trick you envisioned and how it related to Ronan Stone."

Paddy slumped in his chair. "You do know how to spoil a party, Rose," he said. Tara had actually cut off Rose's feed, something she would no doubt pay for later, but she had to focus.

"This isn't a party," Dave said.

"It's not a séance either," Paddy replied as he grudgingly stood up. Uncle Johnny passed him a torch. He held it under his chin. "I gave Ronan a hundred euro to buy a tin of Johnny's Irish soda bread. I had planted one of my magic scarves inside a single tin before it went into the oven while on kitchen duty this morning." Paddy paused for a moment and looked at Johnny. "I would apologize, but we did pay a hundred euro for two tins of Irish soda bread." Johnny shrugged and then nodded.

"How did you plan on identifying the tin with the scarf later?" Tara asked.

"I marked the one with the scarf with a tiny cross—that way I'd be able to spot it and purchase it. I was going to wow the crowd with the trick later in the afternoon. That's why I needed Ronan to purchase it for me—otherwise too many would have accused me of planting the scarf. And I can't count on you lot to keep your gobs shut, now can I? But I did *not* put peanut butter in any of the tins, and I had no reason to wish Ronan dead." He looked to the ceiling. "May you rest in peace. I am truly sorry."

"Thank you, Paddy," Tara said. She turned to Dave. "It's your turn."

Dave looked startled. "Me?"

Tara stared him down. "Were you entirely forthcoming in your interview with Detective Hayes?"

Dave slapped his thighs. "Blame the husband again, is it?" He could not disguise his fury.

"I am simply looking at evidence," Tara said. "I'm sure you'd be interested in knowing that they were able to lift a set of fingerprints off the murder weapon."

"Murder weapon?" several said at once.

Tara nodded. "A jar of peanut butter was found in the dumpster."

Ciara jumped up. "I threw it in the dumpster. I found it in the road just before I pulled into the car park. I swear!"

"She admits it," Dave said. "She admits to handling the murder weapon."

"We'll get to that," Tara said. "But she was wearing gloves. So once again, Dave, I'll ask you. Would you like to admit that it could be your prints on the murder weapon?" Tara could feel the room buzzing. Unbeknownst to most, the guards were watching this on video from Johnny's office. The lighting was dim, but their voices would be clear. Dave was starting to squirm in his seat. "All of your fingerprints will be taken for comparison," Tara said. "But you could save us time if you really want Ronan's killer to be found—"

Dave shot up. "They're mine, so. All right? Is that what you want to hear? The guards will no doubt find my fingerprints on that jar of peanut butter."

Chapter Twelve

The group stared at him, aghast. He held up his hands. "It's not what you think."

"I think you had better start talking," Ciara Moon said. "You were quick enough to throw *me* under the bus." She huffed. "You even *drove* the bus."

"I wouldn't put it that way," Dave said.

"Did you not make a point of telling Detective Hayes that Ciara Moon was the first to arrive?" Tara asked.

"Yes," Dave said. "Because when she exited her car, she was wearing gloves and holding a jar of peanut butter."

Gasps sounded from the circle.

"That is indeed how you first told the story," Tara said. "What did you leave out?"

Dave crossed his arms. "The jar of peanut butter belonged to Ronan." Voices rose in confusion. Dave waited until they died down. "It's the truth. Ronan liked facing his fears. He started keeping a jar of peanut butter close—'facing death' is how he phrased it." Dave shivered. "Peanut butter was only deadly if he ingested it, mind you. He could smell it and touch it. That isn't true for everyone with a food allergy—everyone is different—but Ronan had to actually ingest it for it to cause him any problems. Even so his new experiment made me extremely nervous.

We arrived early this morning. But just as we were pulling into the car park, Ronan took out the jar of peanut butter. I acted on instinct. I snatched the jar out of his hands and threw it out the window."

Ciara Moon jumped up. "You're the one who littered! I arrived next and saw it lying in the middle of the road. I thought it was rude that someone tossed it out right in front of the mill—and what with the event going on—that's why I stopped and picked it up."

"That's two people who handled the murder weapon," Paddy said.

"*You* handled the tin of soda bread, Paddy," Deirdre said. "So don't act all high and mighty."

But Tara wasn't finished questioning Dave. "When you saw Ciara with the jar of peanut butter—marching it to the dumpster—did you assume it was the jar you had thrown out?" she asked.

"I assumed it was, yes," Dave said.

"Then why did you tell the story in a way that made Ciara appear guilty?" Tara asked. "You told the detective that you observed Ciara throw a jar of peanut butter into the dumpster, and you emphasized that she was wearing gloves and that after she threw it away, she sped out of the car park."

"And all that is true," Dave said. He crossed his arms.

"Yet you conveniently left out the fact that Ronan is the one who brought the peanut butter and, more to the point, that you grabbed it and threw it out onto the street." Tara stared him down.

"I only left that bit out because I know I'm innocent and I didn't want to distract the detective." Dave looked around as if trying to garner support from the others. Hardly anyone would make eye contact with him.

"As I said," Ciara said. "You threw me under the bus, then drove right over me!"

"Everything I said was true," Dave said. "You could have scooped out enough peanut butter to kill him *before* throwing the rest in the dumpster!"

"I did no such thing!" Ciara said. "I wouldn't have even had to touch it if you hadn't littered."

"Ciara volunteered her car for a search," Tara said. "There was no whiff of peanut butter found there or in her booth." She turned to Ciara. "Why is it you were wearing gloves?"

Ciara reached into her handbag and held up a pair of leather gloves. "They're me driving gloves. All of you know I wear them." Once more, heads nodded around the circle. Tara was ready to switch focus to Ciara. She kept her attention on her. "When you tossed the jar of peanut butter into the dumpster, did you see a lit cigarette on top?"

Ciara shook her head. "I did not."

"Did you smell cigarette smoke?"

Ciara shook her head. "Not a trace."

"And then what did you do?"

"I left."

Dave sprung from his seat and pointed. "She peeled out of there," he said. "Like she'd just robbed a bank!"

Tara nodded and once more addressed Ciara Moon. "Why did you leave, and is it true that you raced out of the car park?"

"I left because I spotted Dave and Ronan lurking in their car like they were on some kind of stakeout. It made me think of Ronan's crystal ball, and Ronan's crystal ball made me think of my cleansing crystal, and I realize I'd forgotten to bring it. I didn't want to chance a smudge on my aura." She reached into her pocket and this time pulled out a crystal. She held it up. "See?"

"Too bad it didn't work," Sloane said. "I certainly don't feel cleansed."

Tara gave Sloane a look before she could distract everyone. She continued with Ciara. "And why did you peel out of the car park?"

Ciara shrugged. "I was irked to see Ronan and Dave spying on me. I just wanted to kick up a little dust."

"Dave," Tara said. "What do you think of what Ciara just said? Do you think she's telling the truth?"

Dave squirmed. "As far as I know. After she left, I went back to the dumpster and, indeed, the jar of peanut butter was right on top."

"Did you touch it?"

"Of course not. I wouldn't stick me hand in a dumpster."

"Did *you* see any discarded cigarettes lying on top of the dumpster?"

Dave shook his head. "No."

Tara wanted to emphasize this point. The killer was probably on alert by now. "Are you sure?"

"Quite sure."

"Good," Tara said. "One more question for you, Dave. This morning I noticed a smudge on Ronan's crystal ball. It was *before* all the fuss started. Can you tell me why there was a smudge on his crystal ball?"

Dave nodded. "Yes. It wasn't a smudge, but I can see how it appeared to be one from a distance. If you must know—it was writing. Ronan is the one who wrote *Peanut Butter* on his crystal ball—with the aforementioned jar of peanut butter."

Deirdre gasped. "It's like he foresaw his own death."

"Not at all," Dave said. "He was still following his experiment of 'facing death'—he was taking his power back by looking his biggest fear straight in the eye."

A chill went through the group. "At first I thought the killer wrote *Peanut Butter* on the crystal ball as a way of trying to draw attention to the murder," Tara said. "But now that we know it was Ronan who wrote those words, I'm inclined to think that the killer failed to notice those words scrawled on Ronan's crystal ball and *hoped* we would all think Ronan's death was accidental."

"Is there *any* chance that Ronan accidentally licked peanut butter off his own fingers and *that* is how he poisoned himself?" Sloane asked.

"No," Dave said, shaking his head emphatically. "He used disinfectant wipes immediately." Dave looked to Tara. "I've been forthcoming with the guards. I've given them access to everything."

Tara nodded. "I can confirm that Dave offered up his car for a voluntary search and they did indeed find disinfectant wipes in the car, including ones in a makeshift rubbish bag located in the car that had traces of peanut butter on it."

Ciara stood. "It seems to me that we can't be sure Ronan didn't kill himself."

"That's outrageous," Dave said.

Tara was expecting this, and she was prepared. "I have permission to divulge that a deadly amount of peanut butter was found within the tin of Irish soda bread purchased by Ronan Stone."

"I would *never* put peanut butter in Irish soda bread, allergy or no allergy," Johnny said.

"And the only thing I put in one of the tins is me magic scarf," Paddy added.

Ciara sat down once again, presumably satisfied that Ronan did not take his own life.

"Where did Ronan keep his EpiPen?" Tara asked Dave.

Dave didn't hesitate. "He always kept one on him—in the breast pocket of his shirt. Today he was wearing his cape, so it could have been in the cape pocket." He teared up. "I always had an EpiPen on me as well. I believe that's why the fire alarm was pulled. I think the killer knew this and needed me out of the way. Otherwise I could have and would have saved him."

Tara nodded sympathetically. She also believed this to be true. "Is it possible his EpiPen fell out of his pocket and onto the floor?"

"It's possible," Dave said. "Or the killer searched his pockets."

"If I told you that his EpiPen was found inside the jar of peanut butter that was tossed into the dumpster, would this come as a surprise to you?"

"Absolutely" Dave said. "Is that where it was found?"

It was indeed, but Tara didn't directly answer the question, she was here to get information, not give it. "Is there any chance Ronan placed his EpiPen in the peanut butter?" Tara continued.

"Absolutely, not," Dave said. "Not a chance."

"Deirdre," Tara said, switching gears and turning to the palm reader, "tell us about the lawsuit hanging over your head and your financial woes."

Deirdre's eyes widened. "What does that have to do with anything?"

"If you would please indulge me. This case rests on little bits of information from all of you."

Deirdre sighed. "Someone—and I believed it was Ronan—sent phony customers to me for readings. One turned out to be a reporter. I'm being blackmailed—they want fifty thousand euro." Heads turned to see Dave's reaction.

"Is that how Ronan was going to finance our new studio?" Dave said. "I didn't know. I swear I didn't know."

"Sloane," Tara said. "You learned of Deirdre's situation at your birthday party."

"I did," Sloane said. "It was definitely a downer. I don't mind supporting my friends, but it was *my* birthday."

Tara didn't join the pity party but continued along her line of questioning. "Did you ask Johnny Meehan to help Deirdre out financially?"

"What?" Deirdre said. She sounded genuinely shocked. Sloane nodded. "Deirdre was so desperate." She gestured to Johnny. "And he *said* he was a millionaire!"

"I don't have that kind of money," Johnny said. "Sorry, Rose. But in this situation, I need to tell the truth."

"I know that now," Sloane said. "I overheard you earlier today. 'Manifesting.' At the time, I thought you had come into some real money." She looked at Johnny. "I didn't realize how loony you and Rose really are."

Tara knew if she unmuted Rose this very moment, the woman would be losing her mind in Tara's ear.

"There's nothing wrong with manifesting," Johnny said. "We're millionaires!"

"This now sets the stage for this morning," Tara said. "As we know, Ronan had obviously come into money as well—he was promising Dave a lavish new studio."

"Is that a crime?" Dave asked.

"Only if he was copying someone's nefarious way of getting money," Tara said.

"Stop speaking in riddles. Say what you mean!" Dave was losing what little patience he had.

"Ronan wasn't the one who set up Deirdre Palms," Tara said. She turned to Dave. "Despite the fact that the two of you discussed it."

"We discussed a lot of things," Dave said.

"Rose heard your conversation at the pub the night of Sloane's birthday bash. And because she heard you discussing sending in another phony client, she assumed you did. But someone beat you to it."

Deirdre gasped. "Who was it? Who sent that reporter?"

"Let's take this step-by-step," Tara said. "This morning, I heard Ronan make a statement—'A photo is worth a thousand words.'"

"It's *picture*," Dave said.

"Exactly." Tara nodded. "Ronan didn't *accidentally* use the word *photo*—and there's one other person in this room who knows it." Tara began to walk behind the suspects. "I believe Ronan discovered who was behind sending this reporter to Deirdre, and not only did he find out, he secured proof in the form of a photo. What we heard him say—*a photo is worth a thousand words*—is Ronan putting the killer on alert."

Another gasp was heard around the room. "Who is it?" Paddy said. "It's not me."

"I believe once Ronan's victim received this incriminating photo, this person went out, not only to figure out what to do with this photo—and his or her blackmailer— but because this person was also highly stressed. He or she went out to the back dumpster to smoke."

"Nasty habit," Sloane said.

"In times of great stress, people return to their nasty habits," Tara said. "Deirdre. Did you mention the fact that the reporter who visited you—that her clothes reeked of cigarette smoke?"

"I did," Deirdre said. "Because they did."

"Did you ever see the reporter smoke?"

Deirdre shook her head. "No."

"Is it possible her clothing smelled of smoke because whoever sent her to you was a smoker?"

Deirdre gasped. "I never thought of that. But yes, it's possible."

Tara nodded and once more began to pace as she spoke. "I believe the killer went out to the dumpster to smoke after receiving a veiled threat from Ronan. And then just as this person was about to toss his or her cigarette out in the dumpster, he or she saw the jar of peanut butter lying on top."

"An impulsive kill!" Ciara blurted out.

"I'm not here to argue the timeline for premeditation," Tara said, "but when this culprit discovered the peanut butter, I do believe it was at that moment that his or her murderous plan was born. You see, by then Ronan had already purchased two tins of Irish soda bread. He did this in front of an audience. The killer knew Ronan intended to eat at least a slice from *one* of the tins—the one without the tiny cross in it."

"How did the killer know Ronan would eat out of that tin?"

"Because it would have been bad luck to poison the one keeping the devil out," Tara said. "And everyone in this group is superstitious, are they not?"

Paddy jumped up. "I did not do it. I did not!"

"I'm not accusing you, Paddy," Tara said. "I'm simply saying the killer knew which tin Ronan was eating from. The one without a cross. There was clear access to Ronan's tent from the back. Once the peanut butter was in the soda bread, all the killer had to do was take the EpiPen, get rid of the evidence, and clear the mill so that once Ronan was in distress there would be no one to save him. The EpiPen was placed into the jar of peanut butter and put back in the dumpster. Then the killer set the dumpster on fire, thus evacuating the building and ensuring their plan would work out."

"Diabolical," Deirdre said. "But how did the killer put peanut butter in the bread *after* it was baked."

"Only a trace amount would have been necessary," Tara said. "My guess is they went in through the bottom. Ronan wouldn't have noticed it."

"And he could have attributed the scent of peanut butter to the jar he'd been carrying with him that morning," Paddy said. "Once I have a smell in me nose, it stays with me all day." Now that he no longer felt Tara was pointing the finger specifically at him, he was eager to jump in.

"He didn't have the strongest sense of smell to begin with," Dave said. "He might not have detected a thing."

"Ciara Moon was heard yelling 'dumpster fire' this morning," Tara said.

"It's just an expression," Ciara said. "But I do admit, it could have been a premonition."

"You're psychic, you just don't know it?" Dave remarked.

"The killer made a few mistakes," Tara continued. "He or she claimed to see the fire through the back window. Under normal circumstances this killer would have had clear sight lines. But Johnny had to move a lot of stuff out of the way to set up for this psychic fair. He mentioned that he had piled everything in front of the windows. I went to the storage room and saw for myself—there's no way anyone could have seen the dumpster on fire—those windows were obscured."

"You're right!" Ciara said. "I was back there meself. I forgot all about that."

Heads slowly turned to Sloane Stargazer. Sloane took the heat, then stood. "Maybe I *thought* I saw it out the window. But maybe I just *felt* it."

"The killer also needed to disguise the smell of cigarette

smoke," Tara said. "The killer attempted to do this with too much perfume and chewing gum."

"It's not a crime to wear perfume and chew gum!" Sloane said. "This is all conjecture. You have no proof."

"Ronan wasn't the one who set Deirdre up with the reporter. You were." Tara held up a taped-up piece of paper. "This was found in the rubbish bin in Johnny's office. You threw it away right in front of the detective, pretending to be using it to get rid of your gum. Gum you were chewing to hide the cigarette smoke on your breath. And this is the same photo Ronan delivered to your booth this morning with his cryptic warning—*a photo is worth a thousand words*. It's a photo of you and the reporter exchanging money."

"Sloane!" Deirdre cried.

"I'm trying to clean up the community," Sloane wailed. She pointed at Deirdre. "You're the one who was being shady. Every underhanded thing one of you does affects our community!"

Dave struggled to his feet and turned to Sloane. "You turned into a killer to clean up the community?" Sloane swallowed. "If I did do this terrible thing—then *hypothetically*—Ronan had my back against the wall. He was insisting on fifty thousand euro. I don't have that kind of money. Not to mention my reputation as a backstabber would have been sealed. My career would be over. I had planned on borrowing the money from Johnny until I heard him admit he wasn't a real millionaire. He was *manifesting*. I panicked. And yes, I had gone back to my nasty habit. I was smoking by the back dumpster and had just opened the lid to crush and throw out the cigarette, but then—there it was—right there in front of me. A nearly full jar of peanut butter. It was as if the universe *wanted* it to happen." She looked to the ceiling. "I'm sorry, Ronan. But your death was written in the stars."

"And now it's *your* fate that's written in the stars," Tara said to Sloane. "The guards are watching us on camera this very moment. They've heard your confession."

Sloane lunged for the candles and began blowing them out. The room went black. "He deserved it," she shouted. "We'll never survive if we turn on each other." A crack of thunder sounded.

"What's happening?" Ciara yelled. "Has Sloane struck again?"

A scream sounded from their killer, one that gave them all chills. Moments later the lights came on. Sloane, still screaming, had just been handcuffed by Detective Hayes. The detective had snuck into the loft while Sloane was confessing.

"He had to die," Sloane continued saying as they dragged her out of the room. "It was written in the stars."

Chapter Thirteen

"A toast," Danny said, raising his glass. "To my future wife." Danny, Tara, Uncle Johnny, and Rose were sitting outside on the patio watching the setting sun paint the sky orange, red, and pink. It was stunning.

"To Tara," Johnny and Rose echoed. They clinked their glasses of champagne. Hound, Johnny's Irish Wolfhound, put his giant head in Tara's lap. It had been a week since the disastrous psychic fair, and it was nice to take a moment to breathe.

"Next weekend the two of you will be attached," Johnny said. "Welcome to the ball-and-chain club."

Danny roared with laughter while Tara and Rose rolled their eyes. The wedding was going to be spectacular. They'd be married in a gorgeous church in Galway City, then they would watch the Saint Patrick's Day parade while still in their wedding outfits, and finally they would come to the mill for a glorious reception. At first Tara wasn't sure she wanted to hold their celebration where a man had been murdered, but lately a few strange signs made it seem as if Ronan Stone himself was game for the event. Every one of them at some point in the past week had seen a crystal ball. Tara saw one in the window of a curiosity shop, Danny sourced a new one from an estate sale and passed it on to Johnny, and Rose spotted a giant poster of a crystal ball in town. They all believed Ronan was speaking to them. And he always did appreciate a good celebration.

"I'd like to propose a toast," Danny said. "May there be no murder on our wedding day." He grinned. "The same goes for our wedding night."

"No murder," Johnny and Rose said, their glasses raised high.

"You are the strangest folk I've ever met," Tara said. "And I'm so lucky to be stuck with you forever."

"Forever," Danny said, sounding somewhat shell-shocked.

Johnny leaned over. "It's not too late to run," he said.

"Don't listen to him," Rose said. "Marriage is grand." She cocked her head toward Danny. "And divorce is a hundred grand." They laughed again, and as Tara raised her glass for the umpteenth time and the sky turned purplish-red, she turned her head to see something reflecting in the center of the mill. It was one of the crystals from the centerpiece last week, reflecting the sun and beaming it back. She couldn't help but think it was yet another sign. *Rest in peace, Ronan Stone.*

Danny leaned over. "Penny for your thoughts, Ms. America."

"I want to bottle this moment," she said. "It's perfect."

"You're perfect." Danny O'Donnell grinned and then leaned in to kiss her. It was really happening. The self-proclaimed Irish bachelor-for-life was getting married. To *her.* She was under no delusion that it would be a smooth ride, but nevertheless, she couldn't wait to climb aboard and sound the horn. Hound lifted his head and began to howl. Everyone laughed.

"It's a sign," Rose said.

"Good or bad?" Danny asked.

"Whatever we make it," Tara said, looping her arm around him. "Whatever we decide to make it."

Traditional Irish Soda Bread,
Inspired by Darina Allen
https://www.youtube.com/watch?v=p450gWjSKTc

Ingredients
1 pound all-purpose flour
(Irish brands such as *Odlums* can be purchased on
    Amazon)
½ teaspoon salt
1 teaspoon sodium bicarbonate or bicarbonate of soda
You can purchase on Amazon or substitute with
    1 teaspoon of baking soda
12–14 ounces buttermilk—if you can get it, use Jersey
    buttermilk (from Jersey cows)

Author's Note: If desired, a handful of raisins or currants
can be added to the mix.

Directions
Preheat oven to 450 degrees Fahrenheit. In a large mixing bowl, add flour, salt, and bicarbonate of soda. The bicarbonate of soda may have lumps: if it does, use a sieve to break them up and sprinkle into the mix, or use the palm of your hand to break up the lumps. Make a well in the center of the bowl (clear space in the middle). Pour in buttermilk. Using your hand in a claw shape, place in the well of buttermilk and begin to stir outward, thus mixing the buttermilk with the dry mixture. Stir until combined.

Flour a countertop or work surface. Place the combined mixture on top. *Do not knead.* Instead, "tidy it up" with your hands, pat around it, then flip it over. Tuck the dough underneath all around, adding a tad more flour if needed. Dough should be about an inch and a half thick.

Place on a thin baking pan. Cut a deep cross on top of the dough—this is the "blessing," but practically it helps the loaf cook through. Prick the four corners to "let the fairies out" (optional but why not?!). Place in the oven *immediately*.

Bake for 30–35 minutes. Cool on a rack. Slather with good Irish butter.

Author's Note: If you do not wish to make from scratch, you can purchase Odlums soda bread mix, both white and brown, and it will still be delicious.

AN IRISH RECIPE
FOR MURDER

Peggy Ehrhart

Acknowledgments

Abundant thanks to my agent, Evan Marshall, and to my editor at Kensington Books, John Scognamiglio.

Chapter One

"It's going well, don't you think?" Bettina Fraser remarked to Pamela Paterson as she surveyed the scene unfolding in the gymnasium of Arborville's recreation center. Colorful streamers in shades of green and gold fluttered from the ceiling, while garlands composed of foil shamrocks enlivened the walls and cheerful Irish music filled the air. At one end of the room, a table draped in a green cloth and furnished with a chair awaited the main event.

Meanwhile, in a corner of the room, a young man was perched on a low stool regaling an audience with Irish folktales. In another corner, a face-painter was turning children into elves and fairies. Elsewhere, attendees clustered in chatting groups as they nibbled cookies and sipped green punch from plastic cups. A man in a leprechaun costume, including a convincing mask, hopped here and there, shaking hands and chuckling. Earlier events had included an Irish fiddler and a dance troupe demonstrating Irish jigs.

"I'm not quite sure who the leprechaun is," Bettina commented, "and I think leprechauns are supposed to be quite small. But he adds a nice touch. I guess the activities director invited him."

"Is your judge present and accounted for?" Pamela inquired. "It looks like the bakers are here with their loaves."

A long table against the room's back wall served as a staging area for refreshments when the room was used for events like this. At present a large punch bowl, a jumble of plastic cups, and several platters of cookies occupied one end. The rest of the table's surface was taken up by five plates. Each plate held a loaf of Irish soda bread—round, dome-shaped, and golden-brown, with a distinctive crisscross marking the top. Four women and one man hovered nearby. The just-baked aroma of the loaves was so intense that it infused the whole room.

The loaves, submitted by Arborville's home bakers, were to be judged as part of the town's St. Patrick's Day fest. The contest was sponsored by Arborville's weekly newspaper, the *Advocate*, and had been Bettina's idea. In her role as the *Advocate*'s chief reporter, she planned to interview the winner for an article that she was sure would appeal to the *Advocate*'s readers.

She scanned the room, murmuring, "There's Kieran Malone, talking to the bakers. I'm not sure that's fair, but I'm so glad he agreed to judge."

Pamela followed the direction of Bettina's gaze. Kieran Malone was part of a chatting group standing near the punch bowl. He was the focal point of the group, in fact, since all eyes were on him. He seemed to be finishing up a tale that had everyone laughing, and he himself was laughing, rendered all the more handsome by the flash of gleaming teeth.

"Yes," Bettina giggled. "Those dark-haired Irishmen can be awfully good-looking."

"Is that why you invited him to judge?" Pamela nudged her friend. "And you a happily married woman!"

"*Hello!*" Bettina giggled again. "It's *Irish* soda bread. And he's on the town council. It's nice that our leaders are interested in being part of community events."

At that moment, Bettina was distracted by a tug at her elbow, and she turned to greet her friend Marlene Pepper.

"Look at you!" Marlene exclaimed. "Such a perfect outfit for your soda-bread contest. Aren't you just a vision!"

Marlene resembled Bettina in age (mid-fifties) and shape (neither tall nor thin) but, unlike Marlene, Bettina dressed with the flair of a devoted fashionista. Today she was all in green, a bright Kelly green. A fit-and-flare dress with an oversized bow at the neckline hugged her ample curves, and on her feet were green suede pumps. Green jade earrings dangled at her ears. Combined with her scarlet hair, the effect was striking.

"And you too, Pamela!" Marlene added belatedly.

Pamela did not share Bettina's interest in fashion, despite Bettina's frequent observations that her lanky figure deserved a more exciting wardrobe than her usual jeans and simple tops. She had at least made an effort to acknowledge this festive occasion with her choice of sweater. Cowl-necked and blousy, with a lacy texture that resembled moss, it was knit from alpaca blend yarn in a deep forest-green hue.

"It looks like everyone's having fun," Marlene said, bobbing this way and that to survey the room. "And your bakers are all here—five loaves, it looks like, and the children are certainly enjoying that young man's performance . . . awfully handsome . . . no trouble attracting girls, I'll bet."

"That's Whit Sutton," Bettina interjected.

"Oh, and there's Kieran Malone," Marlene went on. "I'm so glad he ran for councilman . . . someone sensible for a change. At least I think he's sensible, not like the mayor—" She seized Bettina's arm. "*He's* not coming, is he? I'd think he'd be afraid to show his face after the comments people have been posting about him on Access-Arborville—not that I spend much time on the listserv . . ." She paused for breath. "Yes, that young man is very . . . and with Kieran standing right there . . . their looks . . . you'd almost think they were related. Pamela!" She seized Pamela's arm with her other hand—"I'm guessing you made that sweater! So talented . . ."

Bettina was listening attentively to Marlene, but Pamela could tell by the slightly glazed look in her friend's hazel eyes that her patience was waning. A burst of applause from the group clustered around Whit Sutton provided a helpful interruption. Bettina detached herself from Marlene and edged aside to gesture to the young man as he rose from his stool.

"That was wonderful!" she cooed as he drew closer. "What an impressive repertoire of stories you've collected!"

"Thank you, ma'am!" He bowed and flashed a charming smile. "We druids aren't taken as seriously as we used to be, but I do what I can. Long before the Celts had an alphabet, the druids kept the culture alive." He tapped the side of his head, which sported a crop of dark, wavy hair. "It was all in here."

"Druids?" Marlene inquired of Bettina after Whit had gone on his way, only to be intercepted by the rec center's activities director. She, too, seemed delighted with his performance.

Bettina laughed. "He's not even Irish, but he's, as they say, into it."

"He's Whitfield Sutton's son, isn't he?" Marlene had watched him depart, and her gaze remained on him. "*Doctor* Whitfield Sutton."

Bettina nodded. "Whit's finishing up his last semester at Wendelstaff, majoring in history."

"Useful," Marlene remarked in a tone that implied it was anything but.

"My Wilfred majored in history, and he had a nice career in the business world," Bettina responded mildly. "Whit's sensible, and he's got plans. He came around to the *Advocate*'s office last week. He thinks he'd like to take photos for a living."

"Kieran's done well with the photography," Marlene said. "Even with everybody using their phones to snap photos, people still need a real photographer sometimes. When our daughter was married . . . the younger one—though the older one is married too, now . . . hope it lasts . . . anyway—"

The timely arrival of the activities director, Fawn Darwin, distracted Marlene from her narrative, though Fawn was seeking Bettina.

"Shall we launch the soda-bread contest now?" she inquired.

Fawn, too, was dressed for the holiday in green, a pea-green jumpsuit that suited her athletic frame and lively expression—as if primed to guide any and every rec center activity to a successful conclusion.

"I'm ready!" Bettina lifted her chin and straightened her spine.

Fawn had already escorted Kieran to the judging table. She collected a microphone from the high school student who had been handling sound for the event and positioned herself in front of the table.

"Welcome, everyone!" she chirped, as the sound system contributed a few chirps of its own. "We've had a great afternoon, thanks to all the people who've contributed their talents, and now I'm going to hand things over to Bettina

Fraser from our own beloved *Arborville Advocate*—and we'll find out which Arborville baker has the magic touch"— her voice rose to a crescendo—"when it comes to that most classic Irish treat, *soda bread*!"

She flung out an arm, beckoned Bettina from the sidelines, and handed over the microphone.

"Let's get started then!" Bettina accompanied the words with a flirtatious wink. "And, remember, everybody will get to sample *all* the entries when the judging concludes." She turned toward the table. "Kieran Malone, are you ready?"

An eager nod greeted her words.

"Loaf number one then, baked by Deirdre McKeon." She glanced toward the table against the room's back wall.

Deirdre was already standing at attention, both hands gripping the plate that bore her loaf. She was a small blond woman with pale eyes and a turned-up nose. Her outfit, too, had been keyed to the occasion—wool pants and a sweater in a pastel green that flattered her delicate looks.

She smiled nervously as she advanced toward the front of the room. When she reached the table, with its festive green cloth, Bettina joined her. From his seat on the opposite side of the table, Kieran offered an encouraging nod and an admiring glance at the loaf that had been set before him. Fawn darted forward, flourishing an impressive-looking bread knife.

After a bit of momentary confusion about who should cut the portion to be sampled, Bettina took the knife. Lining it up with the crisscrossing lines scored into the top of the loaf, she cut the loaf in half and then in quarters, revealing the buttery-gold crumb studded with raisins. From one of the quarters, she cut a slice that Kieran reached for as soon as she pulled the knife away.

"This looks awfully tasty," he commented as he broke off a large piece from the slice and lifted it to his mouth. An encouraging *ummm* emerged as he chewed, and his dark eyes crinkled with pleasure. He took another bite and another and another.

Deirdre appeared to be holding her breath as her lips curved into a tiny smile. Bettina, too, was smiling, as if in vicarious enjoyment of the crusty loaf whose quality had clearly made an impression on Kieran. In fact, he seemed quite transported. He stared straight ahead, his eyes widening, and then he froze. His mouth opened, but no words came out. The only sound was a dry rasp, though his lips moved as if he was trying to speak.

"Kieran!" Deirdre squealed. She circled the table and crouched by his side. "No, no, no!" she moaned as her delicate features twisted into a tragic mask.

Bettina remained where she was standing, but otherwise her reaction was as dramatic as Deirdre's. The lively cheer that normally softened the contours of her face and rosied her cheeks had fled. Pamela stepped closer to her friend's side, a move that Bettina seemed to appreciate as she reached toward Pamela to steady herself.

"What on earth is happening?" Bettina whispered, clearly referring to Kieran's distress, though her gaze strayed to Deirdre. Pamela, too, was puzzled. Anyone would be alarmed if a few bites of something they had baked provoked such a startling reaction. Deirdre's reaction, however, was so *personal*.

Kieran was trying to speak again, but the sounds that emerged from his throat were no more than croaks, as if his tongue was paralyzed. His eyes were still wide, still staring, still focused straight ahead, and it seemed they too were struggling to communicate . . . something. And Deirdre was moaning, no longer crouching but leaning close to Kieran with an arm around his back and a hand caressing his chest.

Barely a minute had passed since Kieran first took ill, though time had slowed in that way it does when an unexpected crisis disrupts the normal workings of things. Fawn had retreated to the edge of the room after handing over the bread knife. Now she darted forward, her expression a more resolute version of the lively competence Pamela had remarked earlier. She produced a phone from somewhere in her jumpsuit and poked at its screen.

"Kieran has had a bad reaction to . . . something," she exclaimed. Without further comment, she raised the phone to her ear and began speaking into it.

Pamela listened with half her attention, aware that Fawn was summoning an ambulance. The other half of her attention was focused on the drama unfolding around Kieran. A few people had surged forward, detaching themselves from the crowd that had gathered near the table to watch the judging. (Other people, less interested in the soda-bread component of the event, were milling about or clustered in chatting groups at the far end of the room.)

"We should lay him on his back," one person, a youngish man, urged.

"No—he could choke!" a middle-aged woman said. "That would be the worst thing."

"But he looks so uncomfortable in that chair," added another woman, younger.

Meanwhile, though Deirdre had continued to moan, she had also been busy, loosening his tie and unbuttoning the top button of his shirt. He seemed unaware of anything around him, no longer even croaking. When Deirdre finished her task and removed her hands, he suddenly slumped sideways, saved from tipping his chair and landing on the floor by the quick action of the youngish man.

The middle-aged woman lurched forward to help, and Kieran was gently disengaged from the chair and lowered to the floor—on his side, at the insistence of the middle-aged woman. Fawn pulled the cloth from the table and rolled it into a sort of pillow that she tucked under his head, though his body had stiffened and he seemed oblivious to anything going on around him.

More people had become aware that something dramatic was happening at the front of the room, and the small crowd that had gathered to watch the judging had grown. It was a silent crowd, however, save for a few low murmurs. Some of the children in attendance were staring curiously at the spectacle of Kieran stretched out motionless on the floor with his head on a rolled-up tablecloth. Others were hovering around their parents, seeking the comfort of a tightly clutched hand or a head pat.

"Is he breathing?" Fawn whispered, and the youngish man crouched down and tipped his head in the direction of Kieran's nose, apparently listening.

"I think he is," was the report.

"Does he have a pulse?" Fawn followed up.

But help had arrived. Pamela had been aware of a sudden, muted ambulance yowl—barely necessary, given that Arborville's EMT squad occupied a building at the edge of the same parking lot that served the rec center. No high-speed dash through traffic-clogged streets had been necessary.

Now the door that led to the parking lot banged open, and through it stepped a sturdy older woman. Her navy blue pants and a zip-front jacket bearing the shield-shaped insignia of her profession identified her as an EMT. Behind her, almost pushing her off balance with its momentum, came a stretcher supported by crisscrossed metal legs that ended in wheels.

"Watch it," she said over her shoulder.

The stretcher made its way through the door, followed by another EMT, an equally sturdy man, who was trying to slow its momentum.

"Back up, back up, all of you!" The woman EMT made shooing motions, first in the direction of the large crowd of onlookers and then at the small group clustered around the figure on the floor. Deirdre was the last to retreat— she'd been kneeling next to Kieran stroking his dark hair.

"What happened to him?" the woman EMT inquired, directing her question to Fawn, who was still holding her phone and thus perhaps identifiable as the person who had called for help.

"Something he ate," Fawn said.

The woman EMT turned toward the stretcher and her partner. As if their motions had been choreographed, they wordlessly propelled the stretcher across the floor until it was lined up parallel with Kieran.

The man lowered himself onto one knee and studied Kieran's face, his eyes serious. He felt for a pulse in Kieran's neck and applied his fingers to Kieran's wrist. The woman manipulated something on the stretcher's underside and then steadied it as it slowly collapsed into a flat pallet. Together, they eased Kieran onto the stretcher, clicked wide belts into place at shoulder, hip, and ankle, and unfolded the stretcher's accordion legs to raise it waist high once again.

Pamela had been as interested in the proceedings as had the other onlookers, who began murmuring among themselves now that the situation appeared to be under control.

She, however, was watching Bettina. Fawn was conferring with the EMTs near the door that led to the parking lot, but Bettina was pacing around the table, now denuded of its cheerful cloth, which still lay bundled into a pillow shape on the floor. Her expression—puckered forehead and pursed lips—suggested that she was puzzled.

As Pamela started toward her, Bettina completed her circuit of the table and veered off toward the far end of the room, dodging among people alternating between looking at their phones and keeping tabs on the movements of the EMTs. Pamela followed.

Four loaves remained lined up on the table, with their creators hovering nearby. Two, a pair of older women who seemed to be friends, had fetched a couple of chairs and were chatting quite companionably. A young man baker, perhaps a high-school student, was looking at his phone, and the fourth baker, an attractive woman Pamela recognized as an officer at one of Arborville's many banks, was craning her neck to keep an eye on the EMTs and their patient.

She spoke first as Bettina approached. "Is it over?" she inquired.

Her expression was neutral, and Pamela couldn't tell from her tone what answer she was hoping for.

Before Bettina could speak, one of the older women said, "What a shame! The contest was such a good idea." The other older woman added, "I'm surprised no one tried the Heimlich maneuver."

True, Pamela reflected—though Kieran hadn't seemed to be choking, and the EMTs—who had presumably seen choking before—hadn't reacted as if that was Kieran's problem.

The young man surveyed the room. Pamela followed his

gaze, noting that the EMTs had gone on their way and Fawn and Deirdre were nowhere to be seen. Perhaps one or both had accompanied Kieran to the hospital.

"Do we just leave now?" he asked, addressing Pamela.

"Do they?" Pamela touched Bettina's arm, and she turned.

"Can we take our bread home?" He addressed Bettina this time.

"The bread!" Bettina blinked. "That's what I was—" She studied the loaves waiting on the table and whispered, "Four." Then she whirled around to face the front of the room. "That table is bare," she whispered again. "Where did Deirdre's loaf go?"

"She carried it up there," the young man said helpfully, nodding toward the table at the front. "Remember? It was loaf number one."

"I know, I know." Bettina was still whispering, as if conversing with herself. "But it's not there now."

It wasn't. That was clear. Whether its disappearance had anything thing to do with Kieran's taking ill was less certain.

At that moment, a quite welcome interruption arrived in the person of Wilfred Fraser. In deference to the occasion, he had traded the bib overalls he had adopted in retirement for a pair of corduroy pants and a flannel shirt, topped by a canvas jacket.

"Am I in time to sample the winning loaf?" he inquired, cheerful anticipation setting his ruddy face aglow. "Or . . ." He stared at Bettina. "Dear wife! What on earth is troubling you?"

Bettina sagged against his comforting bulk, and he wrapped his arms around her as he turned his gaze to Pamela. His expression was question enough without his needing to speak.

"The contest didn't really happen," Pamela said. She described Kieran's reaction after sampling Deirdre's loaf, concluding with, "And Fawn called the EMTs and Kieran's on his way to the hospital, and someone, I guess, should tell all these people to go home."

Chapter Two

In the event, it was the rec center's custodian who did that. Fawn had apparently stopped off to give him a briefing before notifying Kieran's wife that her husband was en route to County Hospital. She had then continued on to the hospital herself in her own car.

Wilfred had driven to the rec center in his ancient but lovingly cared-for Mercedes, and Pamela and Bettina had arrived much earlier in Bettina's Toyota. Now, as Bettina clung mournfully to her husband, Pamela offered to drive the Toyota back to Orchard Street, where she and the Frasers lived in houses that faced each other midway down the block.

The drive was very short—Pamela herself often preferred to walk to destinations in tiny Arborville. Barely five minutes later, she waited as Wilfred nosed the Mercedes into the Frasers' driveway and then pulled up beside him. Still sitting behind the Toyota's steering wheel, she watched as Wilfred circled his car, opened the passenger-side door, and tenderly helped Bettina to her feet. Bettina tapped on the Toyota's window, and Pamela lowered it.

"Come on in," she said, "and stay for dinner."

"I've got work to catch up for the magazine." Pamela smiled a regretful smile. "A book review to finish."

"You're sure?" Bettina leaned closer.

"I'm sure I've got work to finish, yes." Pamela smiled more cheerfully. "And cats. Cats to feed."

Bettina retreated, and Pamela eased out of the Toyota. She slipped between the two cars, and she and Bettina shared a hug at the end of the driveway before she crossed the street. Behind her, the Frasers waved her on her way. She headed toward her big house, alone, as the image of Bettina being comforted by Wilfred lingered in her mind.

Pamela had not always lived alone in her big house. She and her architect husband, Michael Paterson, had bought the house, a very old wood-frame house, as a fixer-upper early in their marriage. They had fixed it up and had had a daughter, Penny. The three of them had inhabited their house happily for several years—until Michael was killed in a tragic construction-site accident. And then, in time, Penny had graduated from college and embarked on her own independent life. Now, just as Bettina had often predicted, Pamela was alone in her big house—except for cats.

As she climbed her front steps, her gaze wandered to the house of her next-door neighbor, Richard Larkin, but she quickly focused instead on extracting her key from her purse. Richard Larkin, too, lived alone in his big house, and his eligibility had often been stressed by Bettina—to the point that Pamela had forbidden the mention of his name.

Stepping onto the worn parquet of her entry and pulling the door closed behind her, she was greeted by two of those cats. Catrina, sleek and black, tiptoed forward and raised her amber eyes with a look that seemed to reprove Pamela for her absence. Ginger, named for her color, traced impetuous figure-eights around Pamela's ankles. Precious, an aloof Siamese, regarded her from the top platform of the cat climber visible through the arch that led to the living room.

"I suppose you all want dinner," Pamela said, as she set her purse on the mail table and continued on toward the kitchen. All three cats joined the procession.

Soon the cats were intent on the contents of their respective bowls, gourmet fish pâté for Precious and beef with gravy in a shared bowl for the other two, who were mother and daughter. Pamela bent into the refrigerator, pondering her own dinner.

Most of a meatloaf remained from the previous night, and part of a roasted chicken from earlier in the week. When Penny was still living at home, Pamela had always cooked real dinners, from scratch, and she'd kept up the habit even when she was only cooking for herself. But a meatloaf or a roast chicken could provide many, many dinners now, with little for her to do after the first appearance but decide which leftover suited her current mood.

She was reaching for the chicken, picturing the ultimate comfort meal of creamed chicken on toast, when the doorbell's chime echoed from the entry. The cats, too, noticed the doorbell but quickly returned to eating. Pamela, however, closed the refrigerator and stepped to the kitchen doorway. From there she could see the front door, with its lace-curtained oval window. Twilight was just falling, and through the delicate filigrees of the curtain she could glimpse the silhouette of her caller—as well as the bright crest of scarlet hair that identified the caller as Bettina.

Bettina began speaking even before the door was fully open.

"Fawn called from the hospital," she panted, breathless from what Pamela pictured as a dash across the street. She stepped over the threshold.

Bettina had changed from the stylish green dress she

had worn that afternoon into a comfortable tunic and leggings ensemble in a flattering shade of lavender, but her jade earrings still dangled at her ears.

"Things don't look good," she continued, still panting. She patted her chest and took a deep breath. "In fact, they look very bad."

"Come in, come in." Pamela beckoned toward the kitchen. Observing Bettina, she herself felt a little breathless. It wasn't hard to guess what "things" Bettina was referring to.

Bettina waved her hands as if to reject the invitation. "I can't stay. I just wanted to let you know . . ."

Pamela slipped an arm around Bettina's shoulders and guided her through the arch that separated the entry from the living room. "At least sit down for a minute," she said.

Without turning on a lamp, she settled Bettina on the sofa, moving a few needlepoint pillows aside to make space for her guest and for herself. The room's dimness seemed more soothing, given Bettina's state.

"It's all my fault," Bettina wailed after Pamela had settled beside her. "The contest, the whole idea of the contest—and now someone has been poisoned." She grabbed Pamela's hand and squeezed. "I'm sure it was poison. What else could it be? The way he reacted . . ."

Pamela squeezed back. She could feel her brow contracting and her lips twisting in sympathy. "Maybe it isn't poison," she suggested. "Maybe he'd been exposed to something, like the flu, and it suddenly came on him while he was sitting there."

"The flu doesn't come that suddenly," Bettina said. "It comes gradually in the night, and you wake up with it." She'd been looking at Pamela, but now she faced straight ahead and tilted her head to focus on the upper reaches of the room.

"Why would Deirdre poison him, though? It was her loaf."

"Good point," Pamela observed. She pictured Deirdre stroking Kieran's hair, as if the intimate gesture came naturally.

"She's a very nice person," Bettina mused. "Not the poisoning type at all, and I've known her for ages."

"She also seemed to . . ." Pamela hesitated.

"Seemed to what?" Bettina was facing Pamela again.

"Be quite fond of him."

"He's married," Bettina said, "to someone else."

Monday morning brought unfortunate news. Back in her kitchen after her dash to the curb for the *County Register*, Pamela tossed the newspaper on the table and clicked off the flame under her hooting kettle. She poured the steaming contents over the fresh-ground coffee in her carafe's filter cone and, as the spicy aroma of brewing coffee filled the room, slipped the newspaper from its flimsy plastic sleeve.

Even before she spread out the front page, the glimpse of a bold headline made the day's lead story clear: AR-BORVILLE COUNCILMAN DIES AFTER TOWN FEST. A smaller headline below read, KIERAN MALONE TAKES ILL AFTER SAMPLING SODA BREAD HE WAS TO JUDGE.

Pamela unfolded the paper and scanned the article, then lowered it to the table with a long sigh, her mind blank but for the thought that Kieran was now dead. Her immobility aroused the cats' curiosity—normally, fetching the *Register* and launching the coffee would lead to the production of toast and then a cozy breakfast session at the table while they themselves went about their business. Now, instead of going about their business, they milled about her slipper-clad feet—all three, though Precious usually affected an aloof detachment.

Bettina! was Pamela's sudden thought. When the *Register* brought startling news, Bettina usually met Pamela at the curb with a preview even before Pamela collected her own newspaper. Surely this news had alarmed her—likely alarmed her more than it had Pamela, given her role in the soda-bread contest.

Abandoning the coffee and ignoring the need for toast, Pamela hurried upstairs and exchanged pajamas, robe, and slippers for jeans, a sweater, and loafers. As the cats watched, even more puzzled, she dashed out of the house and sped across the street.

Wilfred opened the door still enveloped in a plaid flannel robe. Lurking behind him was a large, shaggy dog. As it peered cautiously around its master, Wilfred rested a gentle hand on its head and murmured, "It's okay. You know Pamela." Turning his attention to his caller, he drew back, pulled the door open, and waved Pamela inside. The welcoming nod was cordial, but Wilfred's usual cheer was lacking.

"She's with Clayborn," he said. "Marcy Brewer was here for an interview first thing, even before we brought the *Register* in."

Marcy Brewer was the reporter whose byline had been on the article reporting Kieran's death. Few newsworthy happenings in Arborville escaped her notice.

"How is Bettina?"

Wilfred shrugged and nodded glumly in response. He took a few steps and extended an arm, inviting Pamela to advance. The comforting aroma of coffee intensified as they passed through the arch that separated the living room from the dining room and then entered the kitchen.

The Frasers' house was the oldest house on the block, a Dutch colonial dating from the era when it was the only house among the apple orchards that gave Orchard Street its name. The kitchen, however, had been added when the Frasers moved in some decades earlier. It was a spacious room bisected by a high counter. On one side of the counter was an area for cooking. On the other, a scrubbed pine table surrounded by four chairs served for casual meals. Sliding glass doors looked out on a patio and a backyard where a venerable maple tree was just coming back to life after its winter sleep.

A coffee mug from Bettina's sage-green pottery set shared the table with the Frasers' copy of the *Register*, arranged so that the sports section was uppermost. The dog, a shelter dog named Woofus, had followed them to the kitchen. He was now stationed in a spot by the sliding glass doors where he could watch the squirrels busily excavating the Frasers' lawn.

"Coffee?" Wilfred asked.

Pamela nodded, and he headed toward the stove as she settled into a chair. A few moments later, he was back, setting a steaming mug in front of her. She lifted the mug to her lips and took a careful, grateful sip.

"Did you eat yet?" Wilfred studied her from the other side of the table as if skipping breakfast could manifest in physical signs.

Pamela shook her head. "I was so startled by the headline in the *Register* that I just dashed across the street. Who could ever think that such a fun idea—a soda-bread contest—could lead to such a tragic ending?"

Wilfred shook his head too, with an air of mournful commiseration. "No silver lining for this cloud—and the *Advocate*'s editor hasn't even weighed in yet."

"Bettina loves her job," Pamela said.

"And now," came a familiar voice from the dining room, "everywhere I go people are going to recognize me as the person from the *Advocate* who poisoned one of Arborville's leading citizens. And how will anyone get their wedding photos done with Kieran gone?"

"Dear wife, dear wife!" Wilfred rose, leaning on the table to give himself a boost.

Bettina stepped through the doorway, to be met by Wilfred. He quickly relieved her of the white bakery box she was carrying, handed it to Pamela, and enfolded his wife in a hug. She nestled her scarlet head against the plaid flannel of his robe as he murmured words of comfort. After a bit, she eased herself out of his arms and plopped into a chair.

Despite the fact that she'd been eager to confer with Detective Clayborn, she'd taken the time for careful makeup, though she hadn't been able to hide the dark circles beneath her hazel eyes. Bright Murano glass earrings dangled at her ears, echoing the orange and blue swirls in the scarf that accented her indigo sweater.

Pamela turned to her. "Do they know for sure now that it was poison?" she asked.

"No." Bettina shook her head, setting the earrings in motion. "But what else could it be—the way he reacted after eating the soda bread, and then fading away so fast?"

A mug of coffee appeared in front of her, and three plates, forks, and napkins joined the bakery box in the middle of the table. Wilfred retreated and returned with the sugar and cream set that matched the sage-green mugs. Bettina continued speaking as she spooned sugar into her mug, stirred briskly, and followed with a sizeable dribble of cream.

"The loaf—Deirdre's loaf—vanished while everyone was paying attention to Kieran, so until the autopsy nothing will be known for sure. Still, I think it was poison."

She sipped her coffee and tried for a smile in grateful acknowledgment of its comforting effect. Wilfred, meanwhile, had transferred the newspaper to the high counter, reoccupied his seat, and loosened the string that fastened the bakery box. He folded the flap back to reveal half a dozen large squares of crumb cake.

"I left the house without breakfast," Bettina explained—though no explanation for crumb cake was really necessary. "And the police station is so near the Co-Op . . ."

"It's an ill wind that blows no good," Wilfred observed as he used two forks to ease one of the slices out of the box and onto a plate. The moist cake was a pale gold, and the buttery ripples of crumb topping were a warm golden brown that hinted at cinnamon.

The focus for the next few minutes was the crumb cake, with the welcome accompaniment of Wilfred's coffee. The coffee had already begun to remedy the early morning shock of the headline. Now the crumb cake and the soothing presence of Wilfred restored Pamela to almost her usual state.

"What about the other loaves?" Pamela asked, once the diminished size of the crumb cake squares on the three plates and the more leisurely pace of eating suggested that attention could be spared for conversation once again. "As I recall, the bakers took them home . . ."

"No ill effects have been reported," Bettina replied, "but Clayborn was about to send officers around to check."

"I'd like to know what happened to Deirdre's loaf," Pamela said. "The fact that it vanished—that someone made sure it vanished—certainly points to a . . . *some-*

one . . . who wanted Kieran dead and had a plan to accomplish that."

"Clayborn is going to talk to Deirdre, of course." Bettina teased another forkful of crumb cake from what remained on her plate and lifted it to her mouth. "He has to, naturally, though baking a poisoned loaf and serving it to a person you want to kill is not a very smart plan." She paused to follow the crumb cake with a swallow of coffee and then added, "Unless you don't mind being caught."

After refills of coffee, and second helpings of crumb cake on the part of Wilfred and Bettina, Pamela took her leave. She crossed the street to her own house carrying the white bakery box, now containing the one last piece of crumb cake, and with an invitation to return that evening to share Wilfred's traditional St. Patrick's Day feast.

"Today is really the day," he had pointed out. "The town's fest was a day early so it could be on the weekend."

She greeted the cats and climbed the stairs to her office. Pamela's job as associate editor of *Fiber Craft* magazine had allowed her to work from home long before working from home became possible for so many people. That feature of it had been particularly welcome when Penny was younger.

As she had told Bettina the previous day, there was a book review to finish. The book chronicled the year its author had spent in West Africa studying traditional methods of textile manufacture. She had learned that ancient techniques, like the weaving process used to make Kente cloth, had attracted the interest of young craftspeople, mostly women, in cities like Lagos and Accra—and they were learning the techniques from older practitioners in order to keep the traditions alive, in some cases putting a modern spin on them.

Pamela had already written a draft of a very enthusiastic review. Now she checked it over and added a section praising the many photographs the author had included, photographs of the textiles themselves as well as some of the textile enthusiasts she had met in her travels.

She closed the Word file, attached it to an email, and sent it off to Celine Bramley, her boss at *Fiber Craft*. Pushing back from her desk, she closed her eyes and raised her arms over her head in a luxurious stretch. No sooner had she opened her eyes again than a new message popped up in her inbox. It was from her boss, thanking her for the review and attaching three articles to copyedit, due the following Monday morning. Strung across the top of the email were short titles hinting at the articles' contents: "Feathered Walls," "Rag Rugs," and "Ariadne's Thread."

Her stomach had begun to remind her that one piece of crumb cake and a few cups of black coffee might serve as nourishment for a while, but with noon approaching something more substantial was required. She closed her email program, relinquished her hold on her mouse, and rose from her chair.

Chapter Three

Several hours later, Pamela stepped over the Frasers' threshold into a living room made cozy by a fire burning in the fireplace, complete with Woofus stretched out on the floor below the hearth.

"It was so cold today," Bettina explained, gesturing toward the fire, "not like spring is on the way at all." Despite the cloud that now shadowed the holiday, Bettina had dressed for that evening's St. Patrick's Day feast in a festive ensemble: silky wide-legged pants in bright chartreuse paired with a chartreuse and cream striped blouse in the same silky fabric.

"Stay there." Wilfred spoke from the arch that separated the living room from the dining room. "I'll bring our hors d'oeuvres to the coffee table." His corduroy pants and a flannel shirt were partly hidden by the bib apron tied around his bulky middle.

Pamela had noticed on entering that the house smelled like Wilfred had been baking, not necessarily something sweet, but rather more like . . .

As if Bettina had read her mind, she quickly said, "It's not soda bread. I don't think I could ever look at a loaf of that again."

Pamela settled into one of the peach-colored armchairs,

the one nearest the hearth, as Bettina took a seat on the sofa that faced the armchairs. Both the armchairs and the sofa offered easy access to the coffee table. Neither spoke for a few minutes, enjoying the crackle of the flames and the soft warmth they provided. Wilfred entered then, bearing a wooden tray that held three tall crystal glasses containing a dark liquid crowned with an inch of thick, creamy foam.

"Guinness Stout," he announced, "just the thing to drink with . . . you'll see." He set the glasses on the coffee table, along with a stack of small paper napkins in a bright Kelly green, and retreated, carrying the tray. His expression—a half-suppressed smile—suggested a treat was in store.

"He's been very mysterious," Bettina said. "He's been baking, but he swore it wasn't soda bread."

On its return journey, the tray held an oval platter from Bettina's sage-green pottery set. Arranged on it were rectangles of dense-looking brown bread, topped with glistening slices of smoked salmon nearly the same shade as the armchairs. Feathery sprigs of dill added a pop of contrasting color. Wilfred lowered himself onto the sofa next to his wife and surveyed his creation with pleasure.

"Irish oatcakes," he explained, "made with oatmeal and oat flour, and I drove to Timberley for the smoked salmon." He reached for the closest glass of Guinness and raised it in a wordless toast.

Pamela sampled her own Guinness. The flavor was deep and rich to the point of being almost chocolaty, and she soon discovered how well it complemented the accompanying food. The oatcakes were chewy and substantial, with a texture that indeed invoked oatmeal. That texture and their unassuming taste provided the perfect backdrop for the salmon, which was meltingly tender and lightly salty, with a hint of sea and smoke.

Wilfred nodded happily in response to the delighted praise that followed the first few bites and sips. Once that topic had been exhausted, Bettina seemed uncharacteristically at a loss for words, though eating and drinking proceeded apace. Normally, a social occasion would have brought out her social side. Now, however, in moments when she wasn't aware of being observed, her expression lapsed into a bleak stare aimed at nothing in particular.

As Pamela was searching her mind for a conversational gambit, Wilfred broke the silence. "Has Penny decided where she'll be studying this fall?"

"She's still waiting to hear from Columbia, fingers crossed." Pamela illustrated the phrase with the gesture that it described and continued. "I have to admit I'd like to keep her close by."

"I would too"—Bettina joined the conversation— "though she's living in Manhattan right now, and we don't see her as often as we'd like."

Pamela's daughter hoped to follow in her father's footsteps with a career in architecture and had applied to several graduate programs.

"She's busy with her own life," Pamela said.

"Too busy, I hope, to be paying attention to current events in Arborville." Bettina paused for a deep breath that she exhaled in a drawn-out sigh.

Silence descended once again, a silence filled by renewed interest in the salmon-topped oatcakes remaining on the platter. A very interesting aroma had been drifting in from the direction of the kitchen, overtaking what Pamela now realized had been evidence of oatcake production. It was rich and meaty, with a hint of pepper and bay leaf.

Wilfred was stirring, turning first toward Bettina as if to check on her state. He pushed himself to his feet then, announcing, "Dinner will be on the table very shortly, with refills of Guinness too." Stooping to collect the plates and the platter, he headed toward the dining room arch. Pamela stood too, and turned toward the dining room. Bettina left cooking to her husband, but she loved to set a pretty table. Tonight she had covered her dining room table with an elegant white lace cloth and tucked white linen napkins beside the sage-green dinner plates at each place. The simple lines of her stainless steel flatware echoed the sleek design of the pewter candle holders, which were fitted with tall white tapers. Carrying out the white theme, miniature narcissus, sprouted from bulbs in a low bowl, provided the centerpiece.

"Your table looks beautiful," Pamela commented.

Bettina, on her feet now, nodded in a resigned way and murmured, "It gave me something to do . . . to take my mind off . . ."

She was closer to the dining room and led the way, carrying her half-empty glass. Pamela followed, carrying her glass and Wilfred's.

Five minutes later, they were all settled around the table, with tapers alight and Wilfred's St. Patrick's Day feast laid out before them. A substantial corned beef brisket, plump and glistening pink, occupied an oval platter. Instead of the boiled potatoes that were a customary accompaniment to corned beef, Wilfred had made a fancier dish, which he announced as "Potatoes Bettina." A round casserole held thin potato slices, overlapping from the center outwards like the petals of a flower, buttery golden in color and shading to toasty brown at the edges.

"That's not cabbage, is it?" Pamela inquired, studying the tiny leaves piled into a serving bowl.

"Brussels sprouts," Wilfred said with a delighted laugh. "Think of them as little cabbage. They're in the same family."

"Aren't Brussels sprouts usually round?" Pamela tipped her head closer to the bowl.

"I deconstructed them," Wilfred explained, "and then sautéed them in butter until they started to caramelize." He picked up an impressive carving knife and an oversized fork, then glanced from Pamela to Bettina and back to Pamela. "Who wants to eat?"

He began to slice the meat as Pamela and Bettina picked up their plates, ready to hold them out when the activity changed from slicing to serving. Under Wilfred's skilled hands, the tender meat fell away from each stroke of the knife, juicy inside and even pinker. Soon each plate held a few slices of corned beef and Wilfred was urging the diners to help themselves to the side dishes.

Large scoops of the potato casserole and the sautéed Brussels sprout leaves joined the corned beef on the sage-green plates. Then Wilfred surveyed his dining companions and, with a hearty "Bon appétit," picked up his own fork. He paused, though, to call attention to the small dish of mustard sitting near the salt and pepper shakers, and dabs of bright yellow mustard soon accented the already colorful fare.

Pamela sampled the corned beef first. It was as tender and juicy as it looked, flavored with the brine and spices that had transformed a beef brisket into the centerpiece of Wilfred's feast. The potatoes were an excellent accompaniment, unassertive in taste and almost creamy in texture but for the oven-crisped slices that had been the casserole's uppermost layer. The Brussels sprout leaves—some deep green, others edged with caramelized char—added their slight bitterness as contrast.

Bettina's reaction was a wordless hum of pleasure. She closed her eyes as if to savor the first taste of her meal without distraction. Pamela did speak, though.

"I know I say this every year, but you've outdone your-self, Wilfred!" Wilfred nodded in acknowledgment of the praise, and the eating continued.

The next words spoken were Wilfred's. "There's more of everything." The impetus for this offer had been the sight of plates bare of all but random strips of corned beef fat, morsels of potato, and stray Brussels sprout leaves.

"Yes, please." Bettina handed her plate to her husband, received it back with two overlapping slices of corned beef, and added scoops of potatoes and Brussels sprouts.

Soon all three plates had been refilled, and eating recommenced silently—but at a more leisurely pace, which made the silence seem awkward. Ever since she'd arrived at the Frasers' house that evening, it had been clear to Pamela that Kieran's death and its apparent connection to the soda-bread contest had been weighing heavily on Bettina's mind. A distraction would be welcome, she suspected. Perhaps a suggestion that pansies would soon be available at the garden center, or a reminder that narcissus would soon be popping up in yards all over Arborville without the extra coaxing required to enjoy them indoors in cold months.

It was a surprise, then, when Bettina returned her fork to her plate with a clunk, regarded Pamela across the table, and said, "Who would want to kill Kieran?"

Pamela blinked. Wouldn't Kieran's death be the last topic Bettina would want to introduce at a meal intended to bring pleasure?

"He'll be missed," Wilfred observed from the head of the table. "He was just what Arborville needed, somebody with new ideas and an open mind. I certainly voted for him."

"I did too." Pamela nodded. "He had a very impressive resume, and he must have really loved Arborville to give up a glamorous career as a photojournalist and come back to the town where he was raised."

"He reported from some pretty dangerous places," Wilfred said, "like war zones in the Middle East, and his photos of the damage from that big earthquake in Turkey showed up all over the place."

Bettina's expression as she listened had reverted to the bleak stare in evidence earlier. She joined the conversation, but whispering, as if talking to herself. "And then he decides to settle down . . . gets married . . . returns to a place he thinks of as safe after all his adventures . . . and what happens but . . ." She sighed a lingering sigh. "I just can't see that he had any enemies in Arborville. Who would it be?"

"Detective Clayborn is probably working on that question at this very moment," Wilfred ventured.

"When he finds the answer—or thinks he finds the answer—Marcy Brewer will get first dibs on the story." Bettina's head tipped forward, and she closed her eyes again, but not to enhance the enjoyment of her meal as she had done before. "And what if he thinks the answer is Deirdre?"

Wilfred turned toward his wife, concern lending a particular tenderness to his glance. "How about some carrot slaw?" he inquired. "It's my own special creation."

"Yes, yes," Pamela said, when Bettina didn't respond. "Carrot slaw sounds like the perfect conclusion to this perfect meal."

"Not quite the conclusion." Wilfred was on his feet now. "There's dessert, after the slaw."

Pamela stood up too and together they cleared the table, with Wilfred stacking plates and piling knives, forks, and spoons atop them, and Pamela following him from the room bearing the platter on which a sizeable chunk of corned beef remained.

"She's really upset," Wilfred murmured when they reached the kitchen.

"What happened wasn't her fault," Pamela said. "Whoever did this would have found another time and place to carry out his evil plan."

"His?" Wilfred turned from the refrigerator. He had just removed a covered plastic bin from its depths. "I guess you're sure Deirdre wasn't the culprit."

"I am sure," Pamela responded. "For one thing, I don't see a motive."

She stepped into the dining room to collect the remains of the potatoes and Brussels sprouts, as well as the little dish of mustard. Bettina's posture and expression hadn't changed.

By the time Pamela returned to the kitchen, Wilfred had lined up three small plates from the sage-green set along the counter and was spooning bright orange mounds of shredded carrots onto them.

"Orange isn't really a St. Patrick's Day color," he commented. "In fact a true patriot would be horrified by the idea of serving an orange salad on such a sacred day."

Wilfred, Pamela knew, was a history buff, and she suspected it wouldn't take much prodding to get him to expand on this idea once they were seated again at the table. If nothing else, it would be a good distraction from current events in Arborville.

"Carrots," he went on, "make a good cold-weather salad, and in the old days traditional corned-beef meals in Ireland certainly didn't include the fresh lettuce and tomatoes that we take for granted year-round."

The slaw first had to be delivered to the table and sampled. It was simple—grated carrots, chopped pecans, and a few raisins, tossed with an oil and vinegar dressing. Wilfred had garnished the plates with curly arugula leaves, whose contrasting dark green brought out even more the vibrant shade of the carrots.

"So," Pamela said after complimenting the slaw, "I want to know why the color orange would provoke outrage at a St. Patrick's Day feast."

"The Orange Men—not really orange but wearing orange regalia." Wilfred responded to Pamela's cue with a pleased smile. "The Protestant king William of Orange defeated the Catholic king James II in the seventeenth century, and the Orange Order was founded a century later to support Protestant rule. It still endures in Northern Ireland, much to the detriment of harmonious coexistence between Catholics and Protestants there."

Bettina's eyes widened. She inhaled deeply and seemed to hold her breath.

Was she thinking, Pamela wondered, that sectarian strife could have followed Kieran back to Arborville? Had Northern Ireland been one of the trouble spots he reported from?

She realized that her fork had paused in midair. It still bore a small scoop of slaw, so she lifted it the rest of the way to her mouth, pondering as she savored the sweet crunch of the carrots and the piquant accent of the dressing.

No, she decided. The idea that Kieran had been murdered by agents of the Orange Order who disagreed with his reporting was outlandish. Anyway, as far as she knew, things had been calm in Northern Ireland for quite a while now.

Half an hour later, the group had moved back to the living room. The fire, with a fresh log added, was a welcome sight—given that the view through the windows was sorely lacking in cheer. Night was descending on a landscape where the branches of bare trees traced skeletal shapes against a darkening sky.

Wilfred had served custard tarts, miniature pies whose neatly crimped pastry shells surrounded silky, pale-gold custard garnished with dollops of whipped cream. More whipped cream topped the mugs of fresh, hot coffee enlivened with shots of Irish whiskey.

Pamela crossed the street to her own house some time later, wondering if the next morning's *Register* would bring news of any developments in the mystery of Kieran's death. Of all the lines of investigation it might occur to Detective Clayborn to pursue, she doubted that the machinations of the Orange Men was one.

Chapter Four

The next morning did bring a new development in the mystery of Kieran's death, one that, as Pamela and Bettina learned, Detective Clayborn had been made well aware of.

Pamela had gone upstairs after breakfast and exchanged her pajamas, robe, and slippers for jeans, a sweater, and loafers. She was crossing the hall from her bedroom to her office when the doorbell's chime alerted her to a caller. She veered toward the stairs and headed back down, pausing on the landing to glance toward the front door.

The caller was Bettina—recognizable, through the lace that curtained the oval window in the door, by her pumpkin-colored coat and scarlet hair. Pamela hurried the rest of the way down and pulled the door open to greet her friend.

Bettina's first words were "corned beef." She extended a foil-wrapped parcel and added, "Wilfred meant to send it home with you last night."

"I could have come to fetch it." Pamela laughed. "You didn't have to deliver it." She studied Bettina's face, trying not to be obvious but searching for signs that a good night's sleep—hopefully—had eased her friend's distress.

"We have an errand." Still carrying the foil-wrapped parcel, she darted around Pamela and headed for the kitchen.

Pamela followed, puzzled. In the kitchen, Bettina opened the refrigerator and placed the parcel on one of the shelves. Then she closed the refrigerator and turned.

"Deirdre wants to confess," she said. "She's already confessed to Clayborn, first thing this morning, and now she wants to confess to me."

"What does . . . what . . . what did she . . . ?" Pamela faltered.

"*Duh!* She didn't tell me on the phone. That's why we have an errand. She wants me to meet her at St. Willibrod's Church."

Bettina did look better, Pamela decided, and the effect wasn't due only to her skillful makeup. The errand had the makings of a story, and as a reporter for the *Advocate*, Bettina loved the promise of a story. It wouldn't exactly be a scoop if Deirdre had already confessed to Detective Clayborn, but . . .

"Come on, come on." Bettina stepped toward the doorway, startling Ginger, who sometimes returned to the kitchen a few hours after breakfast in case more food had appeared. "Grab your jacket and let's go—but don't suggest we walk. I'm not wearing the right shoes."

Pamela's gaze roved to Bettina's feet, shod in a fetching pair of maroon booties, with narrow heels and pointed toes.

On bright days the saints that looked down from St. Willibrod's stained glass windows glowed in rich shades of blue, green, ruby, and gold, illuminating the church's dim interior as the sun streamed through them. Today, though, the sky was gloomy, and the small figure sitting in a pew near the church's entrance would have been easily overlooked had she not turned as Pamela and Bettina entered the church's nave.

"You came," she whispered as she climbed to her feet, adding, "Thank you," as they got closer.

Her blond hair, pale blue eyes, and turned-up nose had not changed, but otherwise she barely resembled the person Pamela remembered from the fest. Even as she hovered over Kieran, moaning and stroking his hair, she had seemed charged with vitality. Now that vitality had dimmed, and she sank back onto the pew as if unable to remain on her feet.

Bettina stepped ahead of Pamela and slipped into the pew, settling next to Deirdre and wrapping an arm around her thin shoulders. Deirdre let her head slump against the comfortable puffiness of Bettina's down coat. Pamela edged into the pew behind them, from where she had a view of their two profiles.

After a few moments, Deirdre raised her head and whispered confidingly to Bettina, "I was in love with Kieran."

Bettina blinked and made a sound that resembled a hiccup. As if the context was a genuine confession, Deirdre went on without waiting for a response.

"I knew him long ago," she said. "We both grew up in Arborville and we both went away to college, but we came back here in the summers. So it lasted on and off until I was twenty-two, more seriously on my part, I'm sure. There were others for him but no others for me. And when he moved back to Arborville, I was still single, but he wasn't . . ."

She paused, and she and Bettina, still in profile, studied each other. It was hard for Pamela to tell what Bettina's reaction was. Her mobile features usually made her emotions clear, but the significance of Deirdre's confession was unfolding only gradually in Pamela's mind, and she imagined Bettina was having the same experience.

Deirdre, meanwhile, had begun to weep, raising a delicate hand to dab at the tears dribbling down her cheeks. Bettina turned away in order to probe the depths of her handbag and came up with a little packet of tissues. For a time, the only sounds were Deirdre's sniffling and Bettina's soft murmurs of comfort.

When the sniffling moderated, Bettina spoke, tipping her head slightly as if to better gauge whether Deirdre was ready for more conversation. "You said Clayborn knows about . . . you and Kieran now?"

"I had to tell him," Deirdre whispered. "I was summoned to the police station this morning, and Detective Clayborn asked me all kinds of questions, and I told him about the . . . relationship back when Kieran and I were in high school and college." She stirred and leaned forward. "But nothing happened after Kieran returned to Arborville."

The pew's back hid all but the heads and shoulders of the pew's occupants, but there was a sudden lurch and Pamela imagined Deirdre had seized Bettina's hands. "I swear," she added, her voice rising above a whisper.

"I believe you," Bettina said, and her expression softened.

"I don't know if Detective Clayborn did"—Deirdre shook her head mournfully—"and after he gets the autopsy report, he'll probably have more questions—or the same questions, to see if I give the same answers—unless it turns out that Kieran actually died of natural causes."

"Or that *all* the loaves were potentially lethal," Bettina suggested.

"They weren't." Deirdre shook her head again. "He told me that. The other bakers took their loaves home.

The police tried to track them down and collect them for testing, but they've all been eaten up—with no ill effects. It's all really a mystery."

"Really a mystery," Bettina echoed, and that comment ushered in a deep and mournful silence.

At length, Deirdre raised her head, took a deep breath, and thrust her shoulders back against the pew. "You don't have to stay," she sighed, "but I want to sit here for a while longer."

Bettina, in profile again, said, "You're sure?"

"I'm sure."

"But you'll be in touch? You'll keep me posted on what's happening with Clayborn . . . and . . . other things?"

Seemingly assured, by whatever she saw in Deirdre's face, that the answer was yes, Bettina slid along the pew and joined Pamela, who was already standing. They retreated down the aisle, crossed through the foyer, and pushed open one of the church's substantial wooden doors to step out onto its wide slate porch.

As they descended the steps, Bettina gestured toward the neat garden apartments on the opposite side of Arborville Avenue.

"That's where Deirdre lives," she commented. "So St. Willibrod's was a convenient meeting place."

"Not to mention an appropriate setting for a confession," Pamela added.

"She teaches at the high school," Bettina went on, "but she told me she's been calling in sick. She can't face her students—or her colleagues either, and who can blame her?"

They'd reached the curb, where Bettina's faithful Toyota waited. No more was said until both were settled into their seats and the Toyota had merged into the flow of traffic along Arborville Avenue.

"Arborville didn't used to have so much traffic," Bettina murmured as she braked while a car maneuvered into a parking spot in front of Hyler's Luncheonette. "It's all the fault of the developers, replacing single-family houses with multiples."

"People have to live somewhere, and we can't hog Arborville all to ourselves," Pamela observed.

"I know that." Traffic was flowing again, and Bettina accelerated. "But people write letters to the editor of the *Advocate* about it, and they complain on the listserv."

They were approaching the big intersection that featured the Co-Op Grocery on one of the far corners.

"You can drop me here," Pamela said. "I'm out of cat food, and other things, and I might as well do my shopping now as wait and walk back uptown later."

"You and the walking!" Bettina laughed. "Why don't I come in with you, and then we can drive home together. Cat food is heavy to carry on foot."

Forty-five minutes later, Bettina pulled into Pamela's driveway and announced, "You're *ho-ome!*"

Pamela knew she'd seemed distracted on the short drive from the Co-Op to Orchard Street, and she didn't blame Bettina for acting as if her passenger needed to be roused from a trance. She'd been deep in thought as she pushed her cart over the Co-Op's creaky wooden floors, automatically filling it with staples like cucumbers and tomatoes, and of course cat food.

The inspiration to pick up Swiss cheese, sauerkraut, and rye bread, with the aim of turning Wilfred's corned beef gift into Reubens, had briefly brought her focus back to her shopping. But once her purchases had been paid for and stowed in canvas totes borrowed from Bettina, her thoughts returned to the meeting that had just taken place between Bettina and Deirdre.

She turned to Bettina and said, "Do you think she killed him because she couldn't have him?"

"Oh, Pamela!" Bettina reacted with a mixture of surprise and horror. "Deirdre would *never* do a thing like that. She was in love with Kieran, and the way she reacted when he was taken ill at the fest . . . her emotions were on display for anyone to see."

"That's my point," Pamela said. "She was in love with him all that time, and he came back to Arborville married to someone else. Maybe she was waiting for him, unmarried and waiting. Maybe she imagined she could win him away from his wife, and maybe she tried but discovered that it was hopeless, so . . ."

"Deirdre is a very decent person." Bettina thumped the steering wheel with her fist to emphasize the point. "She would never try to break up a marriage."

"Her emotions *were* on display at the fest," Pamela agreed. "But maybe she was acting . . . or maybe once her poison, or whatever, had worked and she had seen its effect, she was horrified at what she had done."

"She's not the guilty one," Bettina said firmly, "and Clayborn will figure everything out."

Pamela laughed. "You're not usually so confident in his abilities."

"He'll figure it out," Bettina repeated. "I just hope he gives me the story before he talks to Marcy Brewer."

Pamela reached for the door handle. "Knit and Nibble at Nell's tonight." She pushed down, and the door opened with a click. "I'll drive," she added. "It's my turn."

She retrieved the canvas totes stuffed with groceries from Bettina's trunk, climbed the porch steps, collected her mail from the mailbox, and let herself into her house. After putting the groceries away and heating a can of lentil soup for a quick lunch, Pamela climbed the stairs to her office.

The computer screen brightened as the monitor woke from its sleep. Pamela studied the three short titles spread out across the top of Celine Bramley's email, each identifying an attached article to be copyedited: "Feathered Walls," "Rag Rugs," and "Ariadne's Thread." All three were articles that she herself had evaluated and recommended for publication, so no title teased with the promise of a surprise. She opened the first, whose subtitle made its content clearer: "Ancient Peruvian Wall Hangings in the Hanover Collection."

The wall hangings all dated from before 1000 A.D. They had been discovered in the 1940s, in the course of an excavation, rolled up in large ceramic jars and remarkably preserved. They consisted of lengths of cotton cloth, about two feet by seven, to which rows and rows of blue and yellow macaw feathers had been attached. A hand-drawn diagram illustrated the process by which, using slip-knots, the feathers were attached to long strings that were then sewn to the cloth backing. The feathers' iridescence created an otherworldly effect which was particularly suited to the wall hangings' likely function—covering the walls of shrines during funeral ceremonies.

Even though Pamela was already familiar with the article's contents, as well as the striking color photographs in which the hangings looked as bright and fresh as if they were contemporary creations, she was as mesmerized by it as if reading it for the first time. Surrounded by birds with brilliant plumage, of course it would occur to people that feathers could be repurposed to artistic ends.

The article required very little copyediting, except that the author was British and had different ideas about comma usage, not to mention that the word *colour*, which appeared very frequently, needed to be changed to *color*. She went through it a second time, however, lest she'd omitted a necessary correction while marveling at the article's contents.

One article was enough for one day, she decided, pushing her chair back from her desk and raising her arms in a restorative stretch.

Chapter Five

"Did you make a Reuben for dinner?" Bettina inquired as Pamela opened the door to greet her friend that evening. Bettina was bundled in her pumpkin-colored down coat against a chill that gave no hint of spring's approach, even though dusk had not yet fallen.

"I certainly did," Pamela said, tugging on her warmest jacket and reaching for her purse.

They proceeded down the steps and across the grass to where Pamela's serviceable compact waited in the driveway. Nell Bascomb's house, where the Knit and Nibble meeting was to be held, lay to the east, up Orchard Street, a jog to the left on Arborville Avenue, and then—literally—*up* the hill that formed the backside of the cliffs overlooking the Hudson River. Nell's neighborhood was accordingly known as the Palisades.

The house was old and solid, built from natural stone, and reached via a path that meandered up a slope planted with azaleas and rhododendrons. Bettina was panting by the time they alighted on the porch and the doorbell's chime summoned Harold Bascomb to welcome them. He was a vigorous man in his eighties with thick white hair, a forelock of which habitually strayed over his forehead.

"Come in, come in," he urged, adding a sweeping gesture.

They stepped across the threshold into a slate-floored entry that gave a view of the Bascombs' spacious and comfortably furnished living room, with its high, beamed ceiling and natural stone fireplace. Small loveseats upholstered in faded chintz flanked the fireplace, where the remains of a large log in a bed of ash marked a recent attempt to counter the March chill, and facing the fireplace was a long sofa. Roland DeCamp was already settled on the sofa and was knitting busily.

As Harold began to close the door behind Pamela and Bettina, a lively voice from the porch reached them, saying, "We're here too."

He swung the door back again to reveal Holly Perkins and Karen Dowling, the youngest members of the knitting group. Holly made a striking picture in a pair of chartreuse cable-knit leggings that Pamela recognized as one of her recent knitting projects, paired with chunky black boots and a black leather jacket. Karen and Holly were the best of friends, and the friendship perhaps thrived because Karen's retiring personality complemented Holly's exuberance.

Harold waved them into the entry, and for a few moments greetings overlapped as everyone spoke at once. Holly's voice rose above the others, however, once the basic pleasantries had been exchanged.

"We've certainly had some shocking news in the last few days, haven't we!" she exclaimed.

"You don't need to tell me," Bettina responded.

"So unexpected!" Holly's expressive eyes lent emphasis to the statement.

Footsteps approached from the direction of the kitchen,

which lay at the end of a long hall that opened off the entry to the side. It soon became clear that the footsteps belonged to Nell Bascomb, whose age and vigor matched those of her husband.

"What was unexpected?" she demanded by way of a not-too-cordial greeting. "And I thought I heard the word *shocking*—so I suspect you're referring to the recent, tragic . . ."

She surveyed the little group, her pale eyes so probing that Pamela felt herself unconsciously back away. It was well known among the Knit and Nibblers that Nell disapproved of what she considered an unbecoming interest in the sensational.

"The article in the *Register*," Holly said. As Nell's gaze became positively laser-like, she quickly added, "the Lifestyle section, I mean: EVERYTHING'S COMING UP PINK FOR SPRING."

Nell shifted her gaze to her husband, who nodded. "I was shocked! I mean, pink is so last year." His lips twitched in an apparent effort to hide a teasing smile. "My dear, you know I always turn to Lifestyle first thing when I sit down with the *Register*."

"Oh, Harold!" Nell struggled to hide a smile of her own. "You most certainly do not!" She then allowed a glimmer of the smile to appear as she once more surveyed the group. "Welcome, everyone, and please make yourselves comfortable"—she advanced toward the few steps that led down to the living room, beckoning as she went— "but there are certainly more edifying topics to discuss than what happened at the St. Patrick's Day fest."

"Something smells delicious," Bettina commented, directing her gaze down the hall from which Nell had emerged.

"That's as may be," Nell responded, "but I can assure you it will be healthful, and not too sweet."

It *smelled* sweet, though, Pamela reflected as she fell in with the little group following Nell. Cookies maybe, she decided.

Within a few minutes, coats and jackets had been shed and all the knitters were seated, rummaging in their knitting bags for yarn, needles, and in-progress work. Holly and Karen were side by side on one of the loveseats, and Pamela and Bettina were side by side on the other, leaving Nell to share the roomy sofa with Roland. Harold had excused himself and retreated to his den, promising to return when Nell's not-too-sweet treat came forth at break time.

Pamela took from her knitting bag half a skein of indigo yarn and a pair of size 6 needles and cast on twelve stitches. With so many odds and ends of yarn left from other projects, she'd gotten the idea to knit many squares in various colors and assemble them into a boxy patchwork pullover. The project had turned into a joint venture with Penny, and the end product was now a favorite item in Penny's wardrobe. It had, however, made but a small dent in Pamela's surplus yarn, and she was now embarking on a patchwork pullover of her own.

Next to her, Bettina was studying directions for a new project. Pamela was well acquainted with it because she had been consulted about both the pattern itself and the yarn choice. Opposite the page with directions in the knitting magazine open on Bettina's lap was a photo of the garment that would result—a pale peach cardigan sweater in a lacy knit as delicate as the tiny model who wore it. Bettina had sought out a soft yarn exactly the same shade, declaring that it would be perfect with her little granddaughter's fair skin and strawberry blond hair.

"I don't remember it being this cold in March," Holly remarked to break the silence that had descended as everyone got settled with their projects. As a conversational topic, the weather—as opposed to the poisoned soda bread—was unobjectionable, if unoriginal.

"I think it was." Bettina looked up from studying her pattern. "I remember wearing my down coat well into the beginning of April."

"The first day of spring is this Friday," Karen said. "That's why we think it should be warmer."

"Easy to check what the temperature was last year, and as many years before as you want," Roland murmured from the sofa as his gaze remained focused on his busy fingers. "All the records are online . . . at least as far back as official records were kept."

"And of course we could check online to find out when that was too." Bettina's tone was dry, and the look she directed at Roland was sharp.

Ignoring or unaware of her sarcasm, Roland nodded. "Of course."

But Holly apparently *was* aware, and now she leaned toward Roland with a wide, and genuine, smile and said, "Your project is new, isn't it? All those little bobbins— *awesome!*"

"Yes," he responded, raising his head as his fingers slowed. "It *is* new, and they *are* bobbins." He cut something of an incongruous figure as a member of the knitting group, in his expertly tailored pinstripe suit, immaculate white dress shirt, and discreetly patterned silk tie.

Holly's smile widened, and a dimple appeared in her cheek. "It's a sock, I'm guessing, an argyle sock."

"Yes, again." Roland's lean face was serious. "And it requires a lot of concentration, and I talk all day at work, and when I come to Knit and Nibble I come to knit." With that, he bent toward his work once again, and his fingers picked up speed.

"Then why not just knit at home if you don't want to

talk?" Bettina whispered, provoking an admonitory glance from Nell. "Miss Holly!" Bettina quickly added, shifting her gaze from the sofa to the loveseat across the way. "Again with the cable-knit?"

Holly stretched out her legs to display the chartreuse leggings to utmost advantage. "One of my clients at the salon loves these so much she bought me the yarn to make her a pair. Magenta, though, so they won't be exactly like mine."

"You're charging for your time, I hope," came Roland's voice from the sofa. "And keeping track of the hours you put into the work."

"Oh, Roland!" Holly laughed, displaying her perfect teeth. "I'm not a lawyer like you, so I don't have to charge for every minute of my time! I'm just happy to have a new project, and I've been doing her hair for years." Holly and her husband, Desmond, owned a hair salon in a neighboring town.

Perhaps unwilling to be drawn into a conversation that would distract him further from his bobbins, Roland grunted in response.

"I feel the same way," Bettina said. "I'm just happy to have projects—and people to give them to who appreciate them."

"Our Nell is the queen of that." Holly favored Nell with a fond glance. "Knitting projects for people who appreciate them."

The amorphous shape dangling from Nell's needles wasn't immediately recognizable, but Pamela knew it was part of a bunny. Nell devoted all of her knitting industry to projects that she then donated to various worthy groups. In the lead-up to Christmas, she had turned out dozens of knitted stockings that had been filled with toys and goodies and distributed to the children that accompanied their mothers to the women's shelter in nearby Haversack. Now, with Easter on the horizon, she was creating scores of bunnies to be delivered to the shelter.

The in-progress bunny was lavender, but since Nell used odds and ends of leftover yarn for her charitable projects, others were as likely to be a realistic white or gray as they were to be blue or pink or even multicolored.

At this reminder of Nell's exceptional output, the pace of everyone's knitting picked up, and conversation dwindled to a few quiet exchanges between Holly and Karen. Pamela finished her first square, cast on for another, and was halfway through that one when the faint aroma of coffee reached her nostrils. She looked up from her work to see Bettina staring toward the entry, and the entrance to the hall that led to the Bascombs' kitchen.

Not bothering to disguise a smile, Bettina then glanced at Roland and raised her wrist to check the face of her pretty watch. Roland had set his work aside, resting it on the closed lid of the elegant leather briefcase he used in place of a knitting bag. He was staring at his own watch, which peeked from beneath a crisply starched shirt cuff.

At precisely the same moment that Roland announced, "It's eight o'clock," Harold Bascomb emerged from the hall that served the kitchen to announce, "Refreshments are forthcoming."

Four voices chorused, "Let me help," and four people sprang to their feet.

In the Bascombs' kitchen, which seemed like a time capsule from the 1950s with its avocado green appliances and pink Formica counters, Bettina took charge of pouring coffee. Harold had brewed it in his ancient aluminum percolator, and the china cups that received it featured a wildflower and wheat design in faded gold and coral. He had set water to boil for tea as well, and Karen—a tea drinker like Nell—poured the now steaming liquid into a squat brown teapot already furnished with loose tea leaves.

Pamela's guess at the nature of the not-too-sweet treat proved correct. An oval platter from the wildflower and wheat china set waited on the wooden table, heaped with golden-brown cookies. The top of each was marked by a crosshatch pattern seemingly made by pressing the tines of a fork into the unbaked dough and then repeating the process after rotating the cookie ninety degrees.

With so many people pitching in to help, it took no time at all before coffee, tea, and cookies had been transferred to the living room, along with cream and sugar, napkins, plates, and spoons. Harold joined the knitters, taking a seat on the long hearth. The cream and sugar made their way around the coffee table as coffee drinkers and tea drinkers added more or less of either or both, though Pamela was happy to sip her black coffee. Small plates had been provided for cookies. Pamela stacked a few on her plate and set it on the hearth, which was convenient to her end of the loveseat.

"They're certainly sweet enough," was Holly's verdict, delivered as a hand holding a half-eaten cookie still hovered in the air, her chartreuse nail polish contrasting with the cookie's golden brown. "And I taste another flavor too . . ." She took another bite and chewed meditatively.

"Is it peanut butter?" Karen asked in her mild voice.

Brown sugar too, Pamela suspected. There was a subtle depth to the sweetness.

Nell turned to Karen and nodded. "Peanut-butter cookies, like my mother used to make when I was a child, including the crisscross with the fork tines on top."

Bettina was only just now sampling a cookie, having devoted a long moment to transforming her coffee into the pale mocha concoction she preferred. She took a bite, closed her eyes, and made a purring sound as she chewed.

"Perfect," she sighed upon opening her eyes.

"I just had an amazing idea!" Holly exclaimed. "Peanut butter and jelly cookies!"

"A sandwich cookie . . ." Bettina's eyes took on a dreamy expression. "Two of these"—she picked up a peanut butter cookie in each hand—"with a layer of jam between."

"*Strawberry jam*," Harold contributed from his perch on the hearth. "The classic PB and J is always made with strawberry jam."

"I was picturing more of a thumbprint cookie," Holly said, "starting with the same dough that Nell made for these, but rolling balls of it, laying them out on a cookie sheet, pressing a thumbprint into each one, and filling it with a dollop of jelly—or jam."

"Is there a difference?" Karen inquired.

"We could do a quick internet search . . ." Bettina directed a teasing smile at Roland, which he ignored.

"No need for the internet." Nell leaned forward. "Jelly starts with fruit juice, and pectin makes it jell. Jam can be made simply by boiling fruit with sugar and a little water. It's thicker and fruitier."

"Jam would be better for the thumbprints." Holly accompanied the verdict with a dimpled smile. "And I'm inspired to try my idea—if Nell will give me her peanut butter cookie recipe."

"Of course, of course," Nell said. "It's my mother's, really, and when I make them I still consult the recipe card she wrote out ages and ages ago."

Roland, meanwhile, had shifted his position. He set his cup down on the coffee table next to his empty plate, pushed back his shirt cuff to consult his watch, surveyed the group—including Nell, who was right next to him on the sofa, and remarked, "I prefer the classic peanut butter cookie, plain, though I do enjoy the occasional peanut butter and jelly sandwich." He took up his partly finished argyle sock and concluded, "Now I'm going to get back to knitting."

Suppressing a smile that lingered in the twinkle of her pale eyes, Nell took up her work and launched a new row. With their hostess setting an example of industry, the other knitters were soon focused on their projects too as fingers looped strands of yarn over busy needles.

Chapter Six

"Botulism toxin!" Bettina wasted no words in getting to the point of her visit the next morning. She spoke before Pamela's front door was even fully open, and a moment later she was standing on the worn parquet of Pamela's entry, slipping out of her pumpkin-colored down coat. Beneath the coat, a cashmere turtleneck in a hopeful, spring-like yellow topped a pair of woolen pants in the same shade.

"You've read the article, I suppose?" she said. "I didn't see your *Register* on the lawn."

Pamela had indeed read the article, as was clear when they entered the kitchen. The front page of the *Register*, with its screaming headline and Marcy Brewer's byline, lay uppermost on the table. Next to it was a rose-garlanded cup from Pamela's wedding china half full of coffee and a plate empty but for a scattering of crumbs.

"Would there be more coffee?" Bettina inquired, glancing toward the stove, where Pamela's carafe held a few inches of dark liquid. She added a ziplock bag and a jar to the items on the table.

"There could be," Pamela said.

"I don't mind drinking what's there"—Bettina pointed

at the carafe—"unless you want more too." She paused. "I brought some of Wilfred's oatcakes from the other night, and some red clover honey from the Newfield farmers market, and the oatcakes are very good toasted . . ."

"You've convinced me." Pamela laughed. She reached for the kettle.

"Where would a person even get botulism toxin?" Bettina asked as Pamela busied herself at the counter.

A brief clatter and whirring sound interrupted as she ground beans. While arranging the paper filter in the carafe's plastic filter cone, she responded, "I certainly have no idea." The kettle whistled then, and soon the aroma of fresh-brewed coffee began to fill the little kitchen.

Meanwhile, Bettina had split and toasted two oatcakes, buttered the cut sides, and arranged them on small rose-garlanded plates. She'd also made sure Pamela's cut-glass cream pitcher and sugar bowl were at hand.

"I'll let you do your own honey," she said, as Pamela arrived with two steaming cups of coffee.

A few minutes passed in silence as Bettina stirred sugar and cream into her coffee and both spooned the thick amber honey onto the nubbly surface of the oatcakes.

"Clayborn doesn't know either," Bettina commented over the rim of her cup, after taking a long sip, "and he said he had nothing to add to the news report. Apparently Marcy Brewer has been in direct communication with the medical examiner's office."

"She does have ways of finding things out," Pamela said, and then devoted herself to the pleasures of honey on toasted oatcakes with the bracing contrast of black coffee.

Bettina, however, seemed distracted, twisting in her chair to look toward the kitchen doorway. "It's my phone, I think," she murmured.

Just then Catrina scurried in from the entry, perched on her haunches with her tail wrapped around her front paws, and fastened her amber gaze on Bettina.

"It *is* my phone." Bettina climbed to her feet with an assist from the table. "Catrina heard it too." She left the room, with Catrina following.

Pamela continued to eat and sip coffee, but quietly, with one ear tilted toward the doorway. Half a conversation could be heard, faintly—Bettina's half: "Yes, of course I'm interested . . . important, certainly . . . Mayor Olson, I had no idea . . . would be very shocking, yes . . . and him too? . . . too bad, but maybe . . . yes . . ."

Bettina was quite flushed when she stepped back through the doorway. "Could be something," she whispered as she settled back into her chair, fairly vibrating with excitement. Her eyes were bright.

"What kind of a something?" Pamela asked.

"That was Adelaide Malone, Kieran's widow." Bettina took a deep breath and laid both hands palms down on the table as if to steady herself. "Kieran made a recording at the last town council meeting that he said would mean the end of the mayor and another council member if it ever got out."

"Oh, my goodness . . ." Pamela took a deep breath too. "That means there could be somebody, or maybe two somebodies, with a reason for wanting Kieran dead."

"Getting rid of him isn't the same thing as getting rid of the recording, though." Bettina tightened her lips into an apprehensive zigzag.

"Where is it now?"

"On his phone, she thinks." Pamela was about to ask where the phone was, but Bettina anticipated the question and went on speaking. "And his phone was with him at the fest and went with him to the hospital. So now it must be at the medical examiner's with his body."

Each felt the need then for a fortifying swallow of coffee and another bite of honey-covered oatcake, then another and another.

"Adelaide wants me to stop by her house," Bettina said when only a sticky nubbin of oatcake remained. "Not because she has more to reveal, I don't think, though at some point she's going to get that phone back with Kieran's other effects."

"People trust you to know about things"—Pamela directed a fond smile at her friend—"based on the articles you write about police doings for the *Advocate*. She probably wants advice, because whatever's on that phone could be the key to Kieran's murder."

Bettina lifted her cup to her lips and tilted her head back to drain the last bit of coffee.

"Shall we go then?" she inquired as she rose to her feet.

The first stop, however, wasn't Adelaide Malone's residence. "Deirdre is just on the way," Bettina observed as she steered the Toyota north on Arborville Avenue. "I'm curious how she's reacting to this news about the botulism toxin, and I hope Clayborn isn't closing in."

Soon she had nosed into a spot in front of the neat garden apartments that faced St. Willibrod's Church. She and Pamela made their way up the path that led from the street and veered onto a shorter path that took them to Deirdre's front door. Bettina pressed the doorbell, and as they waited, Pamela had the distinct impression of an eyeball peering at them through the small glass peephole embedded in the door's brightly painted surface.

Thus, Deirdre seemed unsurprised when she pulled the door back to greet her visitors.

"I haven't been home," she said. "At least I haven't been home to reporters, especially that pesky Marcy Brewer." She retreated a few steps and pulled the door open wider. "But you're both welcome to come in."

The small living room was furnished more for comfort than for style, with a nondescript sofa whose soft depths beckoned, as well as an armchair complete with matching hassock. A granny-square afghan and a slumbering cat rounded out the picture.

Deirdre seemed grateful for the company. She waved them toward the sofa after Bettina's coat and Pamela's jacket had been shed, then she perched on the hassock but jumped up again to ask if they wanted coffee.

Bettina explained they'd just had coffee. Her face assumed an expression that mingled sympathy with curiosity, hoping—Pamela imagined—that Deirdre was eager enough to speak to not need prodding. The sympathy was certainly in order. If possible, Deirdre appeared even more drained than she had at St. Willibrod's, and nearly colorless with her pale skin, fair hair, and light eyes.

She *was* eager to speak, though, eager to ask the same question Bettina had asked earlier: "Where would a person even get botulism toxin?"

"Someone did." Bettina shook her head sadly, and her earrings, which were amber teardrops, swayed. "And someone figured out how to insert it into an already-baked loaf of soda bread."

"I've read that it's tasteless and odorless," Pamela said, "and it only takes a tiny bit to kill a person. That's why it used to be so dangerous when so many people did their own canning."

"The loaves were set out on that table against the back wall." Deirdre seemed to be talking to herself, so faint was her voice. "People came and went. A lot was going on, with the storytelling and the face painting and the dancing and all . . ."

"Could the toxin have been injected?" Bettina wondered. She focused on Deirdre. "The crust of your loaf looked normal to you, didn't it?"

Deirdre nodded, but commented, "Not that I examined it that closely. Who'd expect what happened . . . to happen?" Her voice thinned to a squeal, and her head slumped forward.

Bettina was on her feet then, after a brief struggle to escape from the all-enveloping grip of the comfortable sofa. She covered the space between the sofa and the hassock in a few quick steps, crouched at Deirdre's side, and extended a comforting arm.

"It wasn't your fault," she murmured. "It was . . . it was . . ." She tilted her head and her eyes met Pamela's. Was she about to declare that Mayor Olson was the culprit? Maybe a bit premature? Pamela frowned.

Seemingly in response to the frown, Bettina backtracked. "It wasn't your fault," she repeated. "He had . . . enemies."

Adelaide was likewise mourning the death of Kieran Malone. Her wan expression, limp hair, and carelessly assembled outfit—pajama bottoms, sweatshirt, and fuzzy slippers—were testimony to that. Pamela recognized her from various town events, where she had appeared proudly on the arm of Councilman Malone, in stylish garments that flattered her willowy figure and with her dark hair arranged in loose waves.

"Thank you for coming," she said after greeting Bettina with a hug and taking Pamela's hand. "I could make coffee, or something . . . I just haven't been able to . . ." She glanced around the room as if pondering what form of hospitality would be appropriate to the circumstances. "We could sit . . ."

Bettina took charge. "Of course," she agreed, as she lowered herself onto the sofa, "and why don't you come and sit next to me?"

The living room was prettily decorated, with a modern look reflecting the fact that Kieran and Adelaide had only recently married and set up housekeeping. The house itself, though, was old—a sturdy brick structure dating, like most of Arborville's housing stock, to the early nineteen hundreds.

Adelaide nodded and sank down beside Bettina, while Pamela took a seat on one of the chic leather and chrome chairs that faced the sofa. Despite the invitation to talk, Adelaide remained silent as Bettina comforted her with soothing murmurs. Pamela, meanwhile, let her gaze wander, particularly to a dramatic black and white photo on one of the shelves that flanked the fireplace.

It had been taken on Adelaide and Kieran's wedding day, she was sure. Kieran was handsome in a dark suit with a white carnation boutonniere, while Adelaide wore a simple white dress. A veil, anchored to her dark updo by a flower wreath, drifted slightly on an apparent breeze. In the background an ancient castle was silhouetted against an overcast sky.

Adelaide noticed her studying the photo. "Yes," she said, "that was our wedding day, in a village on the west coast of Ireland where Kieran's ancestors were from." She sighed. "He had so many dreams, and some of them came true—returning to Arborville and setting up his photography business, and getting involved in the life of the town . . ." Her voice trailed off as she studied the photo. "Children too, but that hadn't happened yet. He would have made such a wonderful dad."

She shook herself, as if casting off a spell, and focused on Bettina. "But what I really want to talk about is, do you think I should tell the police about the recording on Kieran's phone?"

"Clayborn doesn't always believe that clues are really clues." Bettina's expression—brow raised and lips in a knot—reflected years of frustration in her role as the *Advocate*'s police liaison.

"What if he believes that the recording *is* a clue but wants to protect his pals in the town government? Kieran was horrified at some of the doings that went on behind closed doors in the council meetings."

"*I'd* be interested in hearing the recording," Bettina said. "Deirdre McKeon is beside herself, feeling guilty, and for no reason."

Adelaide nodded and then let her head rest against Bettina's shoulder. The silence that followed stretched on for some time, and it seemed to soothe Adelaide.

"I knew you'd have something helpful to say," she murmured at last, bestirring herself. Then, with a change of subject, she added, "We just lost his parents at Christmas, and in a way I'm glad they didn't live to see this."

"I remember," Bettina said. "People paid attention—because the Malones were such long-time residents of Arborville and because their son was a newly elected councilman."

"The house is going on the market soon. Kieran's sister, Caitlin, was living in Ireland, but she came back here to help with things after the parents' deaths." Adelaide paused and inserted a sad little laugh as punctuation. "She hardly expected to be here for her brother's funeral too. It's tomorrow, by the way. Everyone's invited, if that's the right term . . . and to a reception afterwards at the rec center."

Chapter Seven

"Not the best choice of venue," Bettina remarked as she and Pamela stepped through the wide doorway that led to the rec center's gym.

"So many Arborvillians wanted to honor Kieran that they needed a large room," Pamela replied. "At least the decorations from the fest aren't up anymore."

Instead, the room had been arranged to host a postfuneral reception for Kieran Malone. The long table that had held refreshments—and, yes, the loaves of sofa bread for the ill-fated contest—was now draped with a starched white cloth. The profusion of trays, platters, and serving dishes suggested that the caterers had provided enough food to comfort even the most grieving attendee, though it was difficult to see the offerings in much detail because prospective diners were already hovering over the table.

In deference to the occasion, Bettina was dressed all in black—a black crepe skirt suit with a jacket featuring a peplum, and black suede pumps. A triple strand of large pearls and matching pearl earrings accessorized the outfit. Talkative clusters of people crowded the polished floor, but most wore clothing suitable to the jobs they would soon be returning to, and few people seemed to be actively grieving. Despite the respect and affection Kieran had enjoyed, bursts of laughter rose above the echoing voices. Bettina's friend Marlene Pepper detached herself from one particularly jovial group to intercept Pamela and Bettina as they ventured farther into the room.

"It's more of a social occasion," Marlene said, shrugging, as if to explain the smile she'd just suppressed. "The organizers did a good job, though, and on such short notice." She nodded toward a portly man dressed in business casual. "The mayor was especially eager to acknowledge Kieran's contributions to the town, but of course it was left up to the women on the council to actually find a space and book the caterers. Fortunately they were able to get Debbie Does Delicious, from right here in Arborville."

She extended an arm to urge Bettina forward and beckoned to Pamela. "Come and have some food! My stomach was growling all through that funeral mass."

The three of them wove their way among the milling people and joined the line waiting at the end of the table, where plates and napkins had been staged. Snatches of conversation reached them, including an enthusiastic description of the treasures likely to be had as the elder Malones' house was emptied out to be put on the market.

"This weekend," Marlene said, acknowledging what they had just overheard. "A big estate sale. It was all planned before what . . . happened to Kieran . . . happened, and some outside company is handling it, so they wanted to go ahead."

She picked up a plate and a napkin and advanced a few steps. Pamela and Bettina did likewise, and found themselves contemplating a tray of miniature sandwiches, each speared with a frill-topped toothpick.

"Ham and Swiss cheese on rye, I think," Bettina commented, "and this looks like roast beef on sourdough, and chicken salad on whole wheat . . ."

They moved along the table, adding miniature sand-wiches to their plates, as well as jumbo shrimp dipped in cocktail sauce, meatballs, grilled chicken on wooden skew-ers, slices of lox and pastrami, crackers topped with tiny slabs of cheese, bite-sized puff-pastry turnovers, stuffed mushroom caps, cherry tomatoes, olives, and pickles—until no empty spot remained. Soft drinks were available too, but with a hand needed to hold the plate and another to raise food to the mouth, no extra hand remained to man-age a beverage at the same time.

Retreating to an out-of-the-way spot in a corner of the room—not far from where, at the fest, Whit Sutton had been entertaining the children with his Irish folktales—they focused on their overloaded plates for a bit. Pamela surveyed the crowd as she sampled a puff-pastry turnover with its spicy crab filling.

Many faces were familiar: the attractive woman from the bank, the man who handled building permits at bor-ough hall, the young police officer who halted traffic as the grammar-school children crossed Arborville Avenue in the morning, and Vivian Stringfellow, a realtor whose name and image appeared on HOUSE FOR SALE signs all over town.

Marlene's voice interrupted her musings. "It's obvious she's his sister, don't you think?"

The "she" in question was en route to the refreshment table. She was dressed all in black, perhaps in deference to the occasion but perhaps merely aware that black played up the dramatic contrast between her hair, also black, and her porcelain skin. Finely modeled cheekbones added ele-gance to a face that also featured bold lips seemingly poised to shape a teasing smile.

The comment had been addressed to Bettina, who re-sponded, "Good looks certainly run in that family." But

Vivian Stringfellow had sidled up next to Marlene and echoed Bettina's agreement.

"Caitlin Malone," she added. "Back from her wanderings just in time to cash in on the house sale."

"Ummm?" Marlene's eyes brightened, and she nudged Bettina.

Vivian seemed to need little more encouragement. "I don't think she and her brother had spoken in the last five years and, let me tell you, putting a house on the market when the heirs are at each other's throats isn't fun."

"He was such a lovely person," Bettina murmured. "I can't imagine he was responsible for whatever drove them apart."

"They were both very adventurous," Vivian said. "But I gathered she spent whatever she felt like spending and expected her parents to subsidize her glamorous life abroad—when there wasn't a man around to take care of her, which there sometimes was."

"And Kieran felt she'd already spent her half of the estate?" Marlene suggested.

"Precisely." Vivian nodded, and the smooth curves of hair, framing her face like parentheses, swayed. The impression Vivian made in person wasn't far from the polished competence implied by the photos on the HOUSE FOR SALE signs, Pamela thought, though her clients might have been alarmed by her willingness to gossip about their private affairs.

Vivian's trip to the buffet had been more recent, and her plate was still piled high. She lifted a jumbo shrimp, bathed in bright red sauce and speared with a long toothpick, to her carefully lipsticked mouth. As if reminded of the bounty on offer, Marlene excused herself and backtracked to the table for a refill.

"One plateful is really enough," Bettina commented when Marlene was out of earshot, "though"—she twisted around to focus on the doorway behind the table—"I'm sure coffee and dessert will be coming out soon, and Debbie Does Delicious always has those amazing cream puffs."

In fact, most of the trays, platters, and serving dishes lined up along the table were nearly bare but for cheese rinds or decorative sprigs of parsley, and servers were already beginning to clear them away. Pamela watched Marlene arrive just in time to grab a last chicken skewer, a few miniature sandwiches, and a meatball. The door in the back wall stood open, allowing the aroma of brewing coffee to provide assurance that coffee would soon be forthcoming.

"I just noticed something," Marlene announced when she returned with her scantily replenished plate. "Deirdre McKeon didn't come."

"Did you think she would?" Bettina asked.

Marlene's expression—a knowing look involving raised brows and pursed lips—implied that the reason for Deirdre's nonappearance was obvious. But Bettina's attention was elsewhere. Adelaide Malone was approaching, halfway across the floor and pausing frequently as people greeted her with sympathetic pats and handclasps. She was wearing a simple black suit, and her hair looked freshly washed and hung in becoming waves. But her face was still wan and her response to the greetings cheerless.

Bettina set out to meet her, and Pamela followed. En route they were intercepted by a server, tidy in a white shirt and dark pants, who relieved them of their empty plates. Thus unencumbered, Bettina was able to extend her arms to Adelaide and pull her into a hug.

"I'm getting Kieran's phone back tomorrow," Adelaide whispered as Bettina released her. "Come over, or I'll come to you."

She was pulled away then, by a woman Pamela recognized from coverage in the *Advocate* as another member of Arborville's town council. A snatch of conversation— "I'm so, so sorry for your loss . . ."—reached Pamela's ears.

The aroma of coffee had become much stronger and quite suddenly, as if drawn by some magnetic force, nearly everyone in the room turned to face the buffet table and began to advance. Pamela and Bettina joined them. In addition to coffee in a large aluminum urn and hot water for tea in a similar urn, appealing dessert offerings had appeared, including the cream puffs that Bettina had anticipated. A long tray was heaped with them, flaky orbs enclosing a creamy filling and glazed with chocolate. Other trays held delicate petits fours in pastel colors, miniature pecan pies, bite-size brownies, and cheesecake morsels.

Retreating once again to an out-of-the-way spot in a corner of the room, Pamela and Bettina nibbled from a shared plate of goodies and then returned to the buffet table for coffee. After a noisy bustle during which the buffet table was besieged from every side, people drifted back across the floor bearing plates or cups or both and arranged themselves once more into chatting clusters.

Gradually the room began to empty as watches were checked and attendees recalled work awaiting in offices and homes. Adelaide had slipped out some time ago, it seemed—and anyway, the real hosts of the event were Mayor Olson and the councilwomen who had done the organizing. Now, as people left, they paused for a word or two with the mayor who had stationed himself near the wide door.

Pamela and Bettina relinquished their coffee cups to a server circulating with a tray and, with a wave at Marlene Pepper, made their way toward the exit.

People still lingered out on the sidewalk. The route to where Bettina's Toyota waited at the curb about a block away involved zigzagging among other people wending their slow way to their cars.

"Ms. Fraser, Ms. Fraser," called a voice midway along the block.

Chapter Eight

They turned to see Whit Sutton, dressed in a suit and looking quite different from the casually garbed story-teller who had entertained the children at the fest.

"I didn't see you . . . in there." He nodded toward the rec center.

He was accompanied by a woman who looked to be in her early forties, attractive, with tawny curls tamed into a becoming pouf and full lips that seemed poised to smile. She too was dressed in a suit, a classic well-tailored jacket paired with narrow trousers.

"I'm Chloe Sutton." She extended a hand, to Bettina first and then to Pamela. "Thank you so much, Bettina—I hope I can call you that—for your kindness to Whit."

Bettina laughed. "I hardly did anything, and it was a pleasure to become acquainted with him."

"Terribly sad occasion," Chloe said, taking her turn to nod toward the rec center. "Kieran was so kind to Whit too, encouraging his interest in photography and letting him hang around the studio."

"I will definitely miss him." Whit shook his head mournfully. "He was incredibly encouraging—about everything." Chloe stepped aside to chat with a passerby, but Whit focused on Bettina and continued speaking. Bettina had a way of eliciting confidences even when she wasn't in what Pamela thought of as "interview mode."

"My dad has his own plans for me," Whit continued. "I'm the namesake, after all, of Whitfield Sutton, M.D."

"Medicine is a worthy profession," Bettina suggested, "if a person feels a calling for it."

"I don't feel a calling"—Whit laughed, but not happily— "especially I don't feel a calling to do what he does . . . surgery, injections, whatever . . . to keep rich people looking like they're not a day over thirty for the whole rest of their—"

He lifted a hand to cover his mouth as Chloe turned back from her chat, then removed the hand to reveal a smile that accented his good looks. "And so anyway, Ms. Fraser—"

Bettina interrupted to touch his arm and insist, "*Bettina*, please. And you can get in touch any time, and if you've got photos of town events, send them to me and I'll pass them on to the *Advocate*'s editor."

With that, cordial goodbyes were exchanged all around, and Whit and Chloe made their way toward a burnished silver Lexus.

With much to think about, Pamela and Bettina were silent as the Toyota proceeded south on Arborville Avenue. But both spoke at once as soon as Bettina made the turn onto Orchard Street.

"We didn't know about Caitlin before," Pamela said, her voice overlapping with Bettina's comment, "I wonder if word got back to Adelaide about how Deirdre reacted when Kieran was taken ill."

"No, we didn't know about Caitlin," Bettina agreed after Pamela, upon request, repeated herself. "An inheritance could be a real stroke of good fortune for a person who'd been better at spending than saving." Bettina slowed down as the Frasers' driveway drew near. "Do you think Kieran was truly arguing that she'd already gone through her share of their parents' estate?"

"If the will gave half to each, his opinion wouldn't carry any weight."

"Maybe the will left it all to him . . ."

"She wasn't at the fest," Pamela said. "If she had been, I'm sure she would have come forward, at least to *pretend* concern . . . even if she secretly thought her brother's death would benefit her."

Bettina swung the steering wheel to the right and nosed into the spot next to Wilfred's Mercedes. "We'd have noticed her if she was there. She really is quite striking."

"The poison had to go into the loaf, unbeknownst to Deirdre, while the fest was going on—but how?" Pamela fingered the crease that had formed between her brows.

"Unless Deirdre is really the killer." Bettina stepped on the brake and twisted the key in the ignition to silence the Toyota's engine. She didn't move, however, and seemed to be staring at the Frasers' garage door. Her gaze was unfocused, and her lips twitched as if in response to some inner debate.

"What is it?" Pamela rested a hand on her friend's shoulder.

"I'm trying to think," Bettina said without turning, "how I'd react if I lost Wilfred and then I learned that some other woman had been desperately in love with him forever."

"It would depend whether he knew and what he did about it . . . before you lost him." Pamela studied Bettina's profile as she spoke. "Wouldn't it?"

Crossing the street to her own house, Pamela found herself unexpectedly moved by the question Bettina had posed. Unlike Bettina, she actually had lost her husband. It had never occurred to her back then that some other woman, somewhere else, might have learned of the death and might be mourning the loss of the man she had always pined for.

She and Michael Paterson had met in college, and both had had other relationships before they became a couple— but not after they'd committed themselves to one another, at least not on her part. Perhaps she would just feel sorry if she knew of such a woman, sorry for a woman who had pined and pined for a man who would never be hers.

She climbed the steps to her porch, where she collected her mail from the mailbox. In the entry, she greeted Catrina, tossed all the mail except the water bill into the recycling basket, and proceeded up the stairs. Work awaited in her office, but first she changed her clothes, trading the black pants and brown and black striped jacket she'd worn to the funeral and reception for her usual jeans and sweater ensemble. Then she stepped across the hall and settled into her desk chair.

The computer and monitor had been sleeping since that morning, when Pamela had checked her email and responded to a few messages before rendezvousing with Bettina for the drive to the church for the funeral. Now, the mouse responded to the pressure of her hand, the computer chirped, and the monitor screen brightened. Soon she was staring at the image of a humble rag rug that resembled a swirling kaleidoscope but with colors paled by age.

The article was "Rag Rugs: The Art of the Frugal," and the rugs it dealt with had been collected by the author over several years of patronizing thrift stores and flea markets while vacationing in New England. They exemplified an admirable Yankee frugality, the author said, given that they had been created from fabric that had already served one purpose—as garments that had been worn and mended until they could be mended no more. The fabric had then been cut into narrow strips, and the strips sewn end to end to make longer strips. The strips had been grouped into batches of three and braided, and the braids had been coiled into a spiral and stitched around and around.

To illustrate the process of their creation, the author had made her own rag rug and had salvaged the fabric by browsing at yard sales. She admitted, however, that the castoffs she cut into strips would have struck the long-ago creators of the rugs in her collection as too useful still as garments to be transformed into rugs so soon. Among the illustrations that accompanied the article was a series of photos that started with a colorful shirt being cut into strips and ended with a completed rug, though much brighter in color than those in her collection.

The detail that made the article particularly fascinating was the scholarly attention the author had paid to the fabrics in the rugs she had collected—and the fact that she had kept a record of where she found each rug. She pointed out that careful examination—often with the aid of a magnifying glass—revealed the same fabric used in rugs created near each other geographically. Were neighbors sharing odds and ends of cloth they didn't need, she wondered, or had many patrons of the same general store bought fabric from the same bolt of cloth, turned it into garments for their households, and then recycled it into rugs when the garments wore out?

We will never know, the author concluded, but that observation brought to life for Pamela a community of women united by the impulse to make their homes beautiful and comfortable even though the materials of their artistry might be humble. She saved and closed the Word file, pushed her chair back, and lowered her eyelids against the monitor's continued glare. From the doorway came a meek meow, and she opened her eyes to see Catrina peeking hesitantly through the crack between door and doorjamb.

"What time is it?" she asked, speaking more to herself as she consulted the clock. Late, was the answer, though the sky was not yet dark behind the window shades. She'd worked longer than she planned.

Catrina led the way down the stairs and around the corner into the kitchen, the small procession picking up Ginger and Precious as it proceeded. Soon Catrina and Ginger were sharing generous scoops of Feline Feast chicken giblet pâté in their communal bowl while Precious nibbled at a crab and salmon blend. Pamela herself was anticipating a reprise of the Reuben sandwich Wilfred's gift of corned beef—enough for several sandwiches—had made possible.

Once her own dinner had been prepared and eaten, Pamela settled into her accustomed spot on her sofa. A new square for the patchwork sweater, this one burnt orange, was underway, and before her on the screen a British mystery was unfolding in the genteel accents that suited the backdrop of stately homes and well-manicured gardens.

Chapter Nine

On Friday morning Adelaide opened her front door with a weepy greeting and stepped back to allow Pamela and Bettina to enter. She held a crumpled tissue in her hand, and her eyes were moist and red. Her words squeaked out, barely audible.

"Hearing his voice . . . on the recording. I couldn't bear it." She edged toward where a smartphone lay on one of the sofa's pale gray cushions. A disarranged throw pillow nearby suggested that she had settled there to search the phone for the recording Kieran said he had made at the council meeting. She scooped the phone up and passed it to Bettina.

"Go ahead . . . listen. Sit down . . . stand, whatever you want. I'll be outside." And with that, she bolted for the door.

"Shouldn't you wear a coat . . . ?" Bettina ventured.

But it was too late. The front door opened and closed, and Adelaide was gone. Bettina stared at the door and seemed about to go after her. Pamela took the phone from her hand.

"A walk might help," she said, "and she wants us to hear the recording."

She lowered herself onto the sofa and directed an encouraging look at Bettina, who joined her there. A few moments later a voice emerged from the phone, a familiar voice, though rendered tinny by the small device.

"I'm wondering," Kieran's voice said, "how we should address the town's complaints about the plans to demolish the Dykema House. People have noticed that contractor fencing has gone up around it and they're posting on the listserv. The Dykema House predates the Civil War."

"They like to complain," came a dismissive growl. "It's old. So what?"

"I know the council approved the developer's proposal to build an apartment building on the lot, but that was before I took office and I . . ."

"You have a lot to learn, Malone." It was the growl again.

"Sounds like Mayor Olson," Bettina whispered, as the growl continued:

"Ask yourself, who's more likely to reward you—and if you don't know what I mean by *reward*, it's time to educate yourself—a rich developer or one of those nuts on the listserv who worries about squirrels getting stranded on roofs and Styrofoam getting into the drinking water?"

Somebody laughed and added, "Or cooking smells from the back of Hyler's seeping into the library's reading room." More laughter followed.

"We gave the public a chance to weigh in before we took the vote," somebody else said.

"And not enough people objected?" Kieran asked.

"Not very many stuck around for the whole meeting," was the answer, "because the room was kind of small and there weren't very many chairs . . ." A huge chorus of laughter greeted this statement, and a voice added, "Besides, it was summer, and Olson didn't turn on the AC. Smart guy!"

The recording ended then. Bettina touched the screen to

turn off the phone and looked at Pamela with wide eyes. "What a crook!" she exclaimed. "He certainly wasn't my choice for mayor, but I had no idea . . ." She tightened her lips into a firm line and shook her head, setting the tendrils of her scarlet hair atremble. "Taking bribes from developers— not to mention his contempt for his constituents, and it sounds like most of the other people on the council agree with him! Of course he wouldn't want Kieran's recording to go public. None of them would."

A squeak of hinges and a quiet footstep drew their attention to the front door. It swung open, and Adelaide entered, her arms wrapped around her chest. Bettina set the phone aside and pushed herself to her feet. She grabbed her down coat, which she had earlier tossed on one of the leather and chrome chairs, and rushed toward Adelaide. Wrapping her in the coat, she escorted her to the sofa and settled her next to Pamela.

"The mayor is a crook," Bettina repeated, this time to Adelaide, who appeared dazed. "And you're just about frozen." She looked past Adelaide to make eye contact with Pamela.

Reading her friend's mind, Pamela rose, saying, "I'll make coffee."

The kitchen was unfamiliar, but Pamela managed to find a tin of ground coffee and a French press large enough for two or three cups. No kettle was in sight, so a sauce pan would have to serve for boiling water. As she measured coffee into the glass cylinder of the French press and waited for the water to boil, the faint sound of Bettina's soothing murmur reached her.

Some minutes later, she delivered two cups of steaming coffee to the living room, along with a sugar bowl. A search of Adelaide's refrigerator had revealed no cream.

When Pamela returned with her own scant cup, Adelaide was drinking her coffee gratefully, and Bettina was taking tentative sips of what Pamela knew would be woefully unlike the pale concoction her friend preferred.

"I'll be meeting with Clayborn soon," Bettina said, after the soothing murmurs and the coffee had restored Adelaide to some semblance of herself. "I'll be sure to let him know about the recording."

"You really think it will help?" Adelaide sounded surprised. "You don't think Clayborn would ignore anything that might implicate the mayor and the council?"

"I'll do what I can." Bettina had abandoned her coffee and now had both hands free with which to squeeze one of Adelaide's.

"That cooking smell from Hyler's kitchen exhaust really is strong," Bettina commented as she climbed out of the Toyota. "And people do complain about it on the list-serv."

A narrow passageway ran between Hyler's and one of Arborville's three hair salons. It offered a shortcut to people walking to the shops and restaurants on Arborville Avenue from the parking lot that served the library and police station. Bettina had just parked in that lot.

"People like Hyler's, though," Pamela said. "I can't see that there's a remedy."

They crossed the asphalt and walked single file through the shadowy passageway, emerging into chilly sunshine right next to Hyler's thick glass door. The lunchtime rush had already begun, but a table was available near the floor-to-ceiling windows that looked out on the street. As soon as Pamela and Bettina had settled into the wooden chairs that flanked the worn wooden table, a server approached with the oversized menus that were a Hyler's trademark. Shrugging out of her jacket, Pamela opened her menu, and Bettina did likewise.

" 'The chef recommends,' " Bettina murmured, quoting from the printed card clipped to the menu's first page. "Today he's recommending 'Eggplant Parmesan on a Sourdough Sub.' " She lowered the menu and peered at Pamela over its stiff edge. "Would a vanilla milkshake go with that?"

Pamela lowered her own menu and responded, "I don't see why not."

The server, a middle-aged woman who had worked at Hyler's as long as Pamela could remember, was hovering nearby—eager, it was clear, to expedite their order.

"I'll have the eggplant sub," Pamela said, catching her eye. "And a vanilla milkshake."

"Good choice." The server made a quick note on her pad.

Bettina had raised her menu again and was no longer visible, but her voice emerged. "Vanilla milkshake too, and . . . and . . . *tuna melt*." She relinquished her menu, as did Pamela, and the server went on her way.

"The mayor was very much in evidence at the fest," Pamela observed. Thoughts had been percolating in her mind ever since she and Bettina left Adelaide's.

"*Very* much." Bettina nodded. "And the loaves were sitting out in the open and people were distracted by other things."

"Are you really going to tell Detective Clayborn about the recording?"

Bettina shrugged—and seemed to welcome the interruption provided by the arrival of the milkshakes, which the server lowered one at a time onto the paper placemats already on the table. The tips of straws poked out from the frothy crowns that topped the tall, frosted glasses. Bettina pulled her milkshake closer and bent toward the straw.

"*Are* you going to tell Detective Clayborn about the recording?" Pamela repeated as Bettina sipped.

"Do you think I should?" Bettina asked. A bright smudge of lipstick marked the end of her straw.

"The mayor's desire to keep the recording secret could definitely provide a motive for killing Kieran," Pamela said. "*But*"—she raised a finger—"does anybody else know about it? It doesn't sound like Adelaide even listened to the whole thing. She only knew that it was damning because Kieran told her about it."

"Kieran could have told other people he made it too—like the mayor," Bettina suggested. "Threatened them even."

"In that case, Adelaide could be in danger, now that she has the phone."

Bettina's eyes grew wide, and she raised fastidiously manicured fingers to her mouth. "You're right! I'll definitely tell Clayborn."

The sandwiches arrived then, on heavy oval platters, and for the next several minutes attention was focused on the food. The platter in front of Pamela held a crusty oblong roll, sliced in half horizontally and reassembled with strips of eggplant parmesan piled between top and bottom. A long stripe of eggplant, with purple skin intact, and oozing olive oil and tomato sauce, was visible along the side. The sandwich had been halved for more manageable eating, and the cut surfaces showed the eggplant, lustrous and pale, with layers of sourdough above and below. A few curls of arugula and a several olives were tucked alongside.

Bettina's tuna melt was equally appealing. Gobbets of tuna salad and dribbles of melted cheese emerged from between oval slices of rye bread, buttery and golden-brown from the grill. A scoop of coleslaw in a fluted paper cup and a small heap of fries completed the presentation.

"I think this is my favorite thing on the Hyler's menu," Bettina said as she speared the tuna melt with her fork and used her knife to detach a bite-sized piece.

Pamela, meanwhile, lifted half her sandwich to her mouth, aware that the result would be hands liberally anointed with olive oil and tomato sauce as the juicy interior leaked from the confines of its roll. The taste made the messiness worthwhile, however. Being fried in olive oil had rendered the eggplant silky in texture and deepened its flavor, an effect that was enhanced by the sharp hint of aged parmesan and the acidic tang of the tomato sauce. A cool swallow of the milkshake, smooth and sweet, made a striking contrast.

The platters were more than half empty by the time the conversation veered into a channel that wasn't related to the meals in the process of being consumed. Pamela had just finished remarking how well the sourdough, despite its non-Italian roots, complemented the very Italian flavors of eggplant parmesan, when Bettina said, "Amazing what phones can do now."

"Ummm?" The half-sandwich en route to Pamela's mouth halted mid-journey, and she gazed across the table at her friend.

"Photos, of course, and looking things up on the internet, and recording. I don't know how I got along doing interviews for the *Advocate* before I got my smartphone." Bettina pulled her milkshake closer and positioned the straw to access the last melted bit in the depths of the tall glass. "I've never used mine the way Kieran used his, though—to capture somebody saying something they shouldn't." She bent toward the tip of the straw.

"There's always a first time," Pamela remarked.

"Pamela!" Bettina scowled. "I wouldn't!"

Some time later, Pamela and Bettina stepped through Hyler's heavy glass door onto the sidewalk, mingling with passersby dressed as warmly as if spring was still on the distant horizon. Bettina took the lead as they headed through the passageway that led back to the parking lot.

"That estate sale at the Malone parents' house starts to-morrow," Bettina observed, her voice echoing off the walls.

"I remember," Pamela said. "Marlene Pepper told us."

"I know how much you like estate sales."

"You like them too." Pamela laughed. They had reached the parking lot.

"Do you think it would be ghoulish to go . . . given what happened to Kieran?"

"It's not his house," Pamela observed, "though he did grow up there. We might learn something interesting."

"Really? Like what?"

The Toyota was in sight. Bettina's pace quickened, but Pamela was lingering near the edge of the rock garden by the library entrance. Suddenly she stooped, popped back up again, and extended a hand with a coin between her index finger and her thumb.

"It's good luck, you know," she said, "finding money in the street—or parking lot. It's a nice shiny penny too, double good luck." She rejoined Bettina with a few long strides. "I vote we go to the estate sale."

One article remained to be copyedited from the three that were due back the following Monday. With a whole free afternoon stretching ahead, there seemed no excuse for procrastination, so Pamela climbed the stairs to her office and was soon immersed in the text scrolling before her on her monitor's screen.

The article's full title was "Ariadne's Thread: Craft and Context," and the article dealt with the Greek myth of Theseus and the Minotaur. The author, a classics professor who described herself as a lifelong devotee of the fiber arts and crafts, began by reviewing the myth. Tasked with killing the dreaded Minotaur, Theseus had to venture into the labyrinth King Minos had built to contain it. Not only was his survival in question, but also his ability to find his way back out of the labyrinth, should he be successful. To help him with at least the second challenge, the king's daughter, who had fallen in love with Theseus, gave him a ball of thread—probably pictured by those who told and retold the tale as more like the texture of yarn, the author pointed out. Theseus was to tie one end of the thread to the doorpost as he entered the labyrinth and then let it unwind as he made his way through the labyrinth's twists and turns. Once he had slain the Minotaur, he was to follow the thread back to the entrance of the labyrinth. Thanks to Ariadne's help, he killed the Minotaur *and* emerged safely.

The thread was doubtless wool, the author hypothesized, given that the ancient Greeks were known to raise sheep, and that sheep, wool, and fleece were mentioned in Greek literature as well as in other myths. Ariadne had doubtless used a spindle to spin sheared wool into the thread, and one of the illustrations that accompanied the article was of a Greek vase with an image that showed women spinning thread with handheld spindles.

Ariadne, the author went on to point out, had a particular connection with spinning. Her name was even derived from the Greek word for that archetypal spinning creature, the spider (genus Arachnida). Given the importance of, and magical powers attached to, the production of cloth, her cult seemed even to have reached ancient Gaul, where, as a goddess in creation myths, she spins the universe like a spider spins a web. With their well-known love of maze and labyrinth patterns, the author asked, is it possible that the ancient Celts knew a version of the Theseus myth now lost? And is it possible that a British Isles folksong like "Little Ball of Yarn," with its erotic implications, derived from a version of that myth?

"So interesting," Pamela murmured as she pushed her chair back from her desk and closed her eyes. The article was well written too, as would be expected from the author's credentials. She did, though, have a tendency to let her paragraphs stretch on and on, and her sentences too. The readers of *Fiber Craft* expected a livelier style. Pamela scrolled back to the top of the file and set about pruning sentences and dividing paragraphs into shorter units.

She was just turning a long string of words linked by a semicolon into two self-contained sentences when she was interrupted by the telephone, the landline. She swiveled her chair to the side and picked up the handset.

"You're working, aren't you?" was Bettina's greeting. "I tried your other phone, but I know you don't carry it around with you."

"I can stop for a minute." Pamela closed her eyes again, and fragments of white text danced against the sudden darkness like a negative.

"I followed up with Clayborn like I said I would."

"And . . . ?"

"He said they're already keeping an eye on Adelaide, given that they don't know the motive for Kieran's murder."

"And the recording?" Pamela asked. "Did you tell him about that?"

"I tried to . . ." Bettina paused. "He hemmed and hawed . . . he doesn't like clues that he doesn't find himself."

"Or maybe he's protecting his pals. Maybe Adelaide is right."

"He wouldn't suppress evidence on purpose." The statement ended with an uptilt that suggested Bettina wasn't convinced.

"You know him better than I do."

With that and a quick exchange of goodbyes, Pamela returned to "Ariadne's Thread."

Chapter Ten

Kieran's parents, Bridget and Connor Malone, had lived in a rambling white-shingled house along Arborville Avenue at the north end of town. As the Toyota, with Bettina at the wheel, left Arborville's commercial district behind, it was clear even from a few blocks away that the sale of the Malones' worldly possessions had attracted considerable interest. Every parking space along Arborville Avenue was taken, and streams of people were heading toward the house, where a bright pink sign anchored in the lawn advertised ESTATE SALE HERE TODAY. Bettina found a spot on a side street past the house, and she and Pamela joined the eager treasure hunters proceeding along the sidewalk.

Wooden steps led to an expansive porch crowded with outdoor furniture, rusted metal in colors that had once been bright. A tattered doormat made of braided fibers invited visitors to wipe their feet before stepping through the open half of a pair of impressive double doors. Once inside, Pamela and Bettina were greeted by a smiling woman with a large zippered change purse belted around her waist.

"Welcome," she said. "Three floors, including the basement, and check the garage before you leave."

The living room, off to the right, had been rearranged in order to display as many items as possible. Two long tables occupied much of the floor, with sofa, armchairs, and wooden furniture pushed against the walls. They were also for sale, however, as indicated by taped-on prices. The Persian-style rug under their feet, which showed its age in worn spots and faded colors, was also for sale. The buzz of conversation suggested an enthusiastic reception to the offerings.

Pamela waited until a space opened at the nearest table and stepped up alongside an older woman who was examining an impressive crystal vase faceted in a way that made it refract light almost like a diamond.

"Beautiful," the woman murmured to no one in particular, though Pamela nodded in agreement. "Waterford, I'm sure. I'll bet they brought it back from a trip to Ireland."

Other items on the table testified to a link with that country as well. A china teapot, cream and sugar set, and eight cups and saucers in a creamy porcelain dotted with delicate shamrocks proved to be Belleek when Pamela turned over a saucer in quest of the manufacturer. A plaque featured the outline of a harp and a motto in Gaelic, a lace-trimmed tea towel was embroidered with the words *Souvenir of Lismore*, and a row of pottery figurines depicted leprechauns in various poses.

Bettina, meanwhile, had moved on to the dining room and beckoned to Pamela from the doorway that connected it to the living room.

"I'm so tempted," she said, "but I really don't have room to store them."

The dining room table, very long thanks to a few leaves which might have been added just for the occasion, provided a useful surface for display—in this case, china and other things related to the room's purpose. Here was more Belleek, a service for at least twelve in the shamrock-dotted pattern, with stacks of big plates, little plates, bowls, more cups and saucers, platters, and serving bowls. Near it sat a flat wooden chest open to reveal a set of silver flatware in a pattern involving engraved scrolls and scallops. Stemmed crystal glasses in various sizes were clustered here and there.

Bettina, however, had been attracted by some folded table-cloths on the sideboard, with stacks of napkins nearby.

"Irish linen, no doubt," she said as she stroked the top-most one, which was smooth and immaculately white. "And plenty of matching napkins, it looks like." Her other hand landed atop the napkins.

"You'd find a place for them." Pamela smiled encouragingly. "And you'd be rescuing them. Young people aren't so interested in things like that anymore."

"I have that hall closet upstairs . . ." Bettina raised a thoughtful finger to her lips. "Not near the dining room, but I'd only be getting them out on special occasions . . ."

Catching sight of a fellow shopper who was eyeing the offerings displayed on the sideboard, Bettina quickly placed the white napkins on top of the white tablecloth, folded it over to make a compact bundle, and tucked it under her arm.

A glance into the kitchen revealed that anyone seeking to outfit a kitchen from scratch would be in luck, and several people were examining saucepans and rummaging in drawers. One man was holding a potato masher aloft. But Pamela and Bettina circled around to the entry and climbed the stairs that led to the second floor.

Five doors, four ajar, opened onto the upstairs hall. A sign taped to the doorframe of the fifth read ATTIC STILL IN PROGRESS—COME BACK TOMORROW. Two of the other doors revealed rooms furnished with beds and bureaus. Women's clothes were piled on the bed in one, sheets and towels on the bed in the other. A third room had apparently been a craft room—as was evident from the presence of a monumental sewing machine incorporated into a piece of furniture that resembled a fine wooden desk or cabinet, as well as stacks of fabric and plastic bins of yarn.

After browsing in those three rooms and coming away with a tin box of assorted buttons (Pamela) and a vintage silk scarf (Bettina), Pamela and Bettina returned to the hall. The fourth door was open only a crack, but that was enough to allow a haunting melody to escape. Pamela gave the door an experimental push, and it swung open to reveal Whit Sutton lounging in a comfortable armchair and paging through a large book. Two tall bookcases and a wide desk completed the room's furnishings. Stacks of CDs occupied the desk's surface, some with titles like *Traditional Irish Fiddle Tunes* and *Pub Music from the Emerald Isle* and covers that evoked quaint villages, rugged coastlines, cozy firesides, and picturesque villagers. A CD player on the desk was the source of the haunting melody.

"Those lyrics are quite . . ." Pamela commented after listening for a minute. The song recalled an adventure in which a young man wound up a young woman's ball of yarn, and it advised young women to guard their balls of yarn in the future.

"Suggestive?" Whit flashed his charming smile.

"Yes," Pamela said. "Suggestive." Perhaps, she reflected, this song was the one linked with the Theseus and Ariadne story in the article she had just copyedited. Quite coincidental!

"Discovering anything interesting?" he inquired.

Pamela and Bettina displayed their finds, and Bettina asked, "How about you?"

"This book, for sure." Whit closed the book and low-ered it to his lap. "But I'm actually here as a helper. I met Caitlin at the reception after Kieran's funeral, and I could see she was feeling pretty overwhelmed—coming back to Arborville to help her brother settle her parents' estate and then discovering she'd be doing it all alone because he was poisoned a few days after she arrived."

"Poor thing." Bettina nodded, and sympathy softened her gaze, despite what Vivian Stringfellow had said about Caitlin.

"She's in the attic. A lot of her stuff and Kieran's stuff from when they were growing up is still stored there. It has to be sorted, of course, because it's not all for sale." He waved around the room. "Check out these books though—Irish writers, politics, history . . . cookbooks even . . ."

"Wilfred likes history," Bettina commented as she took a few steps toward the closest bookshelf, "all kinds of his-tory."

Pamela, though, was studying the cover of the book on Whit's lap. Swooping letters that trailed elaborate curli-cues announced the title: *Tales from Irish Myth, Legend, and Folklore*. The cover was dominated by a magus-like figure in robes swirled by the wind, brandishing an elabo-rate staff. Behind him, twisted tree branches writhed against a tempestuous sky.

He noticed her interest and said, "A druid." He held the book up to give her a better look at the cover. "Everything about the picture is taken from the artist's imagination, though. Nobody knows much for sure about the ancient Celts. Even the tales come down at second or third hand because the Celts didn't leave behind a written language." He paused for a moment and turned the book around so the cover was facing him. "That's where the druids came in—part of where they came in, at least. They were the repositories of culture, with all the tales stored in their memories."

Pamela smiled. "I believe you described yourself as a druid when Bettina and I met you at the fest."

"I try to do my part"—he nodded, and a wave of dark hair flopped onto his forehead—"learning the old stories and passing them on. I have a long way to go, though. Some druids were thought to be seers, and their role was to advise the rulers as wise councilors, councilmen if you will." He laughed, a short bark, not cheerful. "I could run for office—but look what happened to Kieran."

He lowered the book to his lap and began to page through it. "Everything's here," he said. "Love stories too, like Guinevere and Lancelot, and all the tragedy that led to. People weren't always faithful to their spouses, even way back then."

"What will you do now?" Bettina asked an hour later as the Toyota came to a stop at the end of Pamela's driveway. "Do you have any plans for tonight?" She accompanied the question with a meaningful glance at Richard Larkin's house.

"We agreed that you weren't going to mention Richard Larkin ever again." Pamela addressed the back of Bettina's head, given that Bettina was still focused on the house.

"I didn't mention him." Bettina swiveled to face Pamela. "I just asked if you had plans for tonight and looked at his house."

"I knew what you meant, though." Pamela suppressed the urge to smile. Bettina really was incorrigible.

"So you don't have plans . . ." Bettina studied Pamela's face. "Come for dinner, then. Wilfred is making a batch of his five-alarm chili."

*   *   *

On Sunday morning Pamela had just changed from her pajamas and robe into her cool-weather uniform of jeans and sweater when the doorbell's chime summoned her back downstairs. A figure dressed in bright yellow was visible through the lace that curtained the oval window in the front door. She opened the door to admit Bettina, whose first words were, "Much warmer today, finally."

Bettina had exchanged her down coat for a chic trench coat in a most spring-like color, fashioned from a shiny fabric resembling patent leather. Her hands were empty, so she clearly had something in mind other than a cozy chat over crumb cake and coffee.

"Grab your jacket," she said. "We're going back to the estate sale. Whit texted me to say he found something we might be interested in."

Ten minutes later, Pamela and Bettina were once again climbing the wooden steps of the house where the Malones had raised their children and lived on into their sunset years. The second day of the sale had attracted a smaller crowd—Bettina had been able to park the Toyota right in front—and only a few people were visible browsing in the living room as Pamela and Bettina stepped over the threshold. The woman who had greeted them the previous day was on duty today as well, and her greeting was just as friendly—and much more personal.

"Bettina Fraser," she exclaimed, adding, "That *is* you, isn't it?" When Bettina nodded, she went on. "And this is your friend from yesterday."

"Pamela Paterson." Pamela extended a hand.

The hand that the woman extended in return was holding the end of a strand of red yarn.

"It's for you," the woman said, still focused on Pamela. "Or you." She turned to Bettina. "Or both of you. Whit told me you'd both come."

Pamela took the offered yarn but realized she must look puzzled when the woman shrugged and commented, "Whit seems like quite a character. You're to follow the yarn."

The yarn was easy to follow, given its bright red color. It lay across the scuffed parquet floor of the entry hall and then made a left turn at the stairs leading to the second floor. Almost automatically, Pamela began winding it around her fingers as she pursued the trail it marked, with Bettina close behind.

It guided them upstairs, where the doors leading to the four second-floor rooms were still open, and a buzz of conversation leaked into the hall, but no music. In the rooms with the beds, people rummaged through the clothes and linens on offer. In the room with the armchair, now empty, where Whit had sat, people pondered the books, many of which were no longer neatly shelved but lay scattered among the CDs on the desk. The monumental sewing machine had disappeared from the fourth room, apparently having found a new owner.

The fifth door was ajar today, and the sign inviting people interested in the attic's contents to come back the next day had been removed. The yarn lay in a bright stripe over the dark wooden threshold and continued up the narrow, carpeted stairway. Pamela continued wrapping it around her fingers and led the way, to the landing, where the stairs changed direction and the yarn followed, and on to the attic itself.

The house's peaked roof meant that the attic walls sloped in an inverted V-shape down to little dormer windows barely a foot from the floor. Pamela and Bettina were the only shoppers here, though boxes of books, old magazines, sports equipment, Christmas decorations, luggage, and camping gear were among the things, some useful, that the Malones had stored in their attic. The yarn, however, snaked its way to a far corner, where it disappeared into a massive trunk. A sign taped to the trunk read NOT FOR SALE.

The attic was dim, with the only natural light coming from the low windows, but a bare light bulb hung from the ceiling near the center of the space. Pamela tugged on the string dangling from it, and it cast a vague pool of light below.

"I guess we're supposed to follow the yarn into the trunk," Pamela said.

Bettina giggled. "This is kind of fun, like a treasure hunt. But that corner is still very dark."

With Pamela at one end and Bettina at the other, they dragged and pushed the trunk across the dusty floor until it entered the pool of light cast by the bare bulb. The trunk was a grand thing, covered in mottled leather, with a domed top and reinforced with strips of metal, now dark with tarnish.

The trunk's heavy top opened with a squeak and a creak, revealing the ball of red yarn whose unwound strand they had followed from the front door. Pamela lifted it out and set it aside, along with the circlet of yarn she had looped around her fingers. The first thing that caught her eye within the trunk was a stack of four yearbooks—yearbooks from Arborville High, to be precise—turquoise and gold with cartoon depictions of the aardvark that was the sports mascot. The top one was from 1998 and a quick glance at the index, followed by turning a few pages, showed that Kieran, darkly handsome in his photograph, had been a senior that year.

Yellowing file folders held term papers and other school assignments, from Arborville High and, to judge from the dates, from Kieran's college career. In fact, a deeper layer in the trunk held more yearbooks, yearbooks from Rutgers.

But the trunk also contained evidence that photography had been an early interest. Manila envelopes of various sizes were interspersed with the file folders. Pamela undid the little metal clasp on one large one, peered inside, and pulled out a sheaf of black and white photos. They had a look that suggested they were the products of a home darkroom, an impression that was intensified when she examined them further.

The top one was a portrait of an attractive woman with abundant curly hair, a head shot with one bare shoulder visible. But the one beneath it was not limited to the subject's head. Shoulders and breasts and a great deal more were visible, and bare. Pamela handed the photo to Bettina, who murmured, "Goodness." The rest of the photos were variations on the same theme—tasteful poses and undeniably artistic, but it was clear that, for whatever reasons, the model had been quite willing to disrobe in Kieran's presence.

Bettina shuffled the photos into a neat stack and handed them to Pamela, who slipped them into the envelope and set it aside. As she did, she noticed a date penciled onto its front: *Summer 2003.*

Chapter Eleven

Pamela continued to excavate, pausing once to ask, "Do you think that's what the yarn was leading us to?"

Bettina crept next to Pamela and began lifting things out of the trunk, grouping the yearbooks in one spot, the file folders with the school assignments in another, and the manila envelopes in yet another.

"Concert T-shirts!" Pamela exclaimed. She lifted out a bundle of carelessly folded T-shirts in various colors. The top one featured a streamlined guitar whose neon-yellow hue fairly vibrated against the black background of the shirt. "And underneath them we have"—the concert T-shirts joined the yearbooks and file folders on the floor—"a pair of faded jeans."

Bettina was watching over Pamela's shoulder as she excavated. The bottommost layer of the trunk's contents was once again manila envelopes. Pamela handed one to Bettina, who opened it and declared, "Negatives." She slid a strip out and held it toward the bare light bulb hanging from the ceiling.

"Nothing very dramatic," she announced after a minute of study, "unless a person was a fan of the Arborville Aardvarks in the 1990s."

In fact, the date noted on that envelope, and several others that also contained sports photos and/or negatives of sports photos, corresponded with the years when Kieran would have been at Arborville High.

The trunk was now empty, except for a few dust balls in the corners.

"We didn't look inside the other envelopes from near the top of the trunk," Bettina said, easing herself out of her crouch in favor of sitting, if less than comfortably, on the floor.

She reached for an envelope from that batch, handed it to Pamela—who had adopted a cross-legged pose—and took another for herself. For several minutes there was no sound except for the shuffling of paper against paper as Pamela and Bettina studied the products of Kieran's early forays into photography.

There were street scenes from Manhattan, highlighting uptown elegance and downtown grit. There were character studies—pensive expressions caught as people sipped coffee in diners, laughter as people toasted one another with brimming mugs of beer. Kieran had captured strollers enjoying a snowy day, sunbathers in what looked like Washington Square Park, a street musician fingering the keys of a saxophone.

"Everyone is wearing clothes," Pamela commented as she tucked the last group of photos back into its envelope. "Even the sunbathers."

Bettina, meanwhile, had extracted from its envelope the head shot of the woman who had revealed so much more of herself to Kieran. She held it out at arm's length and commented, "I can't help thinking that she looks familiar, like a younger version of someone we've met right here in Arborville."

Pamela glanced at the photo and nodded, but she was

busy winding the strand of yarn they had followed up the stairs back onto the main ball. She and Bettina returned Kieran's memorabilia to the trunk, and on the way downstairs she stopped in the craft room and nestled the ball among others in one of the bins where Mrs. Malone had stored her yarn.

They returned to the Toyota and settled comfortably into their seats, but Bettina didn't immediately insert her key in the ignition. Instead, she took her phone from her handbag. Pamela watched as she located the text in which Whit said he'd found something interesting at the estate sale, and she watched as Bettina's finger moved over the keyboard she had summoned onto the screen of her phone.

"The red yarn led us to something interesting," Bettina wrote, "or things, really, but what do they mean?"

She exchanged her phone for the Toyota's key, twisted it in the ignition, and the car grumbled until the engine caught. Soon it was humming happily, and they were cruising south on Arborville Avenue, en route to Orchard Street.

"Let's just see . . ." Bettina retrieved her phone from her handbag after she had steered the Toyota into the Frasers' driveway and parked it next to Wilfred's Mercedes. "Let's just see," she repeated as under her finger the screen brightened, and she continued to touch it here and there.

"He answered already!" She looked over at Pamela. "He says, 'They explain everything, along with the ball of yarn. Do what you want with the information. The druid's role is only to advise.' "

"I thought you might be hungry." Wilfred opened the front door before they even reached the porch. An apron was tied around his waist.

The aroma of chili reached them as they drew nearer.

"There was plenty left from last night," he said, as if aware that the appealing aroma made it unnecessary to identify what exactly there was plenty of. "And it's coming up on noon."

Woofus watched from the sofa as Pamela shed her jacket and Bettina her bright yellow trench coat. Then they all proceeded toward the kitchen, where a welcoming sight awaited. Not only had Wilfred warmed a pot of chili, but he had also set three places at the pine table. As if in reference to the recent holiday—though memories of it were not so pleasant—he'd chosen green placemats and green-and-white checked napkins.

"Sit down, sit down," he urged, and Pamela and Bettina complied as he veered toward the stove.

Within a few minutes three steaming bowls of chili had appeared on the placemats, along with a platter of golden cornbread squares in the center of the table. Wilfred's cheery "Bon appétit" was the signal to pick up spoons. Silence broken only by appreciative hums followed.

Wilfred's chili was characterized by a rich depth of flavor, savory and peppery but smoothed out by long simmering that rendered the meat meltingly tender and the beans velvety. After the first few spoonfuls, Pamela transferred a square of cornbread to her bread plate, sliced it horizontally, and buttered its warm surface. Its fragrance as she bit into it evoked sun and a bountiful harvest.

"Did you in fact find something interesting in the Malones' house this morning?" Wilfred inquired as the pace of eating slowed.

Bettina described the yarn trail, the attic trunk, and the memorabilia documenting Kieran's young manhood. "And his talent for photography was obvious even back then," she said, "including portraits of a quite intimate nature."

Bettina and Wilfred continued to chat as Bettina elaborated on the trunk's contents, wondering at one point what would happen to it now.

"His sister might take it," Wilfred suggested. "Souvenirs of her brother could be meaningful."

Pamela, however, was silent. The mention of the intimate portraits had summoned them into her mind, and she studied them as if the very photographs were before her. The woman had looked so familiar, like a younger version of . . . someone. Of course, many people looked alike. Take a handsome dark-haired young man like Whit . . . there are only so many ways to be handsome, and one handsome man with dark hair could look like another handsome man with dark hair . . .

"Pamela?"

Pamela came back to herself with a start. Bettina was leaning across the table staring at her.

"Do you want more chili?"

"No . . . no . . ." Pamela looked down at her bowl. It was empty, but she'd been so caught up in her thoughts she'd been eating unaware. "It was wonderful," she added. "The cornbread too. I'm quite satisfied."

Bettina and Wilfred did want refills. Pamela did her best to be sociable as they tackled fresh bowls and the conversation moved on to Bettina's reporting schedule for the coming week, which included covering an awards ceremony at the grammar school and a talk on nutrition at the senior center.

As Wilfred finished clearing the table, Bettina once again leaned toward Pamela with a quizzical expression on her face. "You're thinking something, aren't you?" she observed.

Pamela nodded. "Whit said he didn't want to be a doctor."

"Yes?"

Bettina's hesitant tone suggested the import of this statement wasn't clear. And why should it be? Pamela realized her mind had been leaping ahead, starting with the portrait in the manila envelope.

"Specifically, not a doctor like his father," she clarified. "His father is . . ."

Pamela jumped up to retrieve her phone from her purse. Returning to the table, she sat down and fingered its screen. In a few moments she was scrolling through the website of Whitfield Sutton, M.D., which included glowing testimonials from women with unlined faces.

"Deirdre is definitely, definitely not the killer." She looked up at Bettina. "But we have to talk to her."

Pamela closed her internet search, found Deirdre in her phone's directory, and touched the screen to place the call. After a brief conversation with Deirdre, she once again focused on Bettina.

"Deirdre's not home now," she said. "She's at her sister's in Philadelphia, and she's spending the night. She'll be back in Arborville by noon tomorrow, and I told her we'd be over."

"What are we talking to her about?" Bettina inquired.

"Kieran's murder, of course."

"Tell him you know who the leprechaun was," Pamela instructed Deirdre.

The two were sitting on Deirdre's sofa, nondescript but for the colorful granny-square afghan draped over its back. Deirdre was holding the phone she had fetched at Pamela's direction.

"And tell him you're willing to keep that information to yourself in return for . . . something you'll discuss in person."

Bettina was watching from the armchair, looking as raptly attentive as Deirdre.

"Why?" Deirdre's voice was a nearly inaudible squeak, but it provoked a puzzled glance from the cat curled up at the sofa's other end.

"If you do this," Pamela explained, "you'll be able to supply Detective Clayborn with definitive proof that you are not the person who killed Kieran. The leprechaun tampered with your loaf of soda bread."

Deirdre shrugged and murmured, "No harm in trying." She fingered her phone's screen as Pamela read off a number.

"He sounded nervous," Deirdre reported after a brief conversation. "*Very* nervous, and he's coming right over."

"He should be nervous." Pamela smiled a pleased smile and sketched out the form Deirdre's conversation with the erstwhile leprechaun should take. Satisfied that Deirdre understood the assignment, Pamela stood up. She beckoned Bettina, and the two retreated around the corner to a small dining nook where a door opened to the kitchen.

"You're recording this on your phone," Pamela told Bettina as they stood side by side against the counter, facing a magnet-bedecked refrigerator. Bettina touched her phone's screen once, and again, and set it at the end of the counter nearest the door.

Soon—very soon—a doorbell's ping signaled that the scene Pamela had imagined was about to commence. Footsteps crossed the living room floor, a door swung back with a creak, and Deirdre's voice—be *assertive*, Pamela had said—invited the caller to enter.

A deep voice took over then, saying, "What's all this foolishness about, anyway? Me? A leprechaun? Where'd you get that idea?"

The door closed with a clunk.

"You don't need to know that," Deirdre responded. "All you need to know is that I know—and it will cost you."

Bettina turned to Pamela. Her wide eyes and crinkled brow indicated surprise and alarm.

"It's just a ploy," Pamela whispered. "If he agrees, that means he's acknowledging he did it."

From the living room came a laugh, like a hoarse rumble, followed by the words, "Clever, clever. So . . . how much will it cost me for you to forget that I was the leprechaun?"

"Quite a bit," Deirdre said. "Because the leprechaun murdered Kieran. My loaf of soda bread was just a loaf of soda bread until you added your lethal poison."

"Hmmm. I certainly wouldn't want that information to get out . . ."

The deep voice paused, and a heavy footfall indicated a sudden movement.

"Let go!" Deirdre squealed.

"I don't think so," came the response. "I wasn't sure what you had in mind, so I came prepared. You're right—botulism toxin is almost always fatal, so get ready!"

Deirdre squealed again and whimpered, "No!"

Pamela's heart made its presence felt with a sudden thump. The scene between Deirdre and the leprechaun wasn't unfolding as she had envisioned, and Deirdre was now in danger. Behind her Bettina whispered, "I'm calling 911, but we have to do something fast to stop him."

Pamela looked around the small kitchen for something . . . anything . . . scanning counters and then the floor—where, next to a bowl holding a few last crunchy nibbles from a serving of cat treats sat a similar bowl filled with water. She stooped, seized the bowl, and stepped toward the doorway.

Deirdre, looking more delicate than ever, was straining to pull away from a bulky, blond-haired man with one large hand clamped around her wrist. He held the other hand aloft, his fingers gripping a fearsome-looking syringe, its needle glinting in the sunlight filtering through the windows. Its plunger was extended, with a finger poised to send the syringe's contents into his next victim.

"Hey!" Pamela shouted, and the man's head jerked in her direction. With a hand on each side of the water bowl, she tilted it and then lifted it and thrust forward, still holding the bowl but sending its contents in a watery arc toward her target.

He stared at her in astonished wetness, blinking, releasing Deirdre in order to dash water from his eyes. The syringe, meanwhile, had landed on the carpet. Pamela tossed the bowl aside, and it landed with a clunk. She stooped to retrieve the syringe, meeting the gaze of the cat, which had just emerged from beneath the sofa.

Deirdre, meanwhile, had vanished, slipping past Pamela to join Bettina in the kitchen as Pamela studied Whitfield Sutton, M.D. He was still blinking as drips continued to trickle from his sodden hair, blond hair—and his eyes, which now seemed defenseless, were pale and ringed by pale lashes. It all seemed so obvious now. How could the Whitfields as a couple—he so fair and she with her tawny hair—have produced the darkly handsome Whit Jr.?

"Police are on their way," Bettina called from the kitchen.

"My son wasn't my son," Dr. Sutton said as if privy to Pamela's thoughts. "And I didn't have a clue until Kieran returned to the town where he had sowed his wild oats twenty years earlier. Whit was growing closer and closer and closer to him, as if he sensed . . ."

The remainder of the sentence was lost in a sob, and Dr. Sutton collapsed onto the hassock that accompanied the armchair. He slumped forward until he was bent nearly double, with his elbows on his knees and his face cradled in his hands.

After a long minute of sobbing, he spoke once again. Muffled words emerged from behind his hands. "I lost so much, my son who wasn't my son . . . what does it matter what else I lose now?"

The doorbell's ping announced that the police had arrived. Pamela crossed the room to greet them as Bettina and Deirdre stepped through the kitchen doorway.

Chapter Twelve

Tuesday's *County Register* had featured not only Marcy Brewer's article detailing the arrest of Dr. Whitfield Sutton for the murder of Kieran Malone but also her interview with Pamela Paterson. Everyone in Arborville—in fact, everyone in the whole county who had read that morning's *Register*—now knew the particulars of Kieran's murder.

Dr. Sutton had infiltrated Arborville's St. Patrick's Day fest disguised as a leprechaun and had injected botulism toxin—which in the form of Botox smoothed the frown lines of his youth-seeking patients—into the loaf of soda bread baked by Deirdre McKeon. He'd had no particular desire to implicate Deirdre but simply chose the loaf at random, with the goal of removing the man he had recently come to realize was the actual father of the son he considered his own.

Pamela's copy of the *Register* was now tucked away in her recycling basket. Her house had been vacuumed and dusted, and the products of an afternoon baking session awaited the Knit and Nibblers on a platter in the kitchen. Bettina, who always arrived early for the Knit and Nibble meetings, was at this very moment inspecting them. She had dressed even more festively than usual, as if to celebrate the fact that Kieran's murder was no longer a mystery and that sweet Deirdre McKeon had been definitely proven innocent.

"I like green again," she had explained in response to Pamela's compliments. "Now that St. Patrick's Day doesn't have such sad connotations anymore—though I'll always be sad about what happened to Kieran."

Bettina was wearing a snug jersey wrap dress in a swirling abstract print involving many shades of green. The effect was stunning in combination with her scarlet hair, all the more so in that she had accessorized the dress with bold emerald earrings and a necklace to match. On her feet were green suede pumps featuring perilously high heels.

"These look amazing," she sighed as she hovered over the platter. "And what is that elusive aroma?" She lifted her head.

"I'm not telling . . . yet." Pamela smiled mysteriously. "I'll just say that, with St. Patrick's Day itself basically spoiled—except that Wilfred did cook that delicious meal on the real day—I decided to celebrate belatedly by baking an Irish-themed goody for the Knit and Nibblers."

The doorbell's chime interrupted then, though seven o'clock had not yet arrived. Bettina turned and advanced toward the entry. "Holly, I think," she reported over her shoulder, "and Karen. I can see them through the lace."

She swung the front door back, and Holly stepped in first, tipping her head to survey the living room. "No sign of Nell yet," she commented. "We offered a ride, but she insisted on walking—and, anyway, I wanted to get here before her, because . . ."

She advanced toward the kitchen doorway and crossed the threshold. "Pamela!" she exclaimed. "The interview you gave Marcy Brewer was so interesting, but you didn't explain everything." She paused to survey the platter and echoed Bettina's earlier pronouncement that its contents looked amazing.

"I answered all Marcy's questions," Pamela said.

Holly laughed, displaying her perfect teeth, a striking effect with her glowing skin and abundant raven hair. "To apply to Marcy Brewer what you often say about Detective Clayborn, perhaps she didn't ask the right ones."

"Such as . . . ?" Pamela had been spooning coffee beans into her grinder. Content that she had spooned enough, she fitted the lid into place.

"Such as exactly how you figured out that Dr. Sutton was the killer—though I must say that, with his motive revealed, his evil deed makes sense." Karen, standing at Holly's side, nodded as Holly spoke.

Pamela pressed down on the grinder's lid, and a raucous clatter took the place of speech as beans jostled in the grinding chamber. The clatter smoothed to a whir, and Pamela let up on the pressure. Meanwhile, Bettina had been staging wedding-china cups and saucers and little plates on the kitchen table.

"Whit looked so much like Kieran," Pamela said, "but without any other puzzle pieces, that piece didn't mean anything."

Bettina chimed in. "Then there was the fact that he seemed so drawn to Kieran. Another puzzle piece—but a young person who wanted to be a photographer would naturally jump at the chance to spend time with a professional photographer, so not significant in itself."

"Whit could have inherited the photographer gene, though," Holly suggested.

"In retrospect, there *was* a like father, like son aspect to it," Pamela agreed, "and it was actually photographs—Kieran's photographs, but Whit steered us to them—that proved to be a really important puzzle piece."

"*Intimate* photographs"—Bettina raised her brows and added a knowing smile—"of a woman who Pamela later realized was Whit's mother, but much younger, photographed long enough ago that Whit, who's now about to graduate from college, could be the product of the extramarital relationship the photos implied."

"Motive." Holly nodded vigorously. "For sure."

Footsteps on the porch signaled that another Knit and Nibbler had arrived. Still nodding, Holly darted into the entry. They heard the door swing open and then her voice. "Come in quick. Pamela's just telling us how she figured out that Dr. Sutton was the killer—and Nell will be here any minute."

"She's three houses up the block," came Roland's voice. "I stopped and offered her a ride, but she said it's warm and still light out and she's enjoying the air."

Holly returned to the kitchen alone. "He wants to get started knitting," she said. "So, anyway, we've got motive now. And you figured out means and opportunity too. Right?"

"Dr. Sutton was disguised as a leprechaun." Bettina added a who-could-imagine-such-a-crazy-thing shrug. "That gave him the opportunity he was looking for. Everybody noticed the leprechaun but likely assumed he was part of the program, and I thought the rec center's activities director had invited him. So Dr. Sutton could wander here and there, and nobody paid much attention."

"Botulism toxin," Holly said with a shiver. "That was the poison . . ." Karen shivered too.

"And as a doctor specializing in cosmetic procedures, he had the means . . ." Pamela looked up from setting forks, spoons, and napkins on the table. "Botox! And he had syringes, so he could inject the toxin into the loaf. Then, in the confusion as people reacted to Kieran being taken ill, he snatched up the remains of the poisoned loaf and slipped out the back door."

Holly's expression as she gazed at Pamela was rapt. "Awesome," she breathed, "and you somehow knew that Dr. Sutton's specialty equipped him particularly to carry out this scheme."

"Whit told us." Bettina spoke up. She had been leaning into the refrigerator while reaching for the heavy cream, and her voice echoed back from its depths. She straightened up and turned around. "Me really, mostly, but Pamela was there, and she heard him. Whit said he didn't want to be a doctor like his father, or at least the man he thought was his father, and he especially didn't want to be a doctor who focused on keeping rich people looking like they're not a day over thirty."

The doorbell chimed just then, and Bettina, Holly, and Karen went to greet Nell. Pamela surveyed the kitchen, making sure everything was ready for eight o'clock, when Roland would consult his impressive watch and declare it was break time.

Not many minutes later, all the knitters were in their accustomed places. Nell had settled into the comfortable armchair at one end of the hearth, and Roland had settled onto the hassock at the other. Bettina, Holly, and Karen were lined up on the sofa, and Pamela was on the rummage sale chair with the carved wooden back and needlepoint seat, which she'd pulled up near where Bettina sat on the sofa.

So much conversation had already occurred in the kitchen, and on such a gripping topic, that Pamela and the early arrivals went silently about the business of extracting yarn and needles from knitting bags and preparing to take up their knitting where they had last left off. Roland was also silent, manipulating his four needles and managing his dangling bobbins, his placid expression testimony to the soothing effect knitting had even on him.

As the silence threatened to become oppressive, Pamela looked up from casting on for a new square to observe that the weather had certainly improved.

"Oh, yes!" Holly was always ready to do her part when sociability was required.

Nell nodded. "It seems March really will go out like a lamb."

Bettina was puzzling over the directions for the lacy cardigan she was knitting for Betty and seemed disinclined to join the conversation. Pamela glanced at Karen, who was focused on a stitch.

Surprisingly, Roland spoke up. "Why isn't anyone saying anything about the big story in the *Register* this morning?"

"He could have joined us in the kitchen," Bettina whispered to Pamela, but Nell surveyed the occupants of the sofa.

"Yes," she said. "Why? Particularly in that Marcy Brewer made sure to highlight Pamela's role in figuring out who poisoned Kieran Malone and how."

"It's water over the bridge now," Bettina remarked placidly, invoking one of Wilfred's favorite garbled sayings. "No point in dwelling on the details."

A muffled giggle came from Holly's direction.

"I suspect . . ." Nell's expression mingled amusement and reproach. "I suspect that the details were dwelled on before I arrived."

"You did insist on walking." Holly accompanied the comment with a fond smile. "And Karen and I were longing to know how Pamela figured everything out." She noticed Karen giving her a look and added, "Well, mostly I was longing."

Nell sighed. "Well, water over the bridge, I suppose, and just as well. Events like Kieran's murder are bad enough without endlessly rehearsing them."

Her attention returned to her work then, another bunny to judge by the oval shape taking shape on her busy needles. Bettina's fingers were in motion too. The knitting magazine that contained her pattern had been set aside, and she was whispering to herself as she followed the complicated directions that created the cardigan's lacy texture.

A muted conversation sprang up between Holly and Karen, snatches of which indicated that they were planning a trip to a vintage shop that featured midcentury modern furniture. Bettina seemed disinclined to talk, beyond the whispers that were prompting her fingers' motions, so Pamela let her mind wander, aided in its reverie by the rhythmic motions of her needles.

Maybe this silence is a blessing, she reflected. They had been spared a detour into one of Roland's favorite topics, the disappointing return on investment represented by the taxes he paid to Arborville, exemplified by amateurs having to solve crimes that should have been solved by the police.

She was startled from her musings by Roland's voice intoning, "Eight o'clock." He was still perched on his hassock, but he had rested his half-finished sock on the hearth and was peering at the watch peeping from beneath his immaculate shirt cuff. Pamela was equally startled to realize that Bettina had vanished while she was deep in thought, rising from the sofa and slipping away silently.

Normally she would have been the one to slip away, far enough in advance of eight o'clock to start water boiling for the coffee and tea. But judging from the seductive aroma drifting from the direction of the kitchen, coffee was already in progress.

She rose from her chair, set her work aside, and made her way to the kitchen. The carafe, with the plastic filter cone balanced atop it, sat on the counter. Coffee brewing was indeed well underway, and Bettina was now tipping the kettle over one of Pamela's vintage teapots, the one that resembled a cat. Cream had still to be whipped, however, to add the final touch to the belated St. Patrick's Day dessert she envisioned. She poured heavy cream into a small bowl, added sugar and a bit of Irish whiskey, and set to work with her electric mixer. Soon the puddle of cream at the bottom of the bowl had been transformed into a sweet cloud that rose nearly to the bowl's rim.

"I tasted one," Bettina confessed, when the mixing was done and conversation was possible again. "But I'll make sure that's the one I end up with." She'd transferred the contents of the platter to the small wedding-china plates. "I think I'd call them whiskey bars."

"That's exactly what I call them," Pamela said. "*Irish* whiskey bars. I made a shortbread crust like the one I make for lemon bars, and then I made a treacle-like topping with brown sugar, corn syrup, eggs, and a few tablespoons of Irish whiskey. That's my special nod to St. Patrick's Day." She surveyed her handiwork. "They're my own invention, and there's Irish whiskey in the whipped cream too."

"Can I help?" came Holly's voice from the doorway that led to the dining room. Without waiting for an answer, she crossed to the counter and removed the filter cone from the top of the carafe. She picked the carafe up, stepped to the table, and began pouring coffee.

Pamela added a dollop of whipped cream to each of the whiskey bars, where it contrasted with the burnished hue of the sugary surface. Karen appeared in the doorway too, and soon coffee, tea, and whiskey bars had been trans-ferred from the kitchen to the living room, along with cream and sugar, napkins, and forks and spoons.

Pamela had sampled one of the whiskey bars in advance too—the recipe made more than needed for the Knit and Nibblers. She was therefore not in suspense about the taste. But she *was* in suspense about what the Knit and Nibblers' reaction would be.

Five forks bearing bites of whiskey bar garnished with whipped cream were raised in near unison. After a few moments of meditative chewing, a chorus of *ummms* echoed around the room.

"Sweet," Nell commented, but she was smiling. "Very, very sweet, and I taste whiskey."

"Irish whiskey," Pamela explained, "for St. Patrick's Day."

She picked up her own fork and nudged a bite off her whiskey bar. The texture was like a crumbly pudding, she had noted on her first sampling, and she noticed it again now. That wasn't surprising, given that the topping was actually a kind of custard, with corn syrup as the liquid and eggs as the thickener, and that the topping had perme-ated the shortbread crust as it baked.

Smiles, nods, and eager forks made it clear that the whiskey bars were a success. More praise followed, words rather than hums of pleasure. The last to speak, Holly pro-nounced the whiskey bars *awesome* and *amazing*, and she wondered aloud how a person could be such a good cook and a crime solver too.

"A recipe is rather like a mystery," Pamela said, without really thinking. But the minute the statement was out of her mouth, she saw its truth and continued speaking. "The ingredients are the clues, sometimes including unexpected things that might seem not to belong—like Coca-Cola in a recipe for baked ham, or chocolate in a recipe for chili, or canned tomato soup in that old-fashioned cake recipe. But once they're put together, it all makes sense."

"Maybe." Roland had listened with particular interest, but frowning, as if absorbing an unexpected legal argument. Then he nodded. "And in both cases," he observed, "the result is very satisfying."

"*Very* satisfying." Holly pointed at the tiny portion of Irish whiskey bar remaining on her plate. "These seem as appropriate to St. Patrick's Day as . . . as . . ."

"Soda bread?" suggested Nell.

Bettina covered her face with her hands. From behind her carefully manicured fingers came the words, "Please don't say those words."

"The soda bread itself turned out not to be at fault," Nell reminded her. With a glance at Pamela, she added, "No unexpected ingredients."

"Wilfred's version is so good," Pamela said. "I missed it this year." She touched Bettina's arm, and Bettina lowered her hands. "We can't let what happened at the fest ruin our enjoyment of a wonderful tradition."

"No," Bettina murmured. "I guess we can't."

Author's Note

We definitely can't. See the BONUS NIBBLE, Peggy's Irish Soda Bread, guaranteed not lethal but with one unexpected ingredient.

KNIT

Knitted Glasses Case

A knitted glasses case is a quick and easy project that makes a fun gift. It's also practical. It can be used for reading glasses, driving glasses, sunglasses, or whatever, and the double layer has a nice cushioning effect. It doesn't take much yarn and is a great way to use odds and ends left from other projects.

For a picture of the completed glasses case as well as some in-progress photos, visit the Knit & Nibble Mysteries page at PeggyEhrhart.com. Click on the cover for *Irish Soda Bread Murder* and scroll down on the page that opens. References in the directions below to photos on my website are to this page.

Use yarn identified on the label as "Medium" and/or #4, and use size 6 needles (though size 5 or 7 is fine if that's what you have). The glasses case requires about 78 yards of yarn. You can also make the lining of the glasses case one color and the outer layer another color. If you do that, you will need about 39 yards of each color.

If you're not already a knitter, watching a video is a great way to master the basics of knitting. Just search the internet for "How to Knit" and you'll have your choice of tutorials that show the process clearly. The glasses case is worked in the stockinette stitch (the stitch you see, for example, in a typical sweater)—though if you wish, you can also use the simpler garter stitch. The directions are the same.

To create the stockinette stitch, you knit one row, then purl going back the other direction, then knit, then purl, knit, purl, back and forth. Again, it's easier to understand "purl" by viewing a video, but essentially when you purl you're creating the backside of "knit." To knit, you insert the right-hand needle front to back through the loop of yarn on the left-hand needle. To purl, you insert the needle back to front.

Casting on and casting off are often included in internet "How to Knit" tutorials, or you can search specifically for "Casting on" and "Casting off." The simple slip-knot casting on technique is fine for the glasses case.

The glasses case consists of a lining and an outer layer, each a rectangle about 7 inches long. The lining is a tiny bit narrower than the outer layer so it will lie smooth once the glasses case is assembled.

Cast on 22 stitches for the lining. Knit, using the stockinette stitch, until you've knitted 7 inches. Cast off. Cast on 24 stitches for the outer layer. Knit, using the stockinette stitch, until you've knitted 7 inches. Cast off.

Lay the lining on top of the outer layer, wrong sides together and with the end of the lining where you cast off aligned with the end of the outer layer where you cast off. This end will be the open end of the glasses case. (You might want to press the pieces very lightly with a steam iron to get them to lie flat.)

Pin the lining to the outer layer along this edge. Thread a yarn needle—a large needle with a large eye and a blunt tip—with more of your yarn or with one of the tails you left when you cast off. Stitch the two edges together using a whip stitch. When you finish the seam, make a knot, cut what's left of the yarn to leave a tail of a few inches, and tuck it between the lining and the outer layer.

Now pin the lining to the outer layer along the remaining three edges, making sure the edge of the lining is very slightly inside the edge of the outer layer. There is a photo of this step on my website. With a regular sewing needle and regular sewing thread in a color that blends with your yarn, stitch the lining to the outer layer around all three sides using a whip stitch.

Fold the double-layer rectangle in half the long way, making sure the outer layer is on the outside, and pin the side and the bottom. There is a photo of this step on my website. With a yarn needle and more of your yarn or with one of the tails left from casting on or off, stitch the long edge and the bottom. To make a neat seam, use a whip stitch and catch only the loops closest to the edge along each side. When you finish the seam, make a knot and work the needle in and out of the seam for an inch or so to hide the tail. Cut off what's left. There is a photo of this process on my website.

Your glasses case is complete.

NIBBLE

Pamela's Irish Whiskey Bars

As Pamela explains to Bettina and the other Knit and Nibblers when she hosts the group at her house, she wanted to celebrate St. Patrick's Day, though belatedly, by serving an Irish-themed goody. Inspired by the popularity of treacle tarts in the British Isles and my fondness for classic lemon bars, I invented this hybrid, which pairs a shortbread crust with a treacle topping to which I added a bit of Irish whiskey. The alcohol in the whiskey evaporates in the baking, but a hint of the flavor remains. I add Irish whiskey to the sweetened whipped cream I top them with as well. That alcohol doesn't evaporate and can be omitted if you wish.

For a picture of Pamela's Irish Whiskey Bars, as well as some in-progress photos, visit the Knit & Nibble Mysteries page at PeggyEhrhart.com. Click on the cover for *Irish Soda Bread Murder* and scroll down on the page that opens.

Ingredients

For the shortbread crust
1½ cups flour
⅓ cup sugar
½ tsp. baking powder
¼ tsp. salt
10 tbsp. butter, melted
1 tsp. vanilla

For the topping
3 eggs
¾ cup brown sugar
¼ tsp. salt
1 cup dark corn syrup
½ tsp. vanilla
2 tbsp. Irish whiskey
2 tbsp. melted butter

For serving
1 cup heavy cream or whipping cream
2 tsp. sugar
2 tbsp. Irish whiskey (optional)

Make the shortbread crust: Combine the dry ingredients in a medium-sized bowl and stir to mix. Add the 10 tbsp. melted butter together with the vanilla, and stir to blend. The dough will be stiff.

Turn the dough into a buttered 8" by 8" baking pan and use your hands to press it down smoothly. It should cover the bottom of the pan.

Bake it at 350 degrees for 20 minutes. It will not be brown when ready to come out.

Make the topping: Beat the eggs in a medium-sized bowl. Beat in the remaining ingredients. Pour the topping over the prepared shortbread crust and bake at 350 degrees for 50 minutes to an hour. The top should not jiggle when baking is finished, and a wooden toothpick inserted in the middle should come out clean.

Let it cool thoroughly. To remove it from the pan, cut all around the edges with a sharp knife, cut it in half, and lift each half out with a pancake turner. Use the pancake turner to make sure it is thoroughly detached from the bottom of the pan before lifting.

Cut each half into 4 bars, ending up with 8 bars for the entire recipe. It's very sweet and dense, though, so you might want to make 16 small squares instead.

Add the sugar and the whiskey, if using, to the cream and whip until the cream forms soft peaks. Serve each bar with a dollop of whipped cream.

BONUS NIBBLE

Peggy's Irish Soda Bread

I've been making soda bread on St. Patrick's Day for ages. My original recipe came from our local paper and was the classic version that calls for buttermilk. The buttermilk is acidic, and the acid reacts with the baking soda and the soda in the baking powder to form the bubbles that act as a leavening agent. Buttermilk seems to be available only in quart-sized cartons, and the recipe called for a cup, so I ended up with a lot of leftover buttermilk. One year I realized that I could get the same leavening effect with yogurt, and I've been making my soda bread with yogurt ever since. I also discovered that kneading, which resulted in very sticky, dough-covered hands, is unnecessary.

For a picture of Peggy's Irish Soda Bread, as well as some in-progress photos, visit the Knit & Nibble Mysteries page at PeggyEhrhart.com. Click on the cover for *Irish Soda Bread Murder* and scroll down on the page that opens. The reference in the directions below to photos on my website is to this page.

Ingredients
2½ cups flour
1 tsp. baking powder
½ tsp. baking soda
½ tsp. salt
5 tbsp. butter
2 tbsp. sugar

1 tbsp. caraway seeds
1 cup raisins
1 egg
1½ cup plain yogurt

Mix together flour, baking soda, baking powder, and salt in a large bowl. Cut the butter in with two knives, your fingers, or a pastry blender until the mixture resembles coarse sand. Mix in the sugar, seeds, and raisins. Beat the egg and yogurt together in a small bowl and add them to the flour mixture. Stir thoroughly.

Using a rubber spatula, turn the dough out onto a greased baking sheet. Sprinkle the dough with flour and pat it into a round, dome-shaped loaf with floured hands. Using a sharp knife, cut an X ¼ to ½ inch deep in the top to mark quarters. There are photos of these steps on my website.

Bake the soda bread at 375 degrees for 50 minutes or until it is nicely brown. It's delicious warm with butter but let it cool at least 15 minutes before slicing. Cut it into quarters first, and then slice the quarters.

MRS. CLAUS AND THE SINISTER SODA BREAD MAN

Liz Ireland

Chapter One

Wwe were still an hour and a half away from our desti-
nation, and the elves were growing impatient. Especially Butterbean, who sat in the back seat of our rented
SUV, feet protruding straight out in front of him like an
excited toddler. "Are we there yet?"

In exasperated mom fashion, Jingles swiveled peevishly
in the passenger seat. "You asked that five minutes ago."

One thing I hadn't expected before I smuggled three
elves from Santaland into Oregon was how restless they
would be. These elves weren't used to road trips, and we'd
traveled all night from the North Pole in an open-air
sleigh. After my husband, Nick—aka Santa Claus—set us
down on Mount Hood and we said our good-byes, Juniper, Jingles, Butterbean, and I snowshoed down to Tim-
berline Lodge. Not an easy trek, especially when we had to
take turns lugging Butterbean's extra-large suitcase. Once
at the lodge, we'd drunk the last of our thermos of hot
chocolate and waited for an Uber to carry us down the
mountain to the nearest rental car company. Then it was a
four-hour drive by SUV through Portland, across the
Coastal Range, and down Oregon's scenic coastal highway to Cloudberry Bay.

The only one of our party still feeling perky was Juniper.

This was her first vacation, and everything she saw delighted her. "Look at that tree!" she'd said a hundred times as we drove across the coastal range. "It's huuuge! What's it called?"

"Um . . ." I'd been looking forward to playing tour guide, but I hadn't anticipated a botanical quiz. I drew a blank. "Some kind of spruce?"

Juniper was agog at the size of the trees and flowering shrubs. The first three trees she'd pointed out, we'd stopped the car so she could take a picture. After that, she had to snap photos through the car window.

By the time we reached the coastal highway, I was pooped. I needed coffee, and my elves were in dire need of sugary carbs. Even Juniper had looked like she was starting to flag, but the sight of the Pacific Ocean put her back on enthusiasm overdrive.

"It's so big—and blue," she'd exclaimed when she first saw the endless expanse of water. "I can't wait to go swimming!"

"I don't really recommend that." The water was shockingly cold.

"I just hope there'll be enough free time to lie on the beach and get a suntan," Jingles declared.

I'd warned them that the beach in Oregon—especially in March—was more suited to long walks than sunbathing. Yet even now, when it had been overcast or drizzly all day, the elves couldn't believe that Cloudberry Bay wasn't Miami Beach.

When I'd contemplated making this quick trip to deal with an emergency at the inn I owned in Cloudberry Bay, Nick had warned me that bringing not just one but three elves to Oregon could prove problematic. Of course, *he* had been my first choice as a traveling companion. Nick was a dream to go places with, probably because he'd had so much experience with travel in the course of his job. Circling a globe once a year in an open sleigh rendered him unflappable in the face of small discomforts on short jaunts. And his normal personality was that of an organizer, a problem solver, a delegator. On this trip, his patience would have made him a perfect candidate for helping me dealing with the contractors I would need to fix up my inn.

Not to mention, I wouldn't have minded a short getaway with my husband.

Unfortunately, Nick had volunteered to be the grand marshal of this year's St. Patrick's Day parade in Christmastown. He'd even been fitted with an elaborate leprechaun suit. He simply couldn't let Santaland down just because a pipe in the kitchen of a small hotel three thousand miles away had sprung a leak. Even if it was the hotel owned by his wife, which we ran during the summer months.

Eager for company, I'd blithely batted away all arguments against substituting elves for Nick.

"Cloudberry Bay is practically a ghost town in the off season," I'd assured him. As acting Santa Claus, Nick often took what I considered an overly paternalistic attitude with elves. "They'll be fine. I bet no one even knows we're there. We'll keep a low profile."

He'd made a face. I hadn't meant that the way it sounded, and thankfully no elf was within earshot. Butterbean and Juniper were short, but Jingles was just a little shy of my height and could be touchy on the subject. "You know what I mean."

"What about that nosy neighbor of yours?"

Damaris Sproat was the eternal fly in the ointment of any activity in Cloudberry Bay. Plus she'd nursed a special resentment toward me ever since I'd inherited the Coast Inn, which she'd intended to buy for herself. She claimed she wanted it for sentimental reasons—her great-uncle had built it. But as she was the proprietor of the Pacific Breeze B&B, my guess was that she'd harbored some vision of herself as the Conrad Hilton of Cloudberry Bay.

It was an email from Damaris that had brought me down to Oregon. Earlier in the week, she'd sent me a message with the subject line **EMERGENCY!**

FYI, April: A water pipe has burst at the Coast Inn. A neighbor said it looked like Niagara Falls inside the kitchen. Assuming your slacker excuse for a caretaker had flown the coop, I had my niece, Muriel, shut off your water at the street. She also jimmied the backdoor lock and made sure there was no more water running in your kitchen. Muriel, you'll recall, is the capable girl I recommended to you instead of that Ernie character you foolishly hired. She asked me to inform you that it looks like your floors are damaged and that your house has a peculiar smell.

Sincerely,

Damaris Sproat

PS: I have brought your situation to the attention of the Cloudberry Bay town council. Flagrant water wastage carries a hefty municipal fine.

No, I didn't dare hope that I would be able to spend a week in Cloudberry Bay without having to contend with Damaris. But neither did I expect her to be dropping by for tea and cookies. Since I'd taken ownership of the Coast Inn, Damaris had never darkened its door.

"We'll have no trouble," I'd assured Nick.

Now I began to worry. For one thing, under the influence of Oreos and a Yoo-hoo bought at the gas station, Butterbean had begun singing every elf's favorite backseat song, "The Twelve Days of Christmas." By the third day of Christmas, Juniper and Jingles had been unable to resist

joining in. Year-round Christmas carols in Santaland? Totally normal.

"The Twelve Days of Christmas" in March everywhere
else in the world? Odd.

I wasn't sure my efforts to dress them like average people were working out, either. I'd bought jeans for them online in children's sizes, but they still had to be rolled up
several times at the ankles. Their new clothes looked stiff
and new—with fold creases from the packaging they'd
been delivered in—giving them the air of tiny actors at
their first dress rehearsal. They'd drawn stares from people wherever we stopped.

I cleared my throat. "Now, you understand that we're
going to have to lay low. You don't have passports or
other ID, so we can't have you being picked up for anything."

"Picked up?" Butterbean stopped singing. "Do people
here go around lifting elves?" His expression turned pan-
icky. "I'm ticklish."

"It's a euphemism for being arrested," I explained. "The
point is, try not to draw attention to yourselves."

"Don't worry, we'll blend in just fine," Jingles assured
me. For his human attire, he'd insisted on wearing a
Hawaiian shirt even though it was still around fifty degrees outside, and his new reflective sunglasses that he'd
picked up at the last gas station just added to the strange-
ness of him. He might have blended in on the Aloha deck
of *The Love Boat*, but in Cloudberry Bay he would stick
out like antlers on a snowman.

Hopefully people would just think he was clueless, not
an elf.

"Remember," I said, "if anyone asks, you're from the

north. If they ask if you're from Canada, just agree with them. And if they mention a specific place in Canada, just say you're from somewhere farther north." I added, "*Never* say the words Santaland, Christmastown, or the North Pole. No singing Christmas carols in public."

They all nodded.

"And it goes without saying," I added, "that you're not elves."

"I'm not an elf," Butterbean repeated. "I'm just Butterbean, average human being."

An average human being named Butterbean . . . "We need to think of temporary names for you, preferably with letters of your real names so they'll be easy for you to remember. Juniper's okay, but Jingles and Butterbean won't fly."

Butterbean bounced in excitement. "How about Button? I've always liked that name."

I nixed it. "Still too elfy."

He thought for a moment, then beamed. "I know—Buddy!"

I groaned. "Forget about B-U names. We'll call you Tad." I looked over at Jingles. "And you can be Jim."

Jingles made a sour face. "Seriously?"

"It's just for a little over a week." I hoped. Ten days was the bare bones minimum I calculated it would take get the inn on the way to being repaired—at least enough to hold it until Nick and I moved down for the summer season. And of course, I'd need to spend part of those ten days finding a new caretaker.

"I'm hungry," Butterbean said. "Can we stop for more snacks?"

I pulled over at the next stop. Juniper was enchanted with service stations. "These places are so cool," she said, as we stood outside, buffeted by wind both from the Pacific and from passing cars. "They sell so much. You never told me about them."

For some reason, during all my years in Santaland, I'd forgotten to wax nostalgic about highway filling stations in Oregon.

Butterbean found a box of pink snack cakes and a book called *Haunted Hotels of the Pacific Northwest*. Once we were on the road again, he devoured both with his typical single-mindedness.

"Is your inn haunted?" he asked.

"Of course not," I said.

It was on the tip of my tongue to add, "I don't believe in ghosts." But a voice in the back of my head taunted me. *Just a few years ago, you didn't believe in Santa Claus, either.* Now I was married to him and hobnobbed regularly with elves, reindeer, and snowmen.

Still, the only thing haunting my inn at the moment was a bad smell. *Mildew*, I hoped. All that water had probably left the interior dank. I put more gruesome explanations—like Ernie, my AWOL caretaker—out of my mind.

"Cloudberry Bay is going to seem very different from what you're used to," I warned. "It's a small, very quiet town. You might even find it a little boring."

Juniper was shocked. "How could this place be boring! Everything's so big and colorful. I feel like I'm in a fairy tale."

"Anyway, it doesn't matter if we have fun or not," Jingles said. "We're here to help you."

They had all volunteered to come down to give me a hand in getting my inn in some kind of order in advance of the opening of the tourist season, which luckily was still two months away.

"It sure would be scary to see a ghost," Butterbean said, almost shivering at the thought.

"You won't," I said.

"Are you sure?" he asked. "According to this book, one resident hotel ghost just moans a lot. For a long time people thought it was the refrigerator compressor."

"I haven't ever heard moaning," I said.

"Maybe you do, and you mistook it for something else. Do you have a refrigerator?"

"Everyone has a refrigerator down here."

"Imagine that!" Juniper said. "Everyone with their individual artificial ice closets."

At the North Pole, refrigeration wasn't a concern. Everyone had a cupboard or closet—at Castle Kringle it was an entire room—which just required an opening to the outdoors. That was all the cooling required.

Butterbean looked disappointed at the lack of a spook at my inn. "If you had a ghost, you could be in this book. I bet lots of people would stay there just for the thrills."

Juniper shook her head. "The Coast Inn is very successful without some phony ghost. You don't need gimmicks when you have hospitality like April offers."

I was starting to puff up with pride until I remembered that Juniper had not yet set foot in the Coast Inn. That was just her natural loyalty speaking.

I continued to try to lower expectations. "In summer, Cloudberry Bay is full of people, but right now you'll find it pretty empty. It should be easy to avoid too many people."

In the old days, I'd always liked the off season in Cloudberry Bay. But that was when it had seemed a nice respite from the busy summer season. And my friend Claire had lived in town then, running the Cloudberry Creamery, and we always had plenty of time to hang out. Now Claire had moved to Santaland and opened an ice-cream store there.

The Cloudberry Creamery was under new management. I almost dreaded driving into the empty town now.

But when the SUV finally cruised down the main drag—Cloudberry Bay was a one-strip town—the place was busy. And transformed. Green-and-white bunting festooned the light poles.

Juniper and the others gazed out the vehicle windows like kids seeing their first Christmas tree.

"Golly doodle!" Juniper exclaimed. "It's just like Christmastown."

For the off season, Cloudberry Bay *was* looking festive and bustling. I even caught sight of a few tourists wandering up and down the awning-covered walkways, peering into the windows of the stores that lined Sandpiper Street: Wicks Candle Company, the Rock Beach Bakery, the Cup and Chapter bookstore-coffeehouse, the Clothes Hanger. Claire's successor at the Cloudberry Creamery had several customers, and the Sea Otter Café was already seating people at outdoor tables. In March!

Of course, it was warm for March, but still . . .

"What's going on?" I wondered aloud. The town was usually dead this time of year.

Jingles pointed to a sign swagged over the street. CLOUDBERRY BAY ST. PATRICK'S DAY FESTIVAL, MARCH 17.

"Fun!" Butterbean had wriggled out of his seatbelt and leaned forward on the armrest between the two front seats like a golden retriever. "Can we go? I could be a leprechaun like I was for the Christmastown St. Patrick's Day festival last year."

Poor Butterbean had harbored hopes of being a leprechaun this year too—and then Nick had stolen his leprechaun thunder by being named the grandmaster of the parade.

Here, though, leprechaun was too close to elf for my comfort. "The festival's just a few days away. They probably have all the leprechauns they need by now."

"Oh, snowballs!" Butterbean said, disappointed.

The car behind me honked, startling us all. I'd become so distracted by a large boulder—was that supposed to be a Blarney Stone?—in front of the Saucy Mermaid Tavern that I'd stopped in the middle of the street. The car behind me probably thought *I* was a tourist.

I'd have to come back and take pictures to show Claire. Cloudberry Bay with tourists in March—she'd be as shocked as I was. I wasn't even aware of many Irish people in the area.

Of course, elves weren't Irish, either, but that didn't stop them from celebrating St. Patrick's Day in Santaland.

The Coast Inn was located on Plover Street, one block back from the main thoroughfare. The large two-story late Victorian with scrolled woodwork and a wraparound front porch was the largest house on the block. If its size hadn't made it stand out, its paint job would have: deep red with creamy yellow trim and gray accents. The side yard had been half paved to make room for guest parking, but the drive was shaded by a line of apple trees which were all in full bloom.

Juniper sucked in her breath. "It's so pretty!"

"Are you sure it's not haunted?" Butterbean asked, hopping out of the backseat.

"Pretty sure." Unless a poltergeist had caused the pipe to burst.

Jingles frowned as he took in the old house. "It's not very big, is it? Not a quarter the size of—"

I cut him off with a sharp look. We weren't supposed to mention Castle Kringle, or any location in Santaland. We should probably cut it out even among ourselves.

"Sorry," he said.

"Come on," I said. "We'd better see what the damage is."

How much destruction could one burst pipe cause?

A lot, it turned out.

Water had flooded the ground floor, damaging the floor-boards and soaking several rugs. The latter would have to be cleaned—or pitched. The floors required sanding and refinishing. Where was Ernie? He'd clearly been inside the house at some point since the flood—who else could have sopped up the water from the floors and left every available towel mildewing in the downstairs bathtub? I doubted Damaris's niece would have taken the trouble to mop up.

During a brief walk-through of the first floor, I envisioned dollars dancing out of my bank account like a manic chorus line shuffling off into the wings. In the front parlor, I collapsed into a wing chair, which released a cloud of dust around me.

Maybe it just wasn't practical to try to be both Mrs. Claus *and* a summer innkeeper.

Jingles sneezed. "I might be allergic to this house." He waved a hand in front of his face. "What's that smell?"

"Mildew." I frowned. "I think." It seemed sharper than mildew, with an undercurrent of livestock smell.

At least it wasn't *dead* livestock smell.

Butterbean rushed in, still bundled in his jacket and gloves. "I heard a ghost!"

At least that was one problem I could dismiss. "There are no ghosts."

"Then what was that sound?" he asked. "Like moaning."

Juniper joined us. "That was probably me, in the kitchen. There's no food except about thirty cans of tuna."

Maybe *that* was the source of the smell. Ernie must not

have been rinsing out his used cans before he put them in the recycling box.

I rubbed my hands together. "It's cold."

Naturally the elves didn't think so. They had North Pole blood running through their veins. But they couldn't resist an opportunity to cozy things up.

"I know—let's build a fire," Butterbean said. "There's a wood pile near where we parked."

I nodded my assent to this plan. A fire would make the elves feel right at home. Me too.

Jingles and Butterbean got busy, and within ten minutes a fire was blazing in the hearth—and smoke was billowing into the living room. It had been so long since I'd lived through a winter in Cloudberry Bay, the fireplaces hadn't been used much. The fire alarm blared—it seemed to be one thing in the house that was functioning well. Juniper leapt to open windows while Jingles fiddled with the flue. Meanwhile I dragged a chair over to climb up to press the OFF button on the fire alarm.

When the alarm suddenly stopped, we could hear the wail of a fire engine heading our way.

I groaned. So much for keeping a low profile. The elves were going to encounter a few locals sooner rather than later.

"Remember the script," I said.

They nodded. "We're just normal humans," Butterbean affirmed in his high-pitched voice.

Normal might be debatable. Human? I had my fingers crossed.

When a sharp knock sounded at the front door, I pulled it open and found myself face-to-face with the leaders of all the emergency services in Cloudberry Bay: Riley Vance, our chief of police, and Brandon Sides, the volunteer fire brigade's fire chief. Riley was in his blue uniform—a little tighter around the gut than it had been last time I'd seen him. Brandon was wearing a beige turnout jacket with Day-Glo yellow strips on it, matching pants, and heavy boots. He looked ready to put out the Towering Inferno.

Riley smiled—in my single days we'd played darts a few times at the Saucy Mermaid. "Didn't know you were back in town, April. We got a call from your neighbor."

I looked around Riley and Brandon and noticed several of my neighbors congregating in the street next to the fire truck and the patrol car. "It's just a stopped-up chimney," I said, loud enough for everyone to hear.

Brandon stepped inside, followed by Riley. "Stopped-up chimneys can be deadly," the fireman said.

The two men strode into the common room, nodding hello to everyone and crossing directly to the fireplace. Brandon quickly doused the smoldering fire with a spray from the extinguisher, sending more plumes of smoke and extinguisher powder into the air, and then fiddled with the flue. Riley, meanwhile, was distracted by Juniper. His eyes were bright with interest. Or maybe it was just the smoke irritating them.

Even through the smoke and extinguisher residue, I could see Juniper blushing to the roots of her hair. "Hi there," she said.

I waved my hand to clear a little of the room's smoky haze. "My friends are visiting Cloudberry Bay for the first time. This is Juniper."

Butterbean bounced on the balls of his feet. "I'm Tad!"

I hitched my clogged throat and turned to Jingles. "And this is—"

"Cosmo," Jingles interrupted, thrusting out his hand to the fireman. As they shook, I sent Jingles a raised-brow glance. *Cosmo?*

He smiled. I should have known Jim was too vanilla for him.

"Nice to meet you all," Riley said. Then he locked gazes with Juniper. "You're a little mite of a thing, aren't you?"

It was such an annoying thing to say, I barely kept myself from rolling my eyes as I looked over at Juniper, who was still tongue-tied. I worried that Riley's condescending remark about her height would make her angry, but no. She was eyeing him as if he were Prince Charming in cop clothes.

"Juniper's a librarian in the town where I live now," I said.

"You don't say!" Riley grinned as if I'd just announced that she could juggle penguins. "I love libraries."

After squinting up the chimney with a flashlight and grunting in ominous dismay, Brandon straightened. "An animal nest blocking the flue, I think. I'll go on the roof and check."

"Maybe that accounts for the peculiar smell," Riley told me. "I was going to suggest you change the litter box."

There was no litter box. I put my hands on my hips. "You picked up on that weird smell even through the smoke?"

"It's pretty strong." He wrinkled his nose. "Probably squirrels. Or raccoons."

"I hope they aren't in there now." Juniper's forehead rippled with worry lines. "They'll be smoked out of their home."

"They'll relocate," Riley assured her.

"Maybe that's the ghost I heard," Butterbean said.

The policeman drew back. "Ghost?"

"Bu—Tad is convinced that the Coast Inn is haunted," I explained. "Or should be."

Riley looked puzzled. "The last thing I want when I stay somewhere is a ghost hectoring me."

"Lots of people *like* ghosts," Butterbean informed him.

"I've got a whole book about them. We bought it at the place April called a gas station."

I winced at his mentioning gas stations as if they were an exotic idea, but Riley didn't seem to notice. He and Juniper had locked gazes again.

"You don't know what's happened to Ernie Wilson, do you?" I asked, interrupting whatever was going on with those two.

His smile faded as he swung toward me. "Is there a problem?"

"He hasn't answered my texts."

"Well, that's Ernie all over," Riley drawled. "Everybody was real surprised when you hired him as caretaker, especially with Muriel Sproat wanting the job."

Did the whole town know my business?

Stupid question. Of course they did. It was Cloudberry Bay.

Brandon clumped back in. "You've got critters, all right," he announced. "Or had them. Squirrels. You'll have to call somebody to get the nest out."

"Right," I said. "But who?"

"Martin Sproat is your best bet," Brandon replied.

Darn it. Did all roads lead to the Sproats?

As the cop and fireman were leaving, Riley turned again to Juniper. "It sure was nice to meet you. You should come down to the police station. I'll give you a tour."

"That sounds fun!" Butterbean said, as if the invitation had been directed at him.

Cheeks still pink, Juniper thanked Riley.

After they were gone, Butterbean said, "They seemed really nice."

"They sure did," Juniper agreed.

I laughed. "I think you made a conquest there, Juniper.

One hour in Cloudberry Bay, and you've caught the eye of the town's most eligible bachelor."

"I think I'm going to *really* like it here," she said.

Jingles flapped a hand in front of his face. "I don't see how you could like it until we get this place aired out." He frowned as he attempted to shove open the sash of the other living room window.

"Let me help you, *Cosmo*," I said.

He lifted his shoulders. "I wouldn't make a believable Jim."

"I'm happy as Tad," Butterbean said. "It's almost as good as Button."

Jingles and I finally forced the window up. The fresh air did help with the smoke. Unfortunately, the open windows also lowered the temperature in the house. Which was why we'd started the fire in the first place. I kicked the heat up a notch. It caused an ominous rumble from the furnace in the basement.

"I'm hungry," Butterbean said. "Could we find another gas station and get some food?"

Juniper said there was nothing but tuna in the kitchen. Elves needed more than that.

I dug in my pocket for the rental car keys and twirled them around my finger. "We'll do better than a gas station. Let's go the grocery store and stock up."

While I was there, maybe I could find some air freshener to deal with the peculiar smell.

Chapter Two

The Grocery Basket in downtown Cloudberry Bay was modest by American supermarket standards, but the size of it made the elves' jaws drop.

"Leaping lemmings!" Juniper exclaimed.

"This is three times the size of the Christmastown Cornucopia!" Butterbean added.

Jingles gave him a sharp poke. "We're not supposed to use the C word."

Butterbean shrank back with wide eyes. "I'm so sorry. It just slipped out." Straightening, he announced in an emphatic voice, "We're just regular humans. From the north."

It took me a moment to realize that we'd left Juniper behind. She'd stalled out at the cereal aisle, which she stared down with awe. She gestured at the shelves and shelves filled with rectangular boxes. "What's all this? It's so colorful!"

"Breakfast cereal," I explained in a quiet voice over the sounds of "Lost in Love" by Air Supply being piped over the loudspeakers. "It's like porridge, only dry."

"Like what I feed my rabbit?" Juniper asked. "People pellets?"

"Sort of. People really like to eat it for breakfast; some brands contain lots of sugar."

I'd said the magic word. Suddenly the elves were laser focused on cereal, combing every box in the aisle and calling out names to each other, even generic brands.

"Sugar O's!"

"Honey Bits!"

While they studied cereal boxes, I darted two aisles over to grab cleaning supplies. I was waylaid by several people I knew who wanted to say hello, ask after Nick, and tell me about the bad smell in my house. Damaris had probably been blabbing that all over town. I grabbed air fresheners, a new mop, a package of reusable cleaning cloths, and floor cleaner.

When I lugged my finds back to the cereal aisle, a woman with a cart full of groceries was eyeing the elves curiously. It didn't help that they were squabbling over the nutritional benefits of Choco-Flakes versus Apple Puffs.

"We're stocking up the inn," I explained. Not that it was any of her business.

"Oh!" Recognition dawned in her eyes. "You must be that woman who runs the Coast Inn. I heard about the fire today—and the smell."

My smile tightened. "Squirrel nest. I'm getting air freshener."

Another shopper gliding by muttered, "It's going to take more than a can of Glade to mask that smell, from what I heard."

I frowned. It wasn't *that* bad.

Was it?

While I was distracted, the elves had loaded up the cart with boxes of cereal—more than they could eat in a month, never mind a week.

"We don't need all of this," I said. "We'll be buying real food, too."

They seemed as stubborn as toddlers when it came to breakfast choices, though. Jingles held up a family-sized package of Apple Puffs. "It's got a full day's supply of vitamins and minerals."

I negotiated them down to three boxes—one choice apiece. No sooner had we compromised on this than Juniper turned and saw a display of her new friend, the toaster tart. "Mm—brown sugar cinnamon!"

I'd been primed to nix the toaster tarts, but she had me at brown sugar cinnamon. They really were the best. I dumped a family-sized box in the trolley. Then Jingles added some iced cherry.

"This stuff really should be in the candy aisle," I grumbled.

Three gazes widened in excitement. "There's a candy aisle?" Butterbean asked.

"Golly flippin' doodle!" Juniper exclaimed. "Could this place be any more amazing?"

By the time we'd navigated the center section of the store, our cart looked as if it had been filled up by sugar fiends . . . or elves. We were finally getting around to the vegetable section at the end of the store when our cart collided with another shopper's.

"I'd heard you were back in town," came the unwelcome voice of my Cloudberry Bay nemesis.

"Hello, Damaris," I said.

Damaris Sproat's appalled gaze focused on our grocery basket filled with toaster pastries, snack cakes, children's cereal, and economy packs of chocolates. I gave the woman grudging credit for not jumping back in horror. In addition to running the Pacific Breeze B&B, Damaris was the long-time leader of the Tummy Trimmers group at the Cloudberry Bay Community Center, where she also led the

Disco Fitness class. Her pipe-cleaner body was encased in Spandex, including a pair of eye-popping pants with pink and white orchids on a purple background.

She gave me a disapproving up and down. "I see you've let yourself go."

That same look had made me give up Tummy Trimmers back in the day. The last person you want weighing you in weekly is Damaris Sproat.

"Hi!" Butterbean hopped out from behind the cart, saving me from having to respond to her offensive statement. "I'm Tad!"

For a moment, Damaris eyed him with the same look of horror that she'd aimed at our economy tub of Neapolitan ice cream.

"So it's true," she said.

My blood froze. Had news of the elves already traveled around Cloudberry Bay?

Trying to hide the anxious quaver in my voice, I asked, "Is what true?"

"You've brought leprechauns."

Wrong mythical beings, Damaris.

"These are friends of mine." I looked around to introduce Jingles and Juniper, only to see them across the store in the bakery section, deep in a discussion next to a pie display.

"I'm not a leprechaun," Butterbean informed Damaris, "but in the past I've pretended to be one with great success."

Her mouth pursed even tighter. She flicked a glare at me. "You just had to do it, didn't you? Who told you?"

Told me what? "Damaris, I have no idea what you're talking about."

Her face darkened as if she believed I was being purposefully obtuse. "I have a leprechaun lined up for my soda bread table at the community center's St. Patrick's Day craft fair. Little Dee-Dee, my great-niece."

"Leprechauns on St. Patrick's Day," I said, trying not to laugh. "So novel—who could have imagined it?"

"So you're telling me it was just a coincidence?" she asked, clearly not believing it.

Juniper and Jingles rejoined us, placing two pies into the cart.

"Damaris, these are my friends—Juniper, Cosmo, and—"

"Tad!" Butterbean interjected again.

Damaris didn't look charmed. She clearly viewed them only as more potential leprechauns to outshine little Dee-Dee.

"Those are very snappy pants," Jingles remarked, clearly unsure what to make of Damaris.

"They'd look good with booties and tunics," Juniper said.

"I'll say," Butterbean agreed. "They're like flowery sausage casings!"

Damaris's eyes narrowed to slits. Taking a step forward, she poked my sternum with a long-nailed finger. "Your first day back and you just can't help trying to show me up, can you? This is just like when you, Claire, and some others ganged up on me during Thursday Night Book Club."

She was still stewing over a long-ago kerfuffle at our library's book club? "That was eight years ago."

"You formed a cabal against me."

"It wasn't a cabal. It was eight women who didn't want to spend a month reading *Atlas Shrugged*."

She sniffed. "It's a great book."

I struggled not to smile. "I've never read it."

As Damaris fumed, Butterbean piped up, "I'd love to be a leprechaun. I even have a costume."

"You do?" Jingles asked.

This was news to me, too.

"It's mid-March," Butterbean said. "I couldn't very well leave my leprechaun costume behind."

So that's why he'd packed so large a suitcase.

"Maybe you *can* be a leprechaun." I swiveled toward Damaris. "Is Heather at the community center still renting booths for the craft fair? I've got an old family soda bread recipe that I could dust off for the contest."

Her face flamed. "I knew it."

I turned my cart toward the checkout lanes. Bemused elves fell into line behind me like ducklings following a mother duck.

Damaris called after me, "I'm going to win that soda bread bakeoff."

We would see about that.

She added, "If you want to drop into Tummy Trimmers—and I assume you do—we still meet Wednesday mornings."

Call me juvenile, but in response I reached over to an end-of-row display and knocked three packages of pudding cups into my cart.

I was eager to leave quickly so that we wouldn't be stuck in line next to Damaris . . . and before the elves realized they'd skipped the cookie aisle.

"That woman was as prickly as a holly bush," Juniper said. "She seems very competitive."

Yet I was the one who'd blurted out that I was going to enter the bakeoff. Every time I came down to Cloudberry Bay, I promised myself that I wouldn't let Damaris get to me. Usually I was able to laugh at her. Today she'd caught me unawares and worked her way under my skin.

The grocery checker, Lynn, who had been with the store forever, flashed a smile at me as if I were a long-lost relation. "Hi, stranger! We weren't expecting you around here for another month or so."

"There's been trouble at the inn."

"That's right—I heard about your pipe trouble." Her bright smile dimmed. "And the smell."

I transferred an armload of cleaning products from the cart to the belt. "Hopefully this will help."

Lynn turned her smile on Jingles, who snapped open one of our reusable bags with a flourish to load up the groceries. "You've picked a fun time for a visit," she told him. "A festival in Cloudberry Bay in March. This'll be the most fun this town's seen since 730 rubber duckies washed up on shore."

The story tickled Butterbean, who jumped up on his toes, startling Lynn. She hadn't noticed him or Juniper, who were both shorter than the top of the register counter.

"Where'd all the rubber duckies come from?" Butterbean asked.

"A giant container fell off a ship from China," Lynn said.

Juniper moved to the bagging area to help Jingles. "What happened to the ducks?"

"They were distributed to everyone in Cloudberry Bay," I said. "I still have mine."

"Me too." Lynn laughed and added, "We called it 'the duck dividend.' "

With geometrical precision, Jingles managed to fit all the groceries into the back of the SUV. It would take the rest of the afternoon just to get the Coast Inn habitable— clean out the first floor and then make up four rooms for us. I usually slept in one of the two bedrooms downstairs, but in the house's current state the upstairs would probably be more comfortable.

An eerie haze still hung in the air when we returned and hauled in our groceries. Butterbean was leading us down the hallway toward the kitchen when he dug in his heels, dropped his bag, and shrieked. "Ghost!"

He whirled and plowed into Juniper, who fell back against Jingles. Luckily the latter stood firm or else we all might have toppled like dominoes. The spectral figure that had terrified Butterbean stood against a halo of light in the kitchen entrance.

"Oh for Pete's sake," I said. My prodigal caretaker did look thin and pale—not to mention a little ghostlike in the smoky gloom—but this was definitely not a ghost. It was Ernie.

"*April?* Is that you?" He sounded startled, too.

I stepped around the others and helped Butterbean to his feet while Jingles and Juniper gathered up groceries.

"What are you doing here?" Ernie asked. As if finding someone in her own house was a mystery.

The bigger mystery was where *he* had been. He looked as he always did, his lanky body swallowed in too-large jeans, T-shirt, and a gray hoodie. "Didn't you get my messages and emails?"

"Er . . . no." He glanced curiously at my companions. Ernie and I communicated by phone and text—at least, we did when he was still bothering to reply. He had no idea where exactly I lived nine months of the year and probably wouldn't have believed me even if I'd told him. "It's been a crazy few weeks around here," he said.

"I can see that. I had to hear about the burst pipe from Damaris Sproat."

"Shoot—sorry about that." He shifted feet. "I didn't have access to my phone. It got, uh, confiscated."

I laughed. "Why? Were you in jail?"

An awkward hiccup followed my question. Evidently, I'd hit the nail on the head. I groaned.

"It was just for car theft," he explained quickly.

"*Just?*"

"*I* didn't know it was stolen. It was this guy I know that did it." He dug his hands into his jeans pockets. "I thought it was weird that Deke was driving a Lexus."

I dropped the bag I was carrying onto the kitchen table. This was one of the things I didn't like about running a business: employee problems. "Did the police sort it out?"

"Yes, ma'am. A, uh, friend bailed me out and said his lawyer would tend to it."

What did "tending to" a stolen car charge entail—disproving the charge? Getting it dropped? Bribing someone?

On second thought, I didn't want to know.

I hated what I had to do, but this couldn't be put off. I'd known Ernie had had problems in the past, but his mother, Misty, who'd worked for me one summer, had sworn he'd straightened up.

Delaying the inevitable would just make things harder. I turned to the elves. "If you all can finish unloading the groceries, I need to talk to Ernie for a moment."

Alarmed, Ernie stepped forward. "I'd be glad to help with the groceries, too, Mrs. C."

"Cosmo and the others can handle it." I pointed Ernie toward the kitchen's swinging door, which connected to the dining room. I hadn't taken more than a few steps into that room, though, when I stopped, frowning. The carpet squelched under my feet.

Ernie winced. "I should've taken this rug up—sorry. We can do it right now . . ."

I stopped him. It could wait till after we'd spoken. "I think the damage has been done. I've got to hire someone to fix the floors, as well as get a plumber out here."

"I've got the pipe all sorted," he said. "Didn't you notice? I wrapped it in duct tape, and it's as good as new."

I blinked, remembering Damaris comparing the leak in the kitchen to Niagara Falls. "You *duct taped* the kitchen pipe?"

"That stuff is magic. Haven't you noticed that the water's back on?"

"That's great." As long as the duct tape held . . . which probably wouldn't be long. I took a breath for patience. "Ernie, I don't want to know what happened—"

"To the pipe?" He shook his head. "I'm not sure. It must've happened while I was, you know, in the clink. And then, when I got out and came back yesterday, there was this mess everywhere. You can look around yourself and see that I was trying to deal with it."

"I saw the bathtub full of towels."

"Exactly—that was me, cleaning up. Then today while I was out tending to other business, somebody told me there'd been a fire over here. So I knew I needed to handle it lickety split and roared over. But everything's fine, right?"

A hysterical bleat of laughter caught in my throat. "Fine? Ernie, the house is a wreck. And there's a peculiar smell."

He lifted his head as if trying to catch a scent on the air. "I don't smell anything."

I crossed my arms. "I *really* hate to do this, but I'm going to have to let you go."

"Where?" he asked.

I explained, "It's a way to say that I'm firing you."

"Well, yeah. I figured *that* was coming. The problem is, I don't have anywhere to go. Plus I gave the Salem police this address." Noting my confusion, he added, "Salem's where the car thing happened. I told them I was a long-time employee at the Coast Inn, which has a 4.5 Google review average."

"Great." Nothing like a felonious employee to bring in a stampede of customers.

I'd only fired one person before—a maid who'd gotten drunk, dressed in a guest's clothes, and passed out in their bathtub. When she sobered up, that woman had been eager to scuttle away. Ernie, on the other hand, seemed to be refusing to leave.

"It would be a humongous help to me if I could stick around here for a little bit," he said. "My stuff's here. I won't be in the way. I just need a couple of days to figure out where to go."

"What about Misty?" His mother had always been his biggest champion.

"Mom's changed the locks." He shook his head. "Talk about tough love."

This wasn't winning me to his cause. "Look, I'm sorry—"

"It wasn't on account of me that she changed them. She told me that as long as I'm hanging out with Deke, she doesn't want me to have the key to her house."

"Well, he did steal a car."

He ran a hand through his mouse-colored hair. "Believe me, I know. I was ready to kill Deke when we were arrested. I told him I didn't want anything more to do with him."

"And have you had anything more to do with him?"

His wince was as good as a confession. "It's not easy to give up on a friend, especially when he's been a loyal friend to *me*."

I sputtered. "He got you arrested."

"Well, yeah, that wasn't great," Ernie admitted, "but there's that whatchamacallit about casting the first stone."

I steeled myself. I couldn't back down. I only wished Ernie looked a little less like an anxious puppy. "I'm sorry, I just can't—"

He interrupted, "I'm getting that pipe fixed."

"You said you duct taped it," I pointed out.

He shook his head. "I mean permanently. I've called my uncle. Uncle Wyatt's an actual licensed plumber. He would have come earlier, but he's been very busy."

Plumbers usually were.

"He said he'll be over here tomorrow."

"Oh. That's . . . good." My desire to push Ernie out the door as soon as possible took a hit. I heard myself asking, "What is the stuff you mentioned having here?"

"Just boxes—a bunch of stuff I got from my aunt's house that I don't even want. You know. Junk. I just need to haul it to the dump or the thrift store, but I haven't had my truck . . ."

His transportation woes reminded me of his brush with the law, which reminded me why I needed to stand firm. "I don't think—"

"Uncle Wyatt said he'd replace the pipe for free," he added quickly. "As a favor to me."

A *free* plumber?

"Two days," I said. "After that, you'll need to clear out."

His face crinkled into a grateful smile. "Thank you, Mrs. C! You're a lifesaver! You won't even know I'm here, I promise."

As Ernie exited the dining room with a spring in his step, I made a note on the to-do list on my phone to line up an appointment in two days with the locksmith to get the locks changed.

Chapter Three

As I lay in an upstairs bedroom at the Coast Inn listening to the shifting sounds of the old frame house at night, I couldn't get comfortable. I'd never actually slept in this room, on this bed. The mattress topper was so deep that it felt like I was in a memory foam sinkhole. Was it too soft? Light from the street shone through the window, illuminating the bluebirds on the old wallpaper. The pattern had never struck me as so busy before; now I wondered why I hadn't replaced all those swooping birds.

Evidently it took a burst pipe to show me what I was putting my guests through.

An animal screeched. Was that a fox outside? I froze, listening.

From down in the driveway, a car door slammed. *What the heck?*

I tossed off the cotton quilt, crept to the window, and looked down. It was dark, and our parking area was partially obscured by the roof's eave, but I did make out the long profile of a truck.

The tops of three men's heads appeared. Ernie was there. One of the others had to be Deke Saunders; with his shock of red hair, he was hard to mistake for anyone else. The third man, as wiry as Ernie but wearing a shiny leather jacket, was totally unknown to me. Deke heaved a large box onto the tailgate and then pushed it back. He said something that caused the third man to give him a sharp shove and start gesticulating wildly. His finger pointed up to my bedroom window.

I hopped back and pivoted to where my phone was charging on the bedside table. When I flipped the cover open, the time showing was 2:43 A.M. What were they doing out there in the middle of the night?

I was just screwing up my courage to go down and ask—they really shouldn't be arguing in my parking lot while my guests and the neighbors were trying to sleep. But as I was shoving my feet into slippers, a vehicle's door slammed. Moments later, the taillights flashed red briefly as the truck braked at the edge of the drive and then peeled onto the street.

I climbed back into bed. Closed my eyes. Didn't fall asleep.

Odd pattering sounds skittered overhead. Had pinecones blown off a nearby tree? They could make a racket as they bumped their way down the steeply sloped shingled roof. Then again, maybe it was squirrels. I frowned at the old medallion light fixture in the middle of the ceiling. I hoped my resident rodents hadn't relocated from the chimney to the attic. I should check up there, but the access to the attic was a rickety pull-down ladder, which always struck me as an ER visit waiting to happen.

In addition to the locksmith, I probably needed to round up a pest control person to take a look around. Good thing Ernie had contacted his uncle the plumber. At least that was one less workman I had to scare up.

I finally drifted off sometime after that and didn't wake until the next morning when I heard the clattering of cutlery. The kitchen was situated directly below the bluebird room, and sound carried.

Once I was dressed, I hurried down to the kitchen. From the looks of things, the elves had been up and busy for several hours. Juniper was standing on the kitchen counter; Jingles was handing things up to her to place in the high cabinets. Across the room, Butterbean perched on a painted step stool to man the toaster.

A few cabinets stood open, and I took a moment to marvel at them. Pans that had been shoved willy-nilly onto shelves now stood in regimented lines like stainless steel soldiers. The glasses on the shelves were in neat rows, too—a column each for four glass sizes. I was almost reluctant to take a water glass out of the new arrangement.

"Toaster tart?" Butterbean asked me.

I shook my head and lurched for the thermos coffee pot. No one had made coffee.

"We had hot cocoa," Jingles explained apologetically.

I nodded and went about brewing a pot for myself—only to discover the shelf that previously held the coffee can had now become the toaster pastry and cereal area. The boxes, alphabetized by name, were all slipped in neatly on their sides.

Jingles opened the cabinet by the coffee pot and pointed. "We thought coffee-making supplies might be handier for you over here."

Of course. Why hadn't I done that years ago?

Jingles was a domestic ringleader par excellence.

As I waited for my coffee to brew, a quick look around the kitchen told me that shelf rearrangement wasn't the first task the elves had tackled this morning. The tiled kitchen floor sparkled, and so did the countertops. Stainless steel appliances gleamed.

"Thank you for all you've done."

"We had to do *something* while you were sleeping away the morning," Butterbean said. Then, at a raised-brow stare from Jingles, he clapped his hand over his mouth. "I didn't mean that you were being lazy."

"I know what you meant." And I *was* being lazy. "I just didn't get much sleep last night. I kept hearing noises."

"Me too," Juniper said. "I could swear I heard the patter of little feet in the attic."

Had she also heard squirrels, or something else? "It might have been the patter of big feet," I said. "Ernie was up late last night moving boxes of his things."

"That's good," Jingles said. "Closet de-cluttering is my next task."

I sank into a chair by the old chrome dinette table. "I know you came down here to help me, but you don't have to work *all* the time."

"Good." Butterbean gave a hop. "Can we go into town for ice cream? Claire asked me to see how the quality was at the Cloudberry Bay Creamery these days."

That sounded like Claire. She'd sold the Creamery and then moved to Santaland and opened the first ice-cream shop there—the Santaland Scoop. Naturally she was curious about how her successor was doing with her old business. If I ever sold the Coast Inn, I'd probably be checking its online reviews for years.

Ernie bumbled in, rubbing his red eyes. Hanging on his thin frame was an Oregon Ducks sweatshirt featuring an angry Donald Duck shaking his feathered fist.

"Good morning!" Butterbean said to him. "I like your shirt. We also have ducks up north."

Ernie blinked at him in confusion. "Well yeah, ducks are, like, all over the place. Aren't they?"

"I guess you're right," Butterbean said. "Even in—"

"Toaster tart, anyone?" I held up a box, trying to distract them both before Butterbean blurted out something he wasn't supposed to.

"Oh, brown sugar cinnamon," Ernie said. "Those are the best."

"You never told us that your home had so many local delicacies, April," Juniper said. "It's so great here!"

Ernie's brow furrowed. "Pop-Tarts are a delicacy?"

I opened the packet and dropped another two into the four-slot toaster. "I'm amazed you're up," I said, to change the subject. "You seemed busy last night."

Two dots of red appeared in his cheeks. "Deke came over."

"I saw three of you."

His eyes widened. "What were you doing—spying on me?"

"No, I just couldn't sleep, and I heard noises. I looked out the window to check it out, but it was dark, so . . ."

"Oh." He deflated as if in relief. "I'm sorry if we woke you up. We were just, uh, hauling boxes out to Victor's truck."

"Victor?"

"He's just some Russian guy I know."

"Why were you moving boxes in the middle of the night? You said you wanted to take the stuff to a thrift store. None of those are open at 2:30 in the morning."

"It was the only time Victor could spare his truck. He's got a job and is busy most days." He reached for a toaster pastry. When his sweatshirt sleeve rode up his forearm, it revealed several deep gashes in his skin, red and angry. It looked as if he'd had a close encounter with razor wire.

I gasped. "What happened there?"

He pulled the cuff of his shirt over the gashes. "Just a few scrapes. You know how it is when you're moving things. There was some broken glass poking out of one of the boxes."

That would be a drawback of loading up stuff in the moonlight, I supposed. Poor visibility could result in accidents. "Well, I guess it's just good that you've got it all done."

"I still have a few other junk boxes tucked here and there," he said anxiously, as if the boxes assured that he wouldn't be forced to leave.

Actually, it was more his uncle the plumber that kept him from being pitched out on the street.

"You should get those cuts looked at by a doctor."

"I poured alcohol on them. I'll be okay."

"You might need a tetanus shot," I said.

Juniper added, "I'm sure the town doctor would come right over and help you if we called them."

Ernie looked at her as if she were a space alien. In Santaland, Doc Honeytree made house calls all day long. The last call in Cloudberry Bay had probably taken place around 1972.

"I could drive you to a doc-in-the-box," I said.

"I'll be fine. Honestly. It's nothing." He dropped into a chair at the table and looked up at the elves on their perches on chairs and on the counter. "You all sure have gotten a lot done this morning. If you're visiting here for the first time, don't you want to walk around town or something?"

Butterbean looked excited. "I'd sure like to—and to go to the beach. I'd never seen a real beach until the drive here. Weeping walruses, the Pacific Ocean's big!"

"The biggest." Ernie's face twisted into a doubtful frown, directed at me. "Right?"

I nodded. "It is."

"Hey, get me." He grinned. "*Jeopardy!*, here I come."

I doubted he'd be dazzling quiz show audiences anytime soon, but he did make a good point. I wasn't being a good hostess to my friends, bringing them all this way and then just letting them work. They might have volunteered to help, but I should show them the sights.

After breakfast, I proposed a stroll down Sandpiper Street. Excited, the elves stopped their kitchen reorganization and hurried to get ready.

Before we left, I poked my head back in the kitchen door. Ernie still hunched over his coffee cup at the table, looking as if the weight of the world were on his shoulders. "Ernie?"

He snapped to attention. "Something wrong?"

"Have you been having trouble here with animals, by any chance?"

"Animals?" His eyes widened. "What kind of animals?"

"I'm not sure. Probably squirrels?" I nodded my head to the room down the hall. "The firemen found a nest in the chimney, and I thought I heard some in the attic last night."

"Oh." He seemed to shake his head and nod at the same time. "I haven't heard any strange sounds myself, but I'll go up there this morning and poke around."

"Thanks," I said. "If you want to wait till I get back—"

"That's okay," he said quickly. "I need to check to see if I put a box in the attic anyway, so it's no biggie."

"Be careful." I tilted a concerned glance at one of the scrapes that extended past his shirt cuff. "The pull-down ladder to get up there's not in the best shape."

"I've been up and down it several times. It's not a problem. I need something to do anyway while I'm waiting for Uncle Wyatt."

The plumber. Once that pipe was all squared away, I'd feel more confident about getting the floors back in shape.

I heard Butterbean hopping restlessly in the foyer, so I left Ernie there.

"I'd like to find a shirt like Ernie's," Butterbean said, skipping along beside me as we set out to explore Cloudberry Bay. "With a duck on it."

"That shouldn't be too difficult." Oregon Ducks-wear seemed ubiquitous in everyone's wardrobe around here.

On the way to Sandpiper Street, we had to practically tug Juniper past every yard. On her own she would have paused to inspect every flower poking out of the ground.

I hadn't meant to stop at the community center, but the activities advertised on the reader board at the end of its walkway halted Juniper and the others in their tracks. PA-RADE START ST PADDY'S RUMMAGE SALE SODA BREAD BKEOFF, the sign said.

Jingles pointed. "This must be where the soda bread competition that lady in the shiny pants mentioned is going to take place." He tipped his sunglasses to the top of his head and with a wry nod to the missing letter, he added, "Unless it's a bikeoff."

They must have run out of *A*s for the sign.

"We should sign you up," Juniper said. "Since you've got a great recipe."

"Um . . ."

One of Jingles's brows arched up knowingly. "You *don't* have a recipe."

"Anybody can make soda bread," I said. "It's just bread. Made with soda. Right? Maybe with some currants thrown in." I frowned. "Or is it raisins that should be in soda bread?"

Heather, who managed the community center, must have seen me through a window. Waving a clipboard, she sailed out the front doors.

"Here's your registration form," she said.

Confused, I looked at the paper flapping in the breeze. "For?"

"Damaris said you're going to be in the soda bread contest." At the mention of her name, I noticed the insistent thump of the Bee Gees' "Night Fever" coming from inside the community center. Disco Fitness must be underway.

Heather smiled at my companions. "And these must be the little friends Damaris was telling everyone about."

Great. I could see Jingles's hackles raise at the "little" description, so I leapt in to make introductions, then started filling out the form. Why not? What did I have to lose?

Heather's glance settled on Juniper. "You know, the Cloudberry Bay Folk Dance Divas are looking for someone else to be on their float."

Juniper smiled. "You mean—me?"

"I don't see why not."

"But I don't know how to dance."

Heather laughed. "Between you and me and the lamppost, neither do they. Mostly they get together and hop around a little until they're ready to go to the Saucy Mermaid."

"That sounds like fun!" Juniper said.

"Great—I'll tell them to expect you at rehearsal tonight. They'll have an extra lady leprechaun costume for you." She lowered her voice and explained to me, "Judy Kaufman's back went out on her again."

"Can I come, too?" Butterbean asked.

"It's an all-woman group. *Lady* leprechauns."

"I don't mind," he said. "And I have my own outfit."

"You do?" Heather smiled. "Well, in that case, I'll tell them to expect you both tonight at seven. They meet right here."

Cloudberry Bay was a friendly place, but evidently never so friendly as when it needed leprechauns.

"That'll be five dollars, April," Heather informed me as she took the clipboard back. "For the bakeoff registration fee."

"Oh." I hadn't read the fine print. I fished a five out of my purse.

Butterbean pointed across the street, to Second Chances on Sandpiper. "Look, there's a store that sells clothing. Maybe they'll have a duck sweatshirt."

It wasn't a bad idea to look for some extra clothes for the elves—and ones that were worn in a little might help them blend in a little better. We went inside, and the elves were soon grabbing garments off racks right and left. Jingles found more Hawaiian shirts, Butterbean managed to nab a child-sized Oregon Ducks hoodie just like he'd wanted, and Juniper found enough for a whole new wardrobe, never mind a single week.

I needed to hit the bank. It was all the way across town—five whole blocks.

Loaded with their purchases, the elves gaped around them as we walked down the sidewalk along Sandpiper. I was catching their enthusiasm. After a long winter at the North Pole, my eyes were still getting used to the explosion of color around me. Fruit trees' buds were just beginning to open up, their blooms peeking out in pink and white. Flowers were everywhere: the hardiest pansies that had survived the winter and all the bulb flowers—daffodils, anemones, ranunculus. And then there was all the green—grass and evergreen and new green leaves.

And of course there were colorful decorations for St. Patrick's Day everywhere: streamers and balloons shaped like shamrocks and shamrock lights. Not to mention, some merchants displayed planters of actual shamrocks. Cutouts of leprechauns appeared in a lot of windows, and the Antique Attic had decked out its old garden gnomes with velvet leprechaun hats and coats.

The elves took it all in, and the citizens of Cloudberry Bay took in the elves. Outside the Cloudberry Creamery, we stopped so I could take a picture of Butterbean in front of Claire's former business. Butterbean—Claire's employee at the Santaland Scoop—leaned against her old cutout of a smiling anthropomorphic ice-cream cone. The new owners had touched up the paint, but otherwise it was the same.

Riley Vance spotted us and strolled over to talk to Juniper. "You might have heard that we're having a parade this week," he said to her.

She laughed. "We figured that out."

There were signs advertising the parade in every shop window.

"The police won't have an actual float, but we're going to drive our new police vehicle. We could use a leprechaun. You could ride on the hood."

And how many traffic laws would that break? I wondered.

"You're too late," Juniper answered with a little disappointment in her voice. "I'm going to appear with the Folk Dance group on theirs."

"*I* could be your leprechaun," Butterbean volunteered. "I was going to be in the one back home, but then they picked San—"

Jingles gave him a quick jab. "You're going to be on the Folk Dance float, too," he reminded him.

Butterbean looked even more disappointed than Riley. "Oh, snowballs! I forgot."

The policeman extended his leprechaun offer to Jingles. Jingles either resented being designated leprechaun material or didn't appreciate being the last to be asked. He gave the offer an unequivocal no. "I think I'll be needed to help someone stress-baking soda bread that day," he told him, nodding at me.

"Maybe I can do both," Butterbean said. "If the vehicles are far enough apart, I'll just dance on the first float, then run back and hop on your vehicle."

Riley smiled. "Perfect. You know where to find us. The police station's just one building down on Tufted Puffin Way."

Juniper watched him wistfully as he walked away. "He's very nice, isn't he?"

I grunted in half-hearted agreement. A suspicion was taking root that his interest in Juniper had been more about her resemblance to a leprechaun than anything else.

"Can we get going?" Jingles asked impatiently. "I'm still hoping to find some beachwear today."

It was on the tip of my tongue to tell him again that March wasn't exactly beach season on the Oregon coast. On the other hand, to a Santaland elf, anything above forty degrees Fahrenheit is practically tropical.

"We should keep moving," I agreed. "Any more leprechaun offers and Tad here will be as overbooked as an airliner during spring break week."

But it was hard to get far in Cloudberry Bay without being stopped by old friends. Ted Lucas, who owned the Saucy Mermaid Tavern, came out to greet me. "Hey there, April. Care to kiss my Blarney Stone?" He gestured to the large stone-like construct blocking half the sidewalk.

"I'm surprised Riley hasn't ticketed you for obstructing a public walkway."

"It's a civic attraction," he said. "How many towns around here have a Blarney Stone?"

I doubted the real stone looked anything like this big

fake boulder. It looked even less rocklike close up than it had from a car window. "What is this thing made of?" I tapped it, and the rock responded with a hollow sound.

"Papier-mâché around chicken wire," Ted said. "My girl-friend made it for me."

"And you think this will bring in customers?" I asked.

He laughed. "Well, I've also got a pot of gold contest going. You should come in and play. Guess how many gold coin candies are in the jar, and you could win free beer for a month."

"Now you're talking," I said. "I'll stop in sometime."

After we'd been to the bank and poked into more stores—and spent more money—I was eager to get back to the inn to see if Uncle Wyatt had shown up to replace the pipe.

When we arrived back at the Coast Inn, however, the pipe in the kitchen was still wrapped in silver duct tape. This was not good. Ernie was there and looked almost frantic at my arrival. The kitchen smelled like tuna.

"I talked to my Uncle Wyatt," he said, before I could start in on him about the pipe. "He had an emergency to deal with today, but I emailed him a picture and he told me what he needed to fix it." He looked at his watch. "Anyway, I'd better run out to the hardware store and get what he'll need before they close."

In the next moment, he was out the door.

Juniper and Butterbean were very excited about their dance rehearsal. To distract them and to give me a chance to show them around a little more, we piled into the car and drove to a little burger joint on the coastal highway. Even though the temperature was only fifty, the elves de-clared it warm enough to eat outside. I huddled in my jacket.

We ate, and then Jingles and Butterbean went inside to

play at an ancient foosball table they'd seen inside. I was getting up to join them when Juniper stopped me.

"Did you really fire Ernie?" she asked.

"I think so." I laughed. "It didn't seem to take, though."

"So you're going to be looking for another caretaker."

"Do you have any suggestions?" I asked, joking.

"Yes—me." And I could tell by her voice that she wasn't joking.

Pain clutched at my chest. "You want to stay here and not return to"—I lowered my voice—"You Know Where?"

She nodded. "I love Cloudberry Bay."

"You just got here."

"It's so different—and the people are all so friendly."

"Sure, but . . . what about your home and your family?" *What about* me? I almost added. I couldn't imagine Christmastown without Juniper. It would be a much less sparkly place without her.

"I've been there forever."

"Of course you have. It's your home."

"*You* changed your life," she pointed out. "Why can't I?"

"I fell in love with Nick."

"Maybe I'll fall in love, too. Or maybe I'll just fall in love with the place. Isn't that enough?"

It might have been, except for one thing. I hesitated to mention it, but how could I not?

"But you're . . . you know." *An elf.*

She shrugged. "There's got to be some way to make it work. Fake IDs or something?"

Ernie would probably know where to get one of those, I thought.

She sent me a pleading look. "At least think about it. I'm very responsible."

She would definitely be an upgrade. But I would miss her like crazy eight months of the year, while I was in

Santaland and she was here. Should I let that color my decision?

Before I could decide, Butterbean came bounding out of the restaurant. "Time for rehearsal!"

It wasn't really, but elves like to arrive places early, and be prepared.

I drove back into town and dropped Butterbean and Juniper at the community center. Then Jingles and I returned to the inn. Ernie wasn't back yet.

A strange yowl nearby curdled my blood. Jingles and I swiveled toward each other, shock and fear in our faces.

"Was that inside the house?" he asked, a tremor of fear in his voice.

"I don't know." The yowl had sounded like the wild animal I'd heard last night. But closer.

Much closer.

Maybe it *was* inside the house.

I grabbed a heavy-duty flashlight from the toolbox and screwed up my courage. In an emergency, the flashlight could double as a weapon. "I'll go look."

I headed upstairs, feeling wobbly. Whatever animal that had been, it sounded distressed. I hoped there wasn't some awful wounded-wildlife scenario unfolding somewhere in the house. I hated to see animals in pain.

A creak on the stairs nearly sent me shooting out of my own skin. Then I turned and realized that it was Jingles, close behind me. "I thought you might need reinforcements."

He wasn't wrong about that, but I was pretty sure the real reason he was following me was that he didn't want to be alone in the event that the wild animal wasn't where I thought it was. I noticed he'd grabbed a can of WD-40 from the cabinet by the utility sink. "Do you intend on lubricating whatever it is into submission?"

"I wouldn't want the stuff sprayed on me, would you?"

Fair enough.

At the top of the stairs, I took a few steps down the hallway and aimed the beam of my flashlight at the cord that pulled down the staircase to the upstairs. Jingles and I tilted our heads.

"Was that a growl?" he whispered.

I felt a gnawing in the pit of my stomach. "I'll go up and take a look."

He jutted out an arm to stop me. "No, I'll go."

"It's my house," I said.

"But you're Mrs. Claus." When I shot him a warning look, he continued, "There's nobody here but us and whatever's up there. For all I know, it's a Sasquatch. If I let you go up and face it alone and something happened to you, how would I explain that to Santa?"

YEEEEEOOOOOW!

Jingles and I both jumped.

Whatever it was, it sounded ferocious. Jingles gulped and traded his can for my flashlight. "I'll go," he repeated bravely.

We pulled the ladder down. A pungent blast of that very bad smell wafted down at us—a sharp animal odor, plus tuna, on top of musty attic smell. Above, something scurried across the plank attic floor. It had been a long time since I'd been up there. As Jingle climbed the rungs, I tried to remember what the space looked like. I know I had a couple of plastic tubs of Christmas decorations piled up and a steamer trunk. There was also an old ping-pong table lying on its side. It had been left there by former owners, and I'd never been able to understand how to remove the table through the small trap door.

Jingles reached the top rung and shone the light into the attic. Something hissed. "Ah."

Beneath him, I asked, "What is it?"

"Cats. Two of them. No wonder my eyes have been so itchy."

Cats? That was all? "What are they doing up here?"

"Not sure. They looked scared."

I heard another hiss.

"And maybe a little ferocious," Jingles added uncertainly.

After he shone his beam around to check the corners to make sure there wasn't a Sasquatch hidden behind the ping-pong table, he climbed the rest of the way up. I followed and pulled the chain on the center light, which was nothing but a bare bulb.

Hovering near some old pink insulation were two cats. They weren't too much larger than house cats, but their black-on-brown tortoiseshell markings were striking, and their big round eyes had the frantic look of wild animals trapped in a domestic world.

"Hey, kitties," I said.

Their response was to press into each other, backs arched, eyes wide, and release another yowl of warning. Then I noticed one of their tails swishing menacingly. It was abnormally long, and bristling.

"If they're just cats," Jingles said, "can't we just shoo them outside? That's what I do with Lynxie."

Lynxie was my sister-in-law Lucia's cat. A house cat-lynx cross, Lynxie was one of those ornery, spitty hellcats that loved to ambush you and sink its teeth into your shin for entertainment. Staring into the wild round eyes of this pair, taking in their flat ears and exotic, marbled coats, I doubted they were even as tame as Lynxie. Small as they were, they looked as if they were sizing us up the way a pair of lions might size up a zebra herd.

Surreptitiously, I removed my phone from my pocket and snapped a photo of the crouched pair. At the flash of light and click, they let out outraged yowls and leapt forward, claws bared.

Yelping, Jingles and I hopped back and then scrambled down faster than I would have thought possible. We hit that ladder like Batman and Robin on the bat pole. Once we thumped down on the second-floor landing, I folded the ladder and pushed the trap door closed.

These weren't animals we could just shoo into the yard to find their way home. These were strange, wild creatures. But where had they come from?

"I think we may have a problem."

Chapter Four

"Have you found it yet?" Jingles asked Juniper. We were all hovering around the desk of the Coast Inn's small reception office. When Juniper and Butterbean had come back from dancing practice, I told them about the cats in the attic. Which were still in the attic, of course. I didn't know what to do with them. Ernie still hadn't returned.

Juniper, a librarian through and through, went into research mode and suggested an internet search. "Before you can figure out what to do, we need to figure out what they are."

I showed her the disappointingly blurry photo I'd taken, and Jingles and I described the animals as best we could. I didn't want to open that attic door again, and I especially didn't want to send Juniper or Butterbean up there. The cats were small, but so were the elves.

Butterbean sat in a corner chair, mainlining Cocoa Crunchies cereal straight from the box. Dancing had given him even more of an appetite than usual. "What if those cats are really ghost cats?"

I leveled a skeptical look on him.

While Juniper was tapping her inner librarian, he was

channeling P.T. Barnum. "You might not believe in ghosts, but I bet you'd believe in the big profit that could be made when you combine ghosts and exotic zoo animals. How many innkeepers do that?"

"We don't even know that the cats are—"

"*Marbled cats!*" Triumphant, Juniper swiveled the computer monitor in our direction. "Look."

I leaned in and squinted at the screen. The photos of the cats *did* look like the ones I'd seen upstairs. I tapped my phone and compared the picture on the small screen to the one on the monitor. Same round ears, long tail, and black stripes on its head. Its back showed elaborate markings like you'd expect to see on an exotic snake.

"Their range is from the eastern Himalayas to Southeast Asia," Juniper said. "They're highly endangered."

"How did they end up here?" I wondered aloud.

But of course I knew. Two exotic cats didn't just walk across the Pacific Ocean and decide to settle at my inn. Someone had smuggled them in, and the only candidate for that had to be Ernie. But why would Ernie do such a thing?

"Maybe Ernie's just keeping them for a friend," Butterbean suggested. "Some wildlife enthusiast."

I shook my head. Ernie had been trying to keep the cats under wraps. That screamed illegal activity to me.

Juniper groaned at something on the screen. "Last week there was a story about the Pacific Coast Zoo missing a pair of marbled cats. The zookeepers call them Tiny and Peepers."

I sighed. Somehow, I still wanted to give Ernie a break. For Misty's sake, if not for his own. But this was straight-up theft. Ludlow Cumberland, the zoo director interviewed in an online news article about the theft, had expressed concern that the average person wouldn't know how to care for and feed the endangered cats.

I thought about the many cans of tuna that the animals must have been living on for the past . . . how long? Days? That couldn't be the diet Tiny and Peepers were used to. I doubted there was a lot of tuna swimming around in the Himalayas.

Hopefully they would manage to stay alive until I could turn them back over to the zoo. I leaned toward the screen. "Can you go to the zoo's website and see if there's contact information for Ludlow Cumberland?"

Juniper did. Ludlow Cumberland didn't have a separate email listed, but there was a general phone number and a *Contact Us!* form. I sat down at the desk, but my hands hesitated over the keyboard. Should I just go ahead and throw Ernie under the bus? He could get in a lot of trouble. Kidnapping an exotic species was probably a federal offense. For all I knew, it was an international offense. A word in the wrong ear might have Interpol knocking on our door.

Or did that only happen in movies?

Convincing Ludlow Cumberland that Ernie was the only one living here involved in the marbled cat theft might be tricky. The zoo director—or the police—might want to question everybody in the house. I glanced at Jingles, Juniper, then Butterbean. No telling how they would hold up to even gentle questioning. And what if the police asked for ID? I'd have three undocumented elves to explain to the authorities.

Juniper, as usual, tried to put a positive spin on the situation. "Maybe Ernie was just trying to *help* the cats."

I couldn't imagine in what world that would be possible, but I didn't possess an optimistic elf brain.

"That's right," Butterbean said. "He might have gone to the zoo and discovered someone mistreating the cats. What at first glance looks like cat theft might actually be cat rescue!"

Juniper's brow pinched. "I'd hate to think that anyone would hurt a helpless animal."

"Helpless?" Jingles crossed his arms. "If you'd had those cats hissing at you, you wouldn't call them that. Their claws looked like little razor blades."

I thought about the cuts I'd seen on Ernie's arms. I should have known then that something was up.

Where was Ernie now? He wasn't answering the phone or text messages I left for him. Surely they gave him back his phone when they released him from jail?

Maybe he was just avoiding me. Given that he was hiding exotic wild animals in my attic, I could understand his not wanting to face me. But he had no way of knowing that I'd found Tiny and Peepers.

"I'll call the zoo in the morning," I said.

That would allow Ernie a chance to show himself and explain what he was doing with two contraband cats. It would also give me much-needed time to think about how I would explain my contraband elves.

I spent a restless night—my second in a row—worrying. About the cats. About Juniper leaving Santaland. About not calling the zoo right away.

How could I rationalize waiting so long to call the zoo to tell them about the whereabouts of Tiny and Peepers? Of course, I could always say that I'd discovered them right before contacting the zoo, but that would be a lie and I'm a terrible liar. Plus, the zoo officials would find my not knowing the cats were in the house hard to believe. *I* found it hard to believe, given the clues I'd had. The sounds coming from above, the smell . . .

All of Cloudberry Bay would be able to testify that I'd known about the smell.

When Ernie didn't appear the next morning, I assumed he must have guessed that the jig was up and taken off. For Misty's sake I didn't want anything terrible to happen to him, but I had to alert the zoo that the cats had been found.

I was expecting Ludlow Cumberland to be a gruff official. My imagination had been conjuring up visions of an angry administrator who would summon a fleet of law enforcement officers to my door. I had nightmares of black helicopters hovering over the Coast Inn and footage of all of us being frog-marched into police vans on the evening news.

In reality, Ludlow Cumberland sounded more relieved than angry. "Are they all right?" he asked after gushing out a sigh.

"Yes." I had to backtrack. "That is, I believe they are. I only saw them once. I didn't get close enough to handle them."

"Very wise, Mrs. . . . ."

"Claus. April Claus." An awkward pause ensued, and I explained quickly, "It's my married name."

He laughed. "At least your husband's name wasn't Showers." When I didn't join in his mirth, there was laughter. "Get it? Then you'd be April Showers."

I let out a listless chuckle. Was this humor schtick a way to soften the blow that I would soon be in federal lockup for theft of an endangered species? "The cats are safely housed in my attic now," I assured him. "I just returned here to Cloudberry Bay to open up my inn for the season, and I heard them up there. They gave me quite a fright. I was expecting squirrels."

"I can well imagine. You did right in calling me. Leave the cats where they are, and I will be there to pick them up soon."

"*You'll* be picking them up?" Not the police, then.

"Tiny and Peepers are my responsibility."

I sagged with relief. No black helicopters. No mentions of filing federal charges.

No having to explain the presence of undocumented elves.

"Thank you. I'll be very happy when they're back where they should be."

"Believe me, Mrs. Claus, so will I." He lowered his voice. "And if I may, I'd like to ask you to keep the news of what happened confidential between us for now. By confidential, I mean out of the newspapers. Don't even tell your neighbors if you can help it."

"Of course." No one could be more eager to keep this story out of the newspapers than I was. Except Ernie, perhaps.

"We'll inform the public in due time, when we've examined the animals and are satisfied that they're in good health."

Please let them be in good health.

"The catnapping has already had negative repercussions for our zoo," he continued. "There's been an outpouring of concern, but donations are down."

"The media won't hear about this from me," I promised, "but wouldn't letting the public know they've been found be a good PR story for the zoo?"

"You would think. Unfortunately, all the public—and

our corporate patrons—will remember from this incident is *zoo lost, lost, lost.*"

He had a point. People loved good news, but it was the bad stuff that tended to stick in their minds.

By the time I'd given him directions to the inn and hung up, I was convinced the whole incident would turn out all right.

There was just one hitch: I didn't want Juniper, Jingles, and Butterbean around when Ludlow Cumberland came to collect his cats. They were completely innocent in all of this, but I wasn't sure it would appear that way to an out-sider. I could defend myself, but I didn't want a cloud of suspicion to fall over my friends in a country that was strange to them.

When I emerged from the office, the elves were working on cleaning out a cluttered downstairs closet in advance of the floor work that would inevitably need to be done. They had stacked a few boxes up in the hallway.

"These boxes must be Ernie's," Jingles said.

"He said he wanted to donate them to the rummage sale." I toed one of them. It didn't budge.

"We could take them over there for him, couldn't we?" Juniper asked.

It wasn't a bad idea. For one thing, I wanted the elves out of the house when Ludlow Cumberland showed up. "I guess so. And afterwards, you can go swimming."

Jingles twisted from removing coats from the hanging rod inside the closet. "Where will you be?"

"I have to wait here for the head of the zoo to come pick up Tiny and Peepers."

"We can't go to the beach without you," Juniper said. "It wouldn't be the same."

Butterbean nodded. "You'll miss out on all the fun."

"And you won't be able to get a tan," Jingles said.

I didn't want to discourage them, but no one would be getting a suntan in Oregon in March.

It took a little more arguing to convince them that they could have a good time without me. When the SUV was loaded with Ernie's boxes and the elves were in beachwear, I drove to the community center. Jingles helped me carry the boxes inside while Juniper and Butterbean remained in the backseat, blowing up a beach ball and other inflatables they'd found in town. I couldn't help noticing that Jingles drew stares. Why not? Of the three friends with me, he might be the least elfy in his appearance, but his mirrored shades, Hawaiian shirt, and striped shorts made him look like something out of a psychedelic 1960s beach movie.

Back in the car, I reiterated to the elves that they needed to maintain their cover even while they were at the beach. "Even when you're just with each other, don't slip and use your Santaland names."

"Except me," Juniper said.

"Right."

"I'm Tad," Butterbean said. "I'm not an elf. Not an elf."

"Don't mention Santaland," I reminded them. "Or even Santa."

"You don't have to worry," Juniper told me. "Nobody's looking at us as if we might be elves."

True. The town was too busy looking at them as possible leprechauns.

Jingles narrowed his eyes at me. "Is everything okay?"

"Of course," I said. "I'm just a little jumpy about the marbled cat handoff." Also, I wished I knew where Ernie was.

"It'll be fine," Juniper assured me. "You said yourself that Mr. Cumberland seemed like a nice person."

Under the circumstances, maybe *too* nice. Is that why I had this creeping sense of dread, like this was all an elaborate sting operation that I was about to be trapped in?

I dropped them off at the beach—with advice not to go in the water, which would be beyond frigid. Even if they didn't feel the cold as acutely as humans did, it might seem weird to onlookers. Though of course the beach was deserted. The tourists in town this week were all there to stroll through the shops, drink green beer, and kiss the papier-mâché Blarney Stone. No local would hang out on the beach in March. At least not like the elves obviously planned to do, lying on towels and playing with beach balls as if this were Waikiki.

I drove directly back to the Coast Inn to wait for the zookeeper. When I got there, Ernie had returned.

"Oh hey, Mrs. C," he said casually. As if there weren't contraband cats in the attic.

And I'd been worried about him.

"Ernie, we need to have a talk."

"I know—my two days are almost up. I've just come to clear out the last of my stuff."

"There's not as much to clear out as there was," I informed him, my voice now tight with irritation. "And there will be even less after Mr. Cumberland from the Pacific Coast Zoo arrives to take his animals back."

"The zoo?" Ernie's face went white. "Cumberland? Why . . . ?"

"I found the two marbled cats you were hiding in the attic. I tried to call you, but you never responded to my messages. So I contacted the zoo."

"When's he getting here?"

I looked at my watch. It was still just 10:30. "He said between eleven and noon."

He ran a hand through his hair. "I'm sorry. I didn't mean to get you involved in all of this."

I bit out something between a sigh and a ragged laugh. "You were hiding stolen exotic animals in my house."

"But you weren't here," he said, as if that excused anything. "And *I* didn't steal them—you have to believe that."

"Just like you didn't steal the Lexus? You have a knack for getting inadvertently involved in criminal activity."

"I'm unlucky, that's for sure. But I didn't mean for my bad luck to wear off on you. I'm sorry. If I hadn't ended up in jail, I never would have . . ." His words trailed off, and he shuddered.

"Ernie, I didn't give the director of the zoo your name. Not yet. I wanted to hear from you first. But if the police do any kind of investigation—"

"The police?" His eyes widened. "Are they going to be here, too?"

"That depends on whether Mr. Cumberland wants to file charges. For your mom's sake, I don't want to bring more trouble down on you, but I'm angry that you involved my property in this criminal scheme."

"It wasn't like what you think."

"I don't want to hear the explanation or more excuses. It doesn't really matter. I'm not going to take the blame for your criminal actions."

He shook his head in frustration. "Well, never mind. I'll grab the last of my things and get out of your hair."

"That's one thing you don't have to worry about. They're gone."

"Gone?" He blinked in alarm. "You mean the cats?"

"No, your things. The boxes. Cosmo and Tad were cleaning out the hall closet this morning. We hauled your boxes to the rummage sale for you."

He froze.

"You did say you intended to donate the stuff," I reminded him.

"Well, yeah, but I probably should've double-checked what was in the boxes first." His leg started to jiggle nervously. "Just at the community center, you said?"

I nodded. "The sale's on St. Patrick's Day. It's going to be huge. You should see the boxes piled up over there. There's not room for it all."

"That's good." He backed toward the front door. "Sure. Why not? It's as good a place as any."

"The proceeds go to charity."

"Great." He was almost to the door now. "I should probably go. Uncle Wyatt says he should be able to get to the repair soon. I'll check back with you later."

Later probably meant after Ludlow Cumberland had come and gone.

I went to the kitchen, ate my second Pop-Tart of the morning, and contemplated how much trouble I was in. Then I picked up my phone and speed-dialed Nick.

"Castle Kringle Sleigh Taxi Service," he answered, deadpan. "Do you require assistance?"

I laughed. "Don't worry. I won't need your services for another week—I hope."

I filled him in regarding the doings in Cloudberry Bay so far—big and small, legal and illegal. It was only fair to warn him that he might need to come bail me out, or at least smuggle the elves back to Santaland and safety.

For some reason, out of all the travails I related, one detail jumped out at him. "Have you ever baked soda bread?" he asked me.

Really? That's what worried him? That was a sign of how accustomed we were to chaos.

Or how wrong my baking projects could go.

"No, I haven't," I said, "but it's not that hard."

"If you haven't ever made it, how do you know?"

"I looked up a recipe online." I tried not to take offense at his lack of faith in my baking prowess. In Santaland I'd acquired the reputation—unfairly, I thought—for kitchen mishaps.

I cut off any further interrogation about my soda bread plans with a reminder of the more perilous situation. "Stolen exotic cats in the attic, Nick. My attic. The only thing standing between me and federal lockup is the generosity of Ludlow Cumberland, which I'm not certain I can rely on." I drummed my fingers. "Maybe I should be baking something for him."

"Don't do that," Nick said quickly.

"What would you recommend instead?"

"Be apologetic and cooperative," he advised. "And if that fails, throw Ernie under the bus."

I nodded. We were on the same wavelength.

A text came in on my phone. I looked down. It was a strange number, but the message was from Jingles. Well, Cosmo.

Stranded at a gas station. Can you pick us up? Cosmo.

"Nick, I have to go. Elf emergency."

"Anything serious?"

"I'm guessing Butterbean had a snack attack."

I signed off and answered the text.

Where?

Dots pulsed while he typed the answer.

On the highway just this side of Florence.

What? How had they gotten all the way over there—by hitchhiking? I didn't want to imagine.

Hold tight. Will be there in twenty minutes.

It was actually more like thirty minutes away, but I was going to gun it.

As I was rushing out the door, I hesitated. It was going on eleven o'clock right now. What if I missed Ludlow Cumberland while I was out?

If those cats were as important to him as all that, he wouldn't mind waiting an hour. Still, I scribbled a note.

Unforeseen emergency. Back soon. You have my number.

I folded the note, wrote *Ludlow Cumberland* across the front, and stuck it between the door and the doorjamb.

My brain was so bent on rescue, it wasn't until I was almost to Florence that questions started to crowd in. How had the elves reached another town? Whose phone had Jingles borrowed to text me?

And then, when I reached the gas station I assumed he meant, there were no elves.

I texted him again.

Where are you?

No pulsing dots this time. No response at all.

I read back over Jingles's messages. He'd identified himself as Cosmo. It was weird that he ID'd himself at all, except that he was using either a new phone or someone else's phone. But would he have called himself Cosmo in a private text to me?

Probably not.

I should have noticed the signature right away.

What the heck was going on? Had my friends been elf-napped?

Heart thumping in my chest, I looped around the three gas stations in town and then raced back to Cloudberry Bay. It didn't matter if the elves had documents or not. If someone had kidnapped them, I would have to go to the police. Maybe I could cut a deal with Riley Vance: free accommodations for visiting friends and family in exchange for not turning over my elves to Immigration. As I hit the Cloudberry Bay city limits, I was even considering just handing him the keys to the inn. I would make any bargain to get Juniper, Jingles, and Butterbean back safe.

And then, as I pulled onto Plover Street, I spotted Jingles and Butterbean. But no Juniper. Jingles was twirling the beach ball on his index finger, and Butterbean walked beside him with an inflatable seahorse around his waist. I slammed on the brakes and lowered the window.

"Where is Juniper?"

Jingles lifted his shoulders. "She said she had to run an errand."

I didn't like this. I looked down at my phone. She had not tried to contact me.

Butterbean tilted his head. "Did everything go okay with Mr. Cumberland?"

"He hasn't shown up yet."

"Where have you been?" Jingles asked.

On a wild elf chase, I thought. "Get in. Something very hinky's going on here."

The elves piled into the car, bringing with them the overpowering scent of coconut tanning lotion. I sped to the inn, explaining what had happened as best as I could in the time it took to drive two blocks.

"Did Juniper say where this errand was?"

The two elves shook their heads.

"She didn't receive a mysterious phone call or message?"

"Not that I know of," Jingles said. "But I'm not her keeper."

No, I should have been. Anything that happened to the elves here would be my fault.

As I pulled into the drive, I got a glimpse of the inn's door ajar, which was odd but made me hopeful. Maybe Juniper had just run back to the inn for something. Or maybe Ernie was back and had propped it open. For all I knew, he still had boxes cached away. Maybe he and Juniper were both here.

But when we stepped onto the inn's porch, what was propping the door open became clear. It was a body. A lifeless one.

Chapter Five

"Who is that?" Jingles asked.

The body was face down just inside the foyer, but I didn't have to turn him over to know his identity.

"It's Deke." That red hair was as sure an ID as his driver's license would have been. "Deke Saunders. He's Ernie's friend."

"But why did he die in our foyer?" Jingles asked.

Just then, footsteps sounded on the porch. Juniper stopped at the doormat, her face white as she looked down at the Deke. "Who is *that*?"

I explained, then added, "Where have you been?"

"I just had to go somewhere." Unable to take her eyes off the man on the floor, she swallowed with obvious difficulty. "Do you think he died from natural causes?"

A hysterical laugh threatened to bubble out of me. Don't get me wrong. Nothing about this was funny. But only Juniper, with her determined optimism, could overlook the fact that there were two gashes in the back of Deke's blood-soaked denim jacket. There was also blood across the hall floor. Deke had been on his way *out*. Probably attempting to escape from whoever did this to him.

Jingles followed the path of my gaze, taking in the gruesome trail of blood. "Good thing we were already planning to get these hardwoods refinished."

I didn't care about the floors. "I just want to know how this could have happened."

"With a knife." Butterbean rocked sagely on his feet. "Or something sharp."

"Murder." Juniper shuddered. "How did your cozy inn turn into such a hotbed of crime?"

I got out my phone. I would have to call Riley Vance. But what was I going to say?

And what had happened to Ludlow Cumberland?

The cats. Hopscotching across the bloodstains, I scurried up the stairs. On the second floor, the ladder was down so that the door to the attic gaped like an open maw. I knew it was hopeless, but I climbed the ladder with shaky legs.

No cats.

Several scenarios crowded into my mind. First, there was the possibility that Deke had come here to retrieve— steal?—the cats, had been followed in by a bad guy who had killed him, and then the cats had subsequently run away.

Or Ludlow Cumberland had come, and in the belief that Deke was the catnapper, had killed him and taken the cats. Maybe Deke *had* been the cat thief. That made sense, given that Ernie had denied being directly involved with the theft of those animals.

Or maybe Ernie had killed Deke and taken the cats. But why would Ernie kill his friend? And why would he want the cats?

I returned downstairs, where the elves still stood surrounding Deke.

"Are we going to be suspects?" Jingles asked anxiously.

"No." Whatever else happened, the elves had an alibi. "You were all at the beach."

Jingles and Butterbean cast anxious glances at Juniper. "We weren't *all* at the beach," Jingles said.

"Jumpin' gingerbread, Juniper," Butterbean said, "you'd better have a good alibi."

"I do." She raised her chin. "I was at the police station."

I couldn't believe it. "What were you doing there?"

"Riley—Sergeant Vance—asked me to drop by, remember?"

"So you just happened to do that *today*?" I asked. "In your beach cover-up?"

"Evidently it's a good thing I did. Otherwise *I'd* need an alibi."

She was right about that. I turned my attention back to Jingles and Butterbean. "It's lucky you two walked home through town. Everyone in Cloudberry Bay must have seen you."

"Unfortunately, we walked down a side street," Jingles admitted. "I was embarrassed because my clothes were wet."

Butterbean said, "We slipped and fell in the water."

I hadn't even noticed. I'd been distracted by the dead body in the doorway.

The elves exchanged worried glances.

I tried to reassure them. "Don't worry. I won't let them arrest you."

"It's not just ourselves we're worried about," Juniper said. "What's your alibi, April?"

"I was—" I frowned. I'd been driving around by myself on a bad tip.

Someone had been trying to get me out of the house . . . and I had a hunch who that was. Ernie. But why?

Anyway, driving around aimlessly was not the greatest

alibi. It wasn't as if I was stopping people at the gas stations to ask about the whereabouts of three lost elves. I
was trying *not* to attract attention. But perhaps someone
had seen me. And I did have the text thread on my phone.

A flash of color outside caught my eye. It was Damaris,
zipping down the sidewalk in orange Spandex, arms pump-
ing at her sides. She looked like a speed-walking traffic
cone. It was possible that her fitness regimen always took
her down Plover Street . . . but equally plausible that she
was passing by my house to be nosy.

Had her eagle eyes been able to make out that we were
huddled around a dead body?

Suddenly paranoid, I toed Deke's arm out of the path of
the door and closed it. Then I belatedly lowered my voice
as if all the neighbors might be listening in. "Before I call
the police station, we have to be rock solid on what we're
going to say to them."

"Are they going to send a SWAT team?" Jingles's hands
fluttered anxiously. "I've heard about those."

I shook my head. "No. There's just Riley Vance, and
maybe a deputy."

Butterbean nodded. "Like Constable Crinkles and Deputy Ollie back home."

"No." While I doubted Riley ran the fiercest law enforcement organization, comparing even the most inept
police department here to the Christmastown Constabulary was like comparing Dirty Harry to Inspector Clou-
seau. Not to mention, the jail at the constabulary would
not be considered a rough punishment anywhere outside
of *Mr. Rogers' Neighborhood.* "This is nothing like back
home. Jailers don't provide soft flannel sheets for prison-
ers here or serve them fresh-baked cookies."

Butterbean registered this bombshell with visible shock.
"No cookies?"

I took a breath. "Try to stay out of the policemen's way. And if they do want to talk to you, don't let questions rattle you. All you have to do is tell Riley the truth . . . mostly. You never met Deke or even laid eyes on him until just now. You were at the beach—someone's bound to have seen you. You don't have your ID with you because you didn't think you'd need it on this trip. Most of all, you're not elves."

"Right," they said in unison.

"Let me do the talking. I'll explain about the cats, the appointment with the zookeeper, and the text I received this afternoon."

They nodded.

I dialed the police station. Then we waited for Riley to arrive.

Juniper decided to make cocoa. "I'm sorry if my disappearing today panicked you," she said when I followed her to the kitchen.

I pulled down the coffee. It wouldn't hurt to have a fresh pot on hand to offer the officers, sweeten them up. I wondered if they liked toaster tarts. "Why *did* you go to the police station?" I asked Juniper.

She tiptoed to reach the milk on the top shelf. "It's so embarrassing. I thought maybe Riley liked me."

"That's not embarrassing. I thought he liked you, too."

"Well, he doesn't. He kept me waiting fifteen minutes. Then, when I was finally escorted into his office, I told him that I could quit the Irish step dancing group and be in the police car for the parade. You know what he said?"

I shook my head.

"He said he didn't care one way or another." Her expression tightened. "Just like that. He told me that as long as he had Tad in the car, that was all the leprechaun he needed."

"That was a jerky thing to say, but it doesn't mean he doesn't like you."

"Right, but it made me not like *him*. He barely spared me a glance, April." She shook her head. "He was leading me on because I resemble a leprechaun."

I crossed my arms. "It was because of Riley that you said you might want to be my new caretaker, wasn't it?"

She sighed. "Partly. I know now that was a bad idea. Let's face it: I'm an elf on vacation. I've never been on a real trip like this before—I think I was just getting carried away by the novelty of everything. But I can see now that it would be really difficult to live here. People are harder to understand than elves. I don't want to wonder whether people are attracted to me only for my leprechauniness."

"There would have been all sorts of problems with your moving here," I said. "But the biggest one would have been for me."

Her eyes widened. "You wouldn't want me here?"

"No, I wouldn't want to be in Santaland without you."

She threw herself at me, and we hugged. I was so relieved that she didn't really want to stay in Cloudberry Bay. I wasn't sure whether I wanted to thank Riley for discouraging Juniper or smack him upside the head for sending her the wrong signals to begin with.

The doorbell rang.

By the time I got back to the hallway, Jingles had already let Riley and his deputy in. The lawmen were staring down at poor Deke. Butterbean had taken my advice and made himself scarce, and now Jingles retreated to the parlor.

Riley pointed at the lifeless body. "Dead?"

"Yes," I said.

"Looks like he was stabbed," his deputy, Tanner Ford, added helpfully.

"Where's Ernie?" Riley looked around as if he might be hiding behind a door. "Looks like I'll need to arrest him."

"Why?" Maybe this police force wasn't so far from the Christmastown Constabulary after all. Constable Crinkles was always jumping to conclusions based on very little evidence, too. "We don't know that Ernie did this. Deke was his friend."

Riley shook his head. "I've been hearing strange stories from Damaris Sproat about what's been going on around here."

I scoffed at that. "What would Damaris know?"

"Everything. She has spies all over town."

Way to make me feel paranoid about my neighbors. I told Riley about my relationship with Damaris, hoping he would see that her words should be taken with a fat grain of salt.

"You don't need to warn me about Damaris," he said. "I know her better than anyone. I was nearly related to her."

This was news to me.

"I dated her niece, Muriel, for several months," he explained. "During that time Damaris almost took proprietorship of the police station. She seems to think the whole town's business is her business."

"But you and Muriel aren't together anymore?"

"No, we broke up." He shook his head. "I still haven't quite figured out how to break up with Damaris, though."

"Well, you can ignore her about this. If there's anyone you should be talking to, it's an administrator at the Pacific Coast Zoo named Ludlow Cumberland." I explained about the stolen cats, my conversation this morning with Mr. Cumberland, and the mysterious message I'd received today.

"Strange that Cumberland wouldn't want to take the matter to the police," Riley said.

"He said he didn't want negative publicity."

Riley snapped his fingers at Tanner, who had fallen into a fugue state staring at Deke's body. Tanner's face took on a greenish hue. I didn't blame him for being squeamish. All the blood was starting to get to me, too.

"Get on the horn and see if you can track down Ludlow Cumberland of the Pacific Coast Zoo," Riley told his deputy.

Tanner eagerly withdrew from the hallway.

Meanwhile, Riley beckoned me out onto the porch. Neighbors were congregating in the street now, drawn by the sight of Riley's car parked in the inn's drive. When I joined him, he lowered his voice. "I hate to bring this up, April. Don't get me wrong. Your little friends seem perfectly nice, but I don't have a lot of faith in *seems*."

I crossed my arms. "I do, when it comes to my friends."

He leaned back against the intricately carved porch railing. "See, this is the problem Damaris has. She *doesn't* trust them."

I hoped the rush of heat I felt in my cheeks didn't mean my face was beet red. "That's ridiculous. She's just jealous because they're going to look more like leprechauns than her grandniece will. Besides, who cares what Damaris thinks? Does she run the law in this town, or do you?"

"That's what I told her. Still, I'll have to question them, even if they are your friends."

"Why? Cosmo and Tad were at the beach today—and you yourself talked to Juniper while the murderer was attacking Deke."

"True." I could see the wheels turning behind his eyes, and his suspicions returning to Ernie.

Then I remembered someone Ernie had mentioned to me. "The other person you should look out for is some Russian guy Ernie and Deke have been hanging out with. His name's Victor."

"Victor what?"

I sighed. "Ernie didn't say."

His eyes narrowed on me. "Did you talk to this man?"

"No . . . I just heard Ernie mention him. I got the sense that Victor's a criminal."

He jerked his head toward the door. "Criminal enough to do that?"

Even as we were focused on it, the door banged open and Tanner rushed out, breathless. "I just had Ludlow Cumberland on the phone."

"What did he say?" I asked. "Why didn't he show up today?"

Tanner looked almost embarrassed. "He said he never talked to you."

My jaw went slack. "That's not true."

Tanner hesitated, then rushed on, "Also, he said we should arrest you for stealing those cats."

Chapter Six

I held my breath. Could I be arrested on the say-so of a zoo administrator over the phone?

Riley looked at me, then shook his head in disgust. "Big shot in Portland. Thinks he can twist little police departments around his finger."

It was a relief not to be facing immediate arrest, but I was still confused. "How can he say that he doesn't know me? I spoke to Mr. Cumberland on the phone. I had an appointment for him to meet me here."

Riley glanced down at the body in the doorway. "Maybe he has an incentive to lie about that now."

"You think a zoo administrator was the murderer?" I asked.

"You said he was supposed to meet you here around the time the murder took place."

"But then where are Tiny and Peepers? Wouldn't he have them?"

He scratched his chin. "I dunno."

Unless . . . "Maybe the cat theft was an inside job."

Riley twisted his mouth in thought. "I don't really have the authority to investigate that. I'd have to involve Portland." He frowned. "Or maybe the zoo police."

"The zoo police?" We were in *Gong Show* territory now.

"The point is, I'm dealing with a murder," Riley continued, "and we've got Ernie going missing in a suspicious way. I'm taking your word that the exotic cats in the attic were stolen. And if they were, then the most obvious suspect for the theft is Ernie. Ernie's confederate is lying dead on the floor here, at the place Ernie's been working."

"Deke and Ernie were friends."

"But you said you thought you saw them both plus some Russian guy loading up a truck in the middle of the night."

"Yeah, but . . ."

Why was I sticking up for Ernie? I'd fired him. He wasn't my responsibility.

Yet something inside me knew he wasn't capable of doing anything this horrible. And when I looked into Riley's eyes, I could tell he wasn't going to look further for suspects as long as Ernie provided him with a plausible suspect to arrest. Part of me was glad. I certainly didn't want him investigating me and the elves.

But it meant that someone needed to find Ernie and get his side of the story before he wound up in jail again.

That someone was me.

The day seemed to drag on forever as we waited for the police and then the coroner to finish at the Coast Inn. When they were gone, the elves and I locked up the house and went to the Sea Otter Cafe for dinner. Of course the news of the suspicious death at the Coast Inn had already spread all over town. In a small town, news didn't have to travel far.

Janine, our waitress, was someone I knew from a school library fund drive several years ago. "Hey," she said to me, then looked curiously at the others sitting at the booth with me. For some reason, even Jingles was looking more elfy than usual. His ears were not large, but they did stick out at an odd angle.

"I heard about the trouble at your place," Janine said. "Just awful. Deke and my little brother, Kevin, went to school together."

"It *is* awful," I said. "I didn't know Deke that well, but he was Ernie's friend."

She nodded. "They were the Two Musketeers at school. At least, that's what Kev says they got called."

All for one, one for all. Would Ernie stab his fellow musketeer in the back?

As we placed our orders, a hush fell over the restaurant. It seemed as if everyone was curious to eavesdrop on us . . . even if it was to know what food we were eating. Maybe coming here hadn't been the best idea. I just hadn't been able to face eating at the inn after what had happened there.

Janine rolled her eyes apologetically for the rubber-necking diners, then beamed a smile at Butterbean and Juniper. "I hear you all are going to be busy on St. Patrick's Day."

Butterbean related his leprechauning activities.

After Janine left us, Jingles tried to return the focus to getting the Coast Inn fixed up. "The floors really need to be lightly sanded and refinished now."

I nodded. I'd done the kitchen myself when I'd first moved in, so I wasn't a stranger to that kind of work. "We'll rent a machine." I thought about all the work involved—including multiple steps of applying stain and varnish. "We might need to get that ball rolling even before Ernie's Uncle Wyatt shows up."

"I'm beginning to wonder if this Uncle Wyatt isn't like the Easter Bunny," Jingles grumbled. "Lots of anticipation, but I'm beginning to doubt we'll ever see him."

"Ernie said we will."

Jingles shot me a pitying look. "Ernie isn't what I would call a trusted source for information."

After all that had happened, I couldn't really argue with that opinion.

Our food arrived, and while we were eating, two women stood up from a booth on the other side of the restaurant. I groaned, which of course made the others swivel to see what had caught my attention. Damaris waved, and then she and her niece, Muriel, made a beeline for our table. The two women shared the same pencil-like shape and short hair, although Muriel didn't dress in the same flamboyant Spandex that her aunt favored. Muriel was wearing a navy pantsuit.

"Terrible about what's happened at your inn, April," Damaris said by way of greeting. "I'm surprised you can sit there calmly eating after the carnage that Sergeant Vance described to me."

I put down my hamburger. "Who says I'm calm?"

"They still haven't found the murder weapon, I hear."

She hadn't wasted any time squeezing information out of Riley. The knife—which probably matched the Cut Pro butcher knife currently missing from the knife block in the inn's kitchen—had not been located.

"But I imagine you're growing used to calamity over there, between the flooding, theft, and murders," she added.

"Only one murder," Butterbean said.

Damaris's lips flattened into a humorless smile. "You'd do well to sell out now before the Coast Inn's reputation as a murder house spreads far and wide."

I twirled the ice in my tea glass. "Who would be doing the spreading, I wonder?"

Damaris sighed. "Well, at the very least, you'll need a new caretaker for all the months you're off jetsetting."

I'd never been able to get it through Damaris's head that I wasn't spending eight months of the year gallivanting around the globe.

Damaris nudged Muriel. "Give them your card."

Muriel dutifully produced a business card: MURIEL SPROAT. LICENSED REALTOR. RESPONSIBLE HOME MANAGEMENT.

"Thanks." I put it on the table next to the ketchup bottle. I had nothing against Muriel—people couldn't pick their relations—but I was dubious of anyone affiliated with Damaris. "I'm not interested in selling now, and I'm still mulling over caretaker options."

Damaris shook her head. "I always knew you were stubborn. I didn't think you were stupid."

It was so hard not to rise to the bait. "Didn't I see you today, Damaris? You were circling my house right around the time Deke was killed." I narrowed my eyes at her. "I'm sure you told Riley Vance about that."

Her mouth snapped shut. "I didn't consider my power-walking route pertinent to the investigation."

"It isn't, unless that's not your usual route. Your being near the scene of the crime makes you a person of interest for the police, I'd say."

She put her hands on her hips. "I was ready to welcome you back with friendship, April, but you just can't help being snippety and competitive, can you? Those are two traits I can't abide in people."

I laughed. "You must hate looking in mirrors."

Muriel, shifting feet uncomfortably, tugged on her aunt's sleeve. "Maybe we should go."

Damaris stood her ground to give me a parting shot. "You're going to regret tangling with me this time. I'm going to win the soda bread contest, and do you know why?"

"I can't wait to hear your theory, Damaris."

"Because I don't think you know how to make soda

bread any more than you know how to run an inn or pick a caretaker who isn't a criminal."

"She does so," Juniper said. "April's got the best idea for soda bread ever."

It was hard not to swivel toward her in surprise and ask "*I do?*" But I crossed my arms and managed to stay collected.

Damaris's gaze narrowed on me. "What is this big idea?"

"A secret," I said.

She brayed out a laugh. "You're making it up."

"Soda bread men!" Butterbean blurted. "That's what she's making—and she'll win, too."

Soda bread men? What the heck were those?

Damaris's face fell. "I've never heard of such a thing." She turned to Muriel. "Have you ever heard of a soda bread man?"

Her niece tilted her head. "No . . ."

Neither had I.

"It sounds odd," Damaris said. "Odd doesn't win prizes."

With that final pronouncement, she hustled Muriel out of the restaurant.

"I'm sensing that you two don't get along," Jingles said, laughing.

"Soda bread men?" I asked Butterbean.

He shrugged. "If you can make gingerbread men, why not soda bread men?"

Well, you couldn't ice soda bread, for one thing. But maybe I could get creative with the raisins. Or was it currants?

After dinner we walked Butterbean and Juniper to the community center for another practice. Jingles told me he wanted to clean up—I wasn't sure if he meant himself or the inn—and was going to head back. We parted ways, and I circled back up Sandpiper Street to the Cup and Chapter.

I had two reasons for going to the bookstore. First, for books. The selection of modern fiction in Santaland was limited, so I always loaded up with reading material while I was in Cloudberry Bay. And now there was an even more important reason for popping into the bookstore: Ernie's mom, Misty, worked there.

It was one of the reasons I'd understood why she'd wanted to leave my employ several years ago. Who wouldn't rather work at the bookstore than serve breakfasts and clean rooms at an inn?

The Cup and Chapter was just a half hour from the posted closing time when I walked through the door, and there weren't any other customers there. Misty spotted me right away. Her brief, warm smile turned quickly into a shake of her head. "I don't know where he is."

She didn't have to explain who *he* was. "Have the police questioned you?"

As she nodded, her halo of frizzy hair seemed to undulate over her scalp. "They came here right after they left your place." She poured me a cup of coffee and pushed the mug across the counter. "On the house."

"Thanks." It was amazing coffee, too. "I'm sorry about everything that's happened."

"Ernie didn't do it. I'm not just saying that. God knows, I know that boy of mine's not the straightest arrow in the quiver. But murder?" She shook her head. "No."

"I don't think he did it, either. Not that my opinion will matter much if the deputy has evidence against him."

"I've told Ernie a million times that he needed to clean up his act. I thought he had. Then Deke led him astray again."

I could understand a mother not wanting to blame her son for his misdeeds, but Ernie was an adult. "Twenty-eight's a little old to use succumbing to peer pressure as an excuse."

"True." She sighed. "I swear. I don't want to sound heartless, but it's a good thing for Ernie that Deke will now be out of his life for good."

"Say that around the police, and they might ask you about *your* alibi." I was starting to wonder if she had one myself.

She let out a short burst of laughter. "They can have it. I've been working here all day, except for my lunch break when I closed the shop for thirty minutes."

"When was that?"

"Just before noon."

Around the time Deke was killed, in other words.

Her level look let told me she knew I'd been fishing for her alibi. "If you're going to look for a murderer around here, you should hunt down that Victor character."

"Do you know Victor's last name?"

She shook her head. "The police asked me that, too. You should have just come over here with them this afternoon. I wouldn't have to repeat myself."

"I'm sorry. I probably sound as nosy as Damaris. Finding that body in my doorway shook me."

She waved a hand dismissively. "If anybody has the right to ask questions about Ernie, it's you. You took a chance on him, and he let you down."

"I just want to find out who did it—and make sure Ernie's not in danger."

Her eyes filled with gratitude. "Thank you. I wish Ernie had more people like you in his life."

I shifted and confessed, "I fired him, you know."

"Oh, hon, I've been expecting that." Before I could protest, she said, "I know he did pretty well for a while. When I recommended him to you, he was full of talk about turning over a new leaf. It's only in the last few months that I could tell he'd fallen in with bad company again. He never did have much of a backbone. Maybe I coddled him too much."

"I doubt that. Anyway, not having a backbone is a far cry from being a murderer."

She reached for her own coffee mug. "He was always a kind-hearted kid. Hated to see other kids bullied, kind to animals, helped carry old ladies' groceries to their car . . ."

Something in what she said snagged my attention. "You said he loved animals. Did he ever have cats?"

She frowned. "No. We had a dog he loved. He also had a box turtle named Larry."

This probably wasn't a productive angle to pursue. But what would be?

I decided to be direct. "Misty, do you have any idea where Ernie could be?"

She stared at her hands. "I worry he's with that Victor fellow, wherever he lives."

"What about his Uncle Wyatt?"

"That's his late father's brother. He tries to help Ernie, but he keeps his distance, you know what I mean?"

"He said he'd replace a cracked pipe in my kitchen for free."

"That sounds like something he'd do. But harbor a fugitive? No way." She sighed sadly. "He's always so conscious of appearances, and his reputation."

"As a plumber?"

"No, as mayor of Marmot Creek."

"Oh, I didn't know." Marmot Creek was a community about a half-hour inland.

"It's only a part-time job, but you know how politicians

are. Image is everything." She sniffed. "A week ago I was giving Ernie a lecture about personal responsibility. Now I just wish I could rescue him."

I nodded. "I have a hunch that he's trying to save himself."

"But does he know how?"

That was the million dollar question.

After draining my coffee cup, I did a quick lap around the bookstore. It seemed as if every author I loved had come out with a new book since I'd been here in the fall. I was scooping up titles left and right. I bought eight books, along with a Cup and Chapter tote bag to lug them home in.

The Coast Inn was ablaze with lights when I came up Plover Street. I didn't blame Jingles for wanting all the lights on. With the image of Deke still in my mind, I doubted I would be sleeping with the lights off tonight. I skittered across the foyer—pushing unpleasant images out of my mind—and dropped my books down on the low step of the staircase. Then I headed back to the kitchen.

Jingles was at the breakfast table, searching through the Yellow Pages. I didn't even know they still produced those.

"There's a big hardware store in that town called Coos Bay," he said. "They might rent floor sanders. Maybe we could go tomorrow."

Tomorrow. There was so much to do. Besides tending to the house and trying to find Ernie, I needed to scare up a foolproof soda bread recipe and make enough to justify having a table at the bakeoff. And now I needed to see if there was a way to shape the dough to make something that would look like a soda bread man.

"Are Butterbean and Juniper here yet?"

"Not yet."

"Maybe I should go pick them up," I said. "I don't like the idea of them walking around at night. There's a murderer loose."

"But I assume whoever killed Deke had a motive for murder," Jingles pointed out. "It's not like there's a serial killer lurking outside the community center."

"Probably not, but—"

The sound of glass shattering followed by a loud thump cut me off. Jingles and I both leapt to our feet. "What was that?" I asked.

We hurtled through the dining room and into the parlor, where the noise had come from. Cool damp air rushed through a square foot hole in the glass of the front bay window. Glass shards littered the window seat, and on the floor nearby lay a rock. It was actually half of a brick. Someone had attached a note to it by winding a rubber band around both the brick and the note several times. I pulled the note free, trying to just touch the tip of one corner.

I read the message and frowned.

"What does it say?" Jingles asked.

I turned the paper so he could read it.

GO BACK TO WHERE YOU CAME FROM!

Chapter Seven

The brick through the window made for an unsettling evening. While Jingles and I waited for Riley to arrive, Juniper and Butterbean returned from their rehearsal, Butterbean carrying his costume in a little garment bag. St. Patrick's Day was just one day away.

"What's going on?" Juniper asked as soon as she saw the glass on the floor in the parlor. I hadn't let Jingles clean up because I thought maybe Riley would want to see the scene of the crime.

"Has there been another murder?" Butterbean asked.

Obviously, a brick and broken glass wasn't as distressing as finding a body in the foyer, but I still felt unnerved. Who could have committed this act of small-scale terrorism?

I kept picturing that message. *GO BACK TO WHERE YOU CAME FROM!* The warning had been carefully hand-lettered with a thick magic marker. Yet some of the letters, like the *B* and *C*, had elaborate curlicues trailing off the ends. The ornamentation created a disturbing impression of formality and menace.

Which of us was the target of this message? Me? Or did someone want the elves out of town?

"I'm sorry I brought you all down here," I told them. "Usually Cloudberry Bay's pleasantly dull and uneventful."

"I can't imagine it being dull here," Butterbean said. "There's so much to do."

"I mean dull as in *no murders*. And no missing persons. And no bricks."

"All those things make me glad we came," Juniper said. "I'd hate to think of you dealing with all this on your own."

"Me too," Jingles said. "Although I could have done without the dead body."

"Tomorrow will be better," Juniper said.

"It sure will," Butterbean agreed. "We can start making soda bread for the bakeoff. I've got a great idea for our table—an extra big soda bread man." He stood on his toes and outlined this colossal soda bread man with his arms.

Although a soda bread creation as big as the one he was envisioning seemed implausible, I appreciated the distraction.

When Riley arrived, he looked as confused by the brick as I was. "What's it mean, 'go back'? You're *from* here."

"That's what I thought," I said.

"Unless it's talking about your friends." He looked from Jingles to Butterbean to Juniper, then scanned the note again. "You don't recognize this handwriting, do you?"

"No," I said.

He folded it and then tucked it in his pocket. "I'd better safeguard this. Evidence."

I got up to walk him to the door. "Might be just kids," he told me in a low voice as I showed him out. "St. Patrick's falling on spring break week, plus all this hoopla with parades and contests, has everybody stirred up."

I comforted myself with this juvenile delinquency theory as I brushed my teeth and got ready for bed. Kids pulled pranks like this out of rowdiness, not hostility.

But then as I lay in bed, doubts bubbled up. Cloudberry Bay had never had trouble with teenage hoodlums . . . ex-

cept, a while ago, Ernie. And why would random teen-
agers target the Coast Inn? How would they know who
was staying here, and why would they care?

Maybe I was being paranoid, but that warning message
seemed personal.

Then again, when it came to people throwing bricks
through windows, could you be too paranoid?

I woke the next morning to laughter floating up from
the kitchen. After a night of troubled dreams, it was a welcome sound.

The kitchen looked as if a baking tornado had hit it.
Butterbean, who was standing on a stool to reach the
counter, blinked through a face dusted with all-purpose
flour. "Good morning!" he said. "We're baking!"

"So I see." I hurried toward the coffeemaker. "I would
have thought you had enough cereal here to last a few
years."

"We're not making breakfast," Juniper said. "It's a surprise for you."

Jingles sent me an apologetic look. "I tried to talk them
out of it."

I laughed. "It's okay. I like surprises." *Just not deadly
ones . . .*

The oven timer buzzed, and Butterbean hopped off his
stool to check his creation. Putting on oven mitts that
reached nearly up to his armpits, he pulled open the oven
door and removed a baking sheet with three soda bread
blobs in ascending sizes baked together. It looked like a
featureless snowman . . . only made from soda bread. "What
do you think?"

"Is that what the smaller ones will look like?" Juniper
asked. "How are we going to decorate them?"

"We're not going to," Butterbean said.

Jingles crossed his arms. "Then how will anyone know what they are?"

"Because we'll have a sign saying that we're selling soda bread men," Butterbean replied.

The doorbell rang, and I left the soda bread discussion to see who was here. When I opened it, I still didn't know. The man, who was wearing overalls and work boots, was a stranger to me. Something about his face did seem familiar, though. The man wore a beard, but if I looked into his eyes . . .

"Are you Uncle Wyatt?" I asked. "Ernie's uncle, I mean?"

His face broke into a smile, and he held out his hand to shake. "Wyatt Wilson—pleased to meet you. I promised Ernie I'd fix your sink."

I practically yanked the man across the threshold. "Do you know where Ernie is?"

"No . . ."

"You haven't heard from him in the past twenty-four hours?"

He tilted his head, suddenly wary. "What's this about? Is Ernie in trouble again?"

Apparently, he hadn't heard about all the goings-on here at the Coast Inn and Ernie's involvement in them. I filled him in as quickly as I could. He also hadn't heard that Ernie was in hiding somewhere.

That is, I *hoped* he was in hiding. Given what happened to Deke, maybe I shouldn't assume.

Wyatt's expression turned grave. "I'm sorry to hear this. I thought Ernie had straightened himself out."

"We don't know exactly what happened," I said.

"People don't disappear for no reason. It's usually because they've done something bad."

"I think Ernie might be *hiding* from something bad."

The man cast a glance out to the front of the inn, where his van was parked. It had his company name in bold letters on the side:

WYATT WILSON

PLUMBER-MAYOR

"VOTE FOR THE MAN WITH EXPERIENCE IN FLUSHING TROUBLES AWAY"

It was hard to know if it was a campaign vehicle doubling as a plumber's van or the other way around.

Beneath his practiced smile, Uncle Wyatt looked poised to flee to his vehicle. "I might have thought twice about coming if I'd known there had been a murder committed here."

Misty had said he cared about appearances more than anything. Could he care about them enough to have done away with the man everyone considered to be a bad influence on his nephew?

I shut the door to cut off the temptation of escape. "The kitchen's back this way."

He followed me, but I could feel his reluctance with every step. When he came into the kitchen and saw the elves, he stopped in his tracks. In their flour-covered bib aprons and no hats to disguise their protruding ears, they looked especially elfy.

Juniper smiled warmly in greeting. "You must be Ernie's uncle."

"We've heard a lot about you," Butterbean said.

Jingles beckoned the newcomer with his hand. "Maybe you can help us. We need to know if you can identify what this is." He pointed to the three blobs of soda bread baked together.

Wyatt tilted his head and gave the creation some consideration. "I don't know . . . but to me it looks a little like a snowman. Only made out of bread?"

"Yes!" Butterbean pumped his fist in triumph. "I told you it would work."

"But it doesn't have a face," Juniper said. "Who's ever heard of a snowman without a face? They wouldn't be able to see or talk."

Wyatt looked thoroughly confused.

"I've entered the soda bread contest," I explained quickly. "We're trying something different."

"Ah—I see! Very clever." He beamed at the three elves, then thrust his hand toward each in turn, asking their names and how long they'd be staying in Cloudberry Bay.

Not long enough to be potential voters, I wanted to tell him.

"We should give Mr. Wilson room to work," I said, looking meaningfully at the elves.

"Maybe I should stay," Butterbean suggested. "I'm very helpful."

Luckily, Juniper and Jingles took the hint and dragged Butterbean away. As Wyatt Wilson approached the sink, I followed.

"Did you know Deke Saunders?" I asked, opening the cabinet for him.

"Who?"

"The man who was killed here."

He reached into the toolbox he'd brought in with him, pulled out a work light, and plugged it into the outlet by the coffeemaker. "No, should I have?"

I wondered briefly if I should be looking at Wyatt Wilson as a suspect. Probably not, I decided.

Maybe I just didn't want to think that the man who could solve my plumbing situation was capable of such evil. And from a purely practical viewpoint, why would he have killed Deke and then come here a few hours later to do this repair?

Unless this was all cover-your-butt theater.

"From talking to Ernie, I thought you had spoken to him enough to know about his friends," I said.

He ducked his head out from under the sink. "Ernie told you that?"

"Actually, I just inferred it."

"I haven't spoken to my nephew directly for a long while. He always calls my office, and most of the time there my phone is answered by Oksana."

"Oksana is your secretary?"

"I call her the office assistant."

"Is she Russian?"

He laughed. "Well, yeah. She just runs the plumbing office, of course. At city hall I've got a girl who's more, you know, American. But Oksana's very organized. She could run the world."

Could she run a criminal enterprise?

My spidey senses were activated. Yes, there were many Russians in the world, even in Oregon. After Spanish, Russian was the most commonly spoken foreign language around Portland. Still, the chances seemed good that there could be a connection between Deke's Russian friend and Wyatt's office assistant.

The plumber sighed. "I left my saw in my van."

"I can get it for you," I offered quickly.

He tilted a glance at me. "You know what a hacksaw looks like?"

"Of course." *Of course not*, I should have said. That was what the internet was for.

He tossed me his van key.

"Back in a jiffy," I said, hurrying out.

I wasn't sure what I expected to find in the van. The murder knife propped in a cup holder? Blood stains? I slid onto the passenger side seat and peered around the cab. There was nothing incriminating that I could see. I got out, closed the door, and went to the back of the van. A second toolbox lay on an old blanket. I found what had to be the hacksaw quick enough, and then my eye caught something else. Hair.

With my thumb and index finger, I pincered a strand from the blanket and held it up to the sunlight. A dark gray-brown hair with a black tip. Tabbies had that color combo. So did wild marbled cats.

"I don't thinks that I know you."

Oksana spoke with a thick Russian accent and not the best grammar. Then again, if you asked me to say something in Russian, I'd be all tapped out after *nyet*.

"I'm looking for Ernie," I said. "Ernie Wilson."

"I do not knows this person."

"He's your boss's nephew. You spoke to him about arranging for Mr. Wilson to go the Coast Inn."

"Mr. Wilson is at Coast Inn presently," she informed me, pronouncing the name *Vilson*.

"I know that. I run the Coast Inn."

"And Mr. Vilson is there?"

"Yes. He's fixing my sink."

"Then what is problem?"

"The problem is that Ernie, his nephew, is missing, and Ernie's friend, Deke, is dead. Would you happen to know anything about that?"

"I know nothing. I make appointment for Mr. Vilson, no more."

"If you know where Ernie is, please let me know. I'm trying to help him."

"I know nothing," she insisted.

"His mother is very worried about him, and so am I—"

"Please do not call here anymore."

She ended the call.

I smacked my phone on my lap in frustration. That was stupid. Why had I thought she would talk to me? And now, if she was involved in Deke's murder, I'd alerted her that the connection between her and Deke had been made.

With a sigh, I dialed the number I had for Riley. He picked up fairly quickly.

"Ernie's uncle, Wyatt Wilson, has a Russian woman working for him."

There was a pause over the line. "Wyatt Wilson, the mayor of Marmot Creek?"

"His non-political job is as a plumber."

"That's a switch. Usually all these politicians are lawyers. Nice to see one with a real job every once in a while."

"I didn't call to talk politics, Riley. I think this woman, Oksana, might know something about Ernie's whereabouts. She was very evasive when I was asking her questions."

"Of course she was. A stranger called out of the blue to ask her questions. Why were you interrogating her?"

"Because I thought maybe hearing from a person concerned about Ernie's welfare might make her tell me what had happened to him."

"That's not how the criminal mind works." There was a sigh on the line. "I'll have a talk with her, but I doubt she'll say anything more to me than she did to you."

I doubted it, too. Her guard would be up.

Before he hung up, I told Riley about the cat hair I found. He didn't seem impressed by that, either.

"Well, I guess if we ever see Ludlow Cumberland,

maybe he'll be able to identify it as belonging to a marbled cat," he said. "I'll drop by and pick it up."

"I'm about to leave for the community center and set up my table for tomorrow," I told him.

"Okay, I'll send Tanner over there to pick it up." There was a moment of silence, then he asked, "What's there to set up?"

"Decorations. Knowing my competition, it's going to be very cutthroat."

"Given the week we're having, cutting throats isn't anything to joke about," he said.

Years of working in the children's library in Christmastown had made Juniper a whiz with construction paper, scissors, and glue. By the time we were setting up our table at the community center, she had fashioned a perfect leprechaun outfit for our soda bread man. We had to prop him up with a little cardboard backing, but once he was upright, we pasted the shamrock-colored hat at a jaunty angle onto his head. His brown and green coat fitted perfectly over the blob of soda bread that constituted his midsection. She finished by gluing a pair of googly eyes on him that gave him a goofy, doleful look.

The soda bread man drew attention even as I was tacking bunting from the dollar store all around the table. Tanner, the deputy, hung around to stare at it after I handed him the plastic sandwich baggy with the cat hair I'd pinched from Wyatt Wilson's van.

"I know that cat hair I found—if it is cat hair—won't be admissible in court as evidence or anything like that," I told him. "But it still might tell us whether Tiny and Peepers were ever in Wyatt Wilson's van."

"Mm." Tanner eyed the soda bread man. He seemed more interested in it than in crime detection.

"Have you and Riley had any luck finding the knife?" I asked him.

"Not yet, but we're pretty sure it's out there somewhere."

Brilliant. With that kind of deductive reasoning, the murderer might be found sometime in the next century.

"Are all your breads going to have eyeballs?" he asked.

"No, just this one," Juniper said.

"That's good. Having food stare back at me makes me uncomfortable."

"He's not food that anyone's going to eat," Juniper said. "He's a holiday decoration."

The deputy shook his head. "He looks real."

I worried Deke's murder might have affected the deputy's mental equilibrium.

It wasn't helping mine, either.

When I finished with the crepe paper, I didn't see any more reason to hang around. I just needed to go home and bake soda bread.

On our way out, Juniper and I stopped by the SODA BREAD BY SPROAT table, which also was all ready for tomorrow. Damaris's hand-lettered sign caught my eye. The *B* had a familiar curlicue finishing it off, just like the lettering on the note sent through my window on a brick.

That was one mystery solved, at least. Even if the brick seemed trivial compared to the murder.

Damaris had also gone berserk with balloons. I made a mental note to stop for some of those on the way home. I'd add them to the booth tomorrow. Even if I didn't win the soda bread contest, I could still score a triumph in the war of mutual irritation with Damaris.

"Now what?" Juniper hiked our shopping bag filled with the craft supplies onto her hip.

"Now we go home and bake like the wind."

But, like a character in a fairy tale, I returned home to

discover that elves had done my work for me. When we got back to the inn, Jingles and Butterbean were just taking the last two baking sheets out of the oven. The aroma of fresh bread made my stomach growl. It was tempting to devour some of our wares right now.

"I think you'll have enough to put on a good showing tomorrow," Jingles said. "We have soda bread with currants and without."

I couldn't thank them enough.

"I'd better go to bed." Butterbean stretched and yawned. "Tomorrow's a big day. I just hope the ghost doesn't keep me up tonight."

I shook my head. "There is no ghost."

"Deke's ghost," he said. "My ghost book is filled with stories of murder victims whose ghosts haunt the places where they breathed their last. Especially if their killer was never found."

We all looked at each other uncomfortably.

"I hope Ernie's Uncle Wyatt isn't involved in the murder," Juniper said. "He seemed nice."

I nodded. "And he fixed the pipe for free."

"Classic deflection," Jingles said. "Guilty people try to act the most innocent."

"Or maybe he was just doing a sincere favor for his nephew," Juniper said.

I tapped my fingers. "A cat hair isn't much to go on."

"But he has a Russian office assistant," Juniper reminded me.

"Her name wasn't Victor, though." I sighed. "I'm afraid Riley's right about one thing. The most obvious suspect is Ernie."

But if Ernie wasn't the murderer, he was also the most likely next victim of Deke's killer.

Butterbean yawned again. "Good night, all."

After he left, I tried to push Jingles out of the kitchen, too. "Let me clean up."

He shook his head. "I'm almost done."

That was a lie. I arched a brow in the direction of the sink stacked with mixing bowls and other pans he and Butterbean had been using. "It's not fair. You three did all the baking, and I'll be sitting at the booth tomorrow taking credit for it."

"Haven't you heard? Behind every successful businessperson, there's an even busier assistant."

Like Oksana . . .

I snapped on a pair of rubber gloves and joined him at the sink. While we worked, Juniper retrieved the laptop from my little reception office and set it down on the kitchen table. After a few moments, I heard her sharp intake of breath and turned around.

"Something's been bothering me about Mr. Cumberland at the Pacific Coast Zoo," she explained. "I couldn't figure out why he would say he never spoke to you. But then Jingle's mentioning assistants got me thinking . . ."

She turned the screen toward us. In a thumbnail on the Leadership and Personnel page, under Assistant to the Director, was listed one Victor Kozlov. He looked to be around thirty years old, with a buzz cut and bright blue eyes. His serious manner was only slightly lightened by the fact that he was pictured next to a seal.

"I *didn't* speak to Ludlow Cumberland," I said, piecing it together. "I must have been speaking to Victor Kozlov pretending to be his boss." I frowned. "But he didn't have an accent."

"Ernie never said the Russian guy was fresh off the boat," Jingles pointed out.

I took my phone out of my pocket and called Riley. He greeted me with a sleepy—or maybe just weary—hello.

"I've got another suspect for you," I said. "Victor Kozlov—he's Ludlow Cumberland's assistant. Someone needs to talk to him."

"We'd like to. There's only one problem. When I talked to Cumberland this evening, he said his assistant called in sick two days ago and hasn't been heard from since. Now Kozlov isn't answering his phone."

Chapter Eight

As if a murder, a disappearing caretaker, and a corrupt zoo administrator turned animal trafficker on the loose weren't bad enough, I woke up the next morning to even more disturbing news.

"You'd better come to the community center right away," Riley told me over the phone. "There's been a stabbing."

My gut clenched. "Who?"

"Your soda bread man."

I hurried downstairs, bumping into Jingles on the staircase.

"I was just bringing you some coffee," he said.

"Can't stop—I need to get to the community center. Have you seen Butterbean and Juniper?"

"They left early to get ready for the parade."

The whole town—and maybe several surrounding towns—seemed to have turned out for the St. Patrick's Day parade. The weather was cooperating, too. It was a glorious sunny day. People clad in various hues of green lined the street in anticipation of the parade, some camped out on lawn furniture they'd brought from home. A band calling itself the Cloudberry Celts was playing "Wild Mountain Thyme." The floats were starting to line up. Juniper, dressed in her lady leprechaun costume, swished her skirts and kicked out a red-and-white stocking-clad leg, laughing. I waved and smiled, hoping my anxiety didn't show. Butterbean wasn't on the float with her. Where was he?

Inside the community center, soft Celtic music was being piped over speakers, and a crowd had gathered around my table—a veritable sea of green. Most of the people there had on green T-shirts or sweaters, and quite a few were also wearing green hats with buckles. The throng parted to reveal the gruesome sight of our poor googly-eyed soda bread man stabbed in the back with a large butcher knife.

Wearing gloves, Riley—in policeman blue, not green—extracted the knife with great care, probably to preserve the evidence, although it looked as if he were trying to spare the soda bread man pain.

"Do you recognize this knife?" Riley asked me.

It was the Pro Cut butcher knife that was missing from the block in my kitchen. It appeared to have streaks of blood on it and had left sinister red smears on the soda bread man.

But wouldn't the blood from Deke's murder be dried by now?

A spiky-haired figure pushed through the crowd. Damaris, of course. She was wearing a Kelly green body suit with a giant foam shamrock over her torso.

"That's quite an outfit, Damaris," I said.

"Since you were being so stubborn about the leprechauns, I decided to switch strategies and come as a shamrock." She lifted her chin. "It nearly broke little DeeDee's heart not to be a leprechaun today, but I explained to her that some selfish people just have to show everybody up."

What a piece of work. I was almost in awe of her awfulness.

Damaris gestured to my table. "But now I see you're leprechaunless *and* you've got some gruesome display here to deflect from your guilt over Deke's death. I've never thought much of your judgment," she said, "but I never thought you'd stoop to murder."

I would have laughed if this hadn't been so serious. Those bloodstains on the knife reminded me of finding Deke in my foyer. I doubted the blood was real, but it was clearly meant to look like it to the police. This was not the time for snark.

"I didn't have anything to do with this, Damaris, and you know it."

"So it's just a coincidence that the knife appeared here?" The question really wasn't directed at me. Like Perry Mason performing for a jury, Damaris pitched her voice to the whole crowd gathered around the table.

"You can't think I'd try to hide a murder weapon by plunging it into my own soda bread man."

"And not only that," she continued as if she hadn't heard me, "according to the gals running the rummage sale, someone broke in last night, stole at least one box of goods that they know of, and made a big mess of their tables. Luckily, some of the boxes that hadn't been emptied were locked in a supply closet."

"And you think *I* did that?" I asked.

She planted hands on her hips, indenting her shamrock costume, and lifted her chin. "I wouldn't put it past you to have lobbed that brick through your own window the other night, either."

"That's funny," I said.

"Funny, why? You know no one wants to stay in your stinky murder house now." She was on a roll, and I let her go. "You were probably just doing it as a twisted play for public sympathy."

I smiled. "Interesting that I would do that by writing the note in *your* handwriting, Damaris."

The woman's face went white. "What are you talking about."

I turned to Riley. "If you compare the note that was tossed through my window with the lettering on the SODA BREAD BY SPROAT sign, you'll find that the lettering is identical."

Damaris opened and closed her mouth like a beached fish. For a moment, the only sound in the hall was a penny whistle version of "Danny Boy."

"All I know is that this is a murder weapon that came from your kitchen, and it was in your soda bread man," Riley said.

"No, it's a Pro Cut knife," I said. "Half the people in town own that same knife set because the Grocery Basket sold them as a promotion a few years ago."

Heads around the table bobbed in agreement. "That's how I got mine," someone said.

"You'll probably find one missing from Damaris's kitchen this morning." I shook my head at her. "You must be *very* desperate to see me disqualified from the competition to give up the best knife in the set."

Tears stood in Damaris's eyes. "It's not fair. You weren't even supposed to be here this week. I should have won this contest in a doddle."

Riley glanced around, obviously unsure what to do next. Sticking a knife in a bread loaf obviously wasn't a crime, and I hadn't said I wanted to press charges for the brick. "Where's my deputy?"

A man with a KISS ME, I'M IRISH shirt stretched over his pot belly called out helpfully, "Tanner's over in the rummage sale room. They found a box of ivory in there. Real valuable stuff."

Ivory? "You can't sell ivory here, can you?" I wondered

aloud. At the same time, though, I remembered how frantic Ernie had been at the idea of his boxes winding up at the rummage sale.

Ernie, what were you mixed up in?

Someone in the crowd pointed a finger at me. "It was one of April's friends who brought it, Margaret Lemmon told me. The little one."

"Tad?" I asked in amazement.

As if I'd summoned him, Butterbean called out my name. "Mrs. Claus! Mrs. Claus!" Tanner held him by the collar of his green velvet leprechaun jacket. The little elf was twisting and kicking out his legs, which were encased in green velvet knee britches and striped stockings. "Tell them I'm innocent!"

I whirled on Riley. It was one thing to suspect me of murder, but to collar poor Butterbean for trafficking in ivory was too much. "Tad didn't do anything."

"Oh yes he did," a stout woman walking behind Tanner declared. "I took the donation myself."

This was Margaret Lemmon, who volunteered on every board in town, including the elder boards of three separate churches. If it was going to be Butterbean's word against hers, we were in trouble.

We were in trouble anyway, for the simple reason that Margaret was telling the truth.

"This is all a mix-up," I said. "*I* told him to bring the boxes here."

Riley pushed his cap back on his head. "So you admit that he did bring them here."

"Yes, but—"

The cop cut me off. "Say no more until we're at the station. Tanner, you take him, and I'll follow."

"But I never even looked at the boxes before I dropped them off," Butterbean protested. "This is all a miscarriage of justice. I just dropped by here this morning to help out before the parade. And to look around for another duck shirt . . ." Tears stood in his eyes.

"You have the right to remain silent," Tanner began.

Butterbean had seen just enough movies to understand that those words meant trouble. His face reddened. "I'm not a criminal! I'm not even a human—I'm an elf!"

"A leprechaun, you mean," someone shouted.

"No, an elf—from Santaland! My name is Butterbean!" The crowd laughed.

"Do you have a cousin named Lima?" someone else asked, to whoops from the people around him.

"It's true, I'm an elf—ask Santa Claus. He'll vouch for me!"

"Unless you've been naughty," Tanner said, pulling his charge toward the door.

"Mrs. Claus—help me! I'm being dragged to the hoose-gow!"

I hurried after them, practically skipping to catch up to Tanner's long-legged stride. We passed through the glass doors to the outside, and a figure caught my eye around the side of the building. *Ernie?* He was wearing a lep-rechaun hat as a disguise. The topper was so oversized, it looked like Mad Hatter headgear.

I peeled off after him as Butterbean's shouts of inno-cence faded into the distance, blending with the sounds of a marching band playing, "When Irish Eyes Are Smiling."

Where was Ernie headed? "Stop!"

He whirled, wide-eyed, and shook his head frantically to warn me off. I sprinted to catch up with him.

"You've got to turn yourself in," I told him, gripping his arm. "They've got Butterbean."

His eyes widened in confusion. "Who?"

"Tad," I translated. "He's not guilty of anything."

He lowered his voice to an urgent growl. "Sh—I'm not the one they want, either. It's Victor." Ernie pointed at a man moving furtively ahead of us along the side of the community center's building.

Victor Kozlov. At least we could tell Cumberland that we'd found his assistant. "What is he doing here?" I asked.

Ernie kept his voice low as we crouched behind a rhododendron. "I told him about the stuff you brought over to the sale, and I think he's here to steal it back. Said the parade would provide a distraction."

"If you're in contact with him, why are you sneaking up behind him?"

"He called me and threatened to do to me what he did to Deke. I told him about the stuff—I didn't care what happened to the boxes of junk. Just the cats."

"He broke in last night, apparently, but didn't find the ivory. That box had been put in a locked storage room."

"I know. I told him he might be able to retrieve it today, while everyone's distracted."

We darted to another clump of bushes. "Are the cats still alive?" I asked.

"Of course. Do you think I'd give up Tiny and Peepers to that barbarian? Now I'm hoping I can catch him stealing."

Had he lost his senses? "Ernie, you don't have to apprehend him. Let the police do that." I got out my phone.

Ernie put his hand over it. "Wait. Unless we catch him in the act, they may think I was in on it."

I shook my head at his confused reasoning, but then up ahead it looked as if Kozlov might be heading for the side door of the community center. When he pulled the handle, it was locked. Thwarted, the man turned, catching sight of me. His blue eyes narrowed to slits as he walked in my direction.

There seemed no point in hiding now.

"Stop!" I yelled. Then, noting that he didn't seem inclined to follow my directive, I added, "You're under arrest!"

My voice must have had unexpected authority, because for a split second he raised his hands to surrender. Then he noticed who I was with. With shocking quickness, he reached into his pocket, pulled out a folded knife, flicked it open, and threw it at us.

Ernie and I hit the ground. By the time I looked up again, Victor was running toward Sandpiper Street. Obviously, he intended to lose himself in the crowd.

"C'mon." I pulled Ernie to his feet. "We can't let him get away now."

If Victor Kozlov got away, Butterbean might be stuck in jail. Eventually it would come out that he really *was* an elf from Santaland. And then the whole house of cards would come tumbling down. I, Mrs. Claus, would be responsible for giving away Santaland's secrets and open up the possibility of curiosity seekers and profiteers heading up north to "discover" Santaland.

Not to mention, it wasn't fair to let Butterbean molder away in custody.

I tugged Ernie along. "How did you get mixed up with this lunatic?"

"It was Deke," Ernie said. "Deke told him that he could use the Coast Inn to store some stuff—totally without my permission. But then once the stuff was there, Victor used the fact that the goods were illegal as leverage. He said if I told anybody what he was doing that I'd end up in the penitentiary right alongside him.

"I was a coward—I went along with it all. But then when I got out of jail after the stolen car thing, I found out that he'd left those zoo cats in the house. He was trying to find some dodgy buyer for them, but that fell through.

Then Victor said that we could sell their pelts on the black market. He knew all about that stuff from his work at the zoo. That's when I threw the cats into cat carriers. Deke tried to stop me, but I took his car and ran with the cats. Victor must have seen me take off in Deke's car. What happened after that, I dunno. Deke must have known I was going to head to Uncle Wyatt's."

"You stayed in his house?"

"Heck no. He'd never allow that. But I hid Deke's car with the cats in the woods nearby and spent the night in Uncle Wyatt's van one night. I also stole some food from his house. Then I headed back here. But when I got to town, Deke was dead."

As he told me this, we kept our heads down, trying to blend in with the crowds of out-of-towners and people with their eyes on the passing parade. Juniper's dance float was queued up to start just behind the fire truck. We'd only been a half a minute behind Victor, but he seemed to have disappeared into thin air. So much for my detective skills.

I was getting out my phone to tell Riley that he had bigger criminal fish to fry than Butterbean/Tad, when half a block away I spotted an odd sight: the papier-mâché Blarney Stone. It was moving.

Working on reflex, I straightened, pointed, and yelled, "Stop that rock!"

Several people around the fake Blarney Stone turned toward it, perplexed, then swung those gazes back at me. The one person who heard and understood was the man under the rock. Suddenly, the rock lifted and jeans-clad legs showed. The rock took off running.

The trouble was, Victor's visibility wasn't very good. As he ran, he careened into several people. Seeking more open ground, he hopped over a few seated children and got into the middle of the street next to a formation of twirlers. The rock knocked one of them over, bringing the ire of the crowd. I hurtled past some seated folks myself, but by the time I reached the rock, Ted Lucas, the owner of the Saucy Mermaid, and a few other men had already laid on the speed and tackled the rock.

Ted smiled as he sat on the rock, imprisoning Victor. Unseen now by the crowd, Kozlov was punching against his papier-mâché prison like the gorilla he was.

No offense to gorillas.

In a Zoom call, Ludlow Cumberland announced that he didn't want either myself or Ernie arrested, as long as Ernie would testify against Victor. After all, Ernie was the one who rescued Tiny and Peepers from becoming kitty stoles around some Russian oligarch's wife's neck.

Cumberland wasn't the only one who turned out to be on Team Ernie. Ernie might have misjudged Deke's penchant for breaking the law on multiple occasions, but his faith in the man's loyalty had not been misplaced. After Ernie ran out of the house, Deke had refused to tell Victor where Ernie would have taken the cats. Victor killed him as the fight escalated and Deke tried to flee.

"It was an accident, though," Victor insisted, until his lawyer arrived and he clammed up completely.

"Sure it was," Riley said. "He just happened to fall forwards with a knife in his back. Happens all the time."

I doubted a jury or a judge would be convinced by that argument, either.

Ernie was amazed to emerge into the sunlight as a free man. Misty was there to greet him—and to lecture him. "You've got another second chance," she said, hugging him. "And you don't have anyone to fall back on as an excuse if you screw things up."

The other person amazed to be free was Butterbean. He was held briefly but never arrested—thank goodness—so we never did have to explain why he had no identification. In the end, Riley took pity on him, and since he was released before the parade ended, Butterbean was able to at least sit in the police car nosing along the parade route driven by Tanner and wave to the crowd.

"It's nice of you to let Butterbean be on the police car," I told Riley.

"I feel sorry for the poor little guy. All that baloney about being an elf from Santaland. He really seemed to believe it."

"Yes, he did," I agreed. "Sad."

The policeman lifted his shoulders. "But crazy or not, he's the most realistic leprechaun I've ever seen."

I was there to watch Butterbean pass by in his leprechaun suit, and so were Jingles and Juniper. Jingles wore his favorite Hawaiian shirt and sunglasses, and Juniper was still in her lady leprechaun dress. I wore just what I had on, with the addition of the Blue Ribbon pin I'd gotten from the soda bread contest. Alas, Damaris had been disqualified.

It really was a glorious day.

My phone vibrated, and I pulled it out. I was treated to a photo of Nick in his leprechaun outfit, smiling and waving at me. I took a snap of Butterbean passing by, and then a selfie of Jingles, Juniper, and me. I sent them to Nick as a reply.

Looks like you're having fun! Nick replied. **Is everything going smoothly there now?**

I nearly choked on my green beer. But then I thought about it. Maybe our time here would go smoothly now that the murder was solved and the contests were done. I still had to fix the floors and decide whether I wanted to give Ernie a second chance as caretaker, but things definitely felt on the upswing now.

All good, I replied.

Rendezvous on Mount Hood in six days? He added a beating heart.

You know you're in love when an animated emoji makes your chest ache with homesickness for the coldest place on earth. I couldn't wait to reunite with Nick.

Make it five, I texted back.

Maybe I had a little elf optimism in me after all.